BENEATH THE SUMMER SKY

T.S. LIEBSACK

To every LGBTQ+ person who has ever felt unseen, unheard, or unloved. This is for the moments you've had to hide, for the strength it takes to be yourself in a world that doesn't always understand. You are brave, you are beautiful, and your story deserves to be told.

Keep fighting, keep hoping, and never stop believing in your worth. This book is for you.

© 2024 by T.S. Liebsack

Introduction: Beneath the Summer Sky
6

PART ONE: AWAKENING
8

Chapter 1: A New Summer
8

Chapter 2: The Struggle Within
17

Chapter 3: Fleeting Glances
22

Chapter 4: A Quiet Realization
30

Chapter 5: A Dangerous Question
35

Chapter 6: The Follow Back
48

Chapter 7: It's Now or Never
57

Chapter 8: Making A Move
61

Chapter 9: Coming to Terms
67

Chapter 10: Fragile Secrets
74

Chapter 11: The First Date
80

Chapter 12: Morning After Uncertainty
95

Chapter 13: Ripples of Truth; Ripples of Hate
111

Chapter 14: Steps Toward Truth
122

Chapter 15: The Weight of Expectations
130

Chapter 16: Conversations and Confessions
135

Chapter 17: Reflections and Decisions
141

Chapter 18: The Moment of Truth
146

Chapter 19: A Step Forward, A Step Back, A Step Forward Again
151

PART TWO: UNRAVELING
168

Chapter 20: Bracing for the Fall
168

Chapter 21: The Rumor
179

Chapter 22: Torn Between Two Worlds
185

Chapter 23: Opening Up
195

Chapter 24: Torn Between Faith and Self
200

Chapter 25: A Voice from the Past
206

Chapter 26: Silence and Fear
212

Chapter 27: Unexpected Support
216

Chapter 28: The Knock on Wyatt's Door
221

Chapter 29: The Stand-Off
227

Chapter 30: Caught in the Crossfire
233

Chapter 31: An Unexpected Message
243

Chapter 32: A Glimmer of Hope
250

Chapter 33: The Pool After Dark
256

Chapter 34: Back in the Water
268

Chapter 35: The Favorite Spot
274

Chapter 36: The Conversation with Mom
281

Chapter 37: A Weekend Away
291

Chapter 38: A Day of Freedom
297

Chapter 39: Coming Back to Reality
317

Chapter 40: The Consequences of Being Seen
323

Chapter 41: The Morning After
330

Chapter 42: The Confrontation
335

Chapter 43: Breaking Point
341

Chapter 44: A Conversation of Hearts
357

Chapter 45: The Incident
364

PART THREE: BECOMING
371

Chapter 46: A Father's Promise
371

Chapter 47: Counting Down the Days
377

Chapter 48: One Last Adventure
383

Chapter 49: Is this the End?
397

Chapter 50: Into the Sunset
403

Introduction: Beneath the Summer Sky

Jesse never imagined that coming home from college would feel like stepping into a different life. Brookwood, the small town where he had spent his entire childhood, felt like a world apart from the life he had started building for himself at school. The familiar streets, the same old faces, the way everything seemed to move at a slower pace—it was all so predictable. But there was a comfort in that, too, even if it felt stifling sometimes.

Jesse had always been the type to fade into the background. In Brookwood, where the same faces had passed each other on the narrow streets for decades, blending in was easy—expected, even. It was the kind of town where nothing ever really changed, and that suited most people just fine. But for Jesse, the sameness was suffocating. The quiet, the predictability, the weight of the unspoken expectations—it all pressed down on him, making him feel like he was living someone else's life.

Brookwood wasn't a place where you talked about your feelings. It was a town of strong, silent types, of men who worked with their hands and women who kept the home running smoothly. Jesse's parents were no exception. His father, a mechanic, had spent his life fixing engines, his hands always greasy and his mind always on the next job. His mother, a nurse, was practical and no-nonsense, the kind of woman who never left the house without her hair perfectly done and her lipstick just so. They loved Jesse, he knew that, but they didn't really understand him. How could they? He didn't even understand himself.

It was in his art that Jesse found a sense of clarity, a way to express the tangled mess of emotions he kept locked inside. His bedroom was filled with sketchpads, each one brimming with drawings of places far from Brookwood–city skylines, crowded streets, and faces of people he'd never met but felt he somehow knew. When he wasn't drawing, he was reading, losing himself in stories that took him away from the stifling familiarity of his life. He dreamed of leaving, of finding a place where he could be more than just "the quiet one," but dreams were all they were. Leaving Brookwood seemed as impossible as the sun not rising in the morning.

It was early June, and the heat was already beginning to settle in for the summer. Brookwood had a way of trapping the heat, the air thick and heavy, clinging to everything in sight. The summer after his first year of college was supposed to be a break–a time to unwind, to recharge before diving back into classes in the fall. But Jesse had quickly realized that "unwinding" wasn't as easy as it sounded, especially when he wasn't quite sure who he was anymore.

College had been an eye-opening experience. He'd left Brookwood feeling excited but terrified, ready to explore what life had to offer but unsure of how he fit into the world beyond the town's borders. The first few months away from home had been full of new experiences, new people, and the freedom to explore parts of himself he had kept hidden for so long. And now, being back in Brookwood, it felt like slipping back into a skin that didn't quite fit anymore.

PART ONE: AWAKENING

Chapter 1: A New Summer

Jesse stared out the window of his bedroom, the same one he'd grown up in, his eyes tracing the familiar streets below. Everything looked exactly the same. The neighbors still parked their cars in the same spots, the lawns were perfectly manicured, and the sound of kids playing in the distance floated through the open window. Nothing had changed, except for Jesse.

He glanced at the clock. Almost time for work.

The Brookwood Community Pool had been Jesse's summer job for as long as he could remember. When he was younger, he'd started out helping with the kids' swim lessons, handing out towels and cleaning up after everyone. Now, at nineteen, he had graduated to working the concession stand and doing maintenance around the pool. It wasn't glamorous work, but it was steady, and it paid enough for him to save up some spending money for when he returned to college in the fall.

As he grabbed his backpack and slung it over his shoulder, Jesse couldn't help but feel the weight of the summer ahead of him. It wasn't that he hated being home–it was just that being home reminded him of everything he hadn't figured out yet. Who he was, what he wanted, and how to navigate the parts of himself that he hadn't yet come to terms with.

His parents didn't ask too many questions about school. They were proud that he was the first in their family to go away for college, and they never missed an opportunity to remind him how lucky he was.

But they didn't know everything. They didn't know about the nights he'd spent lying awake in his dorm, wondering if anyone else felt as lost as he did. They didn't know about the thoughts that had kept him up–thoughts about who he was, about the part of him he hadn't been able to express growing up in a place like Brookwood.

Stepping outside into the heat, Jesse made his way to his car and drove the short distance to the pool. Brookwood wasn't a big town–everything was just a few minutes away, and Jesse knew every street, every turn by heart.

When he arrived at the pool, the gates were open, but the place was mostly quiet. A few lifeguards were scattered around, setting up for the day. The water sparkled under the bright morning sun, and the familiar smell of chlorine hit Jesse the moment he stepped inside. It was the same as it had always been–but he wasn't the same.

He made his way toward the office building for new summer orientation, feeling the familiar nerves bubbling up in his chest. This wasn't his first summer working at the pool, but for some reason, today felt different. Maybe it was the new hires. Maybe it was knowing that he wasn't the same Jesse who had worked here last summer.

Inside the office, a few of the returning staff members had already gathered. Jesse spotted Rachel sitting at one of the benches, her sunglasses perched on her head. She waved him over as soon as he stepped inside.

"Jess!" she called out, her usual easy grin on her face. "You ready for another thrilling summer of snack-selling and sunburns?"

Jesse smiled as he sat down next to her. "Yeah, can't wait to spend my days handing out popsicles to sugar-crazed kids."

Rachel chuckled. "Hey, at least you're inside most of the time. I'll be frying out there on the lifeguard stand."

Jesse shrugged. "Fair point. I'll think of you while I'm in the shade."

As they settled in, a few more of the returning staff wandered in—Matt, one of the lifeguards, and Tori, who worked the front desk. The four of them had spent the last few summers working together, and it didn't take long for them to fall back into their usual banter.

"Looks like it's gonna be another record-breaking summer," Matt said, sitting down across from Jesse and Rachel. "The heat's already insane."

Tori, who had taken a seat next to Matt, rolled her eyes. "You say that every year. We get it. It's hot. It's a pool."

Rachel snorted. "Yeah, you're really breaking new ground with that observation, Matt."

"Hey, I call it like I see it," Matt shot back with a grin. "And I see a lot of sweaty kids coming our way."

Jesse laughed, feeling the tension in his chest ease a little. It was comforting, slipping back into the familiar rhythm of their group. But even as they joked, his thoughts kept drifting back to the new lifeguard he had seen when he walked in—the guy with the dark, tousled hair and easy smile. There was something about him, something that tugged at Jesse's memory, but he couldn't quite place it.

"Who's the new guy?" Jesse asked, glancing toward the door. "The one with the dark hair. He's a lifeguard, right?"

Rachel turned to look where Jesse was nodding, then back to him. "Oh, that's Wyatt. He's new this year."

"Wyatt," Jesse repeated, the name swirling in his mind like a familiar tune he couldn't quite place.

"Yeah, he's cool," Matt chimed in. "Just moved back here for the summer. He was at college in California, I think. He seems to know his stuff."

Tori raised an eyebrow. "You mean he can sit in a chair and blow a whistle? Impressive."

Matt rolled his eyes. "You know what I mean."

Jesse listened, but his mind was still trying to connect the dots. The name "Wyatt" stirred something in him, but it wasn't clicking just yet. There was something familiar about the guy—something Jesse couldn't quite put his finger on.

"Wait," Jesse said slowly, "I feel like I know him from somewhere. Like, maybe we went to school together or something."

Rachel tilted her head, considering it. "You're from Brookwood High, right?"

"Yeah," Jesse said. "But he looks different... like, really different."

The others exchanged glances. "High school's weird like that," Matt said. "People grow up. Change. Maybe that's why you're not recognizing him right away."

Rachel snapped her fingers suddenly. "Oh! Wyatt Roberts! He went to Brookwood, right?"

The name clicked in Jesse's mind like a puzzle piece falling into place. "Wyatt Roberts," he repeated, a strange flutter in his chest. "Yeah... we had a few classes together. But he looks... so different now."

"Different how?" Tori asked, leaning in.

"I don't know," Jesse said, shaking his head. "He was kind of... I don't know, just not like this. Popular, I guess? But, I don't really remember him standing out back then. He wasn't... like this." He gestured vaguely in Wyatt's direction.

Rachel chuckled. "Well, people change. Maybe he hit the gym or something."

Matt grinned. "Definitely looks like he did."

Jesse frowned slightly, feeling a weird knot of nerves twist in his stomach. Wyatt had been just another guy in high school, someone Jesse barely noticed. But now... there was something about him that Jesse couldn't ignore. Something magnetic.

"He didn't really hang out with anyone in our group," Jesse said, more to himself than to the others. "But... yeah, I remember him. He was quiet, kind of kept to himself."

"Well, he's not quiet now," Rachel said with a smirk. "He's already made friends with half the staff, and it's only orientation."

Jesse felt the knot in his stomach tighten. Of course, he's already made friends. Wyatt seemed to glide through life with the kind of effortless charm that Jesse had always envied. And now, he was back–different, confident, and impossible to ignore.

As the conversation drifted to other topics, Jesse's mind kept circling back to Wyatt. He's the same guy, Jesse reminded himself, but something about that didn't feel quite right. Wyatt looked different, acted different. He wasn't the quiet guy Jesse remembered from high school. He was something else now–something that made Jesse's pulse quicken and his thoughts race.

"Alright, everyone, let's get started," Mr. Stevens' voice boomed from the front of the room, snapping Jesse out of his thoughts. Orientation was about to begin, and Jesse forced himself to focus as Mr. Stevens launched into the usual talk about pool safety, schedules, and responsibilities for the summer.

But even as Mr. Stevens droned on, Jesse's thoughts kept drifting back to Wyatt. Why does he look so different now? It wasn't just his appearance–it was the way he carried himself, the way he seemed so at ease, so confident. Jesse wasn't sure what to make of it, but one thing was clear: this summer wasn't going to be like the others.

As orientation wrapped up and the group began to disperse, Jesse found himself lingering near the door, watching as Wyatt moved through the room, laughing and joking with the other lifeguards. It was like high school all over again—Jesse on the outside, watching as Wyatt effortlessly made his way into the center of things.

Rachel nudged him. "You gonna stand there all day, or are you gonna go say hi?"

Jesse blinked, startled. "What? No, I'm... I'm just heading to the concession stand."

"Uh-huh," Rachel said, raising an eyebrow. "Sure you are."

Jesse rolled his eyes but couldn't suppress the smile that tugged at the corners of his mouth. "I'll catch you later."

As he made his way to the concession stand to start his shift, Jesse couldn't shake the feeling that Wyatt's return to Brookwood was going to complicate things.

He doesn't even remember me, Jesse thought, a strange mix of disappointment and nerves settling in his chest.

But the truth was, Jesse couldn't stop thinking about Wyatt. The way he had changed.

As he started his shift behind the counter, the familiar rhythm of the job took over—handing out snacks, cleaning up, restocking supplies. But even with the usual summer chaos around him, Jesse's mind kept drifting back to Wyatt.

"Hey, you're Jesse, right?"

Jesse froze for a split second before turning around. Wyatt stood there, hands casually shoved into the pockets of his swim trunks, looking friendly but curious.

"Yeah, that's me," Jesse replied, trying to sound normal even though his heart was pounding in his chest.

Wyatt smiled, stepping closer. "I thought I recognized you. We went to high school together, didn't we?"

Jesse's throat felt dry. "Uh, yeah. We had a couple classes together."

"Right, right," Wyatt said, nodding. "I was trying to remember where I'd seen you before. It's been a while, huh?"

Jesse forced a smile. "Yeah, it's been a minute."

There was a brief, awkward pause before Wyatt rubbed the back of his neck. "Well, it's cool to see someone from back home here. I wasn't sure if I'd know anyone when I got back."

Jesse nodded, feeling a strange mix of emotions–relief that Wyatt remembered him, but also the familiar insecurity creeping in. "Yeah, it's a small world, I guess."

Wyatt chuckled. "No kidding. Anyway, good to see you again. I'll catch you later?"

"Yeah," Jesse replied quickly, feeling a flush rise to his cheeks. "See you around."

As Wyatt turned and walked back toward the lifeguard stand, Jesse watched him go, his heart still racing. Wyatt had remembered him–

barely–but it was enough to leave Jesse feeling both excited and completely unnerved.

This summer was going to be different. He could feel it.

Chapter 2: The Struggle Within

The early morning light filtered through Jesse's window, casting soft shadows across his bedroom walls. He lay in bed, staring at the ceiling, feeling the familiar weight of dread settle in his chest. It was another summer day in Brookwood, another day he would spend going through the motions, pretending that everything was fine, that he was fine. But Jesse knew better. Inside, a storm was raging, one he didn't know how to weather.

For days now, his thoughts had been consumed by Wyatt–the guy who seemed to have it all: confidence, charisma, and those piercing green eyes that seemed to see right through Jesse. Jesse had tried to ignore the feelings that stirred within him every time Wyatt looked his way, tried to bury them under layers of denial and distraction. But it was no use. Wyatt was always there, lingering in the back of his mind, a constant, nagging presence that Jesse couldn't shake.

He rolled over, reaching for his phone on the nightstand. His fingers hovered over the screen, his heart pounding. He knew he shouldn't do it, knew it would only make things worse, but he couldn't help himself. He unlocked his phone and opened Instagram, typing in Wyatt's name with a shaky hand. His profile popped up immediately, a carefully curated collection of photos that told a story Jesse was desperate to understand.

Jesse hesitated for a moment, his thumb hovering over the screen. He shouldn't be doing this. He knew that. But the urge was too strong, the pull too powerful to resist. With a deep breath, he tapped on Wyatt's profile, and the first photo filled his screen. It was a picture of Wyatt at the beach, the sun setting behind him, casting a warm glow over his tanned skin. He was smiling, that easy, confident smile that made Jesse's stomach twist in knots. His hair was tousled, his eyes bright, and he looked like he belonged there, in that moment, in a way Jesse never felt he belonged anywhere.

Jesse's thumb swiped up, scrolling through photo after photo. Wyatt on a hike, his shirt off, sweat glistening on his skin. Wyatt with friends, laughing, his arm casually draped over someone's shoulder. Wyatt at a concert, his face lit up with joy. Each image was a punch to Jesse's gut, a reminder of everything he wasn't–everything he wanted but could never have.

He knew it was wrong to feel this way, knew it was pointless to torture himself like this. But he couldn't stop. He was obsessed, caught in a cycle of longing and self-loathing that left him feeling dizzy and sick. Why couldn't he be normal? Why couldn't he just push these thoughts away, forget about Wyatt, and focus on something–anything–else?

Jesse's mind raced with intrusive thoughts, dark and suffocating. *I can't be like this. I can't be... gay. What if people find out? What if my parents find out? They'll hate me. They'll be so disappointed.* The thoughts spiraled, each one feeding into the next, building into a crescendo of fear and shame that threatened to swallow him whole.

He tried to remember what he'd learned in his psychology class about intrusive thoughts, about how they were just thoughts and didn't have to mean anything. But it was hard to believe that when every fiber of his being felt like it was screaming at him, telling him he was wrong, that he was broken. He squeezed his eyes shut, trying to block out the images, the feelings, the fear. But it was no use. The thoughts came anyway, like a flood he couldn't control.

I don't want this. I don't want to be this way. The words echoed in his mind, over and over, a mantra of denial. He wanted to reject it, to push it all away. But then he'd see Wyatt's face in his mind's eye, those green eyes looking at him with a kind of understanding that made Jesse's heartache, and all his resolve would crumble.

He opened his eyes and stared at the screen, his thumb frozen over Wyatt's most recent post. It was a photo of him at the pool, his lifeguard whistle hanging around his neck, a playful grin on his face. The caption read: *"Another day in paradise."* Jesse's heart clenched at the sight. Wyatt looked so carefree, so at ease in his own skin. Jesse envied him, envied the way he seemed to move through the world without fear or hesitation.

Jesse found himself wondering what it would be like to be that close to Wyatt, to feel his warmth, to hear his laughter up close. His thumb hovered over the "like" button, his breath catching in his throat. He wanted to reach out, to connect, to let Wyatt know he was thinking about him. But he couldn't. He couldn't risk it. What if Wyatt saw through him? What if he knew?

He tossed his phone aside, frustration boiling up inside him. *Why am I doing this to myself?* he thought, his hands trembling. He buried his face in his hands, his mind swirling with a toxic mix of desire and shame. He hated himself for feeling this way, for wanting something he knew he couldn't have.

But no matter how hard he tried, he couldn't stop thinking about Wyatt. He couldn't stop imagining what it would be like to kiss him, to feel his hands on his skin, to hear him whisper Jesse's name in the dark.

The thoughts were like a drug, pulling him deeper and deeper into a fantasy he knew was dangerous.

Jesse lay back on his bed, staring up at the ceiling. He felt like he was losing his mind, like he was spiraling out of control. He wanted to scream, to cry, to do something–anything–to make the thoughts stop. But he couldn't. They were there, constant and unrelenting, a reminder of everything he was afraid to face.

He knew he couldn't keep going on like this, couldn't keep torturing himself with thoughts of Wyatt. But he didn't know how to stop. He didn't know how to turn off the part of his brain that was so drawn to him, so consumed by him.

Jesse sighed, feeling the familiar weight of despair settle over him. He wished he could talk to someone about it, but who? His parents would never understand. His friends wouldn't either. He was alone in this, trapped in his own mind, with no way out.

He glanced at his phone again, the screen dark now, Wyatt's face no longer staring back at him. For a moment, he considered deleting Instagram altogether, getting rid of the temptation. But he knew it wouldn't help. Wyatt was still there, still in his mind, still in his heart.

And that was the worst part of all.

Jesse rolled over, pressing his face into his pillow. He wanted to cry, but no tears came. He felt empty, hollowed out by the constant battle raging inside him. He didn't know how much longer he could keep fighting, didn't know if he even wanted to.

Maybe, he thought, it would be easier to just give in, to let himself feel what he was feeling, to stop pretending. But then the fear would creep back in, the fear of what people would think, of what his parents would say, of what would happen if he let himself be honest.

He couldn't do it. He couldn't face it.

Not yet.

Jesse closed his eyes, trying to push the thoughts away, trying to find some small measure of peace. But even as he lay there, his body tense and his mind racing, he knew it was only a matter of time before the thoughts came back, stronger than ever.

And when they did, he would have to face them all over again.

Chapter 3: Fleeting Glances

The days after were filled with a series of fleeting interactions, brief but charged with tension. Jesse has always struggled with his body image, a source of quiet insecurity that has shaped much of his inner world. Growing up in Brookwood, where athleticism and ruggedness were often celebrated, Jesse felt he didn't quite fit the mold. He was lean and wiry, with a frame that never seemed to fill out like the other boys in his school, who were broad-shouldered, muscular, and seemed to exude confidence without even trying. Jesse, on the other hand, had always felt a bit awkward in his own skin–a sense that he was somehow less, or that he didn't measure up to the standards set by the world around him.

He often caught himself comparing his body to those of his peers, seeing flaws in every reflection. His arms were too thin, his chest too flat, his skin too pale. He felt as if he lacked the definition or the muscular build that seemed to come so naturally to others. His shoulders slouched a bit, his posture subtly mirroring the way he felt inside–trying to shrink himself, to occupy less space. He found himself wearing oversized shirts and baggy jeans, hiding beneath layers of clothing, a subconscious attempt to make himself less noticeable.

These insecurities were amplified by his fear of judgment, the sense that people saw him the same way he saw himself. Even at the pool, where everyone seemed so comfortable in their bodies, Jesse felt exposed. While he had taken the job for another summer to save money for college, he also knew it would force him to confront his discomfort with his body, something he hoped he might grow out of–or at least learn to live with. But each time he stripped down to his swim trunks, he felt a surge of anxiety, a small voice in his head telling him he was being scrutinized, picked apart by unseen eyes.

Wyatt's presence at the pool only heightened these feelings. Wyatt had a body that seemed to belong on a magazine cover—toned, muscular, with an easy grace that Jesse could only admire from afar. Wyatt was everything Jesse felt he wasn't: strong, confident, self-assured. When Jesse first noticed Wyatt, he felt a mix of admiration and a sharp pang of envy, an awareness of the gulf between them.

But then came the unexpected moments—Wyatt's glances, the casual touches, the compliments that seemed so genuine. Wyatt looked at Jesse differently than anyone else ever had, like he saw something more than Jesse's perceived flaws. This attention was both thrilling and terrifying. It forced Jesse to confront his own self-doubt, to grapple with the idea that maybe, just maybe, someone could find him attractive despite all the things he hated about himself.

Jesse had always been the kind of person who kept his head down, moving through life unnoticed, avoiding attention. But now, something had shifted. Wyatt's presence in his world—at the pool, in his thoughts, and increasingly in his fantasies—was something Jesse couldn't ignore, no matter how hard he tried.

It started with a glance. A simple moment that should have meant nothing but ended up meaning everything.

It was Monday afternoon, and the air hung heavy with heat. The relentless summer sun beat down on the pool deck, shimmering off the surface of the water and making the concrete sizzle underfoot. Jesse stood behind the concession stand, wiping the sweat from his brow, as the line of kids and parents in front of him trickled down to a few scattered customers. Most of the children were in the pool by now, splashing around, shouting, their voices blending into the ambient noise of a typical summer day.

As he filled another order of fries and handed it off to a kid barely tall enough to reach the counter, Jesse's eyes drifted, as they always seemed to do lately, toward the lifeguard chair. Wyatt sat there, perched with a kind of effortless grace, his long, lean legs stretched out in front of him, one hand resting lazily on the arm of the chair. His sunglasses reflected the bright blue of the pool, and his posture was relaxed, like he belonged in the sun, like it was a throne and the pool his kingdom.

Jesse's gaze lingered on Wyatt, on the sharp lines of his jaw, the way his hair curled at the edges, damp from the water. There was something magnetic about him, something that drew Jesse in even when he knew he shouldn't be looking. It felt dangerous, this staring, like he was crossing some unspoken boundary. But no matter how hard Jesse tried to pull his eyes away, they kept drifting back to Wyatt, as if pulled by some invisible force.

And then Wyatt turned his head.

Their eyes met, and for a split second, Jesse's heart stopped. He should have looked away–he knew that–but he couldn't. He was frozen in place, his heart hammering in his chest as Wyatt's gaze lingered on him for just a beat too long. Jesse could see the small smile tugging at the corner of Wyatt's mouth, subtle but unmistakable. It wasn't a cocky smile, not exactly, but there was a knowing look in Wyatt's eyes, like he was aware of exactly what Jesse was thinking, what Jesse was feeling.

Jesse's face burned with embarrassment. He quickly averted his gaze, fumbling with the ketchup packets in front of him as if they were suddenly the most interesting things in the world. He felt like he'd been caught, like Wyatt had seen right through him, and the thought made his stomach twist in knots. What if Wyatt *had* noticed? What if Wyatt knew how often Jesse watched him?

But when Jesse dared to glance back up, Wyatt had already turned his attention to the pool, his body relaxed and casual, as if nothing had happened. Jesse exhaled a breath he didn't realize he'd been holding and tried to calm the frantic beating of his heart.

That night, as he lay in bed, staring at the ceiling, Jesse replayed the moment over and over in his head. He told himself it was nothing, that Wyatt probably hadn't even noticed him looking. But deep down, Jesse knew better. There had been something in the way Wyatt had looked at him, something unspoken but undeniable.

The next day was no better. If anything, the tension between them seemed to grow.

It was a slower afternoon at the pool, with fewer families and kids than usual, and Jesse found himself with more downtime than he knew what to do with. He tried to keep busy, restocking the shelves behind the concession stand, but his thoughts kept drifting back to Wyatt, to the way their eyes had met the day before, to that small, knowing smile that had sent a shiver down his spine.

He was halfway through organizing the bags of chips when he heard Wyatt's voice from across the counter.

"Hey, Jesse."

Jesse jumped, his heart leaping into his throat as he nearly knocked over the box he was holding. He turned to find Wyatt standing on the other side of the counter, leaning against it with that same relaxed posture, his hair damp and tousled, droplets of water still clinging to his skin.

"Got anything cold to drink back there?" Wyatt asked, his voice smooth, casual, but there was a hint of something more in his tone, something that made Jesse's pulse quicken.

"Uh, yeah," Jesse stammered, quickly grabbing a bottle of water from the cooler and handing it over. His hand shook slightly as he extended it, and when Wyatt's fingers brushed against his, Jesse felt a jolt of electricity shoot through him. He hoped Wyatt hadn't noticed the way his hand trembled, but when Wyatt's eyes met his, Jesse knew he had.

"Thanks," Wyatt said, taking a long drink from the bottle. "You're a lifesaver."

Jesse tried to laugh it off, his heart still racing. "That's supposed to be your job, isn't it?"

Wyatt chuckled, the sound low and easy, and for a moment, they stood there in silence, the weight of the unspoken filling the space between them. Jesse could feel the heat rising in his face, his mind scrambling for something to say, anything to break the tension. But all he could do was stand there, caught in Wyatt's gaze, feeling like the ground was slipping out from under him.

Wyatt didn't linger for long. He flashed Jesse another one of those smiles—casual, but with just enough edge to make Jesse wonder what, exactly, Wyatt was thinking—and then he was gone, walking back toward the pool with a confidence Jesse could only dream of.

For the rest of the day, Jesse's mind was a mess. He replayed their brief interaction over and over, analyzing every word, every glance, every touch of their hands. He told himself it didn't mean anything, that it was just a normal conversation, but he couldn't shake the feeling that there was something more beneath the surface, something just out of reach.

The next day brought more of the same—glances exchanged across the pool deck, quick conversations that seemed innocuous on the surface but left Jesse reeling. Each time Wyatt came over to the concession stand, Jesse felt his pulse quicken, felt his skin tingle with the anticipation of what might happen next. And each time Wyatt smiled at him, that small, knowing smile that seemed to see right through him, Jesse felt like he was falling deeper into something he couldn't quite understand.

It was Thursday afternoon when things began to shift even further. The pool was quieter than usual, the sun hanging low in the sky as the afternoon stretched on. Jesse was restocking the snack counter when Wyatt appeared again, leaning against the counter like he had the day before. But this time, there was something different about the way he looked at Jesse—something more deliberate, more intense.

"You ever get bored working back here?" Wyatt asked, his voice casual, but his eyes were locked on Jesse's in a way that made it impossible to look away.

Jesse shrugged, trying to keep his tone light. "I guess. It's not exactly thrilling, but it's better than being stuck at home."

Wyatt tilted his head, his gaze unwavering. "You seem like someone who'd want more than this small-town routine. Like maybe you've got bigger plans."

Jesse blinked, caught off guard by the comment. "How'd you know that?"

Wyatt smiled, a slow, easy smile that made Jesse's heart race. "Just a feeling. You've got that look, like you're always thinking about something else."

Jesse didn't know how to respond. His mind was racing, his thoughts tangled in knots. He wanted to say something, anything, but the words stuck in his throat. Wyatt's gaze was too intense, too focused, and it left Jesse feeling exposed, like Wyatt could see right through him.

"I've seen your drawings," Wyatt said, his voice softer now. "You're good, Jesse. Really good. You ever think about doing something with it?"

Jesse's cheeks flushed with embarrassment. He hadn't realized Wyatt had been paying that much attention. He opened his mouth to respond, but the words wouldn't come.

Before Jesse could say anything, Wyatt gave him another one of those smiles–gentle but full of meaning. "You should think about it."

And with that, Wyatt pushed away from the counter, walking back toward the pool, leaving Jesse standing there, his heart racing and his mind spinning.

As the days passed, the brief interactions between Jesse and Wyatt continued, each one adding fuel to the fire that was slowly building inside Jesse. He couldn't escape it anymore–the way Wyatt made him feel, the way his heart raced whenever Wyatt was near. It was like standing on the edge of a cliff, knowing he was about to fall but unable to stop himself.

Chapter 4: A Quiet Realization

Jesse lay in bed, the soft hum of the ceiling fan the only sound in the quiet of his room. Outside, Brookwood was silent, the world still under the thick weight of a late summer night. Jesse stared up at the ceiling, his mind racing, thoughts tangled in a mess he couldn't quite untangle. It feels like forever that he has been battling the feelings that had crept up on him, feelings he wasn't ready to admit, but they were relentless. No matter how hard he tried to push them away, they came back stronger, more insistent.

He couldn't stop thinking about Wyatt.

Jesse had tried to deny it, tried to convince himself that it was just a phase, that maybe it was just admiration. Wyatt was everything Jesse wasn't—confident, outgoing, effortlessly charismatic. It made sense that Jesse would look up to him, that he would want to be like him. That's all it was, right? But deep down, Jesse knew it wasn't that simple. He didn't just admire Wyatt; he *wanted* him. And that truth, as much as Jesse tried to avoid it, was starting to become undeniable.

Lying there in the darkness, Jesse let out a long, shaky breath. His thoughts were a jumble of emotions—fear, confusion, desire. He had always known, on some level, that he was different, but he had buried it deep, too afraid to face it. Too afraid of what it might mean. Being gay wasn't something people talked about in Brookwood, and the idea of coming to terms with that part of himself had always felt terrifying. But now, lying here, with the memory of Wyatt's smile, Wyatt's touch, Wyatt's gaze lingering in his mind, Jesse realized something else: maybe being gay wouldn't be the end of the world. Maybe it was just... part of who he was.

It was a quiet realization, one that settled in his chest like a small but significant truth. He wasn't ready to tell anyone, wasn't ready to share this part of himself with the world, but he was tired of running from it. Tired of pretending it wasn't there.

With a sigh, Jesse reached for his phone on the nightstand, his fingers trembling slightly as he unlocked it. He told himself he wasn't going to do it—he wasn't going to scroll through Wyatt's Instagram again. But the pull was too strong, and before he knew it, he was searching for Wyatt's profile, his heart already racing in anticipation.

The familiar grid of photos appeared on the screen, each one a snapshot of Wyatt's life—his friends, his adventures, his effortless happiness. Jesse had seen them all before, had studied them late at night when he couldn't sleep, when his mind was filled with thoughts he didn't know how to control. But tonight felt different. Tonight, he wasn't just scrolling out of curiosity. He was admitting, at least to himself, what he'd been too afraid to admit for so long.

He *liked* Wyatt. He wanted him.

His thumb moved over the screen, slowly scrolling through the photos. There was one of Wyatt at the beach, his tanned skin glowing in the sunset, his smile bright and carefree. Jesse's heart skipped a beat, his chest tightening as he stared at the image. Wyatt was beautiful in a way that felt almost unreal, like he had been sculpted by the summer sun itself. And Jesse couldn't look away.

As he scrolled further, his breath caught when he came to a picture of Wyatt shirtless, standing on a hiking trail, his skin slick with sweat, his muscles defined in the soft glow of the afternoon light. Wyatt's head was turned to the side, his grin playful, like he didn't even realize how effortlessly attractive he was. Jesse felt a warmth spread through his body, a slow, simmering heat that settled low in his stomach.

He stared at the photo for a long moment, his mind going blank except for the image of Wyatt. He felt the tension building inside him, his body responding to the sight of Wyatt's bare skin, the way his muscles moved, the way he seemed so... perfect.

Jesse's breath hitched, his heart pounding in his chest. He hadn't meant for this to happen–hadn't planned on letting himself feel this way–but the desire was overwhelming, too powerful to resist. He could feel his body responding further, the sensation both exhilarating and terrifying, like he was crossing some invisible line he could never come back from.

But he didn't want to stop. Not this time.

His hand drifted down to his waistband, his fingers trembling as he hesitated, his mind racing. He knew what he was about to do, knew what it meant, and for a moment, guilt washed over him, sharp and bitter. But then he looked back at the picture of Wyatt–at the way his body seemed to glow in the soft afternoon light, at the playful smile on his lips–and the guilt faded, replaced by something stronger.

Slowly, Jesse slipped his hand beneath his waistband, his fingers brushing against his skin. A soft exhale slipped from him as his hand found its rhythm, the heat building with every deliberate motion, his eyes still locked on the image of Wyatt on the screen. The sensation was intense, more intense than he'd expected, and the thrill of it sent a shiver through his body.

His thoughts were a blur, his mind filled with nothing but Wyatt—Wyatt's smile, Wyatt's touch, Wyatt's body. He imagined what it would feel like to have Wyatt's hands on him, to feel the warmth of his skin against Jesse's own, to hear Wyatt's voice whispering in his ear.

Jesse's breathing grew heavier, his movements faster, more desperate, as the tension inside him built to a breaking point. He could feel the heat spreading through him, the pressure mounting as his body moved closer and closer to release. His eyes stayed fixed on the image of Wyatt, his mind lost in the fantasy of what could never be.

And then, with a sharp intake of breath, Jesse came, his body trembling as the release washed over him, leaving him breathless and exhilarated. For a brief, glorious moment, there was nothing but pleasure, nothing but the overwhelming sensation of finally giving in to the desire he had been fighting for so long.

But as the pleasure faded, it was quickly replaced by something else—guilt. Shame. Jesse lay there, his chest rising and falling rapidly, the sticky evidence still on his hand, and the weight of what he had just done settled over him like a heavy blanket. He quickly grabbed a shirt from the floor, wiping himself off with shaky hands, but the guilt wouldn't go away. It gnawed at him, sharp and relentless, reminding him of the line he had just crossed.

He had touched himself while thinking about Wyatt. He had *wanted* Wyatt.

And now, lying there in the aftermath, Jesse didn't know how to feel. Part of him was exhilarated by the experience, by the realization that maybe, just maybe, it was okay to want someone like Wyatt. Maybe being gay wasn't the end of the world. Maybe it was just... part of who he was.

But another part of him, the part that had been raised in Brookwood, the part that had been taught that certain things weren't *right*, felt guilty. Wrong. He wasn't ready to face that yet, wasn't ready to confront what it all meant.

He closed his eyes, pulling the blankets up over his body, trying to block out the confusion swirling in his mind. Maybe, in the morning, things would feel clearer. Maybe he wouldn't feel so conflicted, so torn between desire and shame.

But for now, as he lay there in the darkness, the only thing Jesse knew for sure was that something inside him had changed. Something had shifted, and there was no going back.

He wasn't sure what that meant yet, wasn't sure what the future held. But for the first time, he wasn't completely terrified of it.

And that, in its own small way, felt like a step forward.

Chapter 5: A Dangerous Question

Jesse sat alone at the far end of the pool, his back pressed against the cool, rough stone of the wall as the sun beat down on the shimmering water. It was his break, a rare moment of quiet in the endless stream of shouts and splashes that filled his days working at the concession stand. Most of the kids had gone home for lunch, leaving the pool nearly empty, except for a few stragglers floating lazily on inflatable rafts. The lifeguards were still on duty, though, perched on their high chairs, scanning the water with a mix of boredom and vigilance.

And, of course, Wyatt was among them.

Jesse's eyes found him almost immediately, as they always seemed to do. Wyatt was sitting with that same effortless posture he seemed to carry everywhere, his sunglasses perched on top of his head, his hair slightly damp from a recent dip in the pool. His sun-kissed skin gleamed under the afternoon sun, and his casual smile was enough to send Jesse's heart into a familiar, uneasy rhythm.

Jesse had been unable to shake his thoughts of Wyatt. It wasn't just attraction–though that was undeniable. It was the way Wyatt moved, the way he laughed, the way he seemed to *belong* wherever he was. Jesse couldn't help but be drawn to him, couldn't help but imagine what it might be like to be close to him, to let the feelings that had been building inside him come to the surface.

But with every fantasy, with every daydream, came the same crippling fear: *Is Wyatt even gay?*

The thought hit him hard, as it always did. Jesse's stomach twisted with anxiety, a knot forming that only grew tighter the longer he considered the possibility. He had no *idea* if Wyatt was gay. For all he knew, Wyatt was just a friendly, charismatic guy who treated everyone the way he treated Jesse. Maybe those smiles, those lingering glances, those casual touches meant nothing at all. Maybe Jesse was reading too much into everything, projecting his own feelings onto someone who wasn't interested in him in that way at all.

The idea that Wyatt could be straight filled Jesse with a kind of dread he hadn't been able to shake. Every time Wyatt smiled at him, every time their conversations felt a little too charged, Jesse found himself spiraling, wondering if he was imagining things. And then there was the terrifying thought of what would happen if he *was* wrong–if he made a move, if he let his feelings show, and Wyatt reacted with confusion, or worse, disgust.

Jesse cringed at the thought, burying his face in his hands as the anxiety clawed at his chest. He could picture it so clearly: the moment he finally worked up the courage to say something–anything–and Wyatt's expression would shift from warmth to bewilderment. Maybe Wyatt would laugh it off, try to be kind about it. Or maybe he wouldn't. Maybe he would recoil, step back, tell Jesse that he wasn't like that. That he wasn't *gay*.

It would be humiliating. Embarrassing. Devastating.

Jesse sighed, leaning his head back against the stone wall. He felt ridiculous. He hadn't even admitted his feelings to himself for that long, and already he was getting ahead of himself, imagining scenarios that hadn't happened–scenarios that might never happen. But that was the problem, wasn't it? He *wanted* something to happen. He wanted to know, once and for all, if there was a chance, if the way Wyatt looked at him sometimes meant something more than just friendliness.

He had tried to watch for signs, tried to catch some clue in Wyatt's behavior that might reveal his sexuality, but it was impossible to tell. Wyatt was a mystery in that way. He was so comfortable in his own skin, so relaxed around everyone, that Jesse couldn't tell if his smiles and touches were flirtations or just... Wyatt being Wyatt. There were no obvious signs, no telltale indications that Wyatt was gay. But then again, there hadn't been any signs that he was straight, either.

Maybe that's a good thing, Jesse thought, trying to push the anxiety down. Maybe the fact that Wyatt hadn't mentioned any girlfriends, hadn't made any comments about girls in general, meant there was hope. Maybe Wyatt was just like him, figuring things out, testing the waters.

But even as Jesse clung to that hope, the fear remained. The thought of making a move and being wrong was enough to keep him paralyzed. He could handle a lot of things, but rejection? Public embarrassment? That was different. That was something he didn't think he could recover from.

What would Wyatt think of him if he made a move? Would he even *understand*? Jesse thought of the people in Brookwood, the way they would react if they ever knew what was going through his head. This wasn't a town where you could openly explore feelings like this. Brookwood wasn't a place where being different was accepted. Jesse had seen how people treated anyone who didn't fit into the mold, and he didn't want to become a target for their sideways glances and whispered comments.

But Wyatt wasn't like the rest of Brookwood. Jesse *knew* that. Wyatt was... different. He didn't seem to care what other people thought, didn't seem to follow the same unspoken rules that everyone else did. And maybe–just maybe–Wyatt was like Jesse, hiding something beneath the surface, waiting for the right moment to let it show.

Jesse's phone buzzed, jolting him out of his thoughts. He pulled it from his pocket, glancing at the screen to see a new notification from Instagram. His heart leapt when he saw that it was a new post from Wyatt–another picture of him at the pool, shirtless and grinning, the caption as simple as ever: *"Summer vibes."*

Jesse's thumb hovered over the screen. He stared at the photo, his chest tightening as a wave of longing washed over him. Wyatt looked perfect, as always. The sun highlighted the definition of his muscles, his skin glowing under its warmth. It wasn't a staged photo–just something casual, something that Wyatt probably hadn't even thought twice about posting. But to Jesse, it felt intimate, like he was seeing something he shouldn't.

Why do I do this to myself? Jesse thought, his stomach churning with a mix of desire and frustration. He knew that going through Wyatt's Instagram was only making things worse, feeding the feelings he was trying so hard to control, but he couldn't help it. The more he looked at Wyatt, the more he wanted to know. The more he wanted *him*.

Jesse's mind raced. He wasn't ready to make a move, wasn't ready to risk it all, but maybe... maybe there was a way to find out without putting himself out there completely. He could test the waters, drop a subtle hint, see how Wyatt reacted. But what would that even look like? How could he possibly find out if Wyatt was gay without making it obvious that he was interested?

He groaned, pressing his palms into his eyes. He didn't know what to do. Every option felt like a risk, and Jesse wasn't sure he was ready to take that leap. But he also knew that if he didn't do something soon, the feelings would only keep growing, and the uncertainty would eat away at him until he couldn't stand it anymore.

His phone buzzed again, and Jesse glanced down to see that someone had liked his most recent post–a photo of one of his sketches, something he had shared without thinking much about. He unlocked his phone and opened Instagram again, scrolling absentmindedly through his feed, trying to distract himself from the thoughts swirling in his head.

But no matter how hard he tried, his mind kept drifting back to Wyatt. To the way Wyatt smiled at him. To the way his heart raced every time their eyes met. To the way he felt when he imagined what it might be like to finally *know*.

Jesse stared down at his phone, his thumb hovering over Wyatt's profile picture. Maybe he would never know for sure. Maybe he would always be left wondering, stuck between desire and fear, too afraid to take the plunge.

But deep down, Jesse knew that eventually, he would have to decide. Because living in the space between wasn't enough. Not anymore.

Jesse was still sitting there, lost in his thoughts, his phone clutched in his hand. His mind kept going in circles, thoughts of Wyatt and the possibility of rejection spinning faster and faster until it felt like his head might explode. He glanced over at the lifeguard chair again. Wyatt was still there, lounging lazily, his sunglasses resting low on the bridge of his nose. He looked relaxed, almost serene, his long legs stretched out in front of him, his body catching the late afternoon sun just right.

God, he looks perfect, Jesse thought, his stomach twisting again.

Before he knew what he was doing, Jesse unlocked his phone and opened the camera app, his heart pounding in his chest. He wasn't sure why–maybe it was a way to hold on to the moment, maybe it was just the need to have something more tangible than the hazy memories he clung to after each day at the pool. Either way, Jesse's thumb hovered over the shutter button, his phone aimed discreetly toward Wyatt.

He could feel his pulse racing, his body buzzing with nervous energy as he tried to frame the shot. Wyatt looked like something out of a magazine, the sun glinting off his skin, the casual confidence in his posture almost hypnotic. It would be so easy, just one quick snap, and Jesse would have the image to look at later, to help him make sense of the mess of emotions swirling inside him.

Jesse's thumb hovered over the button, his breath caught in his throat. He told himself it was harmless, that it didn't mean anything. But deep down, he knew better. Taking this picture–this *secret* picture–felt like crossing a line he wasn't sure he was ready to cross.

And then, just as Jesse was about to snap the photo, Wyatt shifted in his chair, turning his head slightly in Jesse's direction.

Jesse's heart jumped into his throat. He fumbled with his phone, dropping it into his lap as a surge of panic flooded through him. *Did he see me?* The thought sent a wave of fear coursing through his veins. His face flushed hot, his stomach twisted into knots, and for a moment, all he could hear was the deafening sound of his own heartbeat pounding in his ears.

Oh God, what if he saw? What if Wyatt had noticed the phone pointed at him, had seen Jesse staring, had figured it out?

He dared a quick glance in Wyatt's direction, his pulse racing. Wyatt was looking over at him now, his sunglasses perched on top of his head, his eyes hidden in the afternoon glare. For a split second, Jesse was sure that Wyatt had seen the whole thing, that he'd caught Jesse in the act, and that realization made Jesse's stomach churn with dread.

But Wyatt didn't say anything. He just gave a small wave, a casual, easy gesture, like nothing was out of the ordinary. He wasn't frowning, wasn't narrowing his eyes suspiciously. In fact, he didn't seem to be reacting at all.

Maybe he didn't see, Jesse thought, trying to calm the wild thudding in his chest. *Maybe he was just looking over at me because I'm sitting here like a weirdo, staring at him.*

The fear didn't subside completely, though. Even if Wyatt hadn't caught him, the idea of it–that razor-thin moment when Jesse *thought* he had been caught–was enough to send a chill down his spine. He was playing a dangerous game, toeing a line between desire and secrecy, and the realization that he could have been exposed, that Wyatt might know *something*, was enough to leave him feeling shaken.

Jesse forced a smile and waved back at Wyatt, his heart still pounding in his chest. He tried to act casual, like nothing was wrong, like he hadn't just been inches away from doing something incredibly risky and embarrassing. Wyatt gave a lazy grin and a thumbs-up before turning back to the pool, completely unaware of the storm that was raging inside Jesse.

Jesse let out a long, shaky breath, his hands trembling as he picked up his phone again. His camera app was still open, the screen showing an empty shot of the poolside where Wyatt had been sitting. He quickly closed it, his stomach in knots. *What the fuck was I thinking?*

He felt sick with guilt and embarrassment. Even if Wyatt hadn't seen, the fact that Jesse had *almost* done it—that he had come so close to snapping a secret picture—was enough to make him feel queasy. What was wrong with him? Was this what he had become, sneaking pictures like some kind of creep?

Jesse leaned his head back against the stone wall, closing his eyes, trying to calm himself down. The fear that had gripped him so tightly moments before was starting to fade, but the guilt remained. He couldn't keep doing this, couldn't keep obsessing over Wyatt like this. It was driving him crazy, making him reckless. He had to get a grip on himself before he did something even more foolish.

But even as he tried to convince himself of that, the truth lingered, undeniable and heavy: he liked Wyatt. He wanted him. And no matter how hard he tried to fight it, that wasn't going to change.

What scared him most wasn't the fear of getting caught. It was the fear that he was losing control of the feelings he'd tried so hard to suppress.

And if he wasn't careful, those feelings would lead him somewhere he wasn't sure he was ready to go.

Jesse's heart was still racing as he sat there by the pool, trying to calm himself down after that near-disaster. Wyatt had looked over at him, waved casually, and gone about his day, completely oblivious–or so Jesse hoped. But the adrenaline was still pumping through his veins, and the knot of anxiety in his stomach hadn't quite loosened.

He couldn't believe how close he had come to making a fool of himself, and now, all he wanted to do was crawl into a hole and hide. But instead, he sat there, his phone still in his hand, feeling like he was on the edge of something dangerous and exhilarating all at once.

Jesse glanced back at Wyatt, who was still sitting in his lifeguard chair, casually scanning the pool, completely unaware of the internal storm that Jesse was caught in. *Why do I keep doing this to myself?* Jesse thought, feeling the familiar mix of desire and fear wash over him again. Wyatt was *so* out of his league. Even if he *was* gay–which Jesse still wasn't sure of–there was no way Wyatt would be interested in someone like him. Jesse wasn't confident or outgoing. He was awkward, quiet, and constantly second-guessing himself.

But despite all the doubts, all the anxiety, there was a part of Jesse that wanted to push past the fear. He couldn't stop thinking about Wyatt. He couldn't shake the feeling that something was there, something just beneath the surface. Maybe it was just wishful thinking, but the way Wyatt smiled at him, the way their conversations seemed to have an undercurrent of something unspoken... it kept pulling Jesse in, making him want to believe that there was a chance, no matter how slim.

His phone buzzed in his hand, and Jesse looked down, his screen lighting up with a notification from Instagram. He swiped it away and found himself back on Wyatt's profile, staring at that same shirtless picture he'd nearly taken a snapshot of earlier.

For a moment, Jesse just sat there, staring at the photo. His thumb hovered over the screen, hesitating. His stomach twisted with nerves, and his mind raced with a thousand reasons why he shouldn't do what he was about to do. But something inside him was tired of waiting, tired of wondering. He had to take a step–however small–to move forward.

Just follow him, Jesse thought, his heart pounding. *It's just Instagram. It's not like it's a big deal. It doesn't mean anything.*

But, of course, it *did* mean something. Following Wyatt would be a small acknowledgment of the connection Jesse felt between them, even if Wyatt didn't see it that way. It was a move that felt risky, like putting himself out there in a way he wasn't used to. And the fear of rejection, even in something as small as a social media follow, was enough to make his hands shake.

Jesse took a deep breath, steadying himself. He couldn't live in this limbo forever, trapped between fear and desire, constantly wondering but never knowing. He had to take a step, even if it terrified him. And maybe, just maybe, this was the first step.

His thumb hovered over the "Follow" button for a moment longer, his heart hammering in his chest, and then, with a quick, decisive motion, he tapped it.

Followed.

Jesse's breath caught in his throat, his pulse racing as he stared at the screen. It was done. There was no going back now. He had followed Wyatt on Instagram. It was such a small thing, just a tap on a screen, but to Jesse, it felt monumental. He felt like he had crossed some invisible line, taken a step toward something unknown, and the rush of it was both exhilarating and terrifying.

He locked his phone quickly, slipping it into his pocket as if hiding it would somehow make the act less real. But the excitement that surged through him wouldn't be so easily dismissed. He couldn't help but feel a strange thrill, like he had just made a bold move, even though Wyatt might not even notice–or care.

But what if he *did* notice? What if Wyatt saw the follow and followed him back? What if this led to something–anything–that would give Jesse the answer he so desperately craved?

The thought sent a rush of hope through him, and he couldn't help but smile, even as anxiety gnawed at the edges of his mind. He glanced over at Wyatt again, half expecting to see some kind of reaction, but Wyatt was still sitting there, oblivious, scanning the pool like any other day. Jesse felt a strange mix of relief and disappointment.

He stood up, dusting off his shorts and heading back toward the concession stand, trying to focus on the tasks ahead and shake off the lingering nerves. But as he walked, his mind kept drifting back to his phone, back to that small act of following Wyatt and what it might mean.

Every buzz in his pocket made his heart jump, each time wondering if Wyatt had noticed, if he would respond.

Back at the concession stand, Jesse grabbed a soda from the cooler, leaning against the counter as he tried to calm his racing thoughts. But even as he took a sip, his mind wouldn't settle. He could feel his phone burning a hole in his pocket, the temptation to check it almost too strong to resist. What if Wyatt had already seen it? What if he had followed Jesse back?

Jesse set the soda down, pulling out his phone with shaky hands. His heart pounded as he unlocked the screen and opened Instagram, his pulse speeding up as he checked his notifications.

Nothing.

No follow-back. No messages. Just silence.

Jesse's shoulders sagged, a wave of disappointment washing over him. He had been so worked up, so anxious, and now, nothing had happened. Maybe he had been wrong. Maybe Wyatt wasn't interested, wasn't even aware of him beyond their casual interactions at the pool. Maybe this was all in his head.

But even as the doubts crept in, Jesse couldn't help but feel a spark of excitement. He had taken a step, however small. He had followed Wyatt. And while nothing had happened *yet*, the possibility still lingered. He had put himself out there in a way he never had before, and for the first time in a long time, he felt a small sense of pride for doing something so bold.

Jesse tucked his phone back into his pocket, taking another deep breath. He didn't know what would happen next, didn't know if Wyatt would ever notice him the way Jesse noticed him. But at least now,

Jesse wasn't just sitting on the sidelines, watching and wondering. He had made a move–one that could lead to something more.

As he glanced back toward the pool, Wyatt was still there, still relaxed, still unaware of the storm of emotions that had been brewing inside Jesse all this time.

Chapter 6: The Follow Back

Wyatt had been mindlessly scrolling through his phone, lying on his bed in the dim light of his room, when he noticed a notification:

@jesse_lee_art just followed you.

For a second, Wyatt just stared at the screen, his mind almost unable to process what he was seeing. Jesse–*Jesse*–had followed him on Instagram. His heart jumped, and his stomach did a weird, excited flip. It was the moment he had been hoping for, but now that it was here, Wyatt didn't know what to do with it.

He clicked on Jesse's profile, staring at the collection of photos–mostly drawings, some random shots of nature, a few blurry group pictures that looked like they'd been taken at school events. It was Jesse's world laid out in quiet detail, each post feeling like a small window into the mind of someone Wyatt had been thinking about more and more.

Wyatt wasn't surprised by how personal Jesse's account felt. It was exactly how Jesse was in real life–quiet, reserved, but thoughtful. Everything Jesse did seemed intentional, and that made this follow feel even more significant. It wasn't like Jesse was the type of guy to follow people just for the sake of it. He had to think about this. He had to want to make this connection.

But now that Jesse had taken that step, Wyatt was left with a question that sent his thoughts into a spiral: *Should I follow him back?*

It seemed like an obvious answer at first. Of course, he should. It was Instagram—no big deal. But as Wyatt lay there, staring at Jesse's profile, his thumb hovering over the follow button, he hesitated.

This was more than just a follow, wasn't it? At least, it felt that way to Wyatt. Jesse was shy, careful. He wasn't the type to make moves lightly, and that's what this follow was—*a move*. It was Jesse opening a door, even if only a crack, and now Wyatt was left to decide if he wanted to step through it.

But what did that mean? What did following Jesse back *really* mean?

Wyatt's chest tightened as a familiar unease crept into his mind—the same unease he'd been trying to avoid for weeks. Liking Jesse was one thing—something Wyatt had been quietly admitting to himself over time. But liking Jesse in a way that felt like *more*—that was different. That was dangerous. Because if Wyatt followed Jesse back, it wouldn't just be a casual, friendly gesture. It would mean something more. It would mean he was acknowledging the possibility that what was between them wasn't just friendship. That maybe—just maybe—there was something else there.

But what if I'm wrong?

The thought hit Wyatt hard, making him sit up in bed, his phone still in his hand. What if he was misreading everything? What if Jesse followed him because they worked together, because they'd shared a few conversations, but nothing more? What if Wyatt made the mistake of reading too much into it, only to find out that Jesse wasn't into him at all?

Or worse, what if Jesse *was* into him?

That thought made Wyatt's chest tighten even more. If Jesse liked him—*really* liked him—what did that mean for Wyatt? What did that mean for the way he'd been feeling lately, the way he caught himself looking at Jesse more than anyone else, the way his heart seemed to race every time Jesse smiled at him, shy and a little unsure?

Wyatt had never thought of himself as gay. It wasn't something that had ever crossed his mind, not really. He'd dated girls before, casually, nothing serious. He liked girls—he was pretty sure of that. But this thing with Jesse felt different. Wyatt didn't know if it was because Jesse was different or if it was because Wyatt had been pushing down feelings he hadn't wanted to face for years.

He didn't *feel* gay, whatever that meant. He didn't have the same struggle he'd seen other guys go through, figuring out who they were attracted to. It had always seemed simple—until now. Until Jesse.

Wyatt rubbed his face with his hand, feeling the weight of the decision pressing down on him. He could just not follow Jesse back, let it be. Maybe that was the safest option. He didn't have to complicate things. They could stay work friends, and Wyatt wouldn't have to confront whatever was brewing inside him. But the thought of leaving Jesse hanging, of leaving that tiny door unopened, didn't sit right with him.

Wyatt unlocked his phone again and opened Instagram, his thumb hovering over the follow button. His pulse quickened, his chest tightening with the familiar mix of excitement and fear. Finally, he let out a long breath, as if he were diving headfirst into something unknown, and he tapped the button.

Followed.

The moment it happened, Wyatt felt a rush of adrenaline–both exhilarating and terrifying. He had done it. There was no going back now. The connection was made, the door cracked open a little wider, and Wyatt knew that things were about to change, even if he didn't know how.

With a nervous energy buzzing through him, Wyatt began scrolling through Jesse's profile, looking at the photos with a new perspective. The drawings caught his attention first–detailed, intricate sketches that felt like a reflection of Jesse's mind. Each one was so precise, so full of emotion, it was impossible not to admire the talent and care that had gone into them.

There was something intimate about it, seeing Jesse's art like this, seeing the world through his eyes. Wyatt had always known Jesse was talented, but seeing it all laid out like this made him feel like he was discovering a whole new side of him. It made Wyatt want to know more, to understand what made Jesse tick, what he thought about when he was sitting quietly, lost in his own world.

And then there were the pictures of Jesse himself. There weren't many–just a few, scattered among the art and the nature shots–but they stood out to Wyatt. Jesse wasn't the type to take selfies or pose in front of a camera, but in the few photos where he appeared, Wyatt could see a vulnerability that made his chest tighten all over again. Jesse was always so guarded, so careful, but here, in these photos, there was a softness to him, a quietness that Wyatt found himself drawn to more than he wanted to admit.

He kept scrolling, lost in thought, his mind racing with possibilities. The more he looked at Jesse's account, the more he realized how much he wanted to know him–not just as the quiet guy at the pool, but as *Jesse*. The real Jesse. And that scared him.

Because if he admitted that to himself, if he admitted that he *liked* Jesse, then what did that mean for Wyatt? What did that mean for everything he thought he knew about himself?

What if I'm gay? Or maybe bi?

The question hit him like a punch to the gut, and for a second, Wyatt had to close his eyes, the weight of it too much to handle. He had never considered it before, never let himself go there. He had always liked girls. That was the truth, wasn't it? But this–this thing with Jesse– wasn't just friendship. It wasn't just admiration. It was *something else*.

But did liking one guy make him gay? Or was it just that Jesse was different? Wyatt didn't know, and the not knowing was tearing him apart.

He wasn't ready to face that part of himself yet. He wasn't ready to say the words out loud, to even fully admit it in his own head. But lying here, staring at Jesse's profile, his heart racing and his mind spinning, Wyatt couldn't deny it anymore.

He *liked* Jesse. He liked him in a way that felt more than just casual interest. It was more than just wondering. It was attraction, plain and simple, and as much as it scared him, it was also exhilarating.

Wyatt let out a shaky breath, setting his phone aside and staring up at the ceiling again. He didn't know what to do next, didn't know where this would lead, but one thing was certain: following Jesse back was the first real step into something new, something unknown. And whether or not Wyatt was ready to face it, there was no turning back now.

For the first time in his life, Wyatt was starting to understand that maybe, just maybe, things weren't as simple as he had always thought they were. Maybe there was more to him than he had ever let himself see.

And maybe, with Jesse, he was about to find out just how much more there was.

Meanwhile a few miles away, Jesse sat at the dinner table, the familiar clink of forks against plates filling the quiet room as his parents chatted about their days. It was a scene that played out the same way nearly every night: his mom asking about work, his dad grumbling about some minor annoyance at the office, and Jesse giving vague, polite answers when prompted. Tonight was no different. They asked him how the pool shift went, and Jesse responded with the same stock phrases. "Yeah, it was fine," he said, offering a half-hearted smile. "Pretty quiet."

But his mind wasn't really there. It hadn't been for the past hour.

His phone, sitting face down next to his plate, vibrated softly. Jesse's heart jumped, but he didn't move. He couldn't–not yet. His mom was still talking, something about the neighbor's overgrown lawn, and Jesse knew that if he grabbed his phone now, it would only raise suspicion. His parents weren't strict, but they had a way of noticing things–little things like Jesse checking his phone one too many times at the dinner table.

He took a slow bite of mashed potatoes, trying to calm the jittery energy coursing through him. His mind raced with anticipation, the subtle buzz of his phone still echoing in his ears. Could it be? Was that *the* notification he had been waiting for?

Ever since he had wrapped up his shift at the pool, he hadn't been able to shake the odd feeling that something had shifted between him and Wyatt. Wyatt had seemed more nervous than usual today, more distant, and Jesse hadn't missed the way his eyes flickered over to him again and again, like he was holding something back. Jesse wasn't sure what to make of it, but there was a part of him—a part he tried not to think about too much—that *wanted* Wyatt to be thinking about him.

The phone buzzed again, and this time Jesse almost couldn't stop his hand from twitching toward it. *Focus,* he told himself, keeping his gaze firmly on his plate. The last thing he needed was his mom glancing over and asking why he was suddenly so interested in his phone during dinner. She was observant like that—always noticing things Jesse wished she wouldn't.

He nodded along to something his dad said about work, offering a vague, "That sucks," even though he hadn't really been paying attention. His mind was too preoccupied, the anticipation building with every second. He wanted to grab his phone, open Instagram, and see if the follow-back notification he had been secretly hoping for had finally come through.

But he had to wait. He couldn't let them see.

Dinner stretched on, longer than usual, or at least that's how it felt to Jesse. The seconds ticked by like hours, his fingers itching to reach for his phone. Finally, after what felt like an eternity, his mom stood up and began clearing the dishes. Jesse immediately followed, grabbing his plate and heading toward the kitchen, all while keeping his phone in his peripheral vision, resisting the urge to check it just yet.

He rinsed off his plate, mumbled something about needing to finish some work in his room, and made his exit as quickly as he could without drawing attention. His parents barely noticed–too busy caught up in their own conversation–and Jesse finally made his way up the stairs, his heart thudding in his chest.

The second he shut his bedroom door, he practically dove for his phone, flipping it over and unlocking the screen in one smooth motion.

There it was.

@i_am_wyatt_roberts just followed you.

Jesse's breath caught in his throat, his eyes widening as he stared at the notification, the little burst of excitement swelling in his chest so fast he almost couldn't contain it. *Wyatt followed me back.*

For a moment, Jesse just stood there, staring at the screen, his mind reeling. He had been hoping for this–waiting for it, really–but now that it had actually happened, the reality of it hit him harder than he expected. Jesse, the quiet, shy guy from the pool, had finally made a move, even if it was just something as small as following him on Instagram.

And to Jesse, it wasn't small at all. It meant something.

A grin spread across his face, and he quickly pulled up Wyatt's profile, scrolling through his photos. He liked Wyatt. There was no denying it anymore.

Jesse's fingers hovered over the "Message" button, a thousand thoughts running through his mind. Should he say something? Should he just wait and see if Wyatt reached out first? His heart raced with anticipation, and for a second, Jesse felt like a middle schooler again, giddy and nervous, unsure of how to handle his emotions.

But for now, he didn't need to do anything. The simple act of Wyatt following him was enough.

Jesse flopped back onto his bed, staring up at the ceiling, his phone resting on his chest as he tried to wrap his mind around the flood of feelings rushing through him. He felt *good*–better than he had in a long time. And he couldn't help the smile that kept creeping back onto his face, the giddy energy bubbling just beneath the surface.

Whatever happened next, Jesse knew one thing for sure: things between him and Wyatt were about to change. And for the first time in a long time, Jesse couldn't wait to see where it would lead.

He pulled out his phone again, opening Wyatt's profile one more time, unable to stop himself from smiling as he scrolled through the pictures. *Maybe this is the start of something real,* Jesse thought, his excitement growing as he realized how much he wanted that to be true.

For now, though, he would play it cool. He had to. But deep down, he was already imagining the possibilities. And he couldn't wait to see what happened next.

Chapter 7: It's Now or Never

Wyatt woke up with a strange sense of certainty in his chest—a feeling he hadn't had in weeks. His heart thudded in a steady rhythm as the early morning light streamed through his bedroom window, illuminating the corners of his room in soft, golden hues. For the first time in what felt like forever, Wyatt knew exactly what he needed to do.

He was going to make a move.

For days now, Wyatt had been tiptoeing around his feelings, wrestling with questions he didn't have the answers to. Was he really into Jesse? Was he gay? Was he bi? Did Jesse like him back? What would happen if Wyatt just put everything out there? But today, something was different. He had spent too much time overthinking, analyzing every glance, every smile, every awkward interaction. The truth was right in front of him, and he was done pretending he didn't know it.

He liked Jesse. Really liked him. And whether or not that meant something bigger about his sexuality didn't matter right now. What mattered was that Wyatt couldn't spend another day living in uncertainty, wondering what might happen if he just took the leap. He had always lived his life with confidence. And this would be no different.

Tonight, after the pool closed, he was going to make his move.

Wyatt swung his legs out of bed and rubbed his eyes, trying to shake off the remnants of sleep. His mind was racing with plans, with ideas of how the evening would go. He wasn't going to be shy about it. He wasn't going to let fear get in the way. He had to know where Jesse stood, and the only way to do that was to take a chance.

As he got ready for the day, a nervous energy began to buzz beneath his skin, but it wasn't the same crippling anxiety that had been plaguing him before. This was different. It was excitement. Anticipation. He wasn't sure how Jesse would respond, but the thought of finally knowing, of putting all the cards on the table, sent a thrill through Wyatt that made it hard to sit still.

By the time Wyatt arrived at the pool for his shift, the late summer heat was already in full swing. The sun hung high in the sky, casting long shadows across the pool deck as kids splashed and shouted in the water. The usual noise and chaos of the pool surrounded him, but Wyatt barely noticed it. His mind was laser-focused on the night ahead.

Jesse was already at the concession stand when Wyatt walked in, his back turned as he restocked the shelves with bags of chips. Wyatt's stomach did a little flip at the sight of him, and for a moment, he had to stop and steady himself. Jesse looked as calm and composed as always, his movements precise and careful, but there was a quiet intensity about him that Wyatt found himself drawn to more and more. The way Jesse's hair fell just slightly into his eyes, the way his shoulders hunched forward when he was lost in thought—it all felt so familiar now, so *right*.

Wyatt had spent so much time wondering if Jesse felt the same way, but tonight, he was going to find out.

He approached the stand, leaning casually against the counter as Jesse looked up, his eyes widening slightly when he saw Wyatt standing there.

"Hey," Jesse said, his voice soft, his usual shyness creeping into his tone. "You're here early."

Wyatt smiled, feeling his confidence build. "Yeah, I wanted to get a head start on the day." He paused, his heart pounding in his chest, but he kept his voice light. "How's it going?"

Jesse shrugged, glancing back at the shelves he had been restocking. "Same old. Just trying to keep the kids from raiding the snack supply."

Wyatt chuckled, though his mind was already elsewhere. He watched Jesse carefully, searching for any sign that he might be nervous too, that maybe Jesse had been thinking about him as much as Wyatt had been thinking about Jesse. But Jesse seemed calm, if a little distracted, his hands busy with the task at hand.

Not tonight, Wyatt thought to himself. *Tonight, I'm going to get his attention.*

The day dragged on, each hour feeling like an eternity as Wyatt's anticipation built. He tried to focus on his lifeguard duties, on keeping an eye on the kids in the water, but his thoughts kept drifting back to what he would say, how he would make his move. He rehearsed a thousand different scenarios in his head, each one ending with Jesse looking at him with those soft, unsure eyes, finally letting Wyatt know how he felt.

Finally, the sun began to set, casting a warm, golden glow over the pool. The crowd started to thin out as families packed up their towels and kids reluctantly climbed out of the water. Wyatt's pulse quickened with every passing minute. The shift was coming to an end. Soon, the pool would be empty, just him and Jesse.

His heart pounded in his chest as he watched the last few stragglers head out the gate, the echoes of their laughter fading into the summer night. Wyatt wiped his hands on his shorts, trying to calm the nervous energy building inside him. *This is it. As Wyatt heads to the locker room, he wonders if his life will ever be the same.*

Chapter 8: Making A Move

Jesse was in the locker room, wrapping up the last of his duties, when Wyatt walked in from the pool, still dripping wet and wearing only his swim trunks. Jesse's pulse quickened, but he kept his head down, trying to ignore the presence he couldn't deny was affecting him.

"Hey, Jesse," Wyatt said, his voice easygoing but with a trace of something more. "You've been working nonstop. Want to take a break and join me for a swim?"

Jesse looked up, surprised by the offer. His first instinct was to say no–anything to keep a distance. "I don't really swim," he mumbled, his words awkward.

Wyatt gave a casual shrug, but his gaze lingered on Jesse. "Doesn't matter. It's just us here. It's hot, and I thought... maybe you'd want some company."

There was something about the way Wyatt said it that made Jesse pause. After a long moment, he relented with a nod. "Okay. Just for a little while."

They walked out to the pool, and Jesse could feel his nerves rising with every step. Wyatt glanced over at him, his expression unreadable, but when he finally spoke, his words were heavy with meaning. "You know, Jesse... I've noticed you, even when you think no one else has."

Jesse blinked, the comment catching him off guard. "What do you mean?"

Wyatt stopped walking for a second, his lips pressing into a thoughtful line. "I've seen you. The way you look at me. The way you… pull back."

Jesse's heart raced, embarrassment flooding through him. "I don't know what you're talking about."

Wyatt didn't push, just nodded slowly, as if he expected Jesse's response. "I wasn't sure either," Wyatt said quietly, "until I realized I've been doing the same thing. I didn't know what to do with it."

Jesse felt his breath hitch, unsure of how to respond. Wyatt's words were so close to the thoughts Jesse had been fighting off for what felt like an eternity.

They reached the pool, and Wyatt sat down by the edge, letting his feet dangle in the water. Jesse hesitated, feeling the weight of the moment pressing down on him. He sat next to Wyatt, leaving a little distance between them.

For a few minutes, the only sound was the gentle ripple of water and the faint buzz of summer insects. Jesse wasn't sure if he should speak, if he should even look at Wyatt, afraid of what might happen if he did.

"I didn't know if I should say something," Wyatt finally broke the silence, his voice low. "I didn't want to make things weird."

Jesse swallowed hard, his throat tight. "Why did you?"

Wyatt let out a slow breath. "Because it was getting harder not to. And because…" He trailed off, as if searching for the right words, his face tense. "Because it scares me. And I thought maybe you felt the same way."

Jesse's heart thudded in his chest. "Yeah," he whispered, barely able to get the word out. "It scares me too."

Wyatt nodded, as though hearing Jesse's confirmation made him feel less alone. He glanced at Jesse, and this time, Jesse couldn't avoid his gaze. Their eyes met, and Jesse felt the weight of all the things they weren't saying yet, hanging in the air between them.

"I didn't know what this was," Jesse admitted, his voice trembling slightly. "I didn't know how to... how to feel about it."

Wyatt shifted closer, but not too close, giving Jesse space. "I don't know either," Wyatt said, his voice quiet but steady. "I just know that I care about you. And that maybe... that's enough right now."

Jesse looked down at the water, the fear still there, but mixed with something else–hope, maybe. "I didn't think you'd ever feel the same way."

Wyatt's smile was small, almost sad. "I didn't think I was supposed to feel this way," he confessed. "I've spent a lot of time trying to ignore it. But it didn't go away."

Jesse felt the weight of those words, because they mirrored his own feelings so closely. "What if... What if we mess everything up?" he asked, his voice barely above a whisper.

Wyatt glanced out at the water, his face contemplative. "I don't know," he admitted softly. "But I'm tired of pretending like this doesn't matter. Even if it's scary. Even if we don't know what happens next."

Jesse felt his chest tighten. "I don't know what this is," he whispered, almost too afraid to say it out loud. "I don't know how to feel."

Wyatt glanced at him, his eyes soft but full of understanding. "Me neither. I've never felt like this before."

Jesse didn't respond right away, his mind racing with questions and doubts. "What if things are never the same?" he asked, his voice barely audible.

Wyatt was quiet for a moment, then he turned to Jesse, meeting his eyes. "Maybe things will change," he said softly. "But what if that's a good thing? What if it's worth the risk?"

Jesse bit his lip, unsure. The fear of the unknown weighed heavily on him, but so did the possibility that maybe, just maybe, Wyatt was right. He felt a warmth spreading through him that made the fear seem a little less overwhelming.

"What do you want?" Jesse asked, the question hanging between them.

Wyatt looked down, hesitating before he answered. "I want to stop being scared," he admitted, his voice low. "I want to know what this could be."

Jesse felt his heart skip a beat. "Me too," he whispered, almost in disbelief that they were having this conversation.

Wyatt's hand hovered between them before he gently took Jesse's, their fingers intertwining. "We don't have to figure it all out right now," Wyatt said quietly. "We can take it slow."

Jesse looked down at their hands, his heart racing, but this time, it wasn't from fear. He took a deep breath and nodded, feeling a weight lift off his shoulders.

Wyatt smiled, a small, reassuring smile that made Jesse feel safe in a way he hadn't expected. Slowly, Wyatt leaned in, and for a moment, Jesse thought about pulling back. But he didn't. Instead, he let his eyes close as Wyatt pressed a soft, tentative kiss to his lips.

The kiss wasn't long, just a brief, delicate connection, but it sent a warmth through Jesse that made him feel like everything was suddenly clearer. When they pulled apart, Wyatt's face was just inches from his, their foreheads nearly touching.

Jesse opened his eyes, feeling a little breathless, but lighter somehow. "That wasn't so bad," he said with a small smile, his voice trembling but filled with relief.

Wyatt chuckled softly. "Yeah. Not bad at all."

For a moment, they just sat there, the quiet of the summer evening settling around them, the uncertainty still there but now tempered with a sense of hope. Jesse felt like something had shifted, like they had crossed a line he never thought they could. And it felt good.

"What happens now?" Jesse asked, his voice soft, almost afraid to break the peaceful silence.

Wyatt squeezed his hand gently. "Whatever we want. We've got time."

Jesse smiled, his heart still fluttering but no longer with fear. For the first time, he wasn't worried about what came next. Sitting there with

Wyatt, he realized that opening up, even though it scared him, had brought him something he hadn't expected–possibility.

Chapter 9: Coming to Terms

The days after the pool encounter felt like a whirlwind to Jesse. Each day is filled with stolen glances, shared smiles, and brief, secret touches that make his heart race. But at night, when he's alone in his room, the quiet brings thoughts that are harder to ignore.

Jesse lies on his bed, staring at the ceiling, his mind a tangled mess of emotions. The feelings he has for Wyatt are new, intense, and undeniably real. For the first time, he's experiencing something he's always kept buried deep, a part of himself he was afraid to confront.

He thinks back to his childhood, the moments when he felt different but couldn't explain why. Growing up, he was surrounded by kids who seemed to know exactly who they were, who they liked, and where they belonged. But Jesse always felt like he was on the outside looking in, unable to find his place.

In middle school, he had his first crush on a boy in his class. He didn't understand it at the time, didn't even have the words for what he was feeling. He just knew there was a magnetic pull, an unexplainable yearning to be near that boy, to hear his laugh and see his smile. But Jesse quickly learned that those kinds of feelings weren't something you shared, especially not in Brookwood, a small town where everyone knew everyone else's business.

Jesse remembers the fear that gripped him whenever he felt a flutter in his chest around another boy. The shame that would settle in his stomach whenever he overheard his friends making jokes, using words like "gay" and "queer" like they were the worst things you could be. He learned to hide, to pretend, to force himself to look at girls the way his friends did, to try and fit in.

And he was good at it, too. He pushed those feelings down so deep that he almost convinced himself they weren't real, that they were just a phase or something he could outgrow. He dated girls, went to dances, and did everything he was supposed to do. But there was always a sense of emptiness, a feeling that something was missing.

Now, with Wyatt, everything is different. Wyatt makes him feel alive in a way he's never felt before. The way Wyatt looks at him, the way he talks to him—it's as if he's being seen for the first time. But with that new feeling comes fear, the fear of what it means to be truly seen, to be vulnerable and open in a way he's never been before.

Jesse sits up, hugging his knees to his chest, and thinks about what his life has been up until now—a series of safe choices, a life lived in the shadows of other people's expectations. He wonders if he can really be himself, if he has the courage to let go of everything he's been taught to hide.

He thinks of Wyatt, of the way he smiles, the way he says Jesse's name like it's something special. He thinks of how free he felt in Wyatt's arms, how, for just a moment, all the fear and doubt melted away, and he could just be.

Jesse knows he can't go back to pretending. He can't go back to hiding this part of himself anymore. But he also knows that accepting who he is means facing a lot of things he's been afraid of—what his parents might think, what his friends will say, what it will mean for his future.

The next day, Jesse finds himself at his favorite coffee shop on the edge of town, sitting across from his best friend, Liz. Liz has known him since they were kids, they met in 1st grade, and she's always been the one person he could talk to about anything… except this.

Liz looks at him, her brow furrowed in concern. "You've been quiet lately," she says, her voice gentle. "Is everything okay?"

Jesse takes a deep breath, feeling his heart pound in his chest. "I… I think I need to tell you something. Something I've been figuring out about myself."

Liz's eyes soften, and she reaches across the table to take his hand. "You can tell me anything, Jesse. You know that."

Jesse nods, feeling a lump form in his throat. "I think… no, I know I'm… I'm gay."

The words hang in the air between them, heavy and charged with meaning. Jesse watches Liz's face closely, looking for any sign of judgment or rejection. But instead, she smiles, a warm, understanding smile.

"Jesse," she says softly, "I'm so proud of you for saying that. For being honest with yourself. I've always known there was something you were holding back, but I didn't want to push you." "To be honest, I thought that could be the reason."

Relief floods through Jesse, and he feels tears prick at his eyes. "I've been so scared," he admits, his voice trembling. "Scared of what people would think, of not being enough… of everything."

Liz squeezes his hand. "You're enough, Jesse. More than enough. And anyone who doesn't see that isn't worth your time. I'm here for you, no matter what."

"Theres more..."

Liz sipped her iced latte, eyes never leaving his.

"Alright... spill. What's going on?" she finally asked, setting her cup down with a soft clink.

Jesse hesitated. This was Liz – his best friend since forever. If anyone could understand, it would be her. Still, a familiar knot tightened in his stomach.

He glanced out the window, gathering his thoughts, then took a deep breath. "I don't know where to start," he said, his voice barely louder than a whisper.

Liz leaned in, her expression softening. "Hey, start wherever you want. I'm here."

Jesse looked down, taking another deep breath. "You know Wyatt, right? The new lifeguard?"

Liz nodded, a small smile playing on her lips. "Yeah, the one everyone's obsessed with. What about him?"

Jesse's face flushed, and he forced himself to meet her gaze. "Something happened between us. At the pool. A few days ago."

Liz's eyes widened with curiosity. "Something like...?"

Jesse exhaled sharply, a mix of nerves and excitement bubbling up. "We kissed… It was… it was intense, Liz. I didn't expect it, but it just happened."

He could see Liz's face light up with a grin. "No way! That's amazing! So, how did it feel?"

Jesse felt his face burn hotter. "It felt… incredible," he admitted, the words tumbling out before he could stop them. "Like I was finally where I was supposed to be. But also… terrifying. I've never felt anything like that before."

Liz nodded, her smile softening into something more understanding. "I get that. But it sounds like a good kind of terrifying?"

Jesse shrugged, looking down at his hands. "Yeah, but it's also confusing. I mean, I've known I'm gay for a while, but I've never actually been with a guy before, you know? And now, with Wyatt… it's like everything I thought I knew just shifted."

Liz was quiet for a moment, then reached across the table to squeeze his hand. "And how does Wyatt feel about all this?"

Jesse couldn't help the small smile that spread across his lips. "He's… been really great. He told me he noticed the way I looked at him, that he'd been waiting for me to make a move. And he didn't care about all the stuff I've been scared about. He just wanted me."

Liz's grin returned. "Wow, he sounds pretty perfect."

Jesse laughed, but the worry in his chest hadn't entirely disappeared. "Yeah, but that's what scares me, too. What if I'm reading too much into it? What if it's just a summer thing for him? I've barely come to terms with this myself, and now there's Wyatt, and I don't want to mess it up."

Liz squeezed his hand tighter, her expression serious now. "Jesse, it's okay to be scared. But from what you're saying, Wyatt seems like he really likes you. And even if it is just a summer thing, that doesn't mean it's not real or important. What matters is how you feel."

Jesse nodded slowly, Liz's words sinking in. "I feel... like I'm finally not hiding. With him, I feel seen."

Liz's smile widened. "Then that's what you hold onto. Don't overthink it. Just be in the moment and see where it takes you."

Jesse sighed, relief washing over him. "Thanks, Liz. I needed to hear that."

Liz winked. "That's what I'm here for. And if you two end up being the hottest couple at the pool, I expect all the juicy details."

Jesse laughed, feeling the weight in his chest lift a little more. "Deal."

That night, back in his room, Jesse feels a new sense of calm. He knows the road ahead won't be easy, that there will be challenges and moments of doubt. But he also knows that he's taken the first step toward embracing who he truly is.

He looks in the mirror, seeing himself with new eyes. He's not the scared kid who felt different, who worried about fitting in. He's Jesse—a young man learning to love himself, finding the courage to be open and real, to live a life that's true to him.

Jesse thinks of Wyatt again, of his smile, his touch, his quiet confidence. He feels a spark of hope, a belief that maybe, just maybe, he's on the right path. He reaches for his iPhone and sends Wyatt a simple message:

"Hey, can we talk?"

Wyatt's reply comes almost immediately:

"Always. Meet me at the pool?"

Jesse smiles, feeling a weight lift off his shoulders. He grabs his jacket and heads out, feeling the cool night air on his skin. He doesn't know what the future holds, but for the first time in his life, he's ready to face it–one step at a time, hopefully with Wyatt by his side.

Chapter 10: Fragile Secrets

Jesse arrived at the pool well before Wyatt, letting himself into the maintenance room, his nerves a tangled mess. He wasn't sure what he was doing here, why he'd asked Wyatt to meet him after hours when they weren't supposed to be here at all. But the weight of everything had been building for days, and tonight felt like the only chance to say what had been bottled up inside him.

He busied himself by pretending to clean, but his hands were trembling, betraying his anxiety. When he heard the faint creak of the door, his heart leapt into his throat.

Wyatt stepped into the room, still a little damp from his earlier swim, wearing a hoodie over his swim trunks. He leaned casually against the doorframe, though the tension in his body betrayed his casual posture. "Hey," Wyatt said, the word hanging between them with unspoken meaning. His usual smile was there, but it didn't quite reach his eyes, as though he, too, was unsure of what this meeting meant.

Jesse swallowed hard, forcing himself to look at Wyatt. "Hey," he replied, trying to keep his voice steady, though he felt like he was coming apart at the seams. His hands gripped a rag, twisting it nervously.

Wyatt took a few steps closer, his eyes locked on Jesse's. "So... what's up? You texted me, asked me to meet you here after hours," he said, his tone light but the undertone unmistakable. "What's going on?"

Jesse hesitated, his heart pounding in his chest as a flood of thoughts swirled through his mind. He'd rehearsed this conversation a dozen times in his head, but now that Wyatt was standing in front of him, everything felt jumbled, as if his words had escaped him entirely. He shook his head slightly, frustrated with himself. "I just needed to see you," he finally said, his voice quieter than he intended.

Wyatt raised an eyebrow, taking another step forward. "Just to see me, huh?" he said, a teasing smile playing at the corners of his mouth, though his eyes flickered with uncertainty.

Jesse dropped his gaze to the floor, his cheeks flushing. "It's not just that," he muttered, almost to himself. "I don't know what to do with all of this. With you."

For a moment, there was silence between them, thick with tension and the weight of all the things unsaid. Jesse's heart thudded painfully in his chest, and he forced himself to glance up at Wyatt, terrified of what he might see in his expression. But instead of confusion or dismissal, Wyatt's face softened. The usual cocky smirk faded as Wyatt's eyes filled with something else–something more vulnerable, more real.

"You don't have to do anything, Jesse," Wyatt said, stepping closer until there was barely any space between them. His voice had dropped to a gentle whisper, as though they were sharing a fragile secret. He reached out, lifting Jesse's chin so their eyes met. "Just be here with me."

Jesse searched Wyatt's face, looking for any trace of doubt or insincerity. He half-expected Wyatt to laugh it off, to shrug it away like it didn't matter. But what he saw in Wyatt's gaze wasn't what he'd expected. There was a longing there, the same kind that had been building inside him all summer. But there was something else too–fear. Wyatt was just as scared as he was.

Wyatt exhaled slowly, his hand dropping from Jesse's face, and he took a step back, his expression shifting to one of hesitation. "But I need to be honest with you," he said, his voice tinged with uncertainty. "This... this whole thing is complicated. A lot more complicated than I thought it would be."

Jesse's heart sank. He could feel the conversation shifting, the tension between them growing heavier. "What do you mean?" he asked, though he had a sinking feeling he already knew.

Wyatt looked away, running a hand through his damp hair, as if trying to buy himself more time to find the right words. "My parents," he began, his voice tight. "They wouldn't get it. They wouldn't understand this... us. If they found out–" He stopped, shaking his head. "They'd flip out. And I can't–" His voice cracked slightly, and he took a deep breath before continuing. "I can't let them know. It's not that simple."

Jesse's chest tightened, his throat thick with emotion. He'd always known, on some level, that Wyatt's family was a looming presence in his life, but hearing it out loud made the fear more real. "So... what does that mean for us?" Jesse asked, his voice small, the question hanging between them like a weight neither of them wanted to confront.

Wyatt's eyes met his again, and Jesse could see the battle going on behind them. "I don't know," Wyatt admitted, his voice barely audible. "I want this–I want you–but I don't know how to do it without risking everything. I'm scared, Jesse. I don't know how to make it work."

Jesse felt his heart ache. He had thought he was the only one struggling with this, the only one scared of what might happen. But now, seeing

Wyatt's vulnerability laid bare, he realized that they were both standing on the same uncertain ground.

"I'm scared too," Jesse whispered, stepping closer to Wyatt. "But I don't want to walk away from this because we're scared. What if we take it slow? No promises, no pressure. Just... see where it goes."

Wyatt let out a shaky breath, the tension in his shoulders easing ever so slightly. He glanced away for a moment, his brow furrowed in thought, before finally nodding. "Yeah," he said softly. "Okay. No promises. We take it one day at a time."

Jesse felt a flicker of relief, but the uncertainty still loomed over them. He didn't know what the future held–didn't know if they could make this work–but for now, the promise of trying was enough. He reached out tentatively, his hand brushing against Wyatt's, and after a brief hesitation, Wyatt took his hand, his grip warm and steady.

Without thinking, Jesse leaned in, his heart pounding as he pressed his lips to Wyatt's in a soft, tentative kiss. The kiss was slow, gentle, but full of the emotions they had both been too afraid to express. Wyatt responded immediately, his other hand coming up to cup Jesse's face, holding him as if he never wanted to let go.

When they finally pulled apart, their foreheads rested together, both of them breathing heavily in the quiet of the night. Jesse opened his eyes, searching Wyatt's face for any sign of regret, but all he saw was the same mix of fear and hope he felt inside.

"Do you want to get out of here?" Wyatt asked, his voice barely above a whisper, as though the moment was too delicate to disturb.

Jesse nodded, his hand still intertwined with Wyatt's. "Yeah. Let's go."

They left the pool together, walking in silence through the quiet streets of Brookwood. The world around them felt still, almost frozen in time. Jesse glanced over at Wyatt, feeling the warmth of his hand, and for the first time, he didn't feel the need to pull away. When they reached a small, secluded park on the edge of town, Wyatt led him to a quiet spot beneath a large oak tree.

They lay down on the soft grass, the night sky above them a deep canvas of blues and purples, the first stars twinkling faintly in the distance. For a long while, they didn't say anything, just lying there side by side, holding hands and listening to the sounds of the evening.

Eventually, Jesse turned to Wyatt, his voice barely more than a whisper. "Wyatt... what happens when the summer ends?"

Wyatt sighed, his gaze fixed on the sky. "I've been thinking about that," he admitted, his voice quiet. "I know I'm going back to college, and you are too. Things will change. I don't know how it'll work." He paused, his fingers tightening around Jesse's. "I can't tell my parents. Not yet. Maybe not for a long time."

Jesse's chest tightened. "So... what do we do?"

Wyatt turned his head, meeting Jesse's eyes with an intensity that made his heart skip a beat. "I want to try," he said softly. "I can't promise anything. Long distance is going to be hard, and hiding this... it'll be harder. But I don't want to let it go just because it's complicated."

Jesse searched Wyatt's face, trying to find an answer in the uncertainty. He wanted to believe it could work, but he knew the challenges were real. "What if... what if it's not enough? What if we can't handle it?"

Wyatt sighed, brushing a strand of hair from Jesse's face. "Then we'll figure it out. One day at a time. We don't have to have all the answers right now."

Jesse's heart swelled at Wyatt's words, the warmth of his touch easing the fears that had been gnawing at him for weeks. Maybe they didn't have all the answers, but for now, being here–being together–felt like enough.

"Okay," Jesse said, his voice firmer now. "Let's try. Let's see where this goes."

Wyatt smiled, his hand squeezing Jesse's gently. "You won't regret it," he whispered.

They lay there in silence for a while longer, watching the stars slowly brighten in the darkening sky. The world around them felt distant, and for the first time in a long time, Jesse felt a sense of calm settle over him. Whatever the future held, they would face it together.

Chapter 11: The First Date

Jesse's heart thudded in his chest as he stared at his reflection in the mirror. The plain black t-shirt and jeans felt like the safest choice, but he still wondered if he should have worn something else. His parents were out for the night and Wyatt took that opportunity to see Jesse again. The text from Wyatt had been casual – *"Pick you up at 7? Got a plan in mind."* – but the simplicity made it feel even more serious.

When the knock came at the door, Jesse took a deep breath, trying to steady his nerves. He opened it to find Wyatt standing there, leaning casually against the doorframe, his hair slightly tousled from the breeze. He looked effortlessly cool in a fitted, dark green shirt and jeans.

"Hey," Wyatt greeted him with a warm smile that seemed to reach right into Jesse's core. "You ready for this?"

Jesse nodded, managing a nervous smile. "Yeah, I think so. Where are we going?"

Wyatt's smile turned playful. "A little adventure. We're heading out of town. Hope you don't mind a bit of a drive."

Jesse's eyebrows lifted. "Out of town?"

Wyatt nodded. "Figured we could use a change of scenery... and maybe avoid any nosy neighbors," he added with a wink.

Jesse laughed, feeling his nerves ease a little. "That sounds perfect."

They walked to Wyatt's car, an old but reliable sedan that seemed to suit Wyatt's laid-back style. As they pulled out of the driveway, Wyatt reached over, brushing his fingers against Jesse's. It was a small gesture, but it sent a warm thrill through Jesse's entire body.

"You good?" Wyatt asked, glancing over with a concerned expression.

Jesse nodded, looking out at the familiar streets passing by. "Yeah, just... I've never done anything like this before."

Wyatt smiled gently. "Me neither. But I'm glad we're doing it."

They drove for a while, the town of Brookwood slowly fading behind them as they made their way toward the open road. The air in the car felt lighter, the further they got from the town Jesse had always known. He glanced over at Wyatt, who was tapping his fingers on the steering wheel to the beat of a song playing softly on the radio.

"You look like you're having fun," Jesse observed.

Wyatt shot him a quick grin. "I am. And I think you are, too."

Jesse chuckled. "Yeah, maybe I am."

About an hour later, they arrived at a small, quaint town that Jesse had never been to before. The streets were lined with charming storefronts, their windows glowing softly in the fading evening light. Wyatt pulled up to a cozy café at the edge of a little square, where strings of lights hung between trees, illuminating tables scattered with couples and friends.

"This place looks... amazing," Jesse breathed, taking it all in.

Wyatt turned off the engine and smiled at him. "I found it last summer. Figured it would be nice to have a date where no one knows us."

Jesse felt a rush of gratitude. "You're always thinking ahead."

Wyatt chuckled. "I try." He got out of the car and walked around to open Jesse's door, taking his hand as he helped him out. "Come on, let's get something to eat."

They entered the café, which was warm and inviting, filled with the scent of coffee, fresh bread, and pastries. A young hostess greeted them and led them to a quiet corner booth near a window. Jesse couldn't help but notice how Wyatt's hand lingered near his, the brush of his fingers light but steady.

They ordered burgers and milkshakes – Wyatt's suggestion, which he insisted were "legendary" at this place. As they waited for their food, Wyatt's eyes flickered with amusement. "So, what do you think? A little different from Brookwood, right?"

Jesse smiled, relaxing into the seat. "Definitely different. I feel like I'm in a whole other world."

Wyatt nodded. "That's the idea. No one here knows us, so we can just... be."

Jesse's heart swelled at the thought. "I like that."

Their food arrived, and they started to eat. Wyatt kept up a lively conversation, telling stories from his college adventures, his time working at the pool, and even some embarrassing childhood tales. Jesse found himself laughing, genuinely enjoying every minute. He couldn't remember the last time he'd felt this carefree, this happy.

At some point, Wyatt leaned forward, his gaze softening. "You know, I've been wanting to do this for a while. Take you out, I mean. Just us, no one watching."

Jesse looked down at his plate, feeling his cheeks flush. "I'm glad you did. I was so nervous, but... I'm really happy I'm here with you."

Wyatt's smile was warm and reassuring. "Good. Because I want to know everything about you, Jesse. The real you."

Jesse's chest tightened with emotion. "I want that too," he whispered.

They finished their meal, lingering over their milkshakes as the café slowly emptied out. Wyatt reached across the table, taking Jesse's hand in his, his thumb brushing over Jesse's knuckles. The gesture was simple but intimate, and Jesse felt a rush of warmth spread through him.

"You ready for the surprise?" Wyatt asked, his eyes twinkling with excitement.

Jesse grinned, nodding. "Absolutely."

Wyatt drove them out of town, following a winding road that led deeper into the countryside. The sun had set by now, and the sky was a blanket of deep blues and purples, dotted with the first stars of the night.

Jesse was about to ask where they were going when Wyatt pulled onto a narrow dirt road that led to a secluded overlook. He parked the car and hopped out, then walked around to open Jesse's door. "Come on," he said, offering his hand.

Jesse took it, feeling a mix of excitement and nerves. "Where are we?"

Wyatt smiled mysteriously. "Just a spot I found. It's perfect for stargazing."

They walked a short distance to a small clearing where Wyatt had set up a blanket.

Jesse's breath caught in his throat. "Wyatt, this is... this is amazing."

Wyatt rubbed the back of his neck, looking a little shy for the first time that night. "I wanted to do something special. I thought... maybe we could watch the stars and just... talk."

Jesse felt a wave of emotion wash over him. "I've never had anyone do something like this for me before."

Wyatt smiled softly, stepping closer. "Well, get used to it," he said, pulling Jesse gently down onto the blanket beside him.

They lay back, shoulders touching, gazing up at the endless expanse of the sky above them. The night was quiet except for the rustle of leaves and the distant sound of crickets. Jesse could feel Wyatt's body close to his, the warmth radiating between them.

After a long silence, Wyatt spoke. "You know, I meant what I said earlier. I really want to get to know you, Jesse. I don't want this to be some summer fling."

Jesse turned his head to look at him, his heart pounding in his chest. "I want that too, Wyatt. I've never felt this way before... about anyone."

Wyatt's hand found Jesse's, their fingers intertwining. "I know it's all new and scary... but maybe we can figure it out together?"

Jesse nodded, feeling a surge of emotion. "Together sounds good," he whispered.

Wyatt leaned in, pressing his lips to Jesse's in a slow, lingering kiss. It was gentle, filled with promise and tenderness, and Jesse felt himself melt into it. For the first time, he felt completely at ease, like he was exactly where he was meant to be.

They pulled back, resting their foreheads together, breathing in the cool night air. Wyatt's voice was soft, barely a whisper. "No more hiding, okay? Let's just... be ourselves, even if it's just here, under the stars."

Jesse smiled, a tear slipping down his cheek, and he nodded. "No more hiding."

They lay there, holding each other under the vast, starry sky, feeling like they were the only two people in the world.

They lay side by side on the blanket, the world around them fading into a gentle hum. Above, the stars sparkled in an endless sea, and for the first time in a long time, Jesse felt like he could breathe deeply. Like the weight of all his secrets and fears was slowly lifting.

Wyatt shifted slightly, propping himself up on his elbow to look at Jesse. "You ever think about what's out there?" he asked, his voice low and thoughtful.

Jesse followed his gaze up to the stars. "Like in space?"

Wyatt nodded. "Yeah. I used to wonder all the time. Are we alone? Or is there something bigger... something more?"

Jesse turned to him, a grin spreading across his face. "I didn't take you for the philosophical type."

Wyatt laughed softly. "There's a lot you don't know about me yet."

Jesse's smile widened. "I'm starting to find that out."

Wyatt reached out, tracing a finger along Jesse's arm. "What about you? What do you think is out there?"

Jesse hesitated, then shrugged. "I don't know. I guess I never really thought about it. I was too busy trying to figure out what was going on inside me... you know?"

Wyatt nodded, his expression turning serious. "Yeah, I get that. It can be hard to think about the big questions when the little ones feel so... overwhelming."

Jesse felt a swell of emotion at Wyatt's understanding. "It's like... I've spent so much of my life trying to fit in, to be what everyone else wanted me to be. But now... now I just want to figure out who I am. For real."

Wyatt's hand slid down to find Jesse's, squeezing gently. "And who do you think that is?"

Jesse stared up at the stars, the silence stretching between them. "I think... I think I'm still figuring it out. But I know I want to be someone who's not afraid anymore. Someone who can love who he wants to love, without worrying what everyone else thinks."

Wyatt's thumb brushed over Jesse's knuckles. "I think you're already that guy, Jesse. You just have to believe it."

Jesse felt his heart swell. "Maybe I'm getting there. Being with you... it makes me feel like I could be."

Wyatt leaned in closer, his voice a whisper in the night air. "You make me feel that way too."

They lay in comfortable silence for a while, letting the sounds of the night wrap around them. A light breeze rustled through the trees, and somewhere in the distance, an owl hooted. Jesse felt a calm he hadn't known was possible settle over him.

After a while, Wyatt broke the silence. "Do you ever think about what you want... like, really want?"

Jesse turned his head to look at Wyatt. "What do you mean?"

Wyatt shrugged, staring up at the sky. "I mean, I think about it a lot. What I want out of life, out of love, out of... everything. Sometimes it feels like I'm just going through the motions, doing what I'm supposed to do. But with you... I don't know, it feels different."

Jesse's heart ached with the sincerity in Wyatt's voice. "I think about that too," he admitted. "I've always felt like I was waiting for something, but I didn't know what. Maybe... maybe I was waiting for you."

Wyatt's smile was soft, his eyes searching Jesse's face. "Maybe we were both waiting for each other."

They fell silent again, but this time, the quiet was filled with possibility. Jesse felt his chest tighten with hope, with the kind of excitement he hadn't allowed himself to feel in years.

Wyatt suddenly sat up, pulling Jesse with him. "Come on," he said, a playful grin spreading across his face.

Jesse looked confused. "Where are we going?"

Wyatt stood and pulled Jesse to his feet. "I saw a little path back there," he said, pointing toward the edge of the clearing. "Let's go see where it leads."

Jesse hesitated, then smiled, nodding. "Alright, lead the way."

They walked together down the narrow path, their hands still entwined. The trees around them grew denser, the air cooler, and Jesse felt a thrill of adventure coursing through him. It was so rare to feel this kind of freedom, to just be in the moment, without fear or worry.

After a few minutes, they emerged into another small clearing, this one with a tiny, serene pond at its center. The water was so still that it perfectly reflected the stars above. Wyatt stopped and turned to Jesse, his eyes sparkling with mischief.

"Skinny dipping?" Wyatt suggested with a playful grin, his eyes glinting mischievously in the fading light.

Jesse's heart skipped a beat, a rush of adrenaline shooting through him. He stared at Wyatt, wondering if he was serious. "Are you... for real?" Jesse asked, half-laughing to mask his nervousness.

Wyatt shrugged casually, but there was a sparkle of boldness in his eyes as he pulled off his shirt in one swift motion. "Why not? No one's here but us. It's summer. Feels like we should do something crazy."

Jesse hesitated, feeling his stomach twist. The thought of being naked in front of Wyatt made his heart race, and not just from excitement. The anxiety of being so exposed gnawed at him. But then, seeing Wyatt's carefree attitude, Jesse felt a strange pull–a desire to let go of the fear that had been holding him back all his life. He wasn't sure if it was the warm night air, the secret thrill of being alone with Wyatt, or simply the desire to take a leap.

"Alright," Jesse said, his voice wavering slightly but filled with a mix of nerves and excitement. He began to pull off his clothes, pausing to glance at Wyatt to make sure this wasn't some sort of joke.

Wyatt's grin widened, full of mischief and warmth. He tossed his clothes onto the grass, leaving them in a careless heap as he stood there, completely bare under the moonlight. Before Jesse could think too much about it, Wyatt ran to the edge of the pond and leapt in, a loud splash shattering the stillness.

He surfaced, laughing and shaking the water from his hair. "Come on, Jesse! The water's perfect!"

Jesse took a deep breath, his hands trembling slightly as he stripped down to nothing. The cool night air prickled against his skin, and he felt a moment of panic–what if Wyatt saw him differently now? What if this was too much?

But before he could let the fear take over, Jesse ran to the edge of the pond, holding himself as best he could, and jumped in. The cold water was a shock, but it was also a relief–like an escape from everything that had been weighing him down. He came up laughing, the nervous energy leaving his body in waves.

Wyatt swam closer, his smile wide and genuine. "Feels good, doesn't it?"

Jesse nodded, grinning despite himself. "Yeah... it does."

They floated for a while, the water gently rippling around them. The moon reflected off the surface, casting a silvery glow that made the moment feel surreal, like they were in their own world, separate from everything else.

Wyatt swam up to Jesse, his face softening. "You're quiet," he murmured. "You okay?"

Jesse bit his lip, feeling the nervous flutter return. "Yeah, just... I don't usually do stuff like this."

Wyatt chuckled, brushing his arm against Jesse's under the water. "Neither do I. But it feels kinda good to be reckless, right? I mean, what's life without a little risk?"

Jesse smiled at that. "Yeah, maybe you're right."

Wyatt grinned, then his expression turned thoughtful. "Wanna play a game?"

"A game?"

"Yeah. '10 Questions.' We take turns asking each other whatever we want. But the catch is... no dodging the questions. You have to answer honestly."

Jesse laughed nervously. "Alright, but I'm holding you to that too."

Wyatt raised his hands in mock surrender. "Scout's honor. You first."

Jesse thought for a moment, trying to come up with something light to ease the tension. "What's your favorite food?"

Wyatt's smile turned playful. "Easy. Pepperoni pizza. Could eat it every day and never get tired of it. Your turn."

Jesse swam back a little, considering. "Okay. What's your biggest fear?"

Wyatt's smile faded just slightly, and he looked down, letting the water ripple around them in silence for a moment before answering. "Honestly? My parents finding out... about all this. About me. I'm afraid of what they'll think, how they'll react." He glanced up at Jesse, his voice softer now. "But I'm trying not to let that fear control me."

Jesse's heart tightened, hearing Wyatt's vulnerability. He nodded, feeling the weight of his own question. "I get that. I'm scared of that too. Of people knowing."

Wyatt moved closer, his voice gentle. "We don't have to rush it. I just don't want to spend my life hiding." He gave Jesse a small smile. "Okay, my turn. What's your favorite thing to do when no one's around?"

Jesse laughed, relieved at the lighter question. "Probably reading. I like getting lost in books, forgetting about everything else."

Wyatt nodded, smiling. "Yeah? What kind of books?"

Jesse grinned. "Fantasy, mostly. I like the idea of magic and other worlds."

Wyatt's eyes lit up. "That's cool. I can totally see that about you. You're always kinda off in your own world sometimes, in a good way."

They continued playing the game, exchanging questions that ranged from lighthearted ("What's your favorite movie?") to deeper ones that made them pause, revealing bits of themselves in the process.

At one point, Wyatt asked, "What's the one thing you want to do before you die?"

Jesse thought for a moment, staring up at the stars. "I think... I want to be brave. I want to stop letting fear decide everything for me. Or... climb Mount Everest, yes, that sounds cooler" he said with a smile.

Wyatt didn't say anything right away, but when he did, his voice was soft. "You're already braver than you think."

They floated in silence for a while after that, the water cool but comforting. Jesse felt more at ease now, more comfortable in Wyatt's presence, even with the nerves still lingering in the background.

But eventually, the cool air started to nip at their skin, and Wyatt glanced at the shore. "We should probably get out soon. We're gonna freeze if we stay in much longer."

Jesse felt his stomach tighten again. The idea of getting out of the water, standing naked in front of Wyatt, made his heart race. He bit his lip, unsure if he was ready for that level of vulnerability. "Yeah... but... what if it's weird when we get out?"

Wyatt seemed to pick up on Jesse's anxiety, and he smiled reassuringly. "It's only weird if we make it weird. We're already here, right?"

Jesse nodded, taking a deep breath. "Okay... on three?"

Wyatt grinned. "One... two... three!"

They both swam toward the shore and climbed out of the water, standing awkwardly for a moment as the night air chilled their wet skin. Jesse instinctively wrapped his arms around himself, trying to cover up. But when he glanced over at Wyatt, he saw the same flicker of hesitation in his eyes.

For a second, they both stood there, unsure of what to do next.

Then Wyatt laughed, shaking his head as he grabbed his clothes. "It's just us, Jesse. We don't have to be embarrassed."

Jesse hesitated, but then he found himself laughing too, feeling the tension break. He let his arms drop to his sides and grabbed his own clothes, getting dressed as quickly as he could. The embarrassment was still there, but it felt lighter now, more manageable.

After they got dressed, Wyatt turned to Jesse with a grin. "See? Not so bad, right?"

Jesse smiled, the warmth from earlier flooding back. "Yeah. Not so bad... I liked what I saw."

"Hey!" Wyatt said laughing. "But... I did too" he said with the same cute grin.

They walked back toward town, their clothes still a little damp, but Jesse didn't mind. The vulnerability, the thrill of the moment–it had all been worth it. And as Wyatt nudged his shoulder playfully, Jesse realized that for the first time in a long time, he wasn't afraid of what might come next.

Chapter 12: Morning After Uncertainty

The next morning, Jesse awoke with a sense of calm he hadn't felt in a long time. The previous day still lingered in his thoughts – the laughter, the quiet moments under the oak tree, and the feeling of Wyatt's hand in his. For a few precious hours, it had felt like they were the only two people in the world.

But today, something felt different. A subtle, nagging worry crept into his mind as he pulled on his uniform and prepared for another day at the pool. He kept checking his phone, hoping to see a message from Wyatt, but there was nothing. Jesse told himself Wyatt was probably just busy or sleeping in; after all, they had been out late.

As he rode his bike to the pool, the warm summer air did little to calm his nerves. The chatter of the kids playing, the sharp whistle blasts from the lifeguards, and the hum of the concession stand filled the space around him, but Jesse felt strangely disconnected from it all. His eyes kept drifting to the lifeguard chair at the far end, where Wyatt usually sat.

When Jesse finally saw Wyatt, his heart leapt – but just as quickly, it sank. Wyatt was there, perched on the tall lifeguard chair, sunglasses on, his expression serious and distant. He didn't look Jesse's way, not once. It was like a wall had gone up overnight, and Jesse didn't understand why.

Jesse tried to keep himself busy, wiping down tables, organizing the concession stand, anything to keep his mind off the uneasy feeling twisting in his stomach. He wondered if he'd done something wrong.

Had Wyatt changed his mind? Was he regretting what had happened between them?

A couple of times, Jesse caught himself staring at Wyatt, hoping he'd glance over or give some sign that everything was okay. But Wyatt didn't. He stayed focused on his job, occasionally blowing his whistle or shouting instructions to the kids in the pool. Even during breaks, Wyatt kept his distance, chatting with the other lifeguards, his usual carefree smile noticeably absent.

At lunchtime, Jesse took his tray and found a quiet corner near the back of the pool area, hoping Wyatt might join him like he usually did. He picked at his food, glancing up every few moments. But Wyatt stayed where he was, talking with a group of the other lifeguards, his body language closed off. Jesse could feel his heart sinking deeper with each passing minute.

Finally, he couldn't stand it anymore. He stood up, taking a deep breath, and walked over to where Wyatt was sitting with the others. "Hey, Wyatt," he said, trying to keep his voice casual. "You got a minute?"

Wyatt looked up, his expression unreadable behind his sunglasses. He hesitated, then nodded. "Yeah, of course," he replied, standing up and following Jesse to a more secluded spot near the edge of the pool.

Jesse turned to face him, searching for something – anything – in Wyatt's face that would tell him what was going on. "Hey," Jesse started, his voice low. "I... I just wanted to see if everything's okay. You've been kind of... distant today."

Wyatt sighed, glancing around to make sure no one was listening. "Yeah, sorry about that," he said quietly. "Just... have a lot on my mind."

Jesse felt a lump forming in his throat. "Is it about... us? About yesterday?"

Wyatt hesitated, then nodded slowly. "Yeah, I guess so," he admitted. "Look, Jesse... yesterday was amazing and I wouldn't change it for the world. But today, I just... I'm not sure what to do, you know? I don't want people here to... start talking."

Jesse felt a pang of disappointment but tried to hide it. "I get that," he said, forcing a smile. "It's just... I thought maybe things would be different today."

Wyatt looked down, kicking at the ground with his foot. "I know. I'm sorry. I just need some time to figure things out."

Jesse nodded, swallowing hard. "Okay," he said softly. "I understand."

Wyatt offered a small, apologetic smile. "We're good, Jesse. I just... need some space right now. Can you give me that?"

Jesse's heart sank, but he nodded. "Yeah, of course. Take all the time you need."

Wyatt's smile was fleeting, and he turned to walk away, leaving Jesse standing alone by the pool's edge. Jesse watched him go, feeling a mix of confusion, hurt, and longing. He had hoped for more after last night, but instead, he felt more lost than ever.

As the day wore on, Jesse tried to focus on his work, but his mind kept drifting back to Wyatt. Every time he looked over, Wyatt seemed just a little further away, like he was slipping out of Jesse's grasp. By the time the sun began to set, Jesse felt emotionally drained, unsure of what the next day would bring.

He knew he needed to talk to someone, to figure out what was going on in his head. Maybe he'd call Liz later; she always knew how to make sense of things. But for now, he just needed to get through the day and hope that Wyatt would come around.

As the day dragged on, Jesse found himself caught in a loop of overthinking. He kept replaying his conversation with Wyatt in his mind, dissecting every word, every pause. Wyatt had said he needed space, but what did that mean? Was it just a temporary thing, or was Wyatt trying to create distance between them for good? Jesse couldn't help but wonder if Wyatt was regretting everything that had happened between them.

Jesse went through the motions of his tasks at the pool, but his mind was elsewhere. Each smile he forced, each polite nod, felt like a lie. He felt the stares of the other lifeguards and pool staff, or maybe it was just his imagination. A quiet paranoia crept in, whispering that they knew, that they could see right through him – right through them.

When he finally got a break, Jesse retreated to the staff locker room, sitting on the bench with his head in his hands. He thought back to the night before, remembering how alive he had felt with Wyatt, how natural it seemed to just be together. He'd felt seen, really seen, for the first time in his life, like someone had reached inside him and found the parts he kept hidden even from himself. Now, it felt like all of that had been shattered in a single day.

What was I thinking? he thought, frustration and sadness battling in his chest. Maybe he had let himself get too carried away, too fast. He knew he shouldn't have expected anything – shouldn't have let himself hope. But he had, and now he didn't know how to dial it back, how to make himself feel okay again.

Jesse decided to text Liz. She had always been the one person who could get him to talk when he didn't want to, who could find the words he couldn't say.

Can we meet later? Need to talk.

Liz replied almost instantly.

Of course. Come over whenever you're done. I've got ice cream.

Jesse smiled weakly at the screen. Liz knew him too well. Ice cream and a talk sounded like exactly what he needed, but he still felt the knot in his stomach tighten as he thought about what he would say. How could he put into words the confusion, the fear, the longing that tangled together inside him?

He spent the rest of his shift in a daze, avoiding Wyatt's gaze whenever he caught sight of him. Wyatt was back on the lifeguard chair, sunglasses hiding his eyes, his posture tense and distant. It felt like they were miles apart, even though they were only a few feet away.

As the last of the swimmers left and the sun began to dip below the horizon, Jesse packed up his things and headed out. He wanted to say goodbye to Wyatt, to gauge his mood, to see if anything had changed, but Wyatt was busy, laughing with a couple of the other lifeguards. The sound of Wyatt's laughter was like a punch to Jesse's gut. He turned away, deciding it was better to just leave.

Jesse rode his bike to Liz's house, the familiar route giving him a small sense of comfort. When he arrived, Liz was waiting for him on the porch, her face lighting up with a concerned smile.

"Hey, you," she said, pulling him into a tight hug. "You look like you've had a day."

Jesse let out a sigh. "Yeah, you could say that."

They went inside, and Liz led him to the kitchen, where two bowls of ice cream were already waiting. Jesse sat down and stared at the bowl, the cold dessert melting a little around the edges.

"So, what's up?" Liz asked gently, leaning on the counter across from him. "I can tell something's bothering you."

Jesse hesitated, unsure where to begin. "It's... about Wyatt," he finally said.

Liz raised an eyebrow, intrigued. "Wyatt? Your lifeguard boyfriend?" She said with a wink.

"Yeah, him," Jesse replied, feeling his cheeks heat up. "We... um, we went on a date last night. Out of town. And... things happened."

Liz's eyes widened, and she leaned in closer. "Things happened, huh? Good things?"

Jesse nodded, a small smile tugging at his lips. "Yeah. Really good things. But today… it's like he's a different person. He was distant, like he regretted it or something."

Liz sighed, reaching out to put a comforting hand on Jesse's arm. "That sucks, Jess. I'm sorry."

Jesse felt his chest tighten again. "I thought… I thought it meant something to him, you know? And now I'm not so sure. I don't know what I'm supposed to do."

Liz frowned. "Have you talked to him? Like, really talked?"

Jesse shook his head. "I tried, but he just said he needed space. And now I'm scared that maybe he's having second thoughts, or that he doesn't want this… doesn't want me."

Liz squeezed his arm gently. "Hey, don't think like that. He's probably just freaking out, too. It's a lot, right? And it's not like you guys live in some big, accepting city. This place… it's not always easy to figure out who you are."

Jesse nodded, feeling the truth of her words. "I just… I don't want to hide anymore, Liz. I don't want to pretend I'm something I'm not. Not after last night."

Liz smiled softly. "Then don't. Be yourself, Jesse. If he's the right guy for you, he'll come around. And if he doesn't… well, screw him. You deserve someone who's not afraid to be with you."

Jesse felt a small flicker of hope. "You think?"

"I know," Liz replied firmly. "And no matter what, you're not alone in this, okay? You've got me. You've got people who care about you. Don't let anyone make you feel like you're not enough."

Jesse nodded, feeling a little lighter. "Thanks, Liz. I needed that."

"Anytime," she said with a grin. "Now eat your ice cream before it turns into soup."

Jesse laughed, picking up his spoon. As he took a bite, the cold sweetness filled his mouth, and for the first time that day, he felt a small, but real, sense of peace.

Later that night, after his conversation with Liz, Jesse lay on his bed, staring up at the ceiling. The room was dark, except for the faint glow of his phone screen resting on his chest. He had been holding his breath for what felt like hours, his thumb hovering over Wyatt's contact in his messages. He wanted to reach out, to break the silence that had grown between them, but fear kept him paralyzed.

He finally opened their chat, rereading their last exchange from the night before – the sweet, teasing messages they'd sent each other as they lay down for bed. Jesse's heart clenched at the memory. They felt like they were from another world, another lifetime.

Just text him, he thought. *Just ask him what's going on.*

He began typing, his fingers moving quickly over the keys.

Jesse: *Hey. Can we talk?*

He hit send before he could second-guess himself. Immediately, his heart began to pound, and he felt a wave of anxiety wash over him. Minutes passed, and the "typing" bubble did not appear. His nerves grew, and he started typing a new message to fill the void.

Jesse: *I feel like something's off. Did I do something wrong?*

He stared at the words, his thumb hovering over the send button. But something in him hesitated. He didn't want to seem needy or desperate. He deleted the message, frustrated with himself.

His phone buzzed in his hand, and he nearly jumped. Wyatt's name appeared on the screen, and Jesse felt his breath catch.

Wyatt: *Hey. Yeah, we can talk.*

Jesse read the message twice, trying to decipher its tone. He felt a tight knot in his stomach, and a part of him almost wished he hadn't reached out at all.

Jesse: *About today?*

There was a pause, and then Wyatt replied.

Wyatt: *Yeah. I'm sorry if I seemed weird.*

Jesse's fingers flew over the screen.

Jesse: *You did. I was worried I messed things up.*

Wyatt's response came a little quicker this time.

Wyatt: *You didn't mess anything up, Jesse. It's just... overwhelming.*

Jesse frowned, staring at the word "overwhelming." It felt like a wall had just gone up between them, solid and impenetrable.

Jesse: *Overwhlming how?*

There was a longer pause this time, and Jesse felt the tension in his chest tightening. He could almost hear Wyatt sigh through the screen.

Wyatt: *Look, I really like you? But it feels like this is moving at light speed. I'm not sure I'm ready for... everything that comes with this.*

Jesse's heart sank a little. He had feared this – that Wyatt was hesitating, that he wasn't ready to face what this might mean for both of them.

Jesse: *What do you mean?*

Wyatt: *I mean, people are already talking. I heard some of the lifeguards making comments today. I didn't expect it to be this hard, this fast. And I don't know if I'm ready for everyone to know... to judge.*

Jesse closed his eyes, feeling a wave of disappointment and a sting of hurt. He understood where Wyatt was coming from – he did. But it didn't make it any less painful to read those words.

Jesse: *I get it, Wyatt. I do. But I can't go back to hiding, pretending like I'm not... like I don't feel what I feel.*

Wyatt's reply took longer this time.

Wyatt: *I'm not asking you to hide. I just need time to figure this out. I'm not used to being this open... I've never been this open with anyone before.*

Jesse bit his lip, fighting back the frustration. He wanted to say something that would make Wyatt understand, make him see that what they had was worth fighting for. But he also didn't want to push too hard, afraid of pushing him away.

Jesse: *I don't need you to have everything figured out right now. I just need to know if this is real for you. If you feel the same way I do.*

There was another long pause, and Jesse's heart thudded in his chest, waiting.

Wyatt: *It is real, Jesse. But that's what scares me. I've never felt like this before, and I don't want to mess it up.*

Jesse felt a flicker of relief. At least Wyatt wasn't shutting him out completely.

Jesse: *I'm scared too. But we can figure it out together, right?*

Wyatt responded almost immediately.

Wyatt: *Yeah. I want that. I really do. Just... give me a little time, okay?*

Jesse nodded, even though Wyatt couldn't see him. He typed back quickly.

Jesse: *Okay. I can give you time. But I'm not going anywhere, Wyatt. I'm here.*

Wyatt's reply was short, but it made Jesse's chest feel a bit lighter.

Wyatt: *Thanks, Jesse. That means a lot.*

Jesse stared at the screen for a moment, then set his phone down beside him. It wasn't exactly the resolution he wanted, but it was something. He took a deep breath, feeling a small bit of calm settle over him.

Jesse lay in bed, his fingers brushing against the edge of his phone screen as if the lightest touch might break whatever fragile thread still connected him to Wyatt. The shadows on his bedroom wall lengthened with each passing minute, the glow of his phone screen casting a soft, bluish hue that seemed to amplify the silence in the room. Every second without a reply felt like an eternity, stretching time into something unbearable.

He rolled onto his side, staring at the last text Wyatt had sent: *"Thanks, Jesse. That means a lot."* Four simple words, but they carried so much weight. He felt like they were floating in a sea of ambiguity, neither sinking nor swimming, just... stuck.

Jesse's thumb hovered over the screen. He wanted to ask Wyatt so many things. Did Wyatt really mean it when he said he wanted time? Or was it just a gentle way to pull back, to create distance without hurting him? His mind raced through countless scenarios, each one more uncertain than the last.

He opened their chat again and started typing another message.

Jesse: *I know it's not easy. But I don't want to lose what we have. I'm scared too, Wyatt. I'm scared of what this all means, but I know what I feel when I'm with you.*

He hesitated, then added:

Jesse: *I don't want to lose that.*

He read the message over and over, considering whether to send it. The fear of coming off as too needy gnawed at him, but he also couldn't just leave things the way they were. Before he could overthink it any more, he hit send.

The minutes stretched on. Jesse checked the time on his phone – 11:47 PM. He wondered if Wyatt had already gone to bed or if he was lying there, just like Jesse, staring at his phone screen and unsure of what to say next.

Finally, the typing bubble appeared, and Jesse's heart skipped a beat.

Wyatt: *I don't want to lose it either, Jesse. That's the thing… I don't know how to handle this. I've never had to.*

Jesse's fingers moved quickly.

Jesse: *Then let's figure it out together. We don't have to have all the answers right now.*

He stared at the screen, hoping Wyatt would find comfort in those words, that they'd be enough to pull him back from whatever edge he seemed to be teetering on. The typing bubble appeared again, but then disappeared just as quickly. Jesse felt his stomach twist with anxiety.

He took a deep breath, running his hands through his hair, trying to ground himself. He could hear his own heartbeat, loud in the quiet of the room. He thought back to the previous night, the way Wyatt had held his hand during their drive, the warmth of his skin, the way

Wyatt's thumb had traced lazy circles over his knuckles as if trying to memorize the feel of him.

He didn't want to lose that. He didn't want to lose Wyatt.

The typing bubble reappeared, and Wyatt's message came through.

Wyatt: *It's not just about us, though. People are talking already. And I'm not used to being the topic of conversation... not like this.*

Jesse's heart sank a little more. He could hear the fear behind Wyatt's words, the way he was pulling back, retreating into himself.

Jesse: *I know. It's hard, and people can be cruel, but they don't matter. Not really. What matters is what we want.*

There was another pause. Jesse wondered if he was saying the right things or if he was just pushing Wyatt further away. His phone buzzed again.

Wyatt: *I wish I could be as brave as you, Jesse. I see the way you look at me, like you're not afraid of anything. I want that... I just don't know if I'm there yet.*

Jesse felt a pang in his chest. Wyatt saw him as brave? The idea was almost laughable. He had spent so much of his life feeling small and invisible, terrified of what others might think or say if they knew the truth about him.

Jesse: *I'm not brave, Wyatt. I'm scared all the time. But being scared doesn't mean I don't want this. I do. I want you.*

He hesitated, then added:

Jesse: *We don't have to rush anything. We can take it slow. I'm okay with that.*

Jesse sent the message and let out a breath he hadn't realized he'd been holding. He needed Wyatt to understand that they didn't need to figure everything out right away. They could just be two people figuring things out, one step at a time.

Wyatt's response took a little longer this time, and Jesse could feel the anxiety building in his chest again. When the reply finally came, it was longer than he expected.

Wyatt: *I want that too, Jesse. I really do. But I'm scared of what's gonna happen if we don't fit... if things get too hard, and I can't handle it. I've always been the guy who's got it together, who's never been in a situation where I'm not sure of myself. This is new for me. And it's terrifying.*

Jesse could almost feel the vulnerability in Wyatt's words, the raw honesty that lay beneath them. For a moment, he imagined Wyatt alone in his room, maybe staring up at his own ceiling, feeling just as lost and uncertain as he was.

Jesse: *I get it, Wyatt. It's new for me too. I don't know what I'm doing either. But maybe that's okay. Maybe we're not supposed to know everything right now.*

The typing bubble appeared again, and Wyatt replied almost immediately.

Wyatt: *Yeah. Maybe you're right. I guess I'm just scared that I'm going to mess this up... mess us up.*

Jesse's chest tightened, but he tried to stay calm. He typed slowly, choosing his words carefully.

Jesse: *We can't mess up something that hasn't even started yet. We'll figure it out together. If it gets hard, we talk. If we're scared, we lean on each other. No pressure, just... being here for each other.*

There was another pause, and then Wyatt's response came.

Wyatt: *Okay. I like that... no pressure. Just being here.*

Jesse felt a wave of relief wash over him. It wasn't a solution, not really, but it was a step. A small step toward understanding, toward something more solid between them. He felt his heart rate slow, his breath becoming steadier.

Jesse: *Good. So, tomorrow... maybe we can just hang out? No expectations, no labels, just... us?*

Wyatt's response came quicker this time.

Wyatt: *I'd like that. A lot.*

Jesse smiled, a real, genuine smile that he hadn't felt in days. He typed back:

Jesse: *Me too. Goodnight, Wyatt.*

Wyatt: *Goodnight, Jesse. See you tomorrow.*

Jesse set his phone down beside him, feeling lighter than he had in days. Maybe things were still complicated, but for now, that was okay.

Chapter 13: Ripples of Truth; Ripples of Hate

Jesse woke up to the faint light of dawn creeping through his bedroom curtains. He lay there for a few minutes, letting his eyes adjust to the dim glow. His thoughts drifted back to the day before, to Wyatt's distant look at the pool, and the confusing feelings it stirred in him. He reached over to his nightstand and grabbed his phone, immediately checking for any new messages from Wyatt. But the screen was blank except for their last exchange the night before.

Wyatt's last message still lingered in Jesse's mind: *"Goodnight, Jesse."* It had seemed simple, yet he read it over and over, looking for any hidden meaning, any clue that could explain Wyatt's cool demeanor. Jesse felt a strange mix of warmth and anxiety, his stomach twisting with uncertainty.

He tossed his phone back onto the bed, frustrated with himself. Part of him wanted to reach out first, to break the silence and ask Wyatt if they were okay. But another part, the part still raw from years of keeping his true self hidden, was terrified of appearing too needy or desperate. He sighed and ran a hand through his hair, finally deciding to get up and go through the motions of his morning routine.

Downstairs, his mom was already in the kitchen, sipping her coffee and glancing at the newspaper. She looked up as Jesse walked in, a small smile on her face. "Morning, Jesse," she greeted warmly. "You're up early today."

"Yeah, just couldn't sleep much," Jesse replied, grabbing a bowl for cereal. He poured it absently, his mind elsewhere.

"Everything okay?" she asked, noticing the distracted look on his face.

Jesse hesitated for a moment. "Yeah, just... thinking about some stuff," he said vaguely, not wanting to delve into it. His mom nodded, sensing there was more he wasn't saying but respecting his need for space.

"Well, if you ever want to talk, I'm here," she offered gently.

"Thanks, Mom," Jesse said, offering a small smile. "I might take you up on that."

After breakfast, Jesse retreated to his room again, pacing a bit before flopping down on his bed. He picked up his phone and stared at it, his thumb hovering over Wyatt's name. Finally, he opened a new text, typing out a quick message:

"Hey, I was thinking about yesterday... just wanted to check in. Are we good?"

He hesitated for a moment, then hit send. The seconds stretched into minutes as he waited for a response. He tried to distract himself, flipping through a book on his desk, but his mind kept wandering back to his phone, willing it to light up with a reply.

After what felt like an eternity, his phone buzzed. Jesse snatched it up, his heart racing.

"Yeah, we're good. Just needed some time to process, you know? Lets talk later?"

Jesse exhaled, feeling some of the tension ease from his shoulders. He quickly typed back:

"Yeah, I'd like that. Whenever you're ready."

Wyatt's reply came almost instantly. *"Cool. See you later?"*

Jesse smiled at the casualness of the message, sensing a bit of the old Wyatt breaking through. *"Yeah, see you later,"* he responded, feeling a flicker of hope.

Later that morning, Jesse decided he needed to get out of the house. The pool was a safe bet – even though it was his day off, he'd have work to distract him, and he could figure out how to approach Wyatt when he saw him. When he arrived, the sun was already high in the sky, and a small crowd of families and kids was beginning to gather.

Jesse spotted Wyatt immediately, sitting in the lifeguard chair, his sunglasses on, watching over the pool with his usual calm focus. There was something reassuring in seeing him there, the familiar ease in his posture, even if things felt a bit off between them.

Wyatt seemed to notice him, nodding slightly, a flicker of a smile passing over his lips. Jesse waved back, feeling the knot in his stomach loosen just a little.

He busied himself at the concession stand, chatting with coworkers, restocking supplies, and trying to keep his nerves in check. Every now and then, his gaze drifted back to Wyatt, who was still perched on the lifeguard chair, his expression neutral but his posture more relaxed than the day before.

When Wyatt's break finally came, Jesse watched as he climbed down from his chair and made his way toward the locker room. Jesse hesitated, his heart pounding in his chest, then decided to follow. He couldn't keep avoiding this – he needed to know where they stood.

Inside, the locker room was quiet, the cool air a stark contrast to the heat outside. Wyatt was leaning against his locker, sipping from his water bottle. He looked up as Jesse entered, his expression unreadable but not unkind.

"Hey," Jesse said, trying to keep his voice steady.

"Hey," Wyatt replied, his tone cautious but open.

Jesse took a breath. "About yesterday... I just wanted to make sure we're okay. I don't want things to be weird between us."

Wyatt nodded, setting his water bottle down. "Yeah, we're okay, Jesse. I just needed some time to think, you know? About... everything."

Jesse nodded slowly. "I get that. I just... I don't want to lose whatever this is. I don't want to lose you."

Wyatt's face softened, and he stepped a bit closer, his voice quiet but sincere. "You're not gonna lose me, Jesse. I just... sometimes I get in my head. I start worrying about things I can't control, like what people will think, what they'll say... and I forget that what matters is how I feel. How *we* feel."

Jesse felt a surge of emotion at Wyatt's words. "I've been scared too," he admitted. "Scared of what people might think, scared of what this means... but being with you feels right. I don't want to hide that."

Wyatt nodded, a small smile forming on his lips. "Me neither. I don't know where this is going, but I would like to find out."

Jesse's heart soared, and he took a step closer, reaching out to take Wyatt's hand. "Then let's do that," he said softly. "Let's find out."

Wyatt squeezed his hand, his smile widening. "Yeah," he agreed. "Let's do that."

For the first time since their night in the pond, Jesse felt a weight lift off his shoulders. The tension that had been building between them seemed to dissipate, replaced by a quiet understanding, a mutual resolve to face whatever came next together.

They stood there for a moment, hands clasped, sharing a look that spoke of all the things they were too afraid to say. Then, Wyatt broke the silence with a grin. "Come on, let's get back out there before they think we've bailed on them," he joked.

Jesse laughed, feeling lighter than he had in days. "Yeah, let's go."

Jesse and Wyatt walked out of the locker room, the sun bright and hot against their faces. The pool was buzzing with activity – kids splashing in the shallow end, parents lounging under umbrellas, and lifeguards calling out instructions from their posts. For Jesse, everything seemed a little brighter, a little more vivid. He felt a renewed sense of energy, buoyed by the brief but meaningful conversation he'd just had with Wyatt. Things were starting to feel right again, or at least better than they had in the past few days.

As they reached the pool deck, Wyatt glanced over at Jesse and gave him a small, reassuring smile. "You good?" he asked, his tone light but filled with genuine concern.

Jesse nodded, smiling back. "Yeah, I'm good. Better than good, actually."

Wyatt's grin widened, and he gave Jesse a quick, discreet nudge with his elbow. "Glad to hear it. Now, let's make it through this shift without any drama, yeah?"

Jesse chuckled. "Deal."

Wyatt headed back to the lifeguard chair, and Jesse made his way to the concession stand, feeling a sense of calm he hadn't felt in days. As he got to work, he found himself glancing over at Wyatt from time to time. Wyatt seemed more relaxed now, a hint of that old confidence back in his posture. Every now and then, their eyes would meet, and they'd share a brief, knowing smile. It was subtle, just enough to keep the connection alive without drawing attention.

Around midday, as the sun climbed higher and the pool grew busier, Jesse noticed a group of teenagers gathering near the deep end. They were loud, splashing each other, and generally making a scene. Jesse recognized a few of them – kids who were known for stirring up trouble. His stomach tightened slightly, but he tried to push the feeling away.

Wyatt, ever the vigilant lifeguard, blew his whistle and called out, "Hey, guys, keep it down and be mindful of the other swimmers, okay?"

One of the teens, a tall boy with a baseball cap turned backward, glanced up at Wyatt and smirked. "Sure thing, lifeguard," he said, his tone mocking. His friends laughed, and Jesse could see Wyatt's jaw tighten slightly from his perch on the chair.

Jesse watched the exchange, feeling a ripple of tension in the air. He could tell Wyatt was trying to keep his cool, but the snide comment had clearly gotten under his skin. The teens continued to splash around, seemingly ignoring Wyatt's instructions. Jesse felt a surge of protectiveness – not just for Wyatt, but for what they were trying to build together.

Taking a deep breath, Jesse walked over to the group, doing his best to keep his tone calm and friendly. "Hey, guys," he said, "could you keep it down a bit? We've got some younger kids here, and we don't want anyone to get hurt."

The boy with the baseball cap turned his attention to Jesse, his smirk widening. "Oh, look, it's the snack boy," he sneered. "Trying to be a hero, huh?"

Jesse's heart pounded in his chest, but he forced himself to stay calm. "I'm just trying to make sure everyone's safe and has a good time," he replied evenly. "We're all here to enjoy the pool, right?"

The boy rolled his eyes and turned back to his friends, muttering something under his breath. Jesse couldn't hear exactly what he said, but he caught the words "fag" and "queer," followed by a chorus of snickers. His stomach dropped, a cold wave of dread washing over him.

He felt his face flush, a mix of anger and embarrassment flooding through him. He glanced up at Wyatt, who was watching the scene unfold, his expression darkening. Jesse knew Wyatt had heard it too.

Wyatt's eyes locked onto the boy with the baseball cap. "Alright, that's enough," he called out, his voice firm and authoritative. "If you can't follow the rules, you're gonna have to leave."

The boy turned back, his smirk fading into a sneer. "Or what?" he challenged. "You gonna kick us out for telling the truth?"

Jesse felt a surge of fear and frustration. He glanced around, noticing a few other pool-goers watching the exchange, their expressions ranging from curiosity, to concern, to disgust. He could feel the situation escalating, tension hanging in the air like a heavy cloud.

Wyatt climbed down from his chair, his movements calm but deliberate. He walked over to the group, standing tall, his eyes fixed on the boy. "We don't tolerate that kind of language here," he said evenly. "This is a place for everyone to feel safe and welcome. If you can't respect that, you need to leave."

The boy hesitated, glancing around at his friends, who seemed to be losing their nerve. Finally, he shrugged, turning to leave with a dismissive wave. "Whatever, man. This place sucks anyway."

As they walked away, Jesse let out a breath he hadn't realized he'd been holding. He looked at Wyatt, who gave him a small, reassuring nod, his expression softening. Jesse nodded back, a silent exchange of gratitude passing between them.

The rest of the shift went by smoothly, but Jesse couldn't shake the uneasy feeling that lingered in the back of his mind. He kept replaying the incident over and over, the cruel words echoing in his ears. He knew people could be ignorant and hateful, but it still stung to hear it so blatantly, to have it thrown in their faces like that.

When the pool finally closed, Jesse started his usual routine of cleaning up around the concession stand, wiping down the counters and restocking the shelves. He saw Wyatt helping to stack chairs and tidy up the pool deck, his movements easy and unhurried.

As Jesse finished up, he felt a presence behind him and turned to see Wyatt standing there, a thoughtful expression on his face. "You okay?" Wyatt asked, his voice gentle.

Jesse nodded, but his eyes betrayed him. "Yeah, I'm fine. Just… I hate that stuff, you know? I hate that people think it's okay to talk like that."

Wyatt reached out, placing a comforting hand on Jesse's shoulder. "I know," he said softly. "But we can't let it get to us. We have to be stronger than that."

Jesse nodded, feeling a small wave of relief at Wyatt's words. "You handled it really well," he said quietly. "I'm proud of you."

Wyatt smiled, his eyes softening. "Thanks. But I couldn't have done it without you. You were the one who kept your cool."

They stood there for a moment, the tension between them replaced by a quiet understanding. Jesse felt a sense of solidarity, a shared strength that seemed to bind them closer together.

"So… what now?" Jesse asked, trying to lighten the mood. "Any plans for the rest of the evening?"

Wyatt thought for a moment, then his eyes brightened. "Actually, I was thinking we could go grab a bite to eat. Somewhere quiet, out of town. Just us."

Jesse's heart lifted at the suggestion. "I'd like that," he said softly. "A lot."

Wyatt grinned, his eyes crinkling at the corners. "Good. There's this little diner a few towns over. It's not fancy, but it's got great food and no one knows us there. We can just... be ourselves."

Jesse nodded, feeling a rush of excitement. "Sounds perfect."

They finished up their closing duties and headed out to the parking lot, the evening air cool and refreshing after the long, hot day. Wyatt's car was parked under a tree, and he opened the passenger door for Jesse with a playful flourish. "Your chariot awaits," he joked.

Jesse laughed, sliding into the seat. "Such a gentleman," he teased back.

As they drove, the town of Brookwood slowly faded behind them, replaced by the open road and the vast expanse of sky above. The sun was setting, casting a warm, golden glow over the landscape, and Jesse felt a sense of peace settle over him. The tension and uncertainty of the past few days seemed to melt away, replaced by a quiet, hopeful anticipation.

Wyatt reached over, his hand finding Jesse's and giving it a gentle squeeze. "I'm glad we're doing this," he said softly.

"Me too," Jesse replied, his heart swelling with a mix of relief and happiness. "It feels... right."

They drove in comfortable silence for a while, the road stretching out before them, endless and inviting. When they finally reached the diner, a small, cozy place with a neon sign that flickered slightly, Wyatt pulled into the gravel lot and turned off the engine.

Inside, the diner was warm and inviting, with checkered tablecloths and a jukebox playing soft, oldies music in the corner. They slid into a booth near the back, away from the handful of other patrons, and picked up the laminated menus.

Wyatt leaned back, a relaxed smile on his face. "I've heard the burgers here are pretty legendary," he said, glancing over the menu. "What do you think?"

Jesse smiled, feeling the last of his nerves fade away. "I think we should find out."

They ordered their food and settled into easy conversation, talking about everything and nothing. Jesse felt a warmth spreading through him, but in the back of his mind, couldn't shake the feeling of uncertainty, the feeling that everything could change in the blink of an eye.

Chapter 14: Steps Toward Truth

The next morning, Jesse woke up to the sound of birds chirping outside his window. For the first time in days, he felt a sense of calm. The events of the previous day at the pool, the tense exchange with the teenagers, and the quiet, reassuring moments with Wyatt played through his mind, but they didn't weigh him down. Instead, he felt a strange sense of lightness, like he was finally starting to come to terms with everything.

It was his day off, and he had no plans except to relax and maybe spend some time with Liz. He grabbed his phone from the nightstand and shot her a quick text.

Jesse: *Hey, you free today? Thinking we could hang out.*

Liz replied almost instantly.

Liz: *Absolutely. Come over whenever. I've got snacks and bad movies.*

Jesse smiled. Liz always knew how to make a day feel special. He got out of bed, took a quick shower, and threw on some comfortable clothes – a plain gray t-shirt and jeans. As he made his way downstairs, his mom called out from the kitchen.

"Morning, honey," she said, glancing up from her coffee. "Plans for the day?"

"Yeah, I'm gonna hang out with Liz for a bit," Jesse replied, grabbing a granola bar from the counter. "Just take it easy."

His mom nodded, a smile playing on her lips. "Sounds like a good plan. You've been working so hard lately. You deserve a break."

Jesse chuckled. "Thanks, Mom. I'll be back later."

He hopped on his bike and rode over to Liz's house, enjoying the warm morning air and the quiet of the neighborhood. When he arrived, Liz was waiting for him on the porch, a bright grin on her face.

"Hey, stranger," she called out as he walked up. "Ready for some serious relaxation?"

Jesse laughed. "Absolutely. I could use a break from all the drama."

Liz gave him a knowing look as they headed inside. "Drama? I need details."

They settled in the living room, Liz flopping onto the couch and Jesse taking the armchair. A few snacks were already laid out on the coffee table – chips, dip, and a bowl of M&Ms.

Jesse sighed, running a hand through his hair. "It's been a weird couple of days," he began. "Things with Wyatt have been… complicated."

Liz raised an eyebrow, munching on an M&M. "Complicated how?"

Jesse hesitated, unsure where to start. "Well, after our first date, he got distant. I wasn't sure what was going on, and then yesterday, some kids at the pool made some nasty comments… homophobic stuff. It just kind of threw everything into a weird place."

Liz frowned, her expression turning serious. "That sucks, Jess. I'm sorry. Kids can be such jerks."

Jesse nodded, feeling the weight of her words. "Yeah, it wasn't great. But then Wyatt and I talked after our shift, and I think… I think we're getting back on the same page. We went out to this diner out of town, and it was nice. It felt like we were just… us again."

Liz's face brightened. "That's good, though! Sounds like you're figuring it out, even if it's a little messy."

Jesse shrugged. "Yeah, I guess. It's just hard, you know? Trying to be open about this, about who we are, when there's so much… shit to deal with."

Liz reached over, giving his arm a comforting squeeze. "You're doing great, Jesse. Seriously. And Wyatt seems like he could be worth it. Just take it one day at a time, like you said."

Jesse smiled, feeling a bit of the tension ease. "Thanks, Liz. I needed to hear that."

Liz grinned. "Anytime. Now, let's watch something terrible and forget about everything for a while."

She grabbed the remote and flipped through a few streaming options, landing on an old, cheesy horror movie from the '80s. "How about this?" she asked, her eyes gleaming with mischief.

Jesse laughed. "Perfect. The cheesier, the better."

They settled in, the movie's terrible special effects and over-the-top acting providing the perfect distraction. They laughed, threw popcorn at the screen, and made sarcastic comments about the ridiculous plot twists. Jesse felt himself relax more with each passing minute, the heaviness in his chest lifting as he spent time with his best friend.

Halfway through the movie, Liz paused it and turned to Jesse, her expression more serious. "Hey, can I ask you something?"

Jesse nodded. "Sure. What's up?"

Liz bit her lip, choosing her words carefully. "Do you ever think about... coming out more publicly? I mean, I know Brookwood isn't exactly the most open-minded place, but... I don't know. I just wonder if maybe you'd feel better not having to hide."

Jesse considered her question for a moment, feeling a mix of fear and longing. "I think about it a lot," he admitted. "But it's scary. People can be... well, like those kids yesterday. And I don't want to make things harder for Wyatt. He's still figuring things out, too. Plus I'm not sure how my parents will react and I don't think Wyatt's parents will react well."

Liz nodded, her eyes filled with understanding. "That makes sense. I just want you to be happy, you know? To not feel like you have to hide who you are."

Jesse smiled, grateful for her support. "I know, and I appreciate that. I guess I'm just taking it one step at a time. I don't want to rush anything, but I also don't want to keep pretending."

Liz squeezed his hand. "Whatever you decide, I'm here for you. You don't have to do this alone."

Jesse felt a swell of gratitude. "Thanks, Liz. You're the best."

She grinned. "I know. Now, let's finish this movie before I lose my patience with these awful special effects."

They returned their attention to the screen, letting the ridiculousness of the movie wash over them. As the credits finally rolled, Liz turned to Jesse with a playful smirk. "So, what's next on the agenda, Mr. Day-Off?"

Jesse stretched, feeling more relaxed than he had in days. "Honestly? I was thinking we could just hang out, maybe take a walk down by the river. Clear my head a bit."

Liz nodded enthusiastically. "Sounds like a plan. Let's do it."

They grabbed their shoes and headed out, walking down the quiet streets of Brookwood toward the river. The air was warm, a light breeze rustling the leaves overhead. Jesse felt a sense of calm settle over him as they walked, the tension of the past few days slowly melting away.

As they reached the riverbank, Liz turned to him, her expression thoughtful. "You know, Jesse, I'm really proud of you," she said softly. "For everything. For being brave enough to be yourself, even when it's hard."

Jesse felt his heart swell. "Thanks, Liz. That means a lot coming from you."

They stood there for a moment, watching the water flow by, the sun glinting off the surface. Jesse felt a sense of peace, a quiet certainty that, no matter what came next, he could face it with the people he cared about by his side.

He glanced at Liz, a smile spreading across his face. "You know what? I think things are gonna be okay."

Liz smiled back, her eyes shining with warmth. "Yeah, Jess. I think so too."

And for the first time in a long time, Jesse really believed it.

Later that afternoon, Jesse rode his bike back home, the sun beginning to dip low in the sky, casting long shadows on the road. As he pedaled, he felt a quiet contentment settle over him. His time with Liz had helped clear his mind, to remind him that he wasn't alone in this. He had people who cared about him, who wanted him to be happy, to be true to himself.

When he pulled into the driveway, he saw his dad working in the garage, sorting through a box of old tools. His mom was sitting on the front porch, a book in her lap, glancing up as Jesse approached. She gave him a warm smile. "Hey, honey. Have a good time with Liz?"

Jesse nodded, smiling back. "Yeah, it was nice. Just hung out, watched a movie, talked."

His mom nodded, her eyes soft. "That's good. I'm glad you're getting out, spending time with friends."

Jesse hesitated for a moment, standing at the bottom of the porch steps. His mom's face was so open, so kind. He felt a sudden urge to tell her everything, to open up about what had been weighing on him for so long. But the fear was still there, lingering at the edges of his mind. He didn't know how she would react, what she would say. Would she still look at him the same way?

He took a deep breath, steeling himself. "Mom," he began slowly, "can I ask you something?"

She set her book down, giving him her full attention. "Of course, Jesse. What's on your mind?"

He glanced back toward the garage, where his dad was still sorting through tools, unaware of the conversation. Jesse felt his heart start to race. "Have you ever... felt like you were hiding something? Something important?"

His mom's brow furrowed slightly, her expression concerned but patient. "I think everyone feels that way sometimes," she said carefully. "Why do you ask?"

Jesse hesitated, the words catching in his throat. He could feel his palms start to sweat, his heartbeat quickening. He had thought about this moment a hundred times, what he would say, how he would say it. But now that it was here, he wasn't sure he was ready.

"I've just... been thinking about some things," he said finally. "Things I've been keeping to myself."

His mom nodded slowly, her eyes searching his face. "It's okay to keep some things to yourself, Jesse. But if it's something that's weighing on you... you know you can talk to me. To both of us."

Jesse swallowed hard, his mouth dry. He knew she was trying to be supportive, but he also knew this wasn't going to be easy. He glanced back toward the garage again, then took a deep breath, trying to steady himself.

"Yeah," he said quietly. "I know. Maybe... maybe I'll tell you soon. Both of you."

His mom smiled gently. "Whenever you're ready, honey. We're here for you."

Jesse nodded, feeling a mix of relief and anxiety. He wasn't sure when he would find the courage to say the words out loud, to tell his parents the truth about who he was. But he knew he was getting closer. He was tired of hiding, tired of pretending. And for the first time, he felt like maybe – just maybe – he could be brave enough to take that step.

He headed inside, his mind racing with thoughts and emotions. As he climbed the stairs to his room, he felt a small flicker of hope. He didn't have all the answers yet, but he was starting to find his way. One step at a time, he was moving closer to the person he wanted to be – the person he knew he already was.

Chapter 15: The Weight of Expectations

The moon hangs low in the sky, casting a silvery glow over the empty pool. The water shimmers, reflecting the stars above, while the air is thick with the scent of chlorine and summer flowers. Jesse and Wyatt sit on the edge of the pool after a long shift, their legs dangling in the cool water, shoulders almost touching.

The conversation between them has flowed easily tonight, moving from lighthearted topics to deeper musings. There's a comfortable silence now, a pause that feels full rather than awkward. Jesse swirls his foot in the water, watching the ripples spread out in soft, concentric circles.

After a moment, he turns to Wyatt, curiosity getting the better of him. "So... you were saying you wanted a break from everything. From what, exactly?"

Wyatt exhales, looking out over the water, as if trying to find the right words. "From expectations, I guess," he begins slowly. "From feeling like I have to be a certain way to make everyone else happy. You know, I grew up in this house where there was always... pressure. My parents love me, sure, but they have these ideas about who I should be."

He glances over at Jesse, searching his face for understanding. "It's like they see my life as this... checklist. Prestigious college? Check. Sports achievements? Check. An internship that looks great on a resume? Double check. But somewhere in all of that, I lost track of what I actually want."

Jesse nods, feeling a pang of empathy. "I get that," he says quietly. "My parents didn't really have big expectations like yours, but I've always felt this need to fit in, to not stand out too much... almost like I was afraid of being seen for who I really am."

Wyatt smiles softly. "Yeah, that's the thing, isn't it? Being seen. It can be terrifying, but also... I don't know... freeing?"

Jesse meets Wyatt's gaze, sensing a deeper story behind his words. "So, what would you do if there were no expectations? If you could just... be?"

Wyatt laughs a little, but there's a hint of vulnerability in it. "Honestly? I don't even know. I think that's why I'm here. Trying to figure out what that even means."

He pauses, his eyes drifting back to the water. "I've thought about traveling. Seeing places that are different, where nobody knows me. Or maybe going into coaching instead of sports medicine... working with kids, helping them find themselves in a way I never really could."

Jesse leans in a little closer, fascinated. "That sounds amazing. Why haven't you?"

Wyatt's face darkens a bit, a flicker of doubt crossing his features. "Fear, I guess. Fear of disappointing them. Fear of failing. Fear that maybe... I don't really know who I am outside of what I've been told I should be."

There's a quiet vulnerability in Wyatt's voice that Jesse hasn't heard before, and it stirs something deep inside him. He reaches out, hesitantly at first, but then with more confidence, placing his hand on Wyatt's. "I think you're a lot more than that," Jesse says softly. "More than what anyone expects of you."

Wyatt turns to Jesse, his eyes softened by the moonlight, and for a moment, he seems almost lost for words. "You really think that?" he asks, his voice barely a whisper.

Jesse nods, feeling his own heart pounding in his chest. "Yeah, I do. I think… you're just beginning to see yourself for who you really are."

Wyatt's expression shifts, a mix of gratitude and something deeper– maybe hope. "That means a lot coming from you," he says. "I feel like… when I'm with you, I don't have to pretend. Like, I can just… exist. Be Wyatt, not some version of myself that others want me to be."

Jesse smiles, feeling a warmth spread through his chest. "That's how I feel around you, too."

Wyatt's hand squeezes Jesse's gently, and they sit there for a moment, the silence between them filled with unspoken understanding.

After a few moments, Wyatt takes a deep breath, as if gathering courage. "My dad… he was an athlete too, you know. Football star back in his day. He got injured, couldn't go pro. I think that's why he's so hard on me sometimes. He sees what he lost in me. Wants me to have everything he didn't get."

Jesse tilts his head, listening intently. "Do you think he sees you, though? Really sees you, I mean?"

Wyatt's smile is tinged with sadness. "I don't know. Maybe he does in his own way. But sometimes it feels like he's looking at a reflection of himself, not me. He loves me, I know that, but it's like he's always trying to live his life through me. And it's suffocating."

Jesse nods. "I get it. My mom… she's always wanted me to be something I'm not. To be more outgoing, to fit in more. And I've always felt like I was disappointing her by just… being myself."

Wyatt leans closer, his shoulder brushing Jesse's. "You're not disappointing anyone, Jesse. You're just… real. That's more than most people can say."

Jesse blushes slightly, feeling a rush of emotion. "Thanks. I… I wish I could be as confident as you seem to be."

Wyatt chuckles. "Confidence? It's mostly just a show, Jesse. You think I don't get nervous, don't have doubts? Trust me, I do. All the time. I'm just good at hiding it, I guess."

He looks away for a moment, then back at Jesse, a serious expression on his face. "But you… you have this quiet strength. You're not trying to be anything other than who you are, and that's… that's something I really admire."

Jesse feels his heart swell, a mix of surprise and gratitude. "I never thought of it that way," he admits.

Wyatt's smile returns, softer this time. "Maybe you should. You're stronger than you think, Jesse. And maybe… maybe we're both just starting to figure that out."

The air between them feels charged now, not just with the warmth of summer but with a new understanding. Jesse senses that they've crossed a line, moved beyond just a casual attraction into something deeper. He feels a flutter in his stomach, the thrill of being truly seen, and he realizes that he wants more of this, more of Wyatt, more of whatever they are becoming.

Wyatt shifts, turning to face Jesse more fully, his expression open and earnest. "So, what about you?" he asks. "What do you want, Jesse? Not just for this summer, but... for you?"

Jesse hesitates, then takes a deep breath. "I want to be free," he says finally. "I want to stop feeling like I have to hide parts of myself. I want to... I don't know, find a way to love who I am, even the parts that scare me."

Wyatt's eyes soften, and he reaches out, his fingers brushing Jesse's cheek. "I think you're already on your way there," he murmurs. "And I'd like to be there with you... if you'll have me."

Jesse feels a tear prick at the corner of his eye, a mix of fear and hope. "I'd like that," he whispers.

Wyatt smiles, and in that moment, Jesse knows that he's found something special–someone who sees him, truly sees him, in a way he's never felt before. They lean in closer, their foreheads touching, the world around them fading into the background as they simply breathe in the same space, sharing their fears, their hopes, and their dreams under the blanket of a starry summer sky.

Chapter 16: Conversations and Confessions

The next day, Jesse headed to the pool for his shift, feeling a mix of anticipation and nerves. The conversation with his mom lingered in his mind, the possibility of coming out to his parents looming larger than ever. He knew he couldn't keep them in the dark much longer. He wanted to be honest–with himself, with Wyatt, and with the people who cared about him most.

As he arrived at the pool, the morning sun was already warm, casting a golden glow over the water. The pool was bustling with activity, a usual sight on a summer day. He spotted Wyatt near the lifeguard chair, adjusting the umbrella to provide a bit more shade. Wyatt looked up and gave him a small, welcoming smile that sent a familiar flutter through Jesse's chest.

"Hey," Wyatt called out as Jesse approached. "How are you?"

Jesse smiled, feeling a bit of the tension ease just at the sound of Wyatt's voice. "I'm good…"
better now."

Wyatt chuckled. "Oh is that so?"

Jesse nodded, but he could feel the weight of the conversation he wanted to have pressing down on him. He wasn't sure how to bring it up, but he knew he needed to talk to Wyatt about it. He wanted to know where Wyatt stood, how he felt about coming out, and whether they were on the same page.

"Hey," Jesse said after a moment, his voice more serious. "Can we talk? Like, really talk?"

Wyatt's smile faded slightly, replaced by a look of concern. "Yeah, of course," he said. "What's on your mind?"

Jesse glanced around, making sure no one was close enough to overhear. "Not here," he said quietly. "Maybe during our break?"

Wyatt nodded, understanding. "Sure. Let's grab a spot in the back when we get a chance."

They went about their morning routine, but Jesse could feel the tension building in his chest as the minutes ticked by. He watched Wyatt from a distance, wondering what he would say, how he would react. Wyatt seemed calm, focused on his duties, but Jesse knew this conversation was as important to him as it was to Jesse.

Finally, their break arrived, and they headed to a quieter corner of the pool area, away from the lifeguard chairs and the chattering crowds. They found a shady spot under a tree, and Jesse sat down on the grass, his back against the trunk. Wyatt joined him, stretching his legs out in front of him.

"So," Wyatt said, turning to face Jesse, "what's going on?"

Jesse took a deep breath, trying to steady his nerves. "I've been thinking... about coming out," he began. "To my parents."

Wyatt's eyes widened slightly, and he nodded. "Wow. That's a big step."

Jesse nodded, feeling a mix of fear and determination. "Yeah, it is. I talked to my mom yesterday... kind of hinted that I had something on my mind. I think she knows something's up, but I didn't tell her everything. Not yet."

Wyatt was silent for a moment, his expression thoughtful. "How do you feel about it?" he asked softly. "About coming out?"

Jesse hesitated, trying to find the right words. "Scared," he admitted. "But also... kind of relieved? I'm tired of hiding. I want to be honest with them. I want them to know who I really am."

Wyatt nodded slowly, his gaze fixed on the ground. "Yeah, I get that. I've been thinking about it too, you know... coming out to my parents."

Jesse looked at him, surprised. "Really?"

Wyatt nodded again, his expression serious. "Yeah. I mean, they've always been closed-minded, so it's scary. I don't know how they'll react. And I don't want to disappoint them. They are very religious and have always lived by a certain set of... ideas... rules...expectations."

Jesse reached out, placing a hand on Wyatt's arm. "You could never be a disappointment, Wyatt. Not to them, and definitely not to me."

Wyatt smiled softly, but there was a hint of uncertainty in his eyes. "Thanks. It's just... it's a lot to think about. I don't want to rush into anything. I want to make sure I'm ready. If I'll ever be ready."

Jesse nodded, understanding. "I get that. I don't want to pressure you into anything. I just... I wanted to know where you stood. Because if I come out, I want to be able to talk about us. I don't want to hide that."

Wyatt looked at him, his eyes searching Jesse's face. "You want to tell them about us?"

Jesse felt a flutter of anxiety, but he nodded. "Yeah, I do. I don't want to pretend we're just friends, you know? I want to be able to tell them the truth."

Wyatt was silent for a long moment, his gaze shifting to the pool, the sunlight dancing on the water's surface. "I want that too," he said finally, his voice quiet. "I don't want to hide either. I just... I need a little more time to get there."

Jesse felt a wave of relief wash over him. Wyatt wasn't shutting him out; he was just taking things at his own pace. Jesse could understand that. He could be patient.

"That's okay," Jesse said softly. "We'll do this together, whenever we're both ready."

Wyatt nodded, a small smile tugging at his lips. "Together," he agreed. "I like the sound of that."

They sat there for a while, the silence between them comfortable, filled with a sense of shared understanding. Jesse felt a weight lift from his shoulders, knowing that Wyatt was on the same page, even if it would take some time for them to fully get there.

After a few minutes, Wyatt turned to Jesse, his expression more relaxed. "So, when are you thinking about telling them? Your parents, I mean."

Jesse shrugged. "I'm not sure yet. Maybe soon. I don't want to wait too long, but I also want to make sure it's the right time."

Wyatt nodded thoughtfully. "Yeah, that makes sense. And whatever happens... you've got me. I'll be there for you."

Jesse smiled, his heart swelling with gratitude. "Thanks, Wyatt. That means a lot."

Wyatt leaned back against the tree, letting out a deep breath. "I guess we're both navigating a lot, huh?"

Jesse chuckled softly. "Yeah, that's an understatement."

They shared a quiet laugh, the tension between them easing into something softer, more comfortable. Jesse felt a sense of peace, a quiet assurance that they were moving in the right direction, even if the path wasn't entirely clear yet.

As their break came to an end, Wyatt stood up and offered a hand to Jesse. "Come on," he said with a grin. "Let's get back to work before they think we've slacked off too long."

Jesse took his hand, letting Wyatt pull him to his feet. "Yeah, let's go."

They walked back to the pool deck side by side, their shoulders brushing, a quiet confidence settling between them. Jesse knew there were still challenges ahead, but for the first time, he felt like they were facing them together, as a team.

Chapter 17: Reflections and Decisions

The rest of their shift went by quickly. The pool was busy, and Jesse found himself caught up in the rhythm of the day—checking the concession stand, chatting with coworkers, and occasionally catching Wyatt's eye across the pool deck. Each time their eyes met, there was a silent communication between them, a shared understanding that gave Jesse a quiet sense of strength.

But underneath the calm, there was a simmering tension—a fear of the unknown, of what could happen if he took that next step and came out to his parents. Jesse knew his mom and dad loved him, but he also knew that coming out was a huge leap of faith. He wasn't just revealing a secret; he was opening himself up to vulnerability, to potential hurt, to rejection.

As the sun began to set and the pool started to empty, Jesse felt a knot of anxiety form in his stomach. He hadn't planned to talk to his parents tonight, but the thought kept gnawing at him. Maybe it was time to stop thinking and just do it.

After closing duties were wrapped up, Jesse walked over to Wyatt, who was gathering the last of the lifeguard gear. His heart raced as he approached, the decision weighing heavily on his mind.

"Hey," Jesse said softly, catching Wyatt's attention. "I think... I think I'm going to tell them tonight."

Wyatt looked up sharply, surprise flickering in his eyes. "Tonight? Are you sure?" His voice was steady, but Jesse could hear the subtle note of concern.

Jesse nodded, though his pulse quickened with nerves. "Yeah. I've been thinking about it all day. I just... I can't keep pretending. I need them to know."

Wyatt glanced away for a moment, a shadow crossing his face. He took a deep breath before looking back at Jesse, his expression conflicted. "That's a big step. I'm proud of you, but... are you sure you're ready for that?" His words were supportive, but Jesse could sense the underlying anxiety.

"I think so," Jesse said, though his heart raced even faster now. "I'm scared, but I know it's the right thing to do. I've been hiding this part of myself for so long, and I don't want to keep lying to them."

Wyatt stepped closer, placing a hand on Jesse's shoulder, though his grip was a little tighter than usual. "I'm here for you," he said, his voice softer. "But just... be careful. You don't have to do this all at once, you know? Sometimes giving yourself more time isn't a bad thing."

Jesse smiled, appreciating Wyatt's concern. "Thanks, Wyatt. I know it's a huge deal, but I've been thinking about this for a while. It feels like I'm ready."

Wyatt's expression shifted, a flicker of unease passing over his face. He swallowed hard before speaking again, his voice quieter. "I get that, but... what if–I mean, that might put pressure on me?" He paused, his words coming out slower now. "If you tell your parents, then I might feel like I have to tell mine. I don't know if I'm ready for that. I'm still trying to figure things out."

Jesse blinked, caught off guard by Wyatt's honesty. He hadn't considered how his decision might affect Wyatt, hadn't realized that his own courage could make Wyatt feel pressured. A wave of guilt washed over him.

"I didn't think about that," Jesse admitted, his voice softening. "I don't want you to feel like you have to do anything you're not ready for. This is my decision–this is about me and my parents. You don't have to follow my lead."

Wyatt nodded, though his eyes remained clouded with worry. "I know you're not trying to push me. It's just... if you do it, it's gonna be hard for me not to think about it, you know? Like, maybe I should be braver, or maybe I should take that step too. But the idea of telling my parents right now? It terrifies me."

Jesse reached out, gently placing his hand on Wyatt's arm. "Hey, you don't have to do anything you're not ready for. I would never want to pressure you into that. I'm doing this because it feels right for me, but I get that it's different for you. We're on different paths, and that's okay."

Wyatt exhaled, some of the tension easing from his shoulders. "Thanks, Jesse. I just don't want you to think I'm not supporting you. I'm here for you, no matter what. I'm just... I'm scared too. Scared of what my parents might do if they found out."

Jesse nodded, understanding Wyatt's fear all too well. "I get it. And you don't have to explain. We'll both figure this out at our own pace."

Wyatt's eyes softened, and he squeezed Jesse's shoulder. "I'm proud of you, though. For taking this step. Just... don't rush into it, okay?"

Jesse felt a warmth spread through him at Wyatt's words, even though the lingering tension between them remained. "Thanks, Wyatt. That means a lot. And don't worry—I'm not expecting you to do anything you're not ready for. You'll know when it's right for you."

Wyatt gave him a small, unsure smile, but the worry still lingered in his eyes. "I hope so."

They stood there for a moment, the air between them heavy with unspoken worries. Jesse could feel Wyatt's tension, the fear that still clung to him, and he wished he could make it all go away. But he knew that Wyatt's journey was his own, and all Jesse could do was be there for him, just as Wyatt was trying to be there for him now.

As they walked out to the parking lot together, the cool evening breeze seemed to carry a sense of finality with it. Wyatt remained quiet, lost in his thoughts, while Jesse's mind raced with anticipation of the conversation he was about to have with his parents. The weight of their individual fears hung in the air between them, unspoken but deeply felt.

When they reached their cars, Jesse hesitated, feeling a surge of gratitude for Wyatt's support, but also the tug of guilt for the pressure his own decision was putting on him. He wanted to say something to ease Wyatt's worries, but nothing felt right.

"Thanks again," Jesse said quietly, his voice laced with emotion. "For everything."

Wyatt nodded, though his smile was thin, his uncertainty still palpable. "Just... be careful, Jesse. You're doing something brave, but don't feel like you have to rush anything."

Jesse managed a nod, his own heart heavy with the decision ahead. "I'll see you tomorrow?"

"Yeah," Wyatt replied, though his voice held a hint of hesitation. "See you tomorrow."

With that, they parted ways, Wyatt lingering for a moment before getting into his car. Jesse sat in his own car for a moment, watching as Wyatt drove off, a mix of emotions swirling in his chest–gratitude, fear, and the uneasy feeling that things between them were shifting.

As Jesse started the engine and drove home, the weight of the conversation still hung over him. He knew he was about to take a huge step, but Wyatt's anxiousness left him with a lingering doubt. Was he rushing things? Was it too soon?

But as the familiar streets of Brookwood passed by, Jesse knew that no matter what, he had to follow his own path. He couldn't let his fear–or Wyatt's–hold him back from being honest with the people he loved. Still, he couldn't shake the feeling that Wyatt wasn't quite ready to take that leap, and that maybe, their paths were beginning to diverge, even if just for a little while.

Chapter 18: The Moment of Truth

When Jesse pulled into the driveway, the house was quiet, the soft glow of the living room lights spilling out onto the front lawn. He took a deep breath, his hands gripping the steering wheel as he tried to steady himself. He knew his parents were home—his dad's car was in the driveway, and he could see his mom's silhouette through the front window, moving around the kitchen.

He sat in the car for a few moments longer, gathering his courage. Then, with a final breath, he stepped out and walked up to the front door, his heart pounding in his chest. He opened the door slowly, stepping inside and closing it behind him.

"Jesse, is that you?" his mom called from the kitchen.

"Yeah, it's me," Jesse replied, his voice sounding more even than he felt.

"Come on in, I made some dinner," she said, her tone warm and inviting.

Jesse walked into the kitchen, his mom smiling at him as she set a dish on the table. His dad was already seated, glancing up from the newspaper with a nod. "Hey, kiddo," he said. "How was your day?"

Jesse forced a smile, his stomach twisting with nerves. "It was good. Busy, but good."

They sat down to eat, the familiar routine of passing dishes and making small talk providing a small comfort. Jesse waited for the right moment, his mind racing with how to start. He could feel his heart beating faster, the anxiety building in his chest.

Finally, he set his fork down and took a deep breath. "Mom, Dad," he began, his voice trembling slightly. "There's… something I need to tell you."

His mom looked up, her expression softening with concern. "What is it, honey?"

Jesse glanced at his dad, who was watching him with a curious but calm expression. "It's… it's about me," Jesse continued. "Something I've been wanting to tell you for a while now, but I wasn't sure how."

His dad nodded, setting his newspaper aside. "Go ahead, Jesse. Whatever it is, we're here to listen."

Jesse took another deep breath, feeling the weight of the moment pressing down on him. "I… I'm ga.. gay," he said, his voice barely above a whisper. "I've known for a while now, but I didn't know how to tell you. I'm sorry if this is a shock, but… I just needed you to know."

The room fell silent, the words hanging heavy in the air. Jesse's heart pounded in his chest, his hands trembling slightly as he waited for their response. His mom's eyes widened slightly, her hand coming up to cover her mouth. His dad's expression was unreadable, a mix of surprise and contemplation.

For a moment, no one spoke. Jesse felt like he couldn't breathe, the silence stretching out painfully. Then, his mom reached out, taking his hand in hers. "Oh, Jesse," she whispered, her voice filled with emotion. "Why didn't you tell us sooner?"

Jesse felt tears prick at his eyes, his throat tightening with emotion. "I was scared," he admitted. "I didn't know how you'd react. I didn't want to disappoint you."

His mom shook her head, her grip on his hand tightening. "Sweetheart, you could never disappoint us," she said softly. "We love you, no matter what. We always will."

Jesse looked at his dad, who was still quiet, his expression thoughtful. Finally, his dad let out a slow breath, his gaze softening. "Jesse, I don't pretend to know what it's like for you," he said carefully. "But I want you to know that we're here for you. We love you. And we'll support you, no matter what."

Jesse felt a sob rising in his throat, but he swallowed it down, a wave of relief washing over him. "Thank you," he whispered, his voice choked with emotion. "I... I was so scared to tell you. I didn't know what to expect."

His dad gave him a small, reassuring smile. "I'm glad you told us," he said softly. "I can't imagine how hard it must have been for you to keep this inside. But you don't have to do that anymore. Not with us."

His mom squeezed his hand again, tears glistening in her eyes. "We love you, Jesse," she said, her voice thick with emotion. "Nothing will ever change that."

Jesse nodded, tears spilling down his cheeks. He felt a mixture of overwhelming relief and profound gratitude. He had feared this moment for so long, had imagined a hundred different ways it could go wrong. But sitting here, with his parents' love and acceptance surrounding him, he felt a weight lift off his shoulders.

They talked for a while longer, his parents asking questions, their voices filled with a mix of curiosity and concern. Jesse answered as best he could, feeling a sense of openness he hadn't known was possible. He told them about Wyatt, about his fears and his hopes for the future. And as he spoke, he felt a newfound strength building inside him.

Finally, as the conversation began to wind down, his dad reached across the table and placed a hand on his shoulder. "You're brave, Jesse," he said quietly. "I'm proud of you."

Jesse felt a surge of emotion, a warmth spreading through his chest. "Thanks, Dad," he whispered. "That... that means a lot."

After dinner, Jesse excused himself and headed up to his room, feeling a strange mix of exhaustion and elation. He closed the door behind him and collapsed onto his bed, letting out a deep breath. He felt lighter, freer than he had in a long time. He reached for his phone and typed a quick message to Wyatt. But, stopped himself and decided this conversation should be in person. As he drifted off that night, he smiled, his heart swelling with warmth and acceptance. "What was I so worried about?"

Chapter 19: A Step Forward, A Step Back, A Step Forward Again

The sun was already high in the sky when Jesse arrived at the pool, the humid summer air wrapping around him like a blanket. The scent of chlorine hit him as he walked through the gate, his nerves jangling with excitement. Today was different–he could feel it in the pit of his stomach, that nervous, jittery energy that had been building since last night.

He had done it.

Jesse had finally told his parents.

It had been one of the hardest conversations of his life, his heart in his throat the entire time, but once the words were out–*Mom, Dad, I'm gay*–a weight had lifted off his chest that he hadn't even realized he'd been carrying for years. His parents had taken it better than he expected. Sure, there were tears, and his dad had been quieter than usual, but they told him they loved him, no matter what. That was all Jesse needed. The relief was overwhelming.

Now, there was only one person he wanted to tell–Wyatt.

Jesse couldn't stop thinking about him, about how Wyatt had been there for him, about how they were slowly figuring things out together. Jesse had been bursting to tell Wyatt about coming out to his parents, to share the relief and joy he felt. He wanted Wyatt to know, wanted to feel that same closeness between them that they had shared in the pool a few weeks ago, that first kiss still fresh in his memory.

But as Jesse approached the pool deck, his excitement began to waver. What if Wyatt wasn't ready to hear it? What if Wyatt wasn't in the same place as him?

Jesse spotted Wyatt almost immediately. He was sitting in the lifeguard chair, sunglasses on, looking every bit as composed and confident as always. But Jesse knew him well enough by now to see the subtle tension in Wyatt's posture–the way his shoulders were just a little too stiff, the way his jaw was set tight, like he was holding something back.

Jesse waved, his heart skipping a beat as Wyatt's gaze shifted to meet his. Wyatt waved back, but there was something off in his expression– something Jesse couldn't quite place. It wasn't the easy, carefree smile that Jesse was used to. Wyatt's wave was brief, almost mechanical, before he turned back to scan the pool.

Jesse frowned, his excitement dimming just a little. *What's going on with him?*

He made his way over to the concession stand to start his shift, but his thoughts kept drifting back to Wyatt. The plan had been to pull Wyatt aside after their shifts, to tell him everything about last night, about how freeing it felt to finally be honest with his parents. But now, seeing Wyatt so distant, Jesse wasn't sure how to approach it. He wasn't sure if Wyatt even wanted to hear it.

The morning passed in a blur of routine–serving snacks, cleaning up spills, restocking shelves–but Jesse's mind wasn't on his work. He kept glancing over at Wyatt, who seemed to be avoiding him, or at least keeping his distance. Jesse's excitement was slowly being replaced by doubt, the familiar anxiety creeping back into his chest.

Maybe he's just having an off day, Jesse thought, trying to push away the unease that was building inside him. *Maybe he's tired or something.*

But by the time their shifts ended, Jesse couldn't take it anymore. He had to know what was going on.

As soon as the last family left and the pool was quiet again, Jesse approached Wyatt, who was gathering his things from the lifeguard chair. Wyatt didn't look up as Jesse walked over, his movements slower than usual, almost hesitant.

"Hey," Jesse said, his voice tentative but hopeful. "Do you have a minute?"

Wyatt finally looked up, his eyes meeting Jesse's for a brief moment before darting away. "Yeah, sure," he said, but his tone was flat, lacking the warmth Jesse had come to expect from him.

Jesse's heart sank, but he pushed forward. He couldn't hold it in any longer. "I, um… I told my parents last night," he said, his voice quieter than he'd intended, but the words still filled the air between them.

Wyatt's head snapped up, surprise flashing across his face. "You… you did it? You actually did it?"

Jesse nodded, his pulse quickening as he waited for Wyatt's reaction. "Yeah. It was hard, but I did it. They were okay with it, you know? I mean, it wasn't perfect, but they didn't freak out or anything. I feel… I feel like I can finally breathe."

He couldn't help the smile that spread across his face as he spoke. Saying it out loud–telling Wyatt–made it feel even more real, even more freeing. But Wyatt didn't smile back. Instead, he looked away, his jaw tightening as he shifted uncomfortably on his feet.

"That's... that's great, Jesse," Wyatt said, but there was no enthusiasm in his voice. In fact, he sounded almost... distant.

Jesse's smile faltered. "Wyatt? What's going on?"

Wyatt ran a hand through his hair, letting out a frustrated sigh. "I don't know, Jesse. It's just... I'm happy for you, I'm proud of you, and I'm here for you... but... I... I'm just not ready to tell my parents. I don't even know how I feel about all this."

The words hit Jesse like a punch to the gut. He had been so caught up in his own relief, in his own journey.

"I get it," Jesse said softly, stepping closer to Wyatt. "I don't mean to pressure you or anything. I just... I wanted to share it with you."

Wyatt shook his head, his frustration evident. "It's not that, Jesse. It's just... I don't know if I'm ready to do what you did. My parents... it's complicated. I don't even know how to talk to them about something like this."

Jesse felt a pang of guilt, realizing how much pressure Wyatt must be feeling, even if Jesse hadn't meant to make him feel that way. "When I said you don't have to do anything you're not ready for, I meant it, Wyatt," Jesse said, his voice gentle. "I'm here for you, no matter what. You can take your time. I don't expect you to be where I am. This is your journey too."

Wyatt finally looked at Jesse, his expression softening. "I just... I'm still figuring it out, you know? I'm still trying to wrap my head around the fact that I am... that I'm gay."

Jesse reached out, placing a hand on Wyatt's arm. "I know. And that's okay. You don't have to have it all figured out right now. We can take it one step at a time."

Wyatt looked down at where Jesse's hand rested on his arm, and for a moment, the tension between them seemed to ease. But Jesse could still feel the uncertainty radiating from Wyatt, the weight of his internal struggle hanging in the air between them.

"I just don't know how to deal with all this," Wyatt admitted, his voice barely above a whisper. "I'm scared, Jesse. Scared of how they'll react. Scared of what this means for me."

Jesse's heart ached for Wyatt. He knew that fear all too well, had lived with it for so long before finally taking the leap. But hearing it from Wyatt made it all the more real. Wyatt wasn't ready, and that was okay. Jesse had to remind himself that they were on different paths, even if those paths had crossed.

"You don't have to do anything until you're ready," Jesse said softly. "I'm here for you, Wyatt. Whenever you're ready, whether it's tomorrow or next year. I'll be right here."

Wyatt nodded, his eyes meeting Jesse's again, this time with a hint of gratitude. "Thanks, Jesse. I... I appreciate that."

They stood there in the quiet, the pool still and shimmering under the evening sky, the weight of the conversation lingering between them.

Jesse wanted so badly for things to be easy, for Wyatt to be as ready as he was, but he knew that wasn't how it worked. Wyatt had his own journey to take, and Jesse would be there for him every step of the way, no matter how long it took.

Finally, Wyatt broke the silence, his voice a little steadier now. "Do you want to go for a swim? Just... forget about everything for a little while?"

Jesse smiled, nodding. "Yeah. That sounds good."

As they walked towards the edge of the pool, the tension between them began to ease, replaced by the familiar comfort of being together. And though there was still so much to figure out, so much uncertainty ahead, Jesse knew that they would get through it.

The cool water wrapped around them as they eased into the shallow end of the pool, the soft ripples barely breaking the surface. The night air was warm, and the stars above seemed to flicker like they were listening, waiting for the words that hadn't yet been spoken. Jesse swam slowly beside Wyatt, the tension from their earlier conversation still lingering between them, though now muted by the quiet of the empty pool.

They floated in silence for a moment, Jesse stealing glances at Wyatt, who seemed lost in thought, staring down at the water as if it held the answers to everything he was wrestling with. Finally, Jesse spoke, his voice gentle, testing the waters of the conversation just as they both were testing the waters of their relationship.

"I'm sorry if I brought it up too soon," Jesse said quietly, his words almost lost in the stillness of the night. "I just... I was excited, you know? I wanted to share it with you."

Wyatt looked up, his expression softening as he met Jesse's gaze. "No, you didn't do anything wrong," he said, his voice low, but steady. "I'm glad you told me. I just… I wasn't ready to hear it. I thought I was okay with you coming out to your parents, but the pressure I felt when I heard you actually did it was intense."

Jesse nodded, understanding. "I get it. It took me a long time to get there. A lot of sleepless nights, a lot of second-guessing. I didn't think I'd ever be able to say the words out loud."

Wyatt sighed, floating on his back for a moment before he turned to face Jesse again, his brows knitted with the weight of his thoughts. "I want to be there, you know? I want to be where you are. But every time I think about saying something to my parents, I freeze. It's like… what if I say it and everything changes? What if they don't understand?"

Jesse swam closer, his heart aching for Wyatt. "It's scary," he admitted. "I was terrified of how my parents would react. I thought they'd be disappointed or angry. But once I told them, even though it wasn't perfect, it was like… I wasn't hiding anymore".

Wyatt let out a small, frustrated laugh, shaking his head. "You're brave, Jesse. I don't know if I can be that brave."

Jesse floated beside him, watching the way the water glistened on Wyatt's skin, the soft glow of the pool lights casting shadows across his face. "You don't have to do it all at once," Jesse said softly. "There's no rush. You'll get there when you're ready. No one's asking you to be brave right now."

Wyatt stayed quiet for a moment, his eyes fixed on the stars above. "I've never been the type to care what people think, you know? But with this... it's different. I care what my parents think. I don't want to let them down."

Jesse frowned, moving closer, their bodies nearly touching under the water. "You wouldn't be letting them down. You'd be showing them who you really are. That's not a bad thing, Wyatt. That's you being *you*."

Wyatt turned to look at Jesse, his green eyes full of uncertainty, but also something else–something softer, more vulnerable. "What if they don't accept me?" he asked, his voice barely above a whisper.

Jesse reached out, his hand gently brushing Wyatt's arm beneath the water. "Then I'll be here," he said firmly. "No matter what happens, you're not alone in this. I'll be with you every step of the way."

Wyatt's breath caught in his throat, and for a moment, the only sound between them was the gentle lapping of the water. He gave Jesse a small, grateful smile, the tension in his shoulders easing just a bit. "I don't know what I did to deserve someone like you," Wyatt said softly.

Jesse chuckled, though his heart warmed at Wyatt's words. "You didn't have to do anything. We're in this together, remember?"

Wyatt nodded, his gaze lingering on Jesse, the vulnerability still there but slowly being replaced by something deeper, something more sure. He reached out, his fingers brushing Jesse's hand under the water, their touch light but full of meaning.

"You've made this easier," Wyatt said quietly. "I don't know how long it's going to take me to figure everything out, but knowing you're here... that helps."

"I'm not going anywhere," Jesse replied, his voice soft but certain. He squeezed Wyatt's hand gently, letting the warmth of the moment settle over them like a blanket.

They floated there together for a while longer, the silence between them comfortable now, the tension finally fading. It wasn't perfect– Wyatt wasn't ready to take the leap Jesse had, and that was okay. They had time.

"Hey," Jesse said after a few moments, his lips curving into a small smile. "Want to race to the deep end?"

Wyatt raised an eyebrow, a playful smirk spreading across his face. "You think you can beat me?"

Jesse laughed, the sound light and easy in the night air. "Only one way to find out."

And with that, they both launched forward, splashing through the water, their laughter echoing through the empty pool. For now, they weren't thinking about the future or the fear or the uncertainty. For now, it was just the two of them, racing toward something they weren't entirely sure of but were ready to explore together.

The water parted around them as they splashed toward the deep end, their laughter carrying across the still pool deck. For the first time in what felt like weeks, the tension between them melted away, replaced by the easy comfort that had always been there–just below the surface.

Wyatt reached the deep end first, a triumphant grin on his face as he turned to face Jesse, who arrived just a moment later, slightly out of breath but laughing.

"Guess I won," Wyatt teased, pushing his damp hair back from his forehead, his green eyes shining under the soft glow of the pool lights.

Jesse shook his head, still catching his breath. "You always win," he said, though his voice held no bitterness, only warmth. There was something about being around Wyatt that made everything easier, even when Jesse's mind was buzzing with uncertainty. Wyatt had that effect on him—like a calming presence, something solid to hold onto when everything else felt shaky.

For a moment, they just floated there, the cool water lapping gently around them. The sounds of the night—distant crickets, the faint hum of the city beyond the pool gates—faded into the background, leaving just the two of them in the quiet, stillness of the evening.

Jesse's heart began to race, not from the swim, but from the way Wyatt was looking at him. It was the same look he'd seen the night they'd kissed for the first time—uncertain, yes, but also filled with something deeper. Something that made Jesse's pulse quicken and his stomach twist in the most exhilarating way.

Wyatt's gaze softened, his playful grin fading into something more serious, more intense. "I guess I should let you win next time," Wyatt said, his voice quiet now, the playful edge gone.

Jesse shook his head, smiling. "Don't go easy on me," he replied, though his voice had grown softer too, the weight of the moment settling between them.

They floated closer, the space between them shrinking as the water pulled them together. Jesse could feel his heart pounding in his chest, the world narrowing down to just Wyatt—Wyatt's green eyes, the slight curve of his lips, the way the light shimmered off the droplets of water on his skin.

The tension in the air changed, becoming something electric, something Jesse couldn't quite put into words but felt in every inch of his body. The way Wyatt was looking at him—it was different now. There was no more hesitation, no more doubt.

Jesse's breath caught in his throat as Wyatt closed the remaining distance between them, his hand reaching out to gently touch Jesse's arm under the water. The warmth of Wyatt's skin sent a shiver through Jesse, the soft ripple of the pool the only sound between them.

"I want to kiss you," Wyatt whispered, his voice barely audible above the quiet slosh of the water. His eyes were locked on Jesse's, the vulnerability there palpable, but so was the desire.

Jesse's heart surged. He didn't need to think. He didn't need to second-guess. The answer was already there, waiting.

"Then kiss me," Jesse whispered back, his voice trembling, but not from fear.

Wyatt didn't hesitate. His hand slid up Jesse's arm, coming to rest on the back of Jesse's neck, his touch gentle but sure. And then, without another word, Wyatt leaned in, his lips pressing against Jesse's in a kiss that was soft, tender, but filled with the intensity they had both been holding back for so long.

Jesse felt the world tilt, the water swirling around them as he melted into the kiss, his body reacting instinctively, pulling Wyatt closer. His hands found Wyatt's waist under the water, holding onto him as the kiss deepened, the warmth of Wyatt's skin beneath his fingers grounding him, making everything else fall away.

The kiss was slow at first, a gentle exploration, as if they were both still testing the waters, feeling out the connection between them. But soon, it grew more urgent, more intense, like they had both been waiting too long for this moment and could no longer hold back.

Wyatt's other hand slid down to Jesse's waist, pulling him closer, their bodies pressing together under the water. Jesse let out a soft gasp as he felt Wyatt's chest against his, the sensation sending a thrill through him that made his pulse race even faster. His hands gripped Wyatt's sides, pulling him in, needing to be closer, needing to feel more.

Their lips moved together, the kiss deepening as the tension between them finally snapped, giving way to something raw, something real. Jesse's heart pounded in his chest, but it wasn't from fear–it was from the overwhelming rush of being with Wyatt, of feeling Wyatt's hands on him, Wyatt's breath mingling with his own, Wyatt's lips claiming his in a way that felt like everything Jesse had been waiting for.

The world around them faded completely, the pool, the night, everything slipping away as they kissed, their bodies tangled together in the water. Jesse's fingers slid up Wyatt's back, his touch soft but urgent, and he felt the faint tremble in Wyatt's body in response. It was as if they were both trying to hold onto this moment, trying to make it last, even as it threatened to consume them both.

Wyatt pulled back slightly, his breath ragged as he looked at Jesse, their faces just inches apart, the water rippling gently around them. His green eyes were dark with desire, but there was also something else there–something vulnerable, something that made Jesse's heart swell even more.

"I've wanted to do this again for so long," Wyatt murmured, his voice hoarse. "But I was so scared..."

Jesse reached up, brushing his fingers against Wyatt's jaw, his touch soft, reassuring. "Me too," he whispered. "But I'm not scared anymore. Not with you."

Wyatt smiled, the tension in his face easing as he leaned in for another kiss, this one slower, more deliberate, as if he was savoring the moment, taking his time. Jesse melted into it, his body relaxing as the warmth of the kiss spread through him, filling him with a sense of peace he hadn't known he needed.

They stayed like that for what felt like hours, kissing slowly, their bodies floating together in the still water, the world around them forgotten. There was no rush, no urgency anymore–just the two of them, in this moment, exploring each other in a way that felt natural, easy, like they had always been meant to find their way here.

When they finally pulled apart, breathless but smiling, Wyatt rested his forehead against Jesse's, his arms still wrapped around him under the water.

"We'll figure it out," Wyatt whispered, his voice steady now, full of quiet determination. "Together."

Jesse smiled, his heart swelling with the certainty in Wyatt's words. He leaned in, pressing a soft kiss to Wyatt's lips, his voice barely above a whisper as he replied.

"Together."

The world seemed to fade away as Jesse and Wyatt held each other in the quiet embrace of the pool. The stars above shimmered like distant lanterns, casting a gentle glow over the water. Their foreheads rested together, breaths mingling, hearts beating in a synchronized rhythm that spoke of newfound understanding and connection.

"Together," Jesse whispered again, savoring the word.

Wyatt smiled softly, his eyes reflecting the subtle light. "Together," he echoed.

For a moment, everything felt perfect. The fears and uncertainties that had weighed them down seemed distant, replaced by a warm certainty that they were exactly where they were meant to be. Jesse felt a surge of hope—perhaps things could be this simple, this right.

But then, a faint rustling sound shattered the tranquility.

Both boys froze, their gazes snapping toward the direction of the noise. It came from near the chain-link fence that surrounded the pool—a whispered giggle followed by hurried footsteps on gravel.

"Did you hear that?" Jesse asked, his voice barely above a whisper.

Wyatt's eyes widened, panic flickering across his face. "Someone's there," he murmured.

They quickly separated, putting a few feet of water between them. Jesse's heart pounded in his chest as he scanned the perimeter of the pool. Near the gate, two silhouettes were briefly illuminated by a passing car's headlights—teenagers, familiar ones.

"Is that...?" Jesse began.

"Those are the guys from the other day," Wyatt confirmed, his tone edged with anxiety.

Recognition hit Jesse like a cold wave. It was the same group of teens they'd had an altercation with earlier in the summer. But now, the mischievous glint in their eyes was replaced with something more unsettling.

The teens stood there for a moment, one nudging the other, smirking. Then, without a word, they turned and sprinted away, their laughter echoing faintly as they disappeared into the night.

Wyatt's face paled. "They saw us," he said hollowly.

Jesse swallowed hard, trying to steady his own racing heart. "Maybe they didn't recognize us. It was dark," he offered, though he wasn't sure he believed it himself.

Wyatt shook his head, moving toward the pool's edge. "No, they saw us. They knew it was us." He hoisted himself out of the water, grabbing a towel and wrapping it around his shoulders with shaky hands.

Jesse followed suit, concern etched on his face. "Wyatt, it's okay. Even if they did see, it doesn't matter. They can't–"

"You don't understand," Wyatt interrupted, his voice tight. "This is a small town. People talk. If they start spreading rumors..." He trailed off, running a hand through his damp hair in agitation.

Jesse reached out, placing a tentative hand on Wyatt's arm. "Hey, look at me."

Wyatt hesitated before meeting Jesse's gaze, his eyes filled with a mix of fear and confusion.

"We'll handle it," Jesse said firmly. "Whatever happens, we'll face it together."

Wyatt pulled his arm away, stepping back. "I can't– I can't deal with this right now." He grabbed his belongings hastily, stuffing them into his bag. "I shouldn't have– We shouldn't have..."

Jesse felt a pang of hurt but pushed it aside. "Don't say that. You didn't do anything wrong."

Wyatt avoided his eyes, his movements frantic. "I need to go home. I need to..."

"Wyatt, please don't shut me out," Jesse pleaded, his voice tinged with desperation.

"I'm sorry," Wyatt whispered, slinging his bag over his shoulder. "I just... I can't." Without another word, he turned and headed toward the exit, his footsteps echoing against the concrete.

Jesse stood there, water dripping from his hair, watching helplessly as Wyatt disappeared into the night. The warmth of their shared moments had vanished, replaced by a chill that seeped deep into his bones.

He wrapped his arms around himself, the weight of the situation settling heavily on his shoulders. The fear in Wyatt's eyes haunted him. Jesse knew all too well the terror of being exposed before you're ready, the vulnerability that comes with it.

Taking a deep breath, he tried to steady himself. "It'll be okay," he whispered into the empty night, unsure if he was trying to convince himself or hoping that somehow Wyatt would hear him.

The pool lights flickered, and a sudden gust of wind sent a shiver down his spine. Gathering his things, Jesse took one last look around the silent pool–the place that had been a sanctuary just moments before now felt foreign and cold.

As he made his way home, his thoughts were consumed with worry for Wyatt. He wished he could have done more, said more to ease his fears. But deep down, Jesse understood that this was a battle Wyatt needed to face himself.

All he could do now was be there for him, hoping that when Wyatt was ready, he'd let Jesse back in.

The night seemed darker than usual as Jesse walked the quiet streets alone, the distant chirping of crickets the only sound accompanying his footsteps. The stars above offered little comfort, their distant light unable to penetrate the uncertainty that now clouded his heart.

PART TWO: UNRAVELING

Chapter 20: Bracing for the Fall

The morning sunlight streamed through Jesse's window, warm and golden, but he hardly noticed. His phone sat on his nightstand, face down and untouched. It had been hours since the previous night's chaos at the pool, and he hadn't heard a single word from Wyatt. Jesse lay there, staring at the ceiling, replaying everything in his head–over and over. The kiss, the noise, the panic on Wyatt's face as he pulled away, and then the moment those boys ran off, their laughter still echoing in Jesse's ears.

He had barely slept, too tangled in his thoughts, too consumed by what had happened. He'd been ready to face anything with Wyatt, ready to figure it all out together, but Wyatt had freaked out. And now, Jesse had no idea where they stood.

Sighing, Jesse reached for his phone, unlocking it and checking his messages. Still nothing from Wyatt. The pit in his stomach grew heavier, that gnawing anxiety settling deeper as the silence stretched on.

He thought about texting Wyatt, but what would he even say? Would Wyatt want to talk about what happened, or was he still too scared? Jesse couldn't blame him, not after the way those boys had seen them, watched them. But that didn't stop the ache in his chest. He thought they'd been on the same page, slowly figuring things out together, but last night had shown him how different their journeys really were.

Jesse sat up, rubbing his face with his hands. He had to get ready for work–*work,* where Wyatt would be. The thought sent a rush of nervous energy through him. Would Wyatt even show up? Would they talk, or would it be too awkward to even look at each other? Jesse had no idea what to expect, and that uncertainty gnawed at him.

He quickly dressed, the routine mechanical as he tried to shake off the unease that had settled over him. As much as he didn't want to face the day, he didn't have a choice. He had to go to the pool, and whether Wyatt showed up or not, Jesse would have to deal with the aftermath of last night.

By the time he arrived at the pool, the familiar sounds of kids laughing and water splashing greeted him. But today, everything felt off. Jesse scanned the pool deck, his heart thudding in his chest as he looked for Wyatt. He wasn't there. Not yet.

Jesse made his way to the concession stand, his hands trembling as he started his shift. He tried to focus on his tasks–cleaning up from yesterday, organizing the snacks–but his mind kept drifting back to Wyatt. He replayed their conversation in his head, the way Wyatt had panicked, the fear in his voice when he talked about his parents finding out. Jesse had known how scared Wyatt was of coming out, but seeing it in person, hearing the desperation in his voice, had been a gut punch.

He wanted to help Wyatt, wanted to be there for him, but he couldn't force him to be ready. Wyatt had to come to terms with things on his own, and Jesse couldn't speed up that process, no matter how much he wanted to.

Just as Jesse was finishing up restocking the shelves, he heard a familiar voice behind him. It was soft, hesitant.

"Hey."

Jesse turned slowly, his heart leaping into his throat. Wyatt stood at the edge of the concession stand, looking worn out, like he hadn't slept either. His hair was messy, and his eyes were tired, but what really struck Jesse was the tension in his posture–the way Wyatt stood, like he was carrying something too heavy for him to bear.

"Wyatt," Jesse said quietly, relief flooding through him despite the tension in the air. "I wasn't sure if you'd come in today."

Wyatt shifted uncomfortably, glancing around the pool deck before meeting Jesse's gaze. "Yeah, I wasn't sure either." His voice was quiet, strained, like he was still trying to process everything.

Jesse could feel the weight of the unsaid hanging between them. He wanted to reach out, to say something that would make it better, but he didn't know where to start. Everything had changed in an instant last night, and now they were standing here, both unsure of what to do next.

"I'm sorry about last night," Wyatt said, breaking the silence. His voice wavered slightly, and Jesse could see the guilt in his eyes. "I just... I freaked out. Those guys... they saw us, and I panicked. I didn't know what to do."

Jesse nodded slowly, taking a deep breath as he tried to steady his voice. "I get it. It was scary. I freaked out too, but–"

Wyatt shook his head, cutting Jesse off. "No, you handled it better than I did. You're... you're braver than I am. I don't know if I can do this, Jesse. I thought I could, but I'm not ready. Not yet."

The words hit Jesse hard, even though he had been expecting them. He had known that Wyatt was struggling, that he wasn't as ready to face things as Jesse was. But hearing him say it out loud, seeing the fear and uncertainty etched into his face, made it all so much more real.

"I won't push you," Jesse said softly, stepping closer but keeping his voice gentle. "I just thought... I don't know, I thought we were figuring this out together."

Wyatt ran a hand through his hair, his eyes flickering with guilt and frustration. "I thought so too," he admitted, his voice barely above a whisper. "But last night, when they saw us... it made me realize how scared I am. What if they tell people? What if my parents find out? I'm not ready for that, Jesse. I don't know how to handle it."

Jesse felt a pang of guilt, knowing that he'd pushed Wyatt into a situation he wasn't ready for. But at the same time, he couldn't help the frustration bubbling inside him. They had shared something so real last night, something Jesse thought had been a turning point. Now, it felt like Wyatt was retreating, pulling away when Jesse needed him most.

"You don't have to do this right now," Jesse said, trying to keep the edge out of his voice. "I'm not asking you to come out before you're ready.

But Wyatt, I need to know you're not going to shut me out. I'm scared too, but I don't want to go through this alone."

Wyatt's face softened, but the tension in his shoulders didn't ease. He glanced around the pool, as if checking to see if anyone was watching, before he looked back at Jesse. "I'm not shutting you out," he said quietly. "But I don't know if I can be what you need right now. My parents... if they find out, I don't know how they'll react. I'm just... I'm not ready for them to know."

Jesse's chest tightened at the words. He had known Wyatt wasn't ready, but hearing it like this–knowing that Wyatt was pulling away, even if it wasn't intentional–made it feel all the more final. He had thought they were in this together, but now, it felt like they were on different paths, and Jesse wasn't sure how to bring them back to the same place.

"I'm not asking you to tell them," Jesse said, his voice softer now. "But you don't have to deal with this alone. We can figure it out, one step at a time."

Wyatt sighed, his shoulders slumping as he looked down at the ground. "I just don't know if I'm ready to take that first step," he said, his voice barely audible. "I don't think I can."

Jesse reached out, his hand gently brushing against Wyatt's arm. "We'll figure it out together," he said quietly. "I'm here for you, no matter what."

For a moment, Wyatt didn't respond, his gaze still fixed on the ground. But then he looked up, his eyes filled with something close to regret.

"I've got to go, Jesse," he said, his voice breaking slightly. "I need some time to think. I don't... I don't know what to do right now."

Jesse felt his heart sink, but he nodded, understanding. "Okay," he said softly, though the lump in his throat made it hard to speak. "Take the time you need."

Wyatt gave a small, strained smile, but there was no joy in it. "I'll talk to you later, okay?"

Jesse nodded, watching as Wyatt turned and walked away, his figure disappearing through the gate. The sound of laughter and splashing water filled the air around him, but all Jesse could hear was the echo of Wyatt's words—*I'm not ready.*

Jesse stood there for a long moment, his hands trembling as he stared at the empty spot where Wyatt had been. He wanted to believe that Wyatt would come around, that they could face this together. But as the silence stretched on, Jesse couldn't shake the fear that Wyatt was pulling away for good.

The day dragged on, each minute feeling longer than the last as Jesse worked through his shift, his mind constantly drifting back to Wyatt. The weight of it all—the fear, the uncertainty, the possibility that everything could fall apart—pressed down on him like a heavy blanket, suffocating and inescapable.

By the time his shift ended, Jesse was exhausted, both physically and emotionally. He headed home, the familiar streets of Brookwood passing by in a blur, but his thoughts were miles away, stuck.

Later that evening, after what felt like the longest shift of his life, Jesse found himself walking toward Liz's house, his mind still buzzing with everything that had happened. The warm summer breeze did nothing to ease the tension in his chest, and he felt like he was drowning in the mess of his own thoughts.

He needed to talk to someone, and Liz was the only person who really understood him. She had been his best friend since forever, the one constant in his life, the one person who knew him inside and out. Jesse didn't even have to ask if she was free–he knew she'd be there for him, like she always was.

By the time he reached her house, the sun had started to set, casting the sky in shades of pink and orange. Liz was sitting on the porch, as if she'd been waiting for him. She looked up from her phone, her brow furrowing slightly when she saw him.

"You look like crap," she said bluntly, standing up and crossing her arms. But her voice was full of concern, not judgment. "What happened?"

Jesse let out a long sigh, running a hand through his hair. "Can we talk? I need to tell you something."

Liz's expression softened, and she nodded, gesturing for him to come inside. "Of course. Let's go to my room."

They made their way up to Liz's room, a familiar, comforting space filled with posters of her favorite bands and old Polaroid pictures they had taken over the years. Jesse sat down on the edge of her bed, feeling the weight of the day settle over him again. Liz plopped down next to him, sitting cross-legged, her eyes focused on him with a mixture of curiosity and concern.

"So, spill. What's going on?" she asked, her tone softer now. "You look like you've been through hell."

Jesse took a deep breath, not sure where to start. "It's about Wyatt," he said, his voice a little shaky. "And... well, everything."

Liz raised an eyebrow. "Are things still complicated?"

Jesse nodded, his hands fidgeting in his lap. "Yeah. Things have been gotten... crazy."

Liz watched him for a moment, and then realization flickered across her face. "Wait. Did something happen?"

Jesse hesitated, his heart pounding in his chest. He hadn't really talked to Liz about what was going on between him and Wyatt passed their first date. But now, with everything that had happened, he needed her to know.

After a moment of silence, Jesse finally let it out, "I like him, Liz. I really like him. But it's been a mess."

Liz's eyes widened, but she didn't say anything for a moment, clearly trying to wrap her head around it all. "Whoa. Okay, back up. I need details."

Jesse let out a small laugh, though it was tinged with exhaustion. "It's complicated. We've been hanging out more, getting close. And I thought maybe we were both ready to figure things out together."

Liz nodded, listening intently, but her expression was thoughtful. "Okay. But you said it blew up? What happened?"

Jesse's heart sank as he thought back to the previous night. "We were at the pool after it closed. Everything was fine, and then two guys from that altercation earlier in the summer–remember them?–they saw us kissing. They laughed and ran off, and Wyatt freaked. He panicked, and then he just... shut down. He ran off. Today, he told me he's not ready. He's scared."

Liz let out a low whistle, her face a mixture of shock and sympathy. "Damn. That's rough, Jess."

Jesse sighed, running a hand through his hair. "He's terrified of coming out, especially to his parents. He told me he's not ready, and I don't want to push him, but... I thought we were on the same page, you know? And now, it feels like he's pulling away."

Liz frowned, reaching out to squeeze Jesse's hand. "I'm really sorry, Jesse. That sounds awful. It's hard enough figuring out your own feelings without other people making it worse."

Jesse nodded, feeling the knot in his stomach tighten. "I just don't know what to do. I want to be there for him, but it feels like he's shutting me out. And now, with those guys seeing us... what if they tell people? What if this all blows up before he's ready?"

Liz was quiet for a moment, her thumb gently rubbing the back of his hand as she thought. "Honestly? I don't know what's going to happen with those guys. People can be jerks, but they're also cowards. Maybe they'll run their mouths, or maybe they won't say anything. Either way, you can't control that."

Jesse nodded, though the thought still made his stomach churn with anxiety. "I know. I just... I'm scared, Liz. For both of us. I don't want him to get hurt, but I don't know how to help him if he's pushing me away."

Liz bit her lip, thinking. "I think Wyatt's just scared, Jess. He probably doesn't know how to deal with it yet. You've been through a lot, and it sounds like you're ready for this, but he's not. And that's okay. He just needs time."

Jesse sighed, feeling a wave of exhaustion wash over him. "I know. I just don't want to lose him" he said as his voice cracked and his eyes welled up with tears.

Liz smiled softly, her eyes warm with understanding. "You won't. It might take time, but if you care about each other, you'll figure it out. Just give him space to sort through his own stuff. Be patient. If it's meant to be, it'll be."

Jesse leaned back against the bed, staring up at the ceiling, feeling a little lighter now that he had told Liz everything. She always had a way of grounding him, of making things feel a little less overwhelming.

"Thanks, Liz," Jesse said quietly and wiped a single tear off his cheek. "I don't know what I'd do without you."

She grinned, nudging him with her elbow. "Yeah, well, you'd probably be a total mess. Lucky for you, you've got me."

Jesse laughed, the sound coming out a little easier this time. "Yeah, lucky me."

They sat there for a while, the comfortable silence settling between them. Jesse felt the weight of the day starting to lift, the tension easing as he let himself relax, knowing that Liz had his back.

Whatever happened with Wyatt–whether he was ready or not–Jesse knew that he wasn't alone. And that, at least, made everything a little easier to bear.

"Want to watch a movie?" Liz asked after a while, breaking the silence. "I've got some terrible rom-coms we can make fun of."

Jesse smiled, nodding. "Yeah. That sounds good."

Chapter 21: The Rumor

The morning light filtered through the kitchen window, casting long shadows across the table where Jesse sat, his fingers nervously tapping against the edge of his mug. His parents were sitting across from him, both of them with serious expressions etched on their faces. The air in the room felt thick, like something heavy was hanging over them, and Jesse's heart was already pounding in his chest, even though they hadn't said anything yet.

His mom's lips were pressed into a thin line, her coffee untouched in front of her. His dad, usually so laid back, sat stiffly in his chair, his arms crossed over his chest. They had asked him to sit down when he came down for breakfast, and now, the silence stretched uncomfortably between them.

Finally, his mom spoke, her voice quiet but firm. "Jesse, we need to talk about something. Something... we heard."

Jesse's stomach flipped, the nervous energy building inside him. He swallowed hard, bracing himself for whatever was coming. "What's going on?"

His dad let out a slow breath, shaking his head. "We were at the grocery store yesterday," he began, his voice gruff. "And while we were there, we ran into Mrs. Alcott. You know, she's always been a little... gossipy. But what she said, Jesse..." He paused, looking at Jesse with a mix of disappointment and concern. "She said there's been talk around town. About you. And Wyatt."

Jesse's heart sank, the pit in his stomach growing heavier with every word. He could feel the blood draining from his face as he stared at his parents, the weight of what they were saying crashing down on him.

"What–what do you mean?" Jesse asked, his voice shaky. "What did she say?"

His mom leaned forward, her expression softening just a little, but there was still a tension there. "Jesse, she said there are rumors going around. That people are talking. And what they're saying is... well, it's not just that you and Wyatt are together. She said she heard you two were... having sex. In the pool. After hours."

Jesse's stomach dropped like a stone, and he felt his entire body go cold. "What?" he whispered, barely able to get the word out. "That's not true. We didn't–"

His dad held up a hand, cutting him off. "Look, Jesse. I don't know what happened, and frankly, I don't want to know. But this is the kind of thing that gets around fast in a small town. People are already talking. It doesn't matter if it's true or not–what matters is that it's out there. People think you and Wyatt are doing... things. And it's making its way through the community."

Jesse's heart raced, panic setting in. He couldn't believe this was happening. "We didn't do anything like that," he said, his voice rising slightly as the shock turned into frustration. "Yeah, we kissed, but we didn't... we weren't having sex! That's just a stupid rumor!"

His mom sighed, shaking her head. "Jesse, we believe you," she said, her voice gentle but firm. "But it doesn't change the fact that people are talking. This town... you know how people are. They take a little piece of information and turn it into something much bigger."

Jesse felt a surge of anger rising in his chest. "So, what, you're mad at me because some lady made up a rumor about me? I didn't do anything wrong!"

His dad's face tightened, his jaw clenched. "We're not mad about you being gay, Jesse," he said, his voice low but tense. "We're upset because now this is what people are saying. Do you know how hard it is to control rumors in a town like this? And the fact that they're talking about you... it's hard for us to deal with."

Jesse couldn't believe what he was hearing. His parents had always been the kind of people who cared too much about what the community thought, but this? This felt like they were more worried about how the rumors made *them* look than about what Jesse was actually going through.

"So, what do you want me to do?" Jesse asked, his voice sharper now. "You want me to pretend it didn't happen? You want me to stay quiet while people talk about me like that?"

His mom looked pained, her hands clasped tightly in front of her. "We just don't want you to do anything that will make it worse," she said carefully. "We're not saying you should ignore it, but maybe... maybe don't do anything that will add fuel to the fire."

Jesse stared at them, his mind spinning. "So, you're saying I shouldn't see Wyatt anymore? Is that it?"

His dad shifted in his seat, his expression conflicted. "We're not saying that, but maybe... maybe you two should be a little more careful. People in this town can be cruel, Jesse. And we don't want to see you get hurt because of that."

Jesse's chest tightened, the frustration bubbling over. "You don't think I know that?" he snapped. "You don't think I've already been scared of what people will say? But I shouldn't have to hide just because some people don't like it!"

His mom sighed, rubbing her temples. "Jesse, we're not saying you have to hide. We just don't want this to get out of control. People are talking, and we can't stop them, but we don't want this to get worse."

Jesse stood up abruptly, his heart racing, anger and hurt flooding through him. "I can't believe this," he muttered. "You're more worried about what people think than about how I feel."

"Jesse, that's not fair," his dad said, his voice rising in frustration. "We care about you. We just don't want this to make things harder for you than they already are."

Jesse shook his head, his hands trembling. "You say you care, but it doesn't feel like it. It feels like you're just embarrassed."

His mom's face softened, and she reached out toward him, but Jesse stepped back. "Jesse, we love you. We're just trying to protect you."

Jesse's chest heaved as he tried to steady his breathing. "I'm going to the pool," he said abruptly, grabbing his keys from the table. "I can't... I can't deal with this right now."

His parents didn't stop him as he turned and left the kitchen, his heart pounding in his chest as he walked out the door. The cool morning air hit him as soon as he stepped outside, but it did nothing to calm the storm of emotions raging inside him.

He couldn't believe what had just happened. The rumors, the way his parents had handled it–it was too much. He felt betrayed, like the one place he thought he'd find support had crumbled beneath him.

As he walked toward his car, his phone buzzed in his pocket. Jesse pulled it out, half-expecting it to be a message from his parents, but it wasn't.

It was from Wyatt.

Wyatt: *Can we talk?*

Jesse stared at the screen for a moment, his mind spinning. Wyatt. Everything was coming back to Wyatt. And now, Jesse didn't know if he had the strength to face him after everything that had happened. But deep down, he knew he had to.

Taking a deep breath, Jesse typed out a quick reply.

Jesse: *Yeah. We need to talk.*

And with that, he got into his car, the weight of the day already pressing down on him, unsure of what would come next.

Chapter 22: Torn Between Two Worlds

Jesse pulled into the parking lot of the small park on the outskirts of town, his hands gripping the steering wheel tightly. The air was thick with tension, the weight of everything that had happened over the past two days pressing down on him like a vice. He had barely had time to process what his parents had told him that morning, and now he had to face Wyatt, who was likely dealing with even worse fallout.

He glanced at his phone again, checking the message from Wyatt.

Wyatt: *Meet me at Briarwood Park. We need to talk.*

Jesse's stomach churned as he stepped out of the car. Briarwood was the one place they could meet where no one would recognize them—at least not easily. The park was small, secluded, and usually deserted except for the occasional jogger or dog walker. It was the perfect place to have a conversation they didn't want anyone else to hear.

Jesse walked down the narrow, winding path that led toward the back of the park, his heart pounding with each step. He spotted Wyatt sitting on one of the old wooden benches, hunched over, his elbows resting on his knees. Even from a distance, Jesse could see the tension in his posture, the way his shoulders were drawn tight, his head bowed like he was trying to hold himself together.

Jesse's chest tightened as he approached, unsure of what to say, unsure of what Wyatt was going to say. The air between them was heavy with the unsaid, the weight of everything that had happened hanging over them like a storm cloud.

Wyatt didn't look up as Jesse sat down next to him on the bench. For a moment, neither of them spoke. The only sounds were the rustling of leaves in the breeze and the distant chirping of birds, a sharp contrast to the turmoil swirling inside Jesse's mind.

Finally, Wyatt broke the silence, his voice low and raw. "They found out."

Jesse's stomach dropped. He had been expecting it, but hearing the words out loud still hit him like a punch to the gut. "Your parents?"

Wyatt nodded, still not looking at Jesse. "Yeah. That woman–Mrs. Alcott–she told them. I guess she saw them at the high school this morning and made a big deal about it. Said people are talking, that we were... you know... doing stuff at the pool."

Jesse clenched his fists, the anger simmering just beneath the surface. He wanted to scream, to punch something. How could one person cause so much damage with nothing more than a few rumors? He opened his mouth to speak, but before he could say anything, Wyatt continued.

"They're pissed, Jesse. My dad... he barely even looked at me when I got home. My mom was crying. They didn't say much, just that they couldn't believe I would do something like this. That I would..." Wyatt's voice cracked, and he ran a hand through his hair, his entire body shaking with barely contained emotion. "They didn't even give me a chance to explain. It's like they've already decided who I am, and they hate it."

Jesse's heart ached at the pain in Wyatt's voice. He wanted to reach out, to comfort him, but he knew this was deeper than anything he could fix with a few reassuring words. "I'm so sorry, Wyatt. I didn't think it would blow up like this."

Wyatt shook his head, his voice filled with frustration. "I didn't either. And now, I don't know what to do. My dad didn't say it, but I could tell... I could see it in his eyes. He's disgusted with me. He doesn't understand, and he probably never will. I'm so scared, Jesse. I'm scared they'll... I don't know... kick me out or something. What if they can't have me around anymore?"

Jesse's breath caught in his throat. Wyatt had never been this vulnerable before, and seeing him so torn up, so scared, broke Jesse's heart. "They won't disown you," Jesse said, though even as the words left his mouth, he wasn't sure if he believed them. "They're your parents. They love you."

Wyatt let out a bitter laugh, finally turning to look at Jesse. His eyes were red, his face drawn with exhaustion. "You didn't see the way they looked at me, Jesse. My dad wouldn't even talk to me. My mom couldn't stop crying. I'm not sure they *do* love me, at least not like this."

Jesse felt his chest tighten, the knot of anxiety growing tighter with each word. He wanted to tell Wyatt that everything would be okay, that they would figure it out together, but how could he promise that when he didn't know what would happen next?

"I don't know what to say," Jesse admitted, his voice barely above a whisper. "I'm scared too, Wyatt. My parents heard the same rumors this morning. They're upset–not because I'm gay, but because people are talking about it. It's like they care more about what people think than about me."

Wyatt clenched his jaw, his hands gripping the edge of the bench tightly. "I don't know how to do this, Jesse. I don't know how to be... this. I thought I was ready to figure things out with you, but now... now it feels like everything is falling apart. My parents, the rumors, everyone watching us–it's too much."

Jesse's heart sank, fear creeping into the pit of his stomach. "What are you saying?"

Wyatt exhaled slowly, running both hands through his hair in frustration. "I think... I think maybe we need to take a break. I need to figure things out, Jesse. I need to deal with my parents and... and everything else before I can handle this. It's just too much all at once."

Jesse felt like the ground was falling out from under him. His chest tightened, his breath coming in shallow gasps as he tried to process what Wyatt was saying. "You want to stop seeing me?" His voice cracked with the weight of the words.

Wyatt shook his head, his expression pained. "I don't *want* to stop seeing you, but I don't know what else to do. I'm scared, Jesse. I'm scared that if we keep doing this, it's only going to get worse. I'm not ready to come out. I'm not ready to lose my parents. And right now, it feels like being with you is going to make that happen."

Jesse's heart broke at the words. He had known that Wyatt was struggling, but hearing him say it out loud–hearing him say that he was willing to push Jesse away–was like a punch to the gut. "So, what? You're just going to disappear until you figure things out?"

Wyatt winced, his hands trembling as he turned away from Jesse, staring down at the ground. "I don't know what else to do, Jesse. I need time. I need space to figure out what I want and how to deal with this. I don't want to hurt you, but if I don't take a step back now, I'm afraid I'll make everything worse for both of us."

Jesse felt a lump rise in his throat, his chest tight with the weight of Wyatt's words. "What about us? What about everything we've been through together?"

Wyatt's voice cracked as he spoke, barely holding it together. "I care about you so much, Jesse. But right now, I'm drowning. I'm torn between you and my parents, between what I feel for you and what they expect from me. I need time to figure it all out. I just... I need to breathe."

Jesse felt hot tears prickling at the corners of his eyes, his vision blurring as he stared at Wyatt. He wanted to fight for them, to tell Wyatt that they could get through this together, but the fear in Wyatt's voice, the pain in his eyes, told Jesse that Wyatt wasn't ready.

After a long, painful silence, Jesse nodded, though his heart felt like it was shattering. "I get it," he whispered, his voice barely audible. "If you need space, I'll give you space. But just... don't disappear completely, okay?"

Wyatt nodded, though he couldn't meet Jesse's gaze. "I won't. I promise."

They sat there in silence for a while longer, the weight of the conversation pressing down on them like a heavy blanket. Jesse felt like he was drowning, but he knew Wyatt was too. And maybe, for now, they had to let each other go.

Eventually, Wyatt stood up, his movements slow and heavy. "I should go," he said quietly. "My parents are expecting me back."

Jesse nodded, not trusting himself to speak. He watched as Wyatt walked away, his figure disappearing down the path, and with each step Wyatt took, the ache in Jesse's chest grew deeper.

As the sun began to set, casting long shadows across the park, Jesse sat there on the bench, feeling more alone than he had in a long time. The silence around him felt suffocating, the weight of the day crashing down on him.

Jesse sat in his car, staring blankly at the steering wheel, the soft hum of the engine doing nothing to quiet the storm raging inside him. The air felt thick, suffocating, and his chest ached with the weight of everything that had just happened. Wyatt was gone—he had walked away, leaving Jesse sitting there in the park, feeling more lost and broken than he ever had.

The tears came before he could stop them, hot and heavy, spilling down his cheeks in a rush of overwhelming emotion. Jesse leaned forward, pressing his forehead against the steering wheel as sobs wracked his body. His shoulders shook, his breath coming in shallow gasps as the guilt and pain flooded through him.

It felt like everything was his fault. If he hadn't pushed Wyatt, if he hadn't been so eager to explore what they had, maybe things wouldn't have gotten so out of control. Maybe Wyatt wouldn't be facing this horrible decision—choosing between his feelings for Jesse and the expectations of his parents. And now, because of those stupid rumors,

Wyatt was pulling away, and Jesse didn't know how to fix it. He didn't know if it *could* be fixed.

"I ruined everything," Jesse whispered to himself, his voice choked and shaky.

He felt guilty, like he had dragged Wyatt into something he wasn't ready for. Wyatt had told him he wasn't ready to come out, and now everything was spiraling out of control, and Jesse didn't know how to stop it.

Jesse sat there for what felt like hours, the sobs slowly subsiding but the ache in his chest remaining. He wiped his face with the sleeve of his shirt, trying to steady his breathing, but it didn't help. His thoughts kept spiraling, guilt and fear twisting together until he felt like he couldn't breathe.

He needed to talk to someone. He needed to hear a voice that wasn't his own, to feel like he wasn't completely alone in this mess.

With trembling hands, Jesse reached for his phone and called Liz. The line rang twice before she picked up.

"Jesse?" Her voice was soft, concerned, like she could hear the pain in his silence before he even said a word. "What's going on?"

Jesse opened his mouth to speak, but no words came out. His throat tightened, and he could feel the tears welling up again. He tried to hold them back, to keep it together, but the sound of Liz's familiar voice made it even harder to keep everything in.

"Jesse, hey, talk to me," Liz urged, her voice gentle but insistent.

"I... I don't know what to do," Jesse finally choked out, his voice barely a whisper. "Everything's a mess."

Liz was silent for a moment, clearly giving him the space to speak when he was ready. "It's okay, Jesse. Just take your time."

Jesse wiped his eyes again, his hand trembling as he gripped the phone. "Wyatt... he wants to take a break," he said, his voice shaking. "He's scared his parents are going to disown him, and I feel like it's all my fault. Everything's falling apart, Liz."

"Oh, Jess," Liz breathed, her voice full of sympathy. "It's not your fault. None of this is your fault."

Jesse let out a small, bitter laugh. "It feels like it is. I kept pushing, even when I knew he wasn't ready. And now people are talking, and he's terrified, and I just–" He broke off, his breath hitching. "I don't know how to fix it."

"You can't fix everything," Liz said softly. "Sometimes things are just... complicated. And Wyatt's dealing with a lot right now. It's not fair, but it's not your fault either."

Jesse swallowed hard, staring at the dashboard, feeling the weight of Liz's words settle over him. He wanted so badly to make things better, to take away Wyatt's fear and hurt, but deep down, he knew Liz was right. Wyatt's struggles with his parents and coming out weren't something Jesse could fix. And pushing him to figure it out faster wasn't going to help.

"I just... I don't know what to do," Jesse whispered, his voice cracking.

"You've done everything you can," Liz said gently. "You've been there for Wyatt, but right now, he needs to sort through his own stuff. It sucks, but sometimes people just need time. And you need to give yourself a break too. You're carrying way too much guilt over this."

Jesse nodded, though he wasn't sure if he believed her yet. "I'm scared I'm going to lose him, Liz," he admitted, his voice barely audible.

Liz was quiet for a moment, and when she spoke again, her voice was soft but firm. "I don't think you'll lose him. Wyatt's just overwhelmed, and it's not fair that he has to choose between you and his parents. But if he cares about you–and I think he does–he'll come back. He just needs space right now. Don't give up hope."

Jesse sniffled, feeling a flicker of relief at her words. "Thanks, Liz. I don't know what I'd do without you."

"You'd probably spiral into a pit of despair," she said lightly, trying to lift his spirits. "But seriously, you're going to be okay. Just take it one step at a time."

Jesse nodded again, feeling a little steadier, though the ache in his chest remained. "I'll try."

"You don't have to figure it all out right now," Liz reminded him. "Just breathe. You've got me, okay? You're not alone."

"Thanks," Jesse said softly. "I'll call you later, okay?"

"Anytime," Liz said warmly. "And remember–this isn't the end of the world. You've got this."

Jesse hung up, letting out a long, shaky breath as he set his phone down. He still felt like he was drowning, but Liz's words had given him a small lifeline to hold onto. Maybe things weren't as hopeless as they felt right now. Maybe Wyatt would come around once he had time to process everything.

For now, though, Jesse needed to get himself together.

He took a deep breath, wiping the last of the tears from his face as he started the car. The sky had darkened with clouds, the soft glow of the setting sun hidden behind them, casting the park in a muted gray. Jesse stared out at the empty path where he and Wyatt had talked, feeling a pang of sadness wash over him. He wasn't sure what would happen next, but for now, he had to let Wyatt figure things out.

Slowly, he pulled out of the parking lot and headed home, the weight of the day still heavy on his shoulders but the smallest flicker of hope keeping him from breaking completely.

Chapter 23: Opening Up

Jesse pulled into the driveway, his heart heavy as he turned off the car engine. The house was quiet, the soft glow of the living room light spilling out into the dusky evening. He sat there for a moment, gathering his thoughts before stepping out of the car and heading inside.

As he opened the front door, the familiar scent of home greeted him, but tonight it felt different—he felt different. The weight of the conversation with Wyatt, the mess of emotions he'd been carrying, and the fear of what might come next all hung over him like a cloud.

He walked through the hallway and found his mom in the living room, sitting on the couch watching TV. She looked up when she heard him enter, her face softening with concern as she took in his appearance. Jesse knew he still looked a mess—his eyes red from crying, his hair disheveled, his expression worn.

"Jesse?" she asked gently, turning the volume down on the TV. "Are you okay, honey?"

Jesse hesitated at the doorway, his chest tightening. He hadn't expected to find his mom alone—his dad was usually the one who tackled the tough conversations, while his mom often struggled to talk about anything that made her uncomfortable. But here she was, watching him with those familiar, motherly eyes filled with concern.

He took a breath, feeling the emotions bubbling up again. "I… I don't know, Mom. I'm not okay."

Her brow furrowed, and she set the remote down, turning fully toward him. "Come here, sweetheart. Sit with me."

Jesse walked over and sank down onto the couch next to her, feeling the tension in his shoulders, the exhaustion of the day weighing heavily on him. His mom reached out, placing a comforting hand on his knee, waiting for him to speak.

"What's going on?" she asked softly.

Jesse swallowed hard, trying to find the words. He wasn't used to opening up to his parents like this—especially about something so personal—but after everything that had happened, he couldn't hold it in anymore. He needed someone to talk to, someone who might understand, even if only a little.

"It's about Wyatt," Jesse began, his voice shaky. "About the rumors that are going around. About me and him."

His mom nodded, her expression tightening slightly. "I'm really sorry you're going through that, Jesse. It's not fair."

Jesse's heart squeezed at her words, but he pressed on. "Well, it's more than just the rumors. Wyatt... he's scared. His parents found out from that woman—Mrs. Alcott—and now they're really upset. He thinks they might... I don't know, disown him or something. He doesn't know what to do."

His mom's face softened as she listened, though Jesse could see the discomfort flicker in her eyes. "That must be really hard for him," she said carefully. "And for you."

Jesse nodded, the lump in his throat growing larger. "It is. And now Wyatt wants to take a break. He thinks it might be better for him to distance himself from me while he figures everything out."

His mom's hand tightened gently on his knee, her expression filled with sympathy. "Oh, Jesse… I'm so sorry."

Jesse felt the tears welling up again, but he blinked them back, trying to stay composed. "I don't know what to do, Mom. I don't want to lose him, but I also don't want to make things harder for him. I just… I feel like this is all my fault."

His mom's eyes widened with surprise, and she shook her head. "No, sweetheart. This isn't your fault. You can't control how people react, and you certainly can't control the rumors. None of this is your fault."

Jesse looked down at his hands, his voice barely above a whisper. "I just don't know what to do. I don't know how to make things better."

His mom was silent for a moment, clearly trying to find the right words. Jesse knew that talking about his relationship with Wyatt made her uncomfortable–it wasn't something they had ever really discussed in detail before–but there was no judgment in her voice. Just hesitation, like she was still learning how to navigate this part of his life.

"I wish I had all the answers for you," she said softly, "but I don't. I can't tell you what's going to happen with Wyatt or how to fix things. But I do know that you're strong, Jesse. And I know that you care about him, and that's important. Sometimes, though, people need time to figure things out. Maybe that's what Wyatt needs right now."

Jesse nodded, his throat tight. "I just hate that it's because of all this. The rumors, the pressure... I wish things were different."

"I know," his mom said, her voice full of empathy. "And I'm sorry that you're dealing with this. I really am. I know it's hard for you, especially with people in town talking. And I'm sorry if it ever seemed like your dad and I cared more about what people think than about you."

Jesse's chest tightened at the mention of his parents' reaction earlier that morning. "It did feel that way," he admitted quietly. "Like you were more worried about the rumors than about how I was feeling."

His mom sighed, her expression softening even more. "We didn't handle it as well as we should have. Your dad and I... we love you, Jesse. We want you to know that. But this is all new for us too. We're still figuring out how to navigate this, just like you are."

Jesse looked up at her, surprised by the vulnerability in her voice. "But you're okay with me being gay, right?"

She nodded immediately. "Yes. We are. We really are. It's just... it's going to take us some time to fully adjust, to fully get comfortable with everything. But we will, Jesse. I promise you that."

Jesse felt a wave of relief wash over him, though the sadness still lingered. "Thanks, Mom. I just... I didn't know how to talk to you about it."

His mom smiled softly, her hand gently squeezing his knee again. "We're always here for you, even if we're not perfect. You can talk to us about anything, even if it's hard. We'll get there together."

Jesse nodded, the weight on his chest lifting just a little. He still didn't have all the answers, and Wyatt's situation was still a mess, but knowing that his parents were trying–that they loved him despite everything–helped.

"I love you, Jesse," his mom said, her voice full of warmth. "And your dad does too. We're proud of you, no matter what."

Jesse felt the tears welling up again, but this time, they were tears of relief. He leaned in, hugging his mom tightly, feeling the warmth of her embrace as she held him close.

"I love you too," he whispered.

As they sat there in the quiet living room, the tension and fear slowly began to fade, replaced by a sense of calm. Jesse knew things were still uncertain with Wyatt, and he didn't know what the future held, but for the first time in a long while, he felt like he wasn't alone.

He had his parents. He had Liz. And maybe, just maybe, he and Wyatt would figure it out too.

Chapter 24: Torn Between Faith and Self

Wyatt's heart pounded in his chest as he pulled into the driveway, the house looming in front of him like an impending storm. His hands gripped the steering wheel so tightly his knuckles turned white. The conversation with Jesse still weighed heavily on his mind, but the dread of what awaited him inside the house was even worse.

His parents were waiting. They'd made it clear earlier, without saying much, that this wasn't going to be an easy conversation. Wyatt had known his parents would be upset, but he hadn't expected them to find out like this—from gossip, rumors spread around town by people who didn't know the truth.

He stepped out of the car, the cool evening air doing nothing to calm the nerves twisting in his stomach. His hands were trembling as he made his way to the front door, each step heavier than the last. When he finally opened the door, the first thing he saw was his parents sitting at the dining room table, their faces tight with tension. The sight made his breath hitch.

His mom looked more upset than he'd ever seen her, her lips pressed into a thin line, her eyes red and puffy like she'd been crying. His dad sat beside her, arms crossed over his chest, his expression more stoic but no less serious. The weight of their disapproval hit Wyatt like a physical blow.

They were waiting for him.

Wyatt hesitated at the doorway, his body rigid with discomfort, but he knew he couldn't avoid this. His parents had made it clear they wanted to talk, and after everything that had happened today, he had no choice but to face them.

"Wyatt, come in and sit down," his dad said, his voice firm but devoid of warmth.

Wyatt swallowed hard and forced himself to step into the room, his legs feeling like lead. He moved toward the dining table, each step slower than the last, and finally sank into the chair across from his parents. The silence stretched on for what felt like an eternity, thick with tension, until his mom spoke.

"You're nineteen," she said, her voice trembling with a mixture of frustration and sadness. "You're an adult. That means you can make your own choices, but it also means you have to face the consequences of those choices."

Wyatt's stomach twisted into knots, his mouth dry. He could already feel where this conversation was going, but hearing the words out loud made everything so much more real.

His dad leaned forward, his voice calm but firm. "We raised you with certain values, Wyatt. Values we believe in—things we've taught you all your life. And what we've been hearing about you... it goes against everything we believe. We don't approve of this—of what you're doing. This... lifestyle."

Wyatt flinched at the word *lifestyle,* his heart sinking further. He'd expected his parents to be upset, but hearing them talk about it like this—as if it was a choice, as if who he was could be reduced to some lifestyle decision—cut deeper than he'd imagined.

His mom's voice cracked as she continued, her eyes filled with tears. "We love you, Wyatt. We do. But this... this is not how we raised you. And it's not what God wants for you."

Wyatt's throat tightened. He'd known his parents were religious, but he hadn't expected them to bring God into this like a weapon. His mom wiped at her eyes, taking a deep breath.

"You can stay in this house until you go back to college," his dad interrupted, his tone more controlled now. "But you need to understand something, Wyatt. We don't want you seeing Jesse anymore. You're free to do what you want, but not under our roof. And... you need to realize that people who live like this—who choose this path—end up in hell. You need to make things right with God before it's too late."

Wyatt sat there in stunned silence, his mind spinning. He could barely process what they were saying. He'd known they wouldn't accept it easily, but this? Being told he was destined for hell? That he needed to cut Jesse out of his life, to make things "right with God"? It felt like the ground had been ripped out from under him.

"I don't know what to say," Wyatt whispered, his voice barely audible.

His dad leaned back, his arms still crossed. "You don't have to say anything. Just know where we stand."

Wyatt could feel the tears welling up in his eyes, but he forced them back, not wanting to break down in front of his parents. Not here. Not like this.

His mom's expression softened, but her eyes were still filled with sorrow. "We just want what's best for you, Wyatt. And this... this isn't it."

Wyatt couldn't respond. He sat there, frozen, his mind a mess of fear, guilt, and confusion. He had always known his parents were strict, but he was hoping it wouldn't come to this, this kind of ultimatum–to choose between his feelings for Jesse and the love of his family.

After a long, painful silence, Wyatt pushed back his chair and stood up. His parents didn't try to stop him. They just watched as he turned and walked down the hall to his room, the weight of their disapproval crushing him with every step.

Once inside his room, he closed the door behind him and leaned against it, his breath coming in shallow, ragged gasps. The tears he had held back in front of his parents came rushing out, and he collapsed onto the bed, burying his face in his pillow as sobs wracked his body.

It felt like his world was falling apart.

He had no idea what to do. He *wanted* to see Jesse again, to talk to him, to tell him everything, but now... what was the cost? His parents had made it clear–they didn't want him seeing Jesse anymore. They didn't approve of who he was, and they were using God and hell to scare him into submission. And as much as Wyatt wanted to fight back, to argue, he didn't know if he could.

The fear of losing his family was too great.

But the idea of losing Jesse–of pretending to be something he wasn't anymore–was just as painful. He *knew* he was gay. He knew this wasn't something he could change or ignore. But now, the cost of embracing that truth seemed too high, and he didn't know how to reconcile the two parts of his life. How could he be himself when it meant losing the people who had raised him?

Wyatt wiped his eyes, his body shaking with exhaustion. He reached for his phone, instinctively wanting to text Jesse, to tell him everything. But as he stared at the screen, his fingers hovered over the keys.

What could he even say?

Jesse was already dealing with so much, and Wyatt didn't want to add to his pain. Not yet. He couldn't bring himself to send the message, not when everything felt so raw, so fragile.

With a heavy sigh, Wyatt put his phone down and lay back on the bed, staring up at the ceiling. His mind was spinning, his thoughts tangled in a mess of guilt, fear, and heartbreak. He grabbed his phone again, but instead of texting Jesse, he opened Instagram and scrolled through Jesse's profile, his watery eyes lingering on the familiar pictures.

Pictures of Jesse's art, even some of him smiling, laughing, living his life. The same life that now felt so distant from Wyatt's own. He scrolled through the photos, his chest tightening with each one. He missed him. Already. And even though he didn't have the words to say it, he knew that not seeing Jesse, not being with him, was going to break him even more.

But what could he do?

As he stared at Jesse's photos, his vision blurred by tears, Wyatt's heart ached with the weight of the impossible decision he was being forced to make. His family, or Jesse. His parents, or the person who made him feel more like himself than anyone else ever had.

He didn't know what to do. He didn't know if he'd ever figure it out.

Eventually, the exhaustion became too much. His body heavy with grief and confusion, Wyatt closed his eyes, the phone still in his hand, and drifted into an uneasy sleep.

But even in his dreams, the weight of the choice he had to make followed him, haunting him with every breath.

Chapter 25: A Voice from the Past

The next morning, Wyatt sat on the edge of his bed, staring at his phone, his mind racing in circles. The weight of the conversation with his parents still pressed down on him, making it hard to breathe. He wanted to talk to someone–anyone who might understand what he was going through. But everyone in town either knew his parents or would judge him for what he was struggling with. Everyone, except for one person.

Josh.

Josh had been Wyatt's best friend all through high school. They had been inseparable–playing soccer together, staying up late talking about life, sharing their hopes for the future. But in their senior year, Josh's family had moved to another state, and even though they had kept in touch at first, the distance made it harder. Wyatt hadn't reached out to him in months, but Josh had always been the kind of friend who understood Wyatt in a way few people did.

Wyatt hesitated, his finger hovering over Josh's contact. *What if it's weird after all this time?* But Josh had always been there for him, and maybe... maybe he could be there now. Wyatt took a deep breath and hit the call button.

It rang twice before Josh picked up, his voice sounding as familiar and easy as ever. "Wyatt? Dude, it's been forever!"

Wyatt tried to smile, but it felt strained. "Yeah... it's been a while."

"What's going on, man?" Josh asked, his tone light but with an undercurrent of concern. "Everything okay?"

Wyatt's throat tightened, and he felt the flood of emotions rise again. He hadn't planned on breaking down right away, but just hearing Josh's voice was like a release valve for everything he'd been holding in. "No, not really," Wyatt admitted, his voice cracking slightly. "Things are pretty messed up right now."

Josh was quiet for a second, then his tone softened. "Hey, whatever it is, I'm here. Talk to me."

Wyatt took a deep breath, trying to steady himself. He wasn't used to being this vulnerable, but if there was anyone who would listen without judgment, it was Josh. "It's… it's kind of a long story."

"I've got time," Josh said. "Go ahead. I'm all ears."

Wyatt hesitated for a moment before the words spilled out. "So, there's this guy… Jesse. We've been kind of… seeing each other. And my parents just found out, and they're pissed. Like, really pissed."

Josh didn't say anything right away, and Wyatt rushed to fill the silence, his nerves getting the better of him. "They told me they don't approve of… of me being gay. They basically said I'm going to hell and that I can't see Jesse anymore. I don't know what to do, Josh. I care about Jesse, but my parents… they're so disappointed. I'm stuck."

Josh finally spoke, his voice calm and steady. "Man, I'm really sorry. That sounds like a nightmare. I had no idea you were going through all that."

Wyatt let out a shaky breath. "Yeah. I didn't really tell anyone. I wasn't ready to admit it to myself, let alone to them. And now… now it feels like I have to choose between my family and being who I really am."

Josh was quiet for a moment, and Wyatt could almost hear him thinking through the phone. "I can't imagine what that's like, Wyatt. But listen... your happiness, man–that's what's important. I know your parents probably have their reasons for reacting the way they did, but you can't live your whole life trying to make them happy if it means making yourself miserable."

Wyatt swallowed hard, the truth of Josh's words hitting him like a punch. "I know, but... it's my family, you know? What if they never come around? What if I lose them?"

Josh sighed softly. "That's a tough one. I'm not gonna lie to you–it might take them a long time to come around, and maybe they won't. But you can't let fear of losing them control your life. You've got to think about your future, about what makes you happy in the long run."

Wyatt's chest tightened as he listened. Josh had always been good at cutting through the noise and getting to the heart of things, but the idea of putting his own happiness first felt selfish. "It's just... I've always done what they wanted, you know? And now it feels like I'm letting them down."

"You're not letting anyone down by being yourself, Wyatt," Josh said firmly. "I know it's hard to see that right now, especially with everything coming at you so fast. But you deserve to live your life authentically, without hiding."

Wyatt ran a hand through his hair, frustration bubbling up again. "I just wish it didn't have to be like this. I wish I didn't have to choose between them and Jesse."

Josh paused, then spoke again, his tone more thoughtful. "Have you ever heard of affirming churches? Places where people don't have to choose between being gay and their faith?"

Wyatt frowned, caught off guard. "What do you mean?"

"There are churches–like, LGBTQ-affirming churches–that support people like you," Josh explained. "You can still have faith and be true to yourself. You don't have to give up your beliefs or your identity."

Wyatt blinked, the idea foreign but intriguing. "I... I didn't even know that was a thing."

"It is," Josh said. "And I think it might help. You've been raised in this really specific environment where being gay is treated like some huge sin. But there are other ways of thinking about it. You're not alone in this, Wyatt. There are people who've been where you are–dealing with family pressure and faith–and they found a way to live authentically without giving up their beliefs."

Wyatt was silent for a moment, letting Josh's words sink in. The idea of finding a way to reconcile his faith and his sexuality was something he hadn't even considered. It had always felt like an impossible choice– either keep his family and his faith, or embrace who he really was and lose both.

"Do you think that could really help?" Wyatt asked quietly, his voice uncertain but hopeful.

"I think it's worth looking into," Josh said. "You've got options, Wyatt. Don't let anyone make you feel like you have to choose between who you are and what you believe."

Wyatt felt a small spark of hope flicker inside him, something he hadn't felt in days. "Thanks, Josh. I... I didn't know who else to talk to. I felt so alone."

"You're never alone, man," Josh said, his voice full of warmth. "You've got me, and you've got people out there who understand what you're going through. You don't have to figure it all out right now, but just know that you don't have to choose between your happiness and your faith. There's a middle ground."

Wyatt nodded, feeling a weight lift off his shoulders, even if just a little. "I'm going to look into that. It's... it's the first thing that's made sense in a while."

"Good," Josh said, his tone encouraging. "Take your time, figure things out, and don't be afraid to reach out if you need to talk. I'm always here."

Wyatt smiled, grateful for the unexpected support. "Thanks, Josh. Seriously. You have no idea how much this helped."

"That's what friends are for," Josh said lightly. "And hey, maybe once you're out of this mess, we can plan a visit. It's been way too long."

"I'd like that," Wyatt said, feeling a warmth he hadn't felt in days. "I'll keep in touch."

After they said their goodbyes, Wyatt hung up the phone, his mind still racing but with a new sense of direction. He wasn't sure what the future held, but knowing there were people who had found a way to balance faith and identity gave him hope. He wasn't alone, and maybe there was a path forward that didn't involve losing everything he cared about.

For the first time in a long while, Wyatt didn't feel completely lost. He had options. And as he lay back on his bed, staring at the ceiling, he allowed himself to believe that maybe–just maybe–things would get better.

Chapter 26: Silence and Fear

It had been three long days since Jesse had seen Wyatt, since that gut-wrenching conversation at the park where everything felt like it was falling apart. Three days of silence, uncertainty, and unanswered questions. Jesse had gone through every possible scenario in his head, wondering what Wyatt was doing, how he was feeling, and most importantly, if he was okay. The silence was unbearable.

Jesse sat on his bed, his phone in his hand, staring at the blank message thread with Wyatt. He had typed out at least five different texts in the past hour, deleting each one after reading it back. Every time he started to say something, doubt crept in. *What if Wyatt doesn't want to hear from me? What if he's just not ready? What if I'm making things worse?*

His thumb hovered over the send button, his heart pounding in his chest. Finally, he took a deep breath and tapped the screen, sending a simple message:

Jesse: *Hey, just checking in. I hope you're okay.*

It was a short message, vague enough that it didn't seem pushy, but the second it sent, Jesse's stomach twisted into knots. He stared at his phone, waiting–hoping–for those little typing dots to appear on the screen. But they didn't. Minutes passed. Then an hour. Nothing.

Jesse leaned back against his pillow, staring up at the ceiling. His mind raced with all the possibilities of what could be happening on Wyatt's end. *Why isn't he responding?* He knew Wyatt was dealing with a lot–his parents, the rumors, the pressure of being caught between two worlds –but the silence was eating away at Jesse. He hadn't been to work, either. "Out sick" was the story floating around the pool, but Jesse wasn't sure he believed it. Sick could mean anything. *What if his parents sent him away?* The thought made his heart race even faster.

Jesse grabbed his phone again, staring at the empty message thread, the single text he had sent sitting there like an unanswered question. He knew he shouldn't push too hard, but the worry gnawed at him. What if Wyatt wasn't okay? What if things at home were worse than he imagined?

Before he could stop himself, Jesse typed out another message, his fingers shaking as he hit send.

Jesse: *I haven't seen you at the pool. I'm worried about you. Please, let me know if you're okay.*

Again, the silence stretched on, each passing minute feeling like an eternity. Jesse's mind spiraled, imagining the worst. *What if his parents are keeping him from talking to me? What if they sent him away to some place to... fix him?*

The thought of Wyatt being forced into something like that–something meant to change who he was–made Jesse's chest tighten with panic. He tried to push the fear down, telling himself that Wyatt was strong, that he wouldn't let his parents push him into anything he didn't want. But the doubt lingered, gnawing at the edges of his thoughts.

Hours passed. Still no response.

Jesse sat in his room, staring at his phone, the silence of the house pressing down on him like a weight. He felt helpless, like there was nothing he could do. He had always been the one to reach out, the one to try and make things right. But now, he wasn't sure if that was even possible. Wyatt was slipping away, and Jesse didn't know how to hold on.

With a heavy sigh, he typed out one final message.

Jesse: *I'm here when you're ready. Please don't forget that.*

He stared at the message for a long time before sending it. It felt like a goodbye, like a door closing between them. But he didn't know what else to say. Wyatt needed space, and maybe Jesse needed to give it to him, no matter how much it hurt.

The next day at the pool was a blur. Jesse went through the motions of his job, selling snacks, cleaning up, talking to the kids who came by, but his mind was somewhere else entirely. Every time he looked up at the lifeguard chairs, he half-expected to see Wyatt there, flashing him that familiar smile. But the chair was empty. Wyatt hadn't shown up for his shift. Not yesterday, and not today.

Jesse overheard one of the other lifeguards, Rachel, talking to one of the managers. "Wyatt's still out sick?" she asked, her voice full of concern.

"Yeah, that's what his mom said," the manager replied. "I hope he's feeling better soon."

The words hung in the air, but to Jesse, they felt hollow. *Out sick?* He couldn't shake the feeling that it was something more than that. Maybe it was true, and Wyatt was just sick. Maybe he needed time. But the nagging fear in the back of Jesse's mind wouldn't go away.

Jesse finished his shift and headed home, the same knot of worry twisting in his chest. He couldn't get Wyatt out of his head–what he was doing, what his parents were saying to him, whether he was okay. It felt like there was a wall between them now, and Jesse didn't know how to break through it.

That night, after another round of sleepless tossing and turning, Jesse picked up his phone and scrolled through the messages he had sent to Wyatt. They were all still unanswered, sitting there in silence, a painful reminder of the distance between them. Jesse's heart ached with every message, but he knew there was nothing more he could do.

He had said everything he could. Now, it was up to Wyatt.

As Jesse lay in bed, staring at his phone, he felt a deep, sinking sadness settle over him. He missed Wyatt more than he could put into words, and the thought of losing him–of never hearing from him again–was too much to bear.

But he had to let go, at least for now. Wyatt needed time to figure things out, and as much as it hurt, Jesse knew he had to respect that.

With a heavy heart, Jesse turned off his phone and closed his eyes, hoping that maybe tomorrow would bring some kind of answer, some kind of sign that things weren't as hopeless as they seemed.

But for now, all he could do was wait.

Chapter 27: Unexpected Support

The sun was beginning to set, casting long shadows across the pool deck as Jesse finished wiping down the last of the concession stand counters. It had been another long, exhausting day. His mind had barely been in the present—every task he performed felt mechanical, his thoughts always drifting back to Wyatt. The unanswered messages, the empty lifeguard chair, and the growing fear that something was terribly wrong.

It had been days since he had heard from Wyatt. Days of worry, anxiety, and that awful gnawing feeling in the pit of his stomach. The silence was unbearable, and every passing hour without a response chipped away at the small amount of hope Jesse had left.

As he packed up for the day, he noticed that a few of his coworkers were lingering nearby—Rachel, the lifeguard, along with two others, Tori and Matt. They were hanging back by the lifeguard chairs, glancing at Jesse every now and then with a kind of hesitant, unsure look on their faces. Jesse tried to ignore it, focusing on finishing his shift so he could get home, but something about their presence made him pause.

Finally, Rachel approached, her expression soft but serious. "Hey, Jesse," she said, her voice gentle. "Can we talk for a minute?"

Jesse's stomach tightened. He wasn't sure what this was about, but he had a sinking feeling it had something to do with the rumors that had been circulating. He had heard the whispers, the gossip, but so far, no one had said anything directly to him.

"Yeah, sure," Jesse said, trying to keep his voice steady.

The others came over, forming a small circle around him. Rachel glanced at Matt and Tori before looking back at Jesse, her eyes filled with concern.

"We've been meaning to talk to you for a few days," Rachel began, her tone careful. "We've all heard… well, we've heard the rumors going around."

Jesse's heart sank. He had known this was coming, but hearing it out loud made everything feel even more real. He forced himself to nod, though his chest tightened with anxiety.

"I don't know if any of it's true, and honestly, it doesn't matter," Rachel continued. "What matters is that we want you to know that we're here for you. For you and for Wyatt."

Jesse blinked, taken aback by her words. He had been expecting judgment, maybe even more gossip. But instead, there was nothing but kindness in her voice.

"We know things have been rough," Matt chimed in, his expression sincere. "And we know Wyatt hasn't been around. We don't know what's going on with him, but we just wanted to make sure you knew… we've got your back."

Jesse stared at them, his throat tightening. "You're… you're not upset? About the rumors?"

Tori shook her head. "Why would we be upset? It's not our business. What people are saying–it's just gossip. What matters is how you're doing. And if you need anything–anything at all–we're here."

Jesse felt his breath catch in his throat, the unexpected support hitting him like a wave. He had been bracing for the worst, for people to turn their backs on him, but instead, his coworkers were standing with him. It was more than he had expected. More than he could have hoped for.

"I... I don't know what to say," Jesse stammered, his voice thick with emotion. "I thought... I thought people would be judging us."

Rachel smiled gently. "People are always going to talk, Jesse. But we know you and Wyatt. We know who you really are. And we're not here to judge—we're here to help, however we can."

Matt nodded, stepping closer. "If you ever want to talk, or if you need to get away for a while, just let us know. We're all friends here."

Jesse's eyes welled up with tears, and he blinked them away, trying to hold himself together. He had felt so alone these past few days, drowning in worry about Wyatt and overwhelmed by the rumors swirling around them. But hearing this—knowing that there were people who cared, who were willing to stand by him—was like a lifeline.

"Thank you," Jesse said quietly, his voice shaking. "I don't... I don't know what to say. I've just been so worried about him. I don't even know what's going on at his house."

Tori reached out and gently placed a hand on Jesse's shoulder. "We can't imagine what you're going through, but we're here to listen. You don't have to go through this alone."

Jesse nodded, his heart full of gratitude and relief. He had been carrying so much by himself—trying to figure out how to reach Wyatt, how to deal with his own fear and heartbreak—and now, finally, he felt like he wasn't completely alone.

"I've tried to reach him," Jesse said, his voice quieter now. "I've sent him messages, but he hasn't responded. I don't even know if he's okay. He hasn't been to work, and I'm just... scared."

Rachel's face softened with understanding. "I'm sure he's going through a lot right now. Whatever's happening, it's probably overwhelming for him. But you're doing everything you can, Jesse. He knows you're there for him."

Matt gave a small, encouraging nod. "He'll reach out when he's ready. And when he does, you'll be there."

Jesse nodded, feeling a mix of emotions swirling inside him. He didn't know what would happen next—whether Wyatt would come back, whether he'd even want to talk—but knowing that his coworkers had his back made the uncertainty a little easier to bear.

"Thank you," Jesse said again, his voice thick with emotion. "I really mean it. I didn't expect... I didn't expect this."

Rachel smiled, her hand giving his shoulder a reassuring squeeze. "You don't have to go through this alone, Jesse. We're here. And whatever happens, we'll be here for both of you."

Jesse nodded, swallowing hard as he tried to keep his emotions in check. He wasn't sure what the next few days would bring, but for the first time in a while, he didn't feel completely lost. He had people who cared, people who were willing to stand by him no matter what.

And maybe—just maybe—Wyatt would come back. When he was ready.

For now, Jesse would hold onto that hope.

As they wrapped up their conversation and headed out of the pool for the night, Jesse couldn't help but feel a small glimmer of warmth in his chest. It wasn't much, but it was enough to get him through another day.

Chapter 28: The Knock on Wyatt's Door

Jesse woke up with a pit in his stomach, the kind of unease that made it impossible to lie still. The silence from Wyatt had stretched on far too long, and the tension in his chest had become a constant companion. The pool was closed for the day, but his mind wasn't at ease. Every time he replayed their last conversation at the park in his head, the same questions circled relentlessly. *Where is Wyatt? What's happening to him?*

Lying in bed wasn't helping. He hadn't heard from Wyatt since their conversation at the park, and with each passing day, Jesse felt more powerless. He couldn't just wait around anymore. Wyatt was going through something heavy–he knew that much–but being kept in the dark like this was suffocating.

He grabbed his phone off the nightstand, hesitating for a moment before opening the group chat with his coworkers. He had to do something. Wyatt might not respond to him, but maybe, just maybe, if they all showed up, Wyatt's parents might listen.

Taking a deep breath, Jesse typed out a message, his heart racing as he hit send:

Jesse: *Hey, I know the pool's closed today, but would you guys be up for meeting? I need to talk about something important.*

He stared at the screen, waiting, nervous energy buzzing through him. It wasn't long before the replies came in.

Rachel: *Yeah, I'm free. What's up?*

Matt: *Sure, where are we meeting?*

Tori: *I'm in. Everything okay, Jesse?*

Jesse's fingers trembled as he typed his response.

Jesse: *Could you guys come over to my house? I was thinking of going to Wyatt's place... I haven't heard from him, and I'm really worried. I think his parents might be keeping him from reaching out. I thought maybe if we all went together, they might let us in.*

He stared at the message, feeling a mix of dread and hope. He wasn't sure if this plan would work, or if it was even a good idea, but the gnawing worry about Wyatt was driving him to try something–anything.

The replies came back quickly.

Rachel: *If you're worried, we should definitely go. I'm with you.*

Matt: *Let's do it. If his parents won't talk to just you, maybe they'll listen if we're all there.*

Tori: *We've got your back, Jesse. We'll be there soon.*

Jesse breathed out a sigh of relief, though the knot in his stomach didn't ease completely. At least he wouldn't be facing this alone.

Later that morning, Jesse stood on the sidewalk in front of Wyatt's house, his hands shoved deep into his pockets as the anxiety gnawed at him. His coworkers stood next to him, exchanging concerned glances. The air felt thick with uncertainty, the tension almost palpable.

Rachel, Matt, and Tori were with him, just as they had promised, but Jesse felt a surge of nerves as they approached Wyatt's house. His heart pounded in his chest, and the nagging thought that this was a mistake crept into the back of his mind. Wyatt's parents hadn't been kind or understanding about anything so far–there was no guarantee that showing up would change that. But Jesse had to try.

Wyatt's car was parked in the driveway, a clear sign that he was home. But where was he? Why wasn't he responding to Jesse's texts? Why had he disappeared from the pool, from his life?

They reached the front porch, and Matt stepped forward, glancing back at Jesse for reassurance before knocking firmly on the door. Jesse stayed back, his stomach twisting with anxiety. He couldn't bring himself to stand next to his friends. The thought of facing Wyatt's parents–especially his dad–filled him with dread. He didn't want to be the reason Wyatt got in trouble.

After a few moments, the door opened. Wyatt's father stood there, his stern face giving nothing away. His eyes flickered briefly toward Jesse standing on the sidewalk, but he quickly turned his attention back to the group on his porch.

"Yes?" His voice was cold, clipped.

Rachel stepped forward, her expression kind but determined. "Hi, Mr. Roberts. We're friends of Wyatt's. We've been trying to reach him, but we haven't heard from him in a few days. We just wanted to check in and make sure he's okay."

Wyatt's dad's eyes narrowed slightly. "Wyatt's fine," he said, his tone flat. "He's been resting."

Rachel hesitated, clearly sensing that she wasn't getting the full picture. "Is there any way we could see him? Just for a few minutes? We're all really worried."

Jesse felt his heart leap into his throat as he watched the exchange. His fingers tightened into fists in his pockets. Wyatt's car was right there, but there was no sign of him. Was he inside? Could he even hear them?

Wyatt's dad's face darkened, his lips pressing into a thin line. "He's not up for visitors right now," he said firmly. "Like I said, he's resting."

Matt stepped in, trying to defuse the tension. "We don't want to bother him, Mr. Roberts. We just want to let him know we're thinking about him. It'll only take a minute."

But Wyatt's dad didn't budge. His gaze turned hard, colder than before. "I said no," he repeated, his voice sharp. "Now, if you'll excuse me, it's not a good time. You should go."

Jesse's heart sank. His worst fears were being realized—Wyatt's dad was shutting them out completely, not even giving them a chance to see him. It felt like the door was slamming in their faces, just like the door Wyatt's dad had metaphorically slammed on Wyatt's identity.

Rachel opened her mouth to say something else, but Wyatt's dad cut her off. "There's nothing more to discuss," he said, his tone leaving no room for argument. "Please leave."

Jesse watched, helpless, as his friends stepped back. Wyatt's dad gave them one last hard look before closing the door with a firm *click*.

The silence that followed was heavy, suffocating. Jesse stood frozen on the sidewalk, staring at the door, his mind racing. *He's in there.* He had to be. But what was happening behind that closed door? What was Wyatt going through?

Rachel turned back to Jesse, her face a mix of frustration and sadness. "I'm sorry, Jesse," she said softly. "He wouldn't even let us talk to him."

Matt shook his head, frowning. "Something's not right. His car's here. He's home, but his dad wouldn't let us see him?"

"I don't like this," Tori added quietly, her eyes filled with concern. "It feels... wrong."

Jesse's heart ached. He had come so close–Wyatt was just behind that door–but it might as well have been a mile away. He had no idea what was happening inside that house, but the helplessness, the uncertainty, was unbearable.

"I don't know what to do," Jesse whispered, his voice barely audible. "What if something's wrong? What if they're not letting him leave?"

Rachel stepped closer, placing a gentle hand on his arm. "We'll figure something out. We're not giving up, okay? Wyatt knows we're here for him, even if his dad won't let us in."

Jesse nodded, though the emptiness in his chest didn't ease. "I just... I thought maybe if we all came, he'd listen. But it feels like Wyatt's trapped in there."

Matt sighed, his brow furrowed. "Maybe we can try again in a couple of days. Or reach out some other way."

Jesse shook his head, the frustration bubbling up inside him. "I don't know if they'll ever let us in."

The group stood in silence for a moment, the weight of the situation pressing down on them. Jesse felt like he was losing Wyatt all over again, and there was nothing he could do about it.

"We'll keep trying," Rachel said softly. "Whatever it takes."

Jesse nodded again, but the ache in his heart didn't go away. Wyatt was just beyond that door, and yet it felt like he was slipping further and further away.

As they walked back to their cars, Jesse stole one last glance at the house, hoping for some sign, some miracle that would change everything. But the house stood quiet, the door closed, and Wyatt remained out of reach.

For now.

Chapter 29: The Stand-Off

Jesse sat in his car, parked just down the street from Wyatt's house, his fingers drumming anxiously on the steering wheel. His heart raced, his mind a swirl of uncertainty and fear. After their attempt with his coworkers, the sense of helplessness had only grown stronger. He couldn't shake the feeling that Wyatt needed him, that something was happening behind those closed doors–and no one was telling him the truth.

Wyatt's car was still in the driveway. He was home. But why wasn't he reaching out? Was he being forced to stay silent? Was his dad keeping him from responding to Jesse's messages?

Jesse couldn't take it anymore. He had to do something. He couldn't just sit around and let Wyatt disappear from his life without trying one last time. He had to make Wyatt see that he wasn't alone, no matter what his parents thought.

With a deep breath, Jesse opened the car door and stepped out, his heart pounding as he made his way down the quiet street. His stomach twisted with anxiety as he approached the front door, his hands trembling slightly. He knew it wasn't going to be easy–Wyatt's dad had made that perfectly clear–but he couldn't leave without at least trying.

Jesse hesitated for a moment at the front steps, then lifted his hand and knocked firmly on the door. There was no answer. The silence stretched on, heavy and tense, but Jesse wasn't ready to give up.

He knocked again. Harder this time.

Still nothing.

The seconds felt like hours, each one stretching out in uncomfortable silence. Jesse's heart raced, the knot of worry in his chest tightening with every passing moment. He couldn't leave. Not yet.

He knocked again—this time more urgently, the sound echoing down the quiet street. His pulse quickened, his thoughts racing as he imagined Wyatt on the other side of the door. *What's happening in there?*

And then, after what felt like an eternity, the door swung open, revealing Wyatt's father, Mr. Roberts, standing there with an unmistakable look of anger in his eyes. His face was flushed, his expression hard and unyielding as he glared at Jesse.

"I thought I made myself clear earlier," Mr. Roberts said, his voice cold and sharp. "You're not welcome here. Wyatt doesn't need visitors."

Jesse's breath caught in his throat, but he forced himself to stand his ground. He couldn't just walk away now. "Please, Mr. Roberts," Jesse said, his voice trembling slightly but full of urgency. "I just need to see Wyatt. I need to know he's okay."

Mr. Robert's eyes narrowed, his jaw tightening. "He's fine. And you need to leave before this becomes a bigger problem than it already is."

Jesse's heart pounded in his chest, desperation rising inside him. He couldn't leave. Not like this. "I know something's wrong," he pleaded, his voice cracking. "Please, just let me talk to him. I'm not trying to cause trouble—I just want to make sure he's okay."

Mr. Roberts stepped forward, his face twisted with anger now. "You don't know what's best for him, and it's none of your business. He doesn't need you filling his head with ideas that don't belong here."

Jesse flinched at the harsh words, but he didn't back down. "Wyatt and I care about each other," he said, his voice stronger this time. "You can't just keep him from the people who care about him. He deserves to make his own choices."

Mr. Robert's face reddened with fury. "I'm not going to stand here and listen to this nonsense. You need to leave *now*, or I'll make sure you regret coming here."

Just as Jesse was about to respond, a voice from behind Mr. Roberts cut through the tension.

"Dad, stop."

Jesse's heart leaped as Wyatt appeared behind his father, standing in the hallway, looking pale and exhausted but very much there. His eyes met Jesse's for a brief moment, and Jesse felt a surge of relief wash over him.

"Wyatt," Jesse breathed, his voice full of emotion. "Are you okay?"

Mr. Roberts turned, glaring at his son. "You're not talking to him. Go back to your room."

But Wyatt didn't move. He stood his ground, his expression weary but determined. "No, Dad," he said quietly. "I'm going to talk to him."

Jesse's heart raced as Wyatt stepped closer, but there was a tension in his face, a mix of emotions Jesse couldn't quite read. He looked tired, worn down, and even though Jesse was relieved to see him, it was clear Wyatt wasn't happy about the situation.

Mr. Roberts stepped aside, his face tight with anger. "Fine. But this is the last time, Wyatt. You know what's at stake."

Wyatt's face hardened for a brief second, but he didn't respond to his dad. Instead, he turned to Jesse, his expression unreadable.

"Jesse," Wyatt said, his voice low and heavy, "I appreciate you coming, but you shouldn't have."

Jesse blinked, taken aback. He had expected Wyatt to be angry with his dad, not with him. "I was just worried about you," Jesse said, his voice trembling. "You haven't answered any of my texts, and I didn't know if you were okay."

Wyatt sighed, running a hand through his messy hair. He looked down, avoiding Jesse's gaze. "I know. I've been meaning to text you back, but... everything's complicated right now. Things at home are... hard."

Jesse took a tentative step forward, his chest tightening. "You don't have to go through this alone, Wyatt. I'm here for you. We're all here for you."

Wyatt shook his head, his eyes still fixed on the floor. "It's not that simple. My parents... they're not going to change their minds. They don't want me seeing you. They think..." He trailed off, his voice thick with frustration. "They think I'm going down the wrong path."

Jesse's heart ached at Wyatt's words. He wanted to say something, to comfort him, but before he could, Wyatt looked up, his expression pained. "I'm not saying I agree with them, Jesse. But I need time. I need space to figure this out, and I can't do that if you keep showing up like this. It's only going to make things worse."

Jesse felt his stomach drop. "Worse?" he repeated, his voice barely above a whisper. "I thought you wanted to be with me."

Wyatt's face crumpled with emotion. "I do, Jesse. I care about you so much. But I'm being pulled in a hundred different directions right now. I don't know what to do, and I don't want to hurt you."

Jesse's throat tightened as he watched the struggle play out on Wyatt's face. He could see the fear, the uncertainty, the weight of his family's expectations pressing down on him. Wyatt was stuck, trapped between his love for Jesse and the demands of his parents.

"I'm not here to make things harder for you," Jesse said softly. "I just want to help."

Wyatt shook his head, his voice raw. "You can't. Not right now. I need to handle this on my own."

Jesse's heart broke at the words, but he nodded, knowing that pushing any further would only make things worse. "Okay," he whispered, his voice barely audible. "I'll give you space. But… just know I'm here when you're ready."

Wyatt nodded, his eyes filled with a mix of sadness and gratitude. "I know. I'll reach out when I can."

Mr. Roberts cleared his throat, stepping back toward the door, his face still a mask of barely controlled anger. "It's time for you to leave," he said coldly.

Jesse nodded, his chest tight as he took a step back toward the sidewalk. He gave Wyatt one last look, searching for any sign of hope. Wyatt gave him a weak, tired smile, but it was clear the weight of his situation was taking its toll.

Jesse turned and walked away, his heart heavy with the knowledge that, for now, there was nothing more he could do.

As he reached his car, he glanced back one more time at the house, feeling a mix of helplessness and sorrow. Wyatt was still trapped in there, tangled in a web of expectations and fear. And all Jesse could do was wait–wait for the day when Wyatt could break free.

But as he drove away, a small part of him couldn't shake the fear that Wyatt might never be able to.

Chapter 30: Caught in the Crossfire

The pool was alive with the usual sounds of summer–kids splashing in the water, lifeguards calling out to swimmers, and the hum of conversation rising and falling like waves. But for Jesse, the noise felt distant, almost muted. He was back at work, back in the familiar routine, but his mind was somewhere else entirely.

It had only been a day since he'd stood on Wyatt's porch, knocking again and again, desperate to see him. And he had. But the conversation that followed–the tension between Wyatt, his father, and the undeniable strain Wyatt was under–left Jesse feeling more helpless than ever.

He hadn't shared what happened with anyone yet. Not his coworkers, not even Liz. The weight of it all sat heavy in his chest, but he knew he couldn't carry it alone anymore. His friends had been there for him, for both him and Wyatt, and now they deserved to know.

As his shift drew to a close, Jesse wiped down the concession counter, trying to clear his head. Rachel, Matt, and Tori were gathering their things nearby, talking quietly amongst themselves. Jesse took a deep breath, pushing down the knot of anxiety in his stomach, and walked over to them.

"Hey," Jesse started, his voice sounding a little rougher than usual. "Can we talk for a minute?"

Rachel glanced up, immediately noticing the seriousness in his tone. "Yeah, of course," she said, giving him a soft smile. "What's going on?"

Matt and Tori exchanged looks before nodding, their concern clear as they followed Jesse to one of the quieter corners of the pool area, away from the remaining crowd. They sat down at a table, waiting for Jesse to speak.

Jesse rubbed the back of his neck, unsure of where to start. The last thing he wanted was to drag them back into his mess, but he needed to tell them what happened. He needed to talk about Wyatt.

"I went back to Wyatt's house yesterday," Jesse said finally, his voice low. "After we all tried to talk to his dad. I couldn't just leave it like that."

Rachel's eyes widened slightly, and Matt frowned. "You went back? What happened?"

Jesse took a deep breath. "I knocked again. Kept knocking until his dad came to the door. He was... he was pissed. Really pissed."

Tori leaned in, her expression tense. "What did he say?"

"He told me to leave, said I had no business being there. But I just... I couldn't walk away. I told him I needed to see Wyatt, that I had to know if he was okay." Jesse swallowed hard, the memory of Mr. Roberts' cold stare flashing in his mind. "He got angrier, started raising his voice, telling me I didn't know what was best for Wyatt."

Rachel shook her head, her face filled with sympathy. "That man is... intense."

"That's putting it lightly," Matt muttered, crossing his arms. "So, did you see Wyatt?"

Jesse nodded, feeling the familiar ache in his chest as he thought about the moment Wyatt had appeared in the doorway. "Yeah. He came out. He told his dad he was going to talk to me."

The group fell silent, waiting for Jesse to continue.

"Wyatt wasn't... happy I was there. I think he understood why, but he was frustrated. He told me that things were complicated, that he didn't want to make everything worse." Jesse sighed, running a hand through his hair. "He said his parents were putting a lot of pressure on him, and he wasn't sure what to do."

Rachel frowned, concern clouding her eyes. "So he's still stuck with them? Stuck trying to balance what they want with how he feels?"

Jesse nodded. "Yeah. And I could tell he was tired–really tired. He's being pulled in so many directions, and it's like he doesn't know where to go."

"Did you guys talk much?" Matt asked, his voice softer now. "Or was it just a quick conversation?"

Jesse hesitated, the weight of Wyatt's words still fresh in his mind. "It wasn't long. He told me he cared about me, but that he needed space. Said he didn't want to make things harder for me or for himself."

Tori frowned, her voice quiet. "So he's pushing you away?"

Jesse shook his head, though his heart twisted at the thought. "I don't think he's pushing me away for good. It's more like... he's trying to figure out what to do with all of this. He's scared of losing his family, scared of going against his dad. But I think he's also scared of what it means to be himself."

Rachel sighed, leaning back in her chair. "That's a lot of pressure. For anyone. I can't imagine what he's going through."

Matt rubbed the back of his neck, looking frustrated. "His dad's got him locked in a corner. How's he supposed to figure anything out when they're breathing down his neck like that?"

Jesse nodded, feeling the weight of Matt's words. "Exactly. And I don't know how to help him. Every time I try to reach out, I feel like I'm making it worse."

"You're not," Rachel said firmly, leaning forward. "Jesse, you're the only person in his life right now who's trying to help him figure out who he really is. I know it feels like you're not doing much, but just being there for him? That's huge."

"Yeah," Tori agreed, nodding. "Even if he's asking for space right now, he needs to know you're still there. That when he's ready, you'll be there waiting for him."

Jesse looked down at his hands, the tension still gnawing at him. "I hope that's enough. I don't want him to feel like he has to choose between me and his family. But at the same time... I can't just walk away from him."

"And you shouldn't," Matt said, his voice firm. "Wyatt's going to need you when he figures things out. It might take some time, but he's going to need someone who gets it. Someone who understands what he's going through."

Jesse nodded, feeling a small flicker of hope despite the heaviness in his chest. "I just wish I knew what his parents were going to do next. I don't trust his dad, and I'm worried that they're going to push him into something he's not ready for."

Rachel leaned in, her voice low and serious. "If they try to pull some kind of move–like sending him away or something–we'll be there. You won't have to go through this alone, Jesse. And neither will Wyatt."

The group sat in silence for a moment, the weight of the situation hanging in the air. Jesse felt a surge of gratitude for his friends–for their support, their willingness to stand by him and Wyatt even when things were messy and uncertain. It made the unbearable silence from Wyatt a little more bearable, knowing that he wasn't alone in this.

"Thanks," Jesse said quietly, his voice thick with emotion. "I don't know what's going to happen, but... it helps knowing you guys are here."

"We've got your back," Rachel said, her voice warm. "And we've got Wyatt's, too. No matter how long it takes."

Jesse nodded, feeling a little lighter for the first time in days. The road ahead was still unclear, and Wyatt was still stuck in a battle with his family, but at least now Jesse knew he wasn't fighting alone.

As the group wrapped up their conversation and started to gather their things, Jesse felt a renewed sense of determination. He couldn't force Wyatt to make a choice, but he could be there, waiting for him on the other side–whenever Wyatt was ready to break free.

And until then, Jesse would keep fighting for him.

After his shift, Jesse drove home feeling emotionally drained, his mind still stuck on the conversation he'd had with his coworkers. It was good to talk to them–to know they had his back–but it didn't ease the ache in his chest or the worry that gnawed at him. Wyatt was still trapped, still struggling, and Jesse couldn't shake the feeling that time was running out.

When Jesse pulled into the driveway, he sat in the car for a moment, staring at the house. His parents were inside, probably getting dinner ready or watching TV. He hadn't told them the full story of what had happened with Wyatt's father yet, and the thought of it made his stomach twist with anxiety. But he knew he couldn't keep it to himself. They deserved to know what was going on, and maybe, just maybe, they'd have some advice.

Jesse climbed out of the car and headed inside, the weight of the day still heavy on his shoulders. The familiar smell of his mom's cooking wafted through the air as he stepped into the kitchen, where his mom was at the stove and his dad was reading the newspaper at the table.

"Hey, Jesse," his dad greeted him, looking up from the paper with a smile. "How was work?"

Jesse managed a small smile back, but he could tell his parents sensed something was off. His mom glanced over her shoulder, her brow furrowing slightly when she saw his face.

"Everything okay?" she asked, turning the heat down on the stove.

Jesse took a deep breath, leaning against the counter. "I need to talk to you guys. About Wyatt. And his dad."

His mom wiped her hands on a towel and turned to face him, while his dad set the newspaper aside, giving Jesse his full attention. The concern in their eyes was immediate, and Jesse felt the knot in his stomach tighten.

"What happened?" his dad asked, his voice calm but laced with worry.

Jesse ran a hand through his hair, trying to find the right words. "I went to Wyatt's house yesterday. After we all tried to talk to his dad, I went back on my own. I knocked, and Wyatt's dad came to the door. He was... really angry."

His mom frowned, stepping closer. "Angry how? Did he threaten you?"

Jesse shook his head. "Not physically, but he definitely wasn't happy to see me. He told me to leave, said I didn't know what was best for Wyatt. I tried to tell him I just wanted to make sure Wyatt was okay, but he wouldn't listen."

His dad's face darkened with concern. "And Wyatt? Did you see him?"

Jesse nodded, feeling the familiar ache in his chest. "Yeah. He came out and told his dad he was going to talk to me. But... he wasn't happy that I was there. He said things at home were really hard, that his parents were putting a lot of pressure on him. He said he needed space to figure things out."

His mom's face softened with concern. "That poor boy... he must be going through so much."

Jesse's throat tightened. "Yeah. He's scared of disappointing his parents, but he's also scared of being himself. And I don't know how to help him. I don't even know if I'm making things worse."

His dad sighed, rubbing his temples. "Jesse, I'm worried about you. I don't like the sound of Wyatt's father. He seems like the type of man who won't let this go easily, and if he's angry now, it could get worse."

Jesse's heart sank. He had been trying not to think about that possibility, but his dad's words brought it to the surface. What if Wyatt's father did escalate things? What if he tried to keep Jesse away from Wyatt entirely?

"I know," Jesse admitted, his voice barely above a whisper. "I'm scared for Wyatt. His dad is so set in his ways, and I don't think he'll ever accept who Wyatt really is. I'm worried he's going to push Wyatt into something he's not ready for."

His mom sat down at the kitchen table, her face filled with concern. "Jesse, honey, I know you care about Wyatt, but you need to be careful. If his father's that angry, we don't know what he's capable of. You could get caught in the middle of something really dangerous."

Jesse bit his lip, feeling the fear and guilt rising inside him. "I just... I don't want to leave Wyatt to deal with all of this on his own. He needs someone to be there for him."

"We're not saying you shouldn't be there for him," his dad said gently, standing up and walking over to him. "But you also need to protect yourself. His father already doesn't like you being around, and if you keep pushing, it could get ugly."

Jesse looked down, the weight of the conversation pressing on his chest. He knew his parents were right. Wyatt's father wasn't going to take this lying down, and if Jesse kept showing up, things could spiral out of control. But the thought of leaving Wyatt alone, of not being there when he needed someone the most, was unbearable.

"I just don't know what to do," Jesse said quietly. "I don't want to push Wyatt away by giving him too much space, but I don't want to make things worse by being around."

His mom reached across the table and took his hand, her touch gentle and reassuring. "Jesse, you've done everything you can for him. Wyatt knows you care. But sometimes, giving someone space is the best thing you can do. It doesn't mean you're abandoning him–it just means you're letting him figure things out in his own time."

Jesse nodded, though the knot of worry in his chest didn't ease. "I hope you're right."

His dad patted his shoulder, his voice steady. "We're concerned for both of you. Wyatt's situation sounds tough, and we don't want either of you getting hurt. But you're not alone in this. If things get worse, we'll figure it out together. Okay?"

Jesse nodded again, the warmth of his parents' support sinking in despite his fear. "Okay."

His mom squeezed his hand before letting go. "Just keep us in the loop, alright? If anything changes, or if you feel like something's wrong, you come to us. We'll help however we can."

Jesse stood up, feeling a little lighter after the conversation, though the worry for Wyatt still clung to him like a shadow. "I will. Thanks, Mom. Thanks, Dad."

As he headed upstairs to his room, Jesse couldn't stop thinking about Wyatt. He hadn't heard from him since their conversation at the door, and the silence weighed heavy on his heart. But he knew one thing for sure: no matter how long it took, he wasn't going to give up on Wyatt.

And even though Wyatt was trapped in his father's world, Jesse would be there, waiting for the day Wyatt was ready to step out of it.

Chapter 31: An Unexpected Message

The house was quiet, but Jesse's thoughts weren't. He paced around his room, glancing at his phone every few seconds, hoping for a message from Wyatt that never came. The silence had stretched on too long. Days had passed since their tense encounter with Wyatt's father, and Jesse was running out of ways to push down the gnawing worry that something was terribly wrong.

He tossed his phone onto the bed and sat at the edge, his hands running through his hair. The tension, the fear of losing Wyatt, was becoming unbearable. Every text he sent remained unanswered, and every second of silence felt like another step further away from Wyatt. He picked up his phone again, scrolling through their old messages, reading and re-reading the last words Wyatt had sent before everything fell apart.

As Jesse was about to put his phone down, it buzzed, breaking the stillness of the room. His heart jumped. For a moment, he let himself believe it was Wyatt finally reaching out. But when he opened the message, it wasn't from Wyatt.

It was from an unknown number.

Unknown Number: *Hi Jesse, this is Wyatt's mom. I'd like to speak with you. Can we meet tomorrow? There are some things I need to talk to you about.*

Jesse's heart sank. Wyatt's mom? Of all the people to reach out, she was the last one he expected. The last time he'd seen her, standing behind Wyatt's father on their porch, she'd been silent, letting Mr. Roberts do the talking. She hadn't defended Wyatt, hadn't said a word in his favor. And now she wanted to meet?

He stared at the message, his mind racing. Was this some kind of trap? Was she going to ask him to stay away from Wyatt for good? Or was there something more to her message? Something softer beneath the surface?

Taking a deep breath, Jesse typed a response.

Jesse: *Okay. Where do you want to meet?*

A minute later, her reply came.

Wyatt's Mom: *The diner on Route 7, 10 a.m. tomorrow.*

The diner was out of the way, far enough from town that they wouldn't run into anyone. Jesse felt a mix of unease and curiosity. What did she want to talk about? And why now?

He set his phone down and exhaled, knowing tomorrow's conversation could either bring him the answers he so desperately needed–or make everything worse.

The next morning, Jesse arrived at the diner a few minutes early. His stomach was in knots as he parked the car, the nerves twisting tighter with each step he took toward the door. He hadn't slept much the night before, his mind replaying every possible scenario of what Wyatt's mom might say. Would she be cold and distant like Wyatt's dad, or was there something else going on?

Inside, the diner was quiet. The usual breakfast crowd had come and gone, leaving only a few scattered customers sipping coffee or reading newspapers. Jesse scanned the room, spotting Wyatt's mom sitting alone in a corner booth. She was stirring her coffee, staring out the window, her face drawn and tired. Jesse hesitated at the door before making his way over, unsure of how this conversation would unfold.

As he approached, she looked up and gave him a small, uncertain smile. It wasn't the hardened expression he'd seen before. There was something softer in her eyes, but also something deeply conflicted.

"Hi, Jesse," she said quietly as he slid into the booth across from her.

"Hi, Mrs. Roberts," he replied, his voice cautious.

For a moment, neither of them spoke. The silence between them was thick with tension. The waitress came by and poured him a cup of coffee, which Jesse didn't touch. Wyatt's mom sipped hers slowly, as if trying to gather her thoughts.

Finally, she broke the silence.

"I've been thinking a lot about everything that's happened," she began, her voice calm but laced with uncertainty. "About Wyatt. About you." She paused, glancing down at her hands. "I know things haven't been easy lately."

Jesse nodded, unsure of where she was going with this. "It's been hard for both of us," he said carefully. "But I care about Wyatt. I just want to make sure he's okay."

Wyatt's mom sighed, setting her coffee cup down. "I know you care about him. I've seen it. And I don't doubt that he cares about you, too. But Jesse, you have to understand, this is... difficult for our family."

Jesse could feel the weight of her words, the hesitation that lingered just beneath the surface. He wasn't sure if she was about to ask him to stay away from Wyatt or if there was something more she wanted to say.

"We've raised Wyatt with certain values," she continued, her voice soft but steady. "His father and I... we've always believed in those values. And this... this part of him," she said, her voice faltering for a moment, "it doesn't fit with what we've taught him."

Jesse braced himself. This was exactly what he'd feared. Wyatt's parents were trying to force him into a mold he didn't fit into, trying to erase the parts of him that didn't align with their beliefs. And now she was here, asking him to let it happen.

"I'm not here to tell you to stop seeing him," she added suddenly, as if sensing Jesse's thoughts. "I know I can't control that. And I know trying to would probably only push him further away." She sighed again, a deep, tired sound. "But I'm scared, Jesse. Scared of what this is doing to our family. Scared of what might happen if his father never comes around."

Jesse's breath caught in his throat. This wasn't what he expected. Wyatt's mom wasn't angry or trying to control the situation—she was scared. Scared of losing her son, scared of what would happen if Wyatt's father never changed. It was the first time Jesse had seen any crack in her stoic exterior.

"Mrs. Roberts," Jesse said carefully, choosing his words, "I understand that this is hard for you. I do. But Wyatt is hurting because he feels like he has to choose between being himself and being your son. That's not fair to him."

Her eyes flickered with pain. "I know that. And I wish... I wish things were different. But his father–he's never going to accept this. He's too set in his ways. And that terrifies me."

Jesse leaned forward, his voice gentle but firm. "You don't have to accept everything all at once. I know it's hard to change what you've believed your whole life. But Wyatt needs to know that at least one of you is willing to try."

Wyatt's mom was silent for a moment, her eyes dropping to her coffee cup. "I want to try," she said quietly. "I love him, and I don't want to lose him. But I'm afraid that if I stand by him, it'll break this family apart. His father... he's not going to come around. I know that much. And if I take Wyatt's side, it'll tear us apart."

Jesse could feel the weight of her words. She was trapped, caught between her love for her son and the fear of losing her husband. He understood now that this wasn't just about religion or values–it was about the fear of losing everything she had built with her family.

"I don't think it's about taking sides," Jesse said gently. "It's about letting Wyatt know he's not alone. Even if his dad doesn't accept him, you can show him that you still love him no matter what. He needs to hear that from you."

She looked up, her eyes misting over for a moment. "I don't want him to feel like he's alone. But I'm scared, Jesse. I'm scared that if I show him too much support, his father will think I'm choosing him over our family. And that could ruin everything."

Jesse leaned back, feeling the enormity of her struggle. It wasn't just about Wyatt–it was about everything Wyatt's mom stood to lose by standing up for him. Her marriage, her home, her place in the family.

"I can't tell you what to do," Jesse said softly. "But I know Wyatt is terrified of losing you both. He doesn't want to break this family apart either. He just wants to be himself without feeling like he's betraying you."

Mrs. Roberts closed her eyes for a moment, her hand trembling as she gripped her coffee cup. "I'm trying to figure out how to balance it all," she whispered. "But it's so hard. So much harder than I ever thought it would be."

Jesse watched her, feeling a mixture of sympathy and frustration. He wanted to tell her to choose Wyatt, to stand up for him and fight against the pressure from her husband. But he knew that wasn't his place. She had to come to that decision on her own.

After a long silence, she finally spoke again.

"I don't know if I'll ever be able to fully accept this," she admitted, her voice fragile. "But I don't want to lose my son. I'll... I'll try. But I need you to give him some space, Jesse. Let him work through this without the pressure of being caught between us and you. He's overwhelmed, and I think he just needs time to figure out where he stands."

Jesse felt a lump form in his throat. He had been bracing for this–the request to back off, to give Wyatt space. But hearing it from Wyatt's mom, seeing the conflict in her eyes, made it harder to say no.

"I don't want to make things harder for Wyatt," Jesse said quietly. "I just want to be there for him. But I'll give him space if that's what he needs."

Mrs. Roberts nodded, her face softening with gratitude. "Thank you, Jesse. I know this isn't easy. But I appreciate you listening."

Jesse stood up to leave, feeling the weight of the conversation settle deep in his chest. As he walked out of the diner, he couldn't shake the feeling that while Wyatt's mom was trying to come around, there was still a long road ahead–for her, for Wyatt, and for their family.

That night, after sitting with his thoughts for hours, Jesse sent a final text to Wyatt.

Jesse: *I talked to your mom today. She's worried about you. I'm here when you're ready.*

As the minutes ticked by in silence, Jesse stared at his phone, hoping for a response that never came. Wyatt was still trapped in his world of fear and expectations, and all Jesse could do now was wait.

Chapter 32: A Glimmer of Hope

Jesse sat at his desk, staring blankly at the notebook in front of him, trying and failing to focus on anything but Wyatt. His mind was consumed by the last few days–the weight of everything between them, the painful conversation with Wyatt's mother, and the endless silence that followed his texts.

It had been two long days since Jesse sent his message to Wyatt after meeting with his mom, and every passing hour of no response chipped away at him. Wyatt had said he needed space, but how much space? And for how long? Jesse couldn't shake the fear that maybe Wyatt's silence was becoming permanent. Maybe his parents had succeeded in pulling him away for good.

Jesse glanced down at his phone, where the screen remained blank, mocking his impatience. He tried to distract himself–watching TV, going through his summer reading list, that no longer seemed important–but nothing worked. His thoughts kept drifting back to Wyatt, back to the unknown.

Just as Jesse was about to give up, his phone buzzed, startling him out of his daze. For a split second, hope flared in his chest, but he tried to temper his expectations. It could be anyone. But when he looked down and saw Wyatt's name, his heart skipped a beat.

He fumbled with the phone, quickly unlocking it to see the message.

Wyatt: *I spoke with my mom.*

Jesse blinked, his breath catching in his throat. Wyatt was reaching out –finally. The relief was almost overwhelming, but there was something guarded about Wyatt's words. Jesse quickly typed out a response, his fingers trembling slightly.

Jesse: *Yeah. She reached out. I wasn't sure what to expect, but... I think she's trying. She's worried about you, Wyatt. Also, hi, glad you're alive!*

He hit send and stared at the screen, his heart pounding as he waited. After what felt like an eternity, the familiar dots appeared, and Jesse held his breath. Wyatt was typing.

Wyatt: *She told me. Said she's scared of what my dad's going to do if she supports me. She doesn't know what to believe anymore. I know it's been a while, I'm sorry, I needed time to think.*

Jesse's chest tightened as he read Wyatt's words. He could almost feel the exhaustion in Wyatt's voice, the deep weariness that came from trying to balance his identity and his family's expectations. The thought of Wyatt feeling so torn made Jesse's heart ache.

Jesse: *I know she's scared. But I think she's trying to understand. She doesn't want to lose you. She told me that herself.*

Another long pause followed, the dots appearing and disappearing as Wyatt seemed to struggle with what to say next.

Wyatt: *I don't know what to think anymore. I feel like I'm stuck between two worlds, and I don't know how to make them both work.*

Jesse stared at the screen, feeling a mix of sorrow and frustration. He wished there was something he could say to make it all better, to fix it for Wyatt, but he knew that wasn't possible. Wyatt was fighting a battle that only he could truly navigate.

Jesse: *You don't have to make both worlds work. You don't have to choose between being yourself and being part of your family. Your mom's trying to figure it out, and I know your dad...* He hesitated for a second before continuing. *Your dad might never understand, but that doesn't mean you have to lose yourself.*

The silence after Jesse sent the message felt like it stretched on forever. He stared at his phone, his mind racing, wondering if his words had hit the mark or if they had only deepened Wyatt's confusion. The dots appeared again, and Jesse held his breath.

Wyatt: *I feel like if I try to be myself, I'll lose them. And if I don't... I'll lose me. It's like no matter what I do, I'm going to end up alone.*

Jesse's heart ached reading the message. He had always known Wyatt was struggling, but seeing it laid out so plainly made it feel all the more real. Wyatt was being torn apart by his parents' expectations and his own identity, and it was breaking him.

Jesse: *You're not going to end up alone. You've got people who care about you, Wyatt. People who see you for who you really are. I'm one of them. And no matter what happens with your family, I'm here for you.*

The dots reappeared quickly this time, but the pause still felt heavy with tension.

Wyatt: *I've been thinking about that. About you. I didn't mean to push you away, Jesse. I just didn't know what to do. I didn't want to drag you into this mess with my family.*

Jesse's heart fluttered at the words. Wyatt hadn't forgotten him. He was still thinking about them–about *them*. And as much as Wyatt was hurting, he hadn't given up.

Jesse: *I get it. You're going through a lot. But I've missed you, Wyatt. And I've been worried.*

There was a long pause after Jesse's message, and his anxiety started to creep back in. What if Wyatt couldn't handle it? What if he was about to pull away again? The dots danced on the screen, and finally, Wyatt's next message came through.

Wyatt: *I miss you too. I just don't know how to deal with my dad. If he finds out we're talking… it's only going to make things worse. For both of us.*

Jesse could feel the fear in Wyatt's words, the deep sense of dread that his father's control had instilled in him. Wyatt wasn't just scared of losing his family–he was scared of what his father might do if he found out about them.

Jesse: *I know it's hard. I know your dad's got a lot of control over you right now. But he doesn't get to decide who you are, Wyatt. And he doesn't get to stop us from talking. I care about you, and I'm not going to let him tear us apart.*

The dots appeared again, and Jesse's heart pounded in his chest. He hoped his words were enough to get through to Wyatt, enough to show him that he didn't have to carry this burden alone.

Wyatt: *It's not just him. It's everything. I don't want to drag you into this mess. My parents are never going to understand. I don't want them to hurt you.*

Jesse frowned at his phone, feeling Wyatt's struggle as if it were his own. Wyatt was trying to protect him, but what Wyatt didn't seem to understand was that Jesse was already in the middle of it. Walking away now wasn't an option–not for Jesse.

Jesse: *I'm already in this, Wyatt. I'm not going anywhere. I don't care what your parents think–I'm here for you. We can figure this out together, no matter how messy it gets.*

The dots danced on the screen again, and Jesse's heart raced, the anticipation nearly overwhelming. Finally, another message appeared.

Wyatt: *I don't know how this is going to work, but I don't want to lose you. And I don't want to lose myself either. Maybe... maybe I'm ready to stop hiding.*

Jesse's breath caught in his throat. Wyatt wasn't just reaching out–he was taking a step forward, even though it terrified him. For the first time in days, Jesse felt a flicker of hope, like maybe they could actually figure this out together.

Jesse: *You don't have to hide anymore, Wyatt. Not from me. I'm here, whenever you're ready to take that step.*

There was a long pause this time, and Jesse's fingers hovered over the phone, waiting. He couldn't tell if Wyatt was trying to figure out what to say next or if he was reconsidering everything.

Then the next message came, and Jesse's heart soared.

Wyatt: *I want to meet. In person. Can we do that?*

Jesse's chest tightened with a mix of relief and excitement. This was what he had been waiting for–what he had hoped for. Wyatt wanted to meet. He wasn't pulling away anymore. He was ready to take that step.

Jesse: *Of course. Just say when and where, and I'll be there.*

The dots appeared once more, and Wyatt's response came quickly.

Wyatt: *Tomorrow night? After the pool closes?*

Jesse felt his heart race with anticipation. Tomorrow night. They would finally see each other again, and maybe, just maybe, they could start figuring this out together.

Jesse: *I'll be there. I've missed you, Wyatt.*

There was a brief pause before Wyatt's final message came through.

Wyatt: *I've missed you too. See you tomorrow.*

Jesse stared at the screen for a moment, a small smile tugging at his lips. It wasn't the end of their struggles–there was still so much to figure out–but it was a start. Wyatt was ready to stop hiding, and that meant everything.

Chapter 33: The Pool After Dark

The day seemed endless. Each minute dragged on, slow and excruciating, as Jesse went through the motions at work. It was like time had slowed down deliberately to taunt him, every tick of the clock a reminder of how much longer he had to wait before he could see Wyatt again. He restocked shelves, wiped down the concession counter, and made half-hearted conversation with his coworkers, but his mind was far away—already at the pool, in the quiet after dark, waiting for Wyatt.

Ever since Wyatt had texted the night before, saying he wanted to meet, Jesse's nerves had been a constant, buzzing undercurrent. He tried to stay calm, to focus on the mundane tasks of his shift, but it was impossible. His mind kept spinning in circles, wondering how the meeting would go. What would Wyatt say? How would he look at him? What if the weight of everything between them was too much?

The anticipation was agonizing. The pool, bustling with families and lifeguards during the day, felt like an entirely different place now that it was almost empty. It was late afternoon, the sun low in the sky, casting long shadows across the water. The kids had gone home, the lifeguards had packed up, and the pool was slowly becoming a quiet, deserted sanctuary—just the way Jesse had imagined it would be when Wyatt finally arrived.

Jesse wiped his sweaty palms on his jeans and glanced at the empty lifeguard chair where Wyatt usually sat. The chair had been unoccupied for days, and Wyatt's absence was like a missing piece of the puzzle. Jesse had heard whispers among the staff—people wondering where Wyatt had gone, why he hadn't been back. "Out sick," was the story, but no one knew for sure. Jesse had spent the last several days in a fog, worrying about Wyatt, imagining the worst, and now the moment was finally here.

After what felt like an eternity, the pool finally closed for the night. Jesse stayed behind after the other workers left, loitering in the back of the locker room where the dim lights flickered overhead. The air outside had cooled slightly, though the heat of the day still lingered. The stillness of the evening was unsettling–too quiet, too empty.

Jesse checked his phone for the hundredth time, the screen glowing softly in the darkened room. There were no new messages from Wyatt, no updates, no signs that he was on his way. Jesse's mind swirled with anxiety, a thousand "what-ifs" spinning in his head. *What if he doesn't show? What if he changes his mind? What if his dad found out and stopped him from coming?*

Just when Jesse thought he couldn't take the suspense any longer, he heard faint footsteps outside, followed by the creak of the locker room door opening. Jesse's heart jumped into his throat. He turned, holding his breath, and there he was–Wyatt.

Wyatt stepped inside, his figure half-hidden in the dim light of the room. His hair was a little messy, and his usual confident demeanor was missing, replaced by an air of quiet exhaustion. He wore a simple t-shirt and shorts, more casual than Jesse was used to seeing him, and the sight of him–real and present–sent a wave of relief and anxiety crashing over Jesse all at once.

They stood there for a moment, neither of them speaking, just taking each other in. Jesse could see the tension in Wyatt's shoulders, the weariness in his eyes, but there was also something else there—something softer, more vulnerable.

"Hey," Jesse finally said, his voice barely above a whisper. It felt surreal to be standing in front of Wyatt again after days of silence and uncertainty.

"Hey," Wyatt replied, his voice equally soft, though there was a roughness to it that hadn't been there before. He looked down at the ground for a moment, then back up at Jesse, his lips twitching into the faintest of smiles.

They were only a few feet apart, but the space between them felt like a chasm. The weight of everything that had happened—the silence, the fear, the uncertainty—hung heavy in the air. Jesse wanted to close the distance, to reach out and touch Wyatt, but he wasn't sure how. He wasn't sure if Wyatt even wanted that.

"I wasn't sure you were going to come," Jesse admitted, his voice trembling slightly as he took a cautious step forward.

Wyatt let out a breath, running a hand through his hair. "I almost didn't," he confessed, his eyes flickering with emotion. "But... I knew I had to."

Jesse's heart clenched at the words. Wyatt had almost backed out, almost let the fear and the pressure stop him, but he had come anyway. That meant something. It had to mean something.

"I'm glad you did," Jesse said, taking another small step closer. "I've missed you."

Wyatt's eyes softened at that, though the tension in his body didn't completely disappear. "I've missed you too," he said quietly, the words coming out like they had been trapped inside him for days. "More than I thought I would."

They were only a foot apart now, standing close enough that Jesse could see the faint lines of exhaustion around Wyatt's eyes, the way his shoulders slumped ever so slightly. He wanted to reach out, to touch Wyatt, to reassure him that everything was going to be okay–but he didn't want to push. Not after everything Wyatt had been through.

"I've been worried about you," Jesse said softly, his eyes searching Wyatt's face for some hint of what he was feeling. "You haven't been at the pool, and I didn't know what was going on with your parents. I didn't want to push, but I couldn't stop thinking about you."

Wyatt looked away for a moment, his jaw tightening. "It's been hard," he admitted, his voice rough. "My dad's... he's never going to change. He's made that pretty clear. But... my mom... she's trying. She's stuck between him and me, and it's killing her."

Jesse's heart ached for him. He could hear the exhaustion in Wyatt's voice, the weight of the struggle he had been carrying alone for too long. Jesse wanted to take that weight from him, to make it easier, but he knew that wasn't possible. Wyatt had to navigate this himself–but Jesse could be there to help him.

"You don't have to choose between being yourself and being their son," Jesse said gently, taking another step closer until they were only inches apart. "I know it feels like that, but you don't have to lose yourself for them."

Wyatt's gaze flicked up to meet Jesse's, and for a moment, the vulnerability in his eyes was almost too much to bear. He looked so tired—tired of pretending, tired of the fight. Jesse could see it all in his expression, the way his shoulders drooped, the way his jaw clenched with uncertainty.

"I'm scared," Wyatt said, his voice barely above a whisper. "I'm scared of what's going to happen if I stop pretending. I'm scared of what my dad will do."

Jesse felt a lump rise in his throat. He could hear the fear in Wyatt's voice, the pain of trying to be someone he wasn't just to keep his family intact. It wasn't fair. None of it was fair.

"You don't have to be scared," Jesse said softly, reaching out and gently placing his hand on Wyatt's arm. Wyatt flinched slightly at the touch, but he didn't pull away. Jesse's heart raced, but he kept his hand there, offering whatever comfort he could. "I'm here, Wyatt. I'm not going anywhere. We can figure this out together."

Wyatt stared at Jesse for a long moment, his eyes flickering with a mix of emotions—fear, hope, longing. Jesse could feel the tension between them, the weight of everything they had been holding back for days.

Finally, Wyatt let out a long, shaky breath, stepping closer to Jesse until the space between them disappeared. "I don't know how this is going to work," Wyatt said, his voice barely audible. "But I don't want to keep hiding. Not from you."

Jesse's heart pounded in his chest at Wyatt's words. This was it—Wyatt was ready. Ready to stop hiding, ready to let go of the fear that had been holding him back. Jesse could feel the pull between them, the magnetic connection that had always been there, stronger now than ever before.

"You don't have to hide from me," Jesse whispered, his voice thick with emotion. "You never have to hide from me."

In that moment, the world outside the pool faded away. The tension, the fear, the uncertainty–it all melted into the background as Wyatt leaned in, closing the final distance between them. Their lips met in a soft, tentative kiss, a kiss filled with all the emotion they had been holding back for so long.

Jesse's hand slid from Wyatt's arm to his back, pulling him closer as the kiss deepened. Wyatt responded in kind, his hands gripping Jesse's shirt as if he were afraid to let go. The kiss was slow, deliberate, and when they finally pulled apart, they were both breathless, their foreheads resting against each other.

"I don't know what's going to happen next," Wyatt murmured, his breath warm against Jesse's lips.

"Neither do I," Jesse replied softly, his hand still resting on Wyatt's back. "But we'll figure it out. Together."

For the first time in what felt like forever, Wyatt smiled–a real, genuine smile–and Jesse's heart swelled with hope. The future was uncertain, and the road ahead was full of obstacles, but in that moment, with Wyatt in his arms, Jesse knew one thing for sure: they weren't alone. They would face whatever came next, together.

They stayed like that for a while, wrapped in each other's presence, the quiet of the night settling around them. The pool, once a place filled with noise and chaos, now felt like a sanctuary–just the two of them, standing close, feeling the weight of the world lift, if only for a moment.

Eventually, Wyatt pulled back, his eyes still soft but more focused now. "I don't know how we're going to make this work with my dad," he said, his voice full of worry again. "He's not going to change, Jesse. And if he finds out we're together…"

"We'll figure it out," Jesse interrupted, his voice steady and sure. "We don't have to have all the answers right now. We just have to take it one step at a time. And I'll be with you every step of the way."

Wyatt looked at him for a long moment, as if searching for something in Jesse's eyes. Whatever he found must have been enough, because he nodded, a quiet determination settling over him.

"Okay," Wyatt said, his voice stronger now. "One step at a time."

Jesse smiled, feeling the warmth of hope spread through him. It wasn't going to be easy, but it didn't matter. They had each other, and for now, that was enough.

Wyatt's gaze flickered toward the pool entrance, his expression shifting to something more guarded, more cautious. "I should probably head out," he said softly, his voice breaking the quiet between them. "I don't want my parents to get suspicious if I'm out too late."

Jesse's chest tightened, knowing that Wyatt was right. Their time together tonight was limited, and though he wished it could last forever, he knew it couldn't. "Yeah, I get it," Jesse replied, his voice tinged with disappointment. "But I'm really glad we did this."

Wyatt smiled, though it was a little sad. "Me too." He glanced at Jesse one more time before adding, "We'll talk more. When we can."

Jesse nodded, understanding the unspoken constraints that Wyatt was under. "Text me when you get home," he said, his voice gentle. "I want to make sure you're okay."

Wyatt hesitated for a moment, then nodded, his eyes softening. "I will."

With that, they shared one last lingering glance, the weight of the night hanging between them. Then, without another word, Wyatt turned and began walking toward the exit, his footsteps echoing softly in the stillness of the evening.

Jesse watched him go, his heart heavy with a mix of emotions–relief, sadness, hope. He knew this wasn't the end of their struggles, but tonight had given him something to hold onto. Wyatt had opened up, and they had shared something real. That was enough for now.

After a few moments, Jesse turned and made his way toward the opposite direction, slipping out through the side gate that led to the quiet street. The walk home was a blur of thoughts and emotions, his mind replaying the kiss, Wyatt's words, the feeling of closeness they had shared. It felt like a small victory, even if there was still so much uncertainty ahead.

By the time Jesse reached his house, the night had fully settled in, the stars faintly visible through the suburban glow of streetlights. He unlocked the front door quietly and slipped inside, careful not to wake his parents. The house was silent, and the dim glow of the kitchen light was the only indication that anyone had been up at all.

He headed up to his room, the tension in his shoulders easing slightly now that he was home. As soon as he sat down on the edge of his bed, he grabbed his phone and checked for a message from Wyatt. His chest tightened when he saw nothing. Jesse hesitated for a second, wondering if Wyatt had gotten home yet–or if something had happened.

A few minutes passed before his phone buzzed, and Jesse's heart leaped in his chest. Wyatt's name flashed across the screen.

Wyatt: *I'm home.*

Jesse exhaled, a sense of relief washing over him. He quickly typed out a response.

Jesse: *Good. I was worried.*

The dots appeared almost instantly, signaling Wyatt's reply.

Wyatt: *Yeah, I made it. My mom asked where I'd been, but I told her I was just out for a walk.*

Jesse smiled to himself, imagining the tightrope Wyatt had to walk at home. He wished Wyatt didn't have to lie to his parents, but he understood why it was necessary right now. Wyatt wasn't ready to confront everything, not yet.

Jesse: *Did she believe you?*

Wyatt: *I think so. She didn't push too much. It's my dad I have to worry about.*

Jesse frowned, his fingers pausing over the keyboard. He hated the constant fear Wyatt had to live with, the looming presence of his father and what he might do if he found out the truth. Jesse wanted to protect Wyatt from that, but he knew there was only so much he could do.

Jesse: *I'm glad you're okay. I was thinking about tonight… It felt good, didn't it?*

There was a long pause before Wyatt replied.

Wyatt: *Yeah. It did. I was nervous at first, but… I don't know. Being with you feels different. Easier.*

Jesse's heart skipped a beat at the words. He hadn't expected Wyatt to say something so honest, so vulnerable. It made everything they had shared tonight feel even more significant.

Jesse: *I feel the same way. I've missed you so much. I know things are complicated with your parents, but… tonight felt like the start of something better.*

Another pause, this time longer, and Jesse wondered if Wyatt was trying to find the right words to respond. Finally, the message came.

Wyatt: *It did. I've been so scared of what my dad might do, of losing everything I know. But being with you tonight made me realize something– I can't keep pretending forever. It's killing me.*

Jesse's heart ached as he read the message. He could hear the pain in Wyatt's words, the internal battle that had been raging inside him for so long. Wyatt was being pulled in two directions–toward his family and their expectations, and toward his true self.

Jesse: *You don't have to pretend with me. You never have to hide with me.*

Wyatt: *I know. That's why I want to keep seeing you, even if it has to be in secret for now. I don't know what's going to happen, Jesse, but I want to try. I'm just not ready to deal with my dad yet.*

Jesse's chest tightened, his heart full of conflicting emotions. He wanted so badly to be with Wyatt openly, for them to not have to hide. But he also knew that Wyatt was dealing with a pressure Jesse could only imagine.

Jesse: *I get it. We'll take it slow, one step at a time. We don't have to rush anything. I'm just glad we're talking again. That we're trying.*

The dots appeared again, and Jesse waited, holding his breath.

Wyatt: *Me too. I don't want to lose this. I don't want to lose you.*

Jesse's heart swelled with warmth. Even though they were texting, the words felt real—like a bridge between the distance that had grown between them. Wyatt wasn't ready to confront everything yet, but the fact that he wanted to keep seeing Jesse, that he didn't want to lose him, was enough for now.

Jesse: *You won't lose me. I'm here, whenever you're ready.*

There was a long pause, and Jesse wondered if Wyatt was trying to find the right words—or if he was thinking about the weight of the situation they were both in. Finally, Wyatt's message came through.

Wyatt: *Thanks, Jesse. I'm gonna head to bed, but I'll text you tomorrow. Okay?*

Jesse: *Okay. Sleep well.*

Wyatt: *You too.*

As the conversation ended, Jesse put his phone down, his heart still racing from the intensity of the night. He lay back on his bed, staring up at the ceiling, letting the emotions of the evening settle over him.

They hadn't solved everything. There was still so much uncertainty, so many battles ahead, but they had taken a step forward. And that was more than Jesse could have hoped for a few days ago.

He could still feel the warmth of Wyatt's touch, the softness of his kiss, the quiet promise of something real between them. And for the first time in days, Jesse allowed himself to feel hopeful.

As he drifted off to sleep, his phone buzzed one last time, and Jesse's eyes fluttered open to see a new message from Wyatt.

Wyatt: *Thanks for tonight.*

Jesse smiled, a soft, contented smile, and typed back quickly before closing his eyes again.

Jesse: *Anytime.*

Tonight was just the beginning. And for the first time, it felt like they were both ready to face whatever came next–together.

Chapter 34: Back in the Water

Jesse stood behind the concession stand, wiping down the counter for what felt like the millionth time. His eyes kept flicking toward the entrance of the pool, where families and kids were filtering in for another hot day. But that wasn't what he was watching for.

Today was the day.

After days of waiting, wondering, and worrying, Wyatt was finally coming back to work. Jesse's stomach had been doing flips all morning—excited, anxious, and nervous all at once. He couldn't stop thinking about their text conversation from the other night, the way they'd opened up to each other. And now Wyatt was going to be back, in person, with all their coworkers around. Jesse had to remind himself that they had to keep it low-key, that they couldn't let on about anything.

But still, his heart raced every time he thought about seeing Wyatt walk through those gates.

He was lost in thought when Rachel walked up beside him, her sunglasses perched on top of her head, and nudged him with her elbow. "You've been cleaning that same spot for ten minutes, dude."

Jesse blinked, snapping out of it. "Huh? Oh." He set down the cloth and gave her a sheepish grin. "Guess I'm just distracted."

"Clearly." Rachel raised an eyebrow, smirking. "Or are you just nervous because someone's coming back today?"

Jesse's stomach flipped again, and he tried to play it cool. "I don't know what you're talking about."

Rachel laughed, leaning against the counter. "Sure you don't. But we're all happy Wyatt's coming back today. It's not just you."

Jesse smiled at that, his chest tightening with a mix of nerves and excitement. He hadn't told Rachel or anyone else about the details of what had been going on between him and Wyatt–about the nights they'd spent talking, the moments they'd shared. But his friends knew enough to pick up on his feelings. And they knew how much Wyatt had been missed at the pool.

"He's had a rough time," Jesse said quietly, glancing over at Rachel. "I just hope today goes okay for him."

Rachel nodded, her expression softening. "He'll be fine. We'll all make sure of it."

As if on cue, the pool gate creaked open, and Jesse's heart immediately kicked into overdrive. He turned toward the entrance, holding his breath, and there he was–Wyatt.

Wyatt walked in with his lifeguard bag slung over his shoulder, his dark hair slightly messy, sunglasses perched on his nose. He looked just like he always did–confident, calm–but Jesse could tell there was a hint of tension in his posture, like he was bracing himself. But even with the weight of everything hanging over him, Wyatt looked good. Really good.

Jesse's breath caught in his throat as he watched Wyatt make his way across the pool deck, heading toward the lifeguard station. His heart pounded in his chest, the urge to rush over and say something–anything–almost overwhelming. But he couldn't. Not like that. They had to be careful.

Rachel gave him a knowing look and nudged him again. "Don't blow your cover, Jesse. Play it cool."

Jesse forced himself to relax, nodding as he took a deep breath. "Right. Cool. I can do that."

Wyatt reached the lifeguard chair, and almost immediately, their coworkers began to notice. Matt, who had been setting up the pool chairs, waved over enthusiastically. "Wyatt! Good to have you back, man!"

Tori, who had been prepping the snack stand, looked up and grinned. "Hey! The place hasn't been the same without you!"

Wyatt smiled at them, though it was a little more reserved than usual. "Thanks. It's good to be back."

Jesse watched from behind the counter, his heart racing as his friends gathered around Wyatt, welcoming him back. He wanted so badly to join them, to throw his arms around Wyatt and tell him how much he'd missed him, but he couldn't. Not yet. Not like that.

Wyatt glanced toward the concession stand, his eyes flickering in Jesse's direction for the briefest of moments. Their eyes met for just a second, and in that second, everything else seemed to fade away. Jesse felt his chest tighten, warmth spreading through him. It was the first time they'd seen each other since that night, since the kiss by the pool.

Wyatt gave him the smallest of smiles–a smile only Jesse would have noticed–before turning back to the others. It was a subtle gesture, but it was enough to make Jesse's heart leap.

He turned back to the counter, pretending to be busy again, though his mind was racing. Rachel shot him another amused look.

"I saw that," she whispered, her tone teasing but kind. "You two are terrible at this whole 'discreet' thing."

Jesse blushed, quickly adjusting the bottles in the cooler. "We're trying," he muttered under his breath. "But it's hard."

Rachel chuckled. "I can tell. Just… be careful, okay? I don't want you guys getting into trouble."

Jesse nodded, grateful for her understanding. "We will. Thanks."

Throughout the morning, Jesse kept sneaking glances at Wyatt, watching him settle back into his routine. Wyatt seemed quieter than usual, but his coworkers were happy to have him back, and it didn't take long for the easy flow of conversation to return. Matt cracked a joke about Wyatt's tan being "too perfect," and Tori kept throwing in comments about how "bored" they had all been without him. Wyatt smiled along with them, but Jesse could tell that something was still weighing on him.

As the day wore on, Jesse found it harder to stay focused. The need to talk to Wyatt, to ask how he was really doing, was gnawing at him. But every time their eyes met, Wyatt gave him a look—a soft, almost reassuring look that said *not now*.

They would talk later. Jesse just had to be patient.

By the time the afternoon lull hit and most of the pool-goers had either left for lunch or were lounging in the sun, Jesse found himself alone behind the counter, wiping down the already-clean surface for what felt like the hundredth time. His mind was still swirling with thoughts of Wyatt—how good it felt to see him again, how badly he wanted to pull him aside and talk, even if it was just for a minute.

He didn't realize Wyatt had made his way over to the concession stand until he heard a quiet voice.

"Hey."

Jesse looked up, his heart skipping a beat. Wyatt stood there, leaning casually against the counter, his sunglasses pushed up onto his head. He gave Jesse a small, almost shy smile—the kind of smile that made Jesse's chest tighten.

"Hey," Jesse said, trying to keep his voice steady. "How's your first day back going?"

Wyatt shrugged, glancing around to make sure no one was too close. "It's... good. Weird, but good."

"I'm glad you're here," Jesse said softly, his eyes searching Wyatt's. "I missed you."

Wyatt's expression softened, and for a brief moment, the tension between them disappeared. "I missed you too. More than I thought I would."

Jesse felt a flutter in his chest, the same warmth from the other night flooding back. But before he could say anything else, Wyatt straightened up, his expression shifting back to something more guarded.

"We can't... you know," Wyatt said, his voice low. "Not here."

"I know," Jesse replied quickly. "I get it."

Wyatt's eyes flicked toward the lifeguard chair where the others were sitting, then back to Jesse. "We'll talk later. After work."

Jesse nodded, his pulse quickening. "Yeah. After work."

Wyatt smiled again—just a small, private smile—and then, just as quickly as he'd appeared, he turned and walked back toward the lifeguard station.

Jesse watched him go, his heart racing, feeling the familiar mix of anticipation and anxiety settle in his chest. It wasn't much—just a few words, a couple of stolen glances—but it was enough.

For now, they had to be careful. They had to keep things under wraps, especially with Wyatt's dad still looming over everything. But later—after work—there would be time. Time to talk, time to figure out what came next.

Chapter 35: The Favorite Spot

The day had felt like a slow burn, anticipation building with every hour that passed. Jesse had spent the entire shift with his heart racing, stealing glances at Wyatt whenever he could. Each time their eyes met, there was a silent promise–a promise that something more was coming after work. They had to keep it discreet, but the knowledge that they'd be alone after the pool closed made the long day bearable.

As the sun set and the pool began to empty out, Jesse could hardly contain his excitement. When the last of the families had packed up and the staff started to clean up, Jesse wiped down the counter, heart pounding in his chest. He could feel the electricity in the air, the tension building between him and Wyatt.

His phone buzzed in his pocket, and Jesse pulled it out, already knowing who it was.

Wyatt: *Meet me by the side gate in five minutes.*

Jesse smiled, quickly texting back.

Jesse: *On my way.*

He finished up, made sure everything at the concession stand was in order, and then slipped away, heading toward the quiet side gate. It was a small, hidden entrance near the back of the pool that was rarely used –perfect for sneaking away unnoticed. His pulse quickened as he reached the gate, his mind spinning with thoughts of what was about to happen.

When Jesse arrived, Wyatt was already there, leaning casually against the fence. The golden light from the setting sun cast soft shadows on his face, making him look even more effortlessly handsome than usual. His hair was slightly messy from the day, and his lips curved into a small, knowing smile when he saw Jesse approaching.

"Ready?" Wyatt asked quietly, his voice low and intimate.

Jesse nodded, feeling the familiar flutter in his stomach. "Yeah. Where are we going?"

Wyatt grinned, that mischievous glint in his eyes returning. "You'll see. Come on."

With a quick glance around to make sure no one was watching, Wyatt led Jesse through the gate and out into the warm summer evening. The town was beginning to wind down, the streets quiet and bathed in the last light of the day. Wyatt moved with purpose, leading Jesse down a path that had become familiar.

Jesse's heart skipped a beat when he realized where they were going. Wyatt's favorite spot–the quiet, secluded clearing just outside of town. It was the place where they'd first shared real moments together, away from the eyes of the world, a place where they could just *be* without any pressure.

When they finally reached the clearing, it was like stepping into another world. The trees formed a natural wall around them, blocking out the sounds of the town. The sky above was a deep, fading blue, stars beginning to peek through as the night settled in. It was peaceful, serene–just the two of them.

Wyatt stopped at the edge of the clearing, turning to Jesse with a soft smile. "It's still as quiet as ever," he said, his voice almost a whisper.

Jesse nodded, his heart full. "Yeah. I missed this place."

"Me too," Wyatt murmured, stepping closer. There was something different in his eyes now–a vulnerability, a rawness that Jesse hadn't seen before. It made the moment feel even more intimate, like they were both standing on the edge of something big.

Wyatt took a deep breath, his gaze locking with Jesse's. "I've been thinking a lot about us," he said, his voice quieter now, more hesitant. "About how we're going to make this work. And I know it's not going to be easy, but... I want to try. I don't want to keep pretending."

Jesse's chest tightened at the words, emotion swelling in his throat. He stepped closer, closing the small distance between them, until they were almost touching. "I don't want to pretend either," Jesse said softly, his eyes never leaving Wyatt's. "I want to be with you. Whatever it takes."

Wyatt let out a shaky breath, his eyes flickering with uncertainty and hope. "I'm scared, Jesse," he admitted, his voice barely above a whisper. "I'm scared of what my dad will do. I'm scared of what happens if he finds out... but I'm more scared of losing you. I don't want to lose this."

Hearing those words–so raw and honest–made Jesse's heart swell with a mixture of love and sorrow. Wyatt had been carrying so much fear, so much pressure, but here he was, standing in front of Jesse, choosing *them* despite it all.

"You won't lose me," Jesse whispered, reaching out and gently taking Wyatt's hand in his. "I'm not going anywhere. We'll figure it out, one step at a time."

Wyatt's grip tightened on Jesse's hand, and for the first time in days, he seemed to relax. His shoulders softened, and he let out a slow breath, as if he'd been holding it in for far too long.

"I want to tell my mom," Wyatt said after a moment, his voice still quiet but steadier now. "She's been trying to understand, and I think... I think if I tell her about us, she might come around. But I'm not ready to tell my dad. Not yet."

Jesse nodded, understanding the weight of Wyatt's decision. He knew how much Wyatt's family meant to him, how hard it would be to face his father's disapproval. "You don't have to tell him yet. We can take it slow. There's no rush."

Wyatt smiled softly, his eyes filled with gratitude. "Thank you. For being patient with me."

"I'd wait forever for you," Jesse whispered, stepping even closer, their bodies almost touching now.

Wyatt's eyes darkened with emotion, and before Jesse could say anything else, Wyatt reached out and gently cupped his face, pulling him into a kiss. It was soft at first, tentative, like they were both testing the waters. But then the kiss deepened, and all the longing, all the desire they'd been holding back for days poured out in that one moment.

Jesse's hands slid up Wyatt's sides, feeling the warmth of his body through his shirt. Wyatt responded by wrapping his arms around Jesse's waist, pulling him closer until their bodies were pressed tightly together. The kiss was slow, deliberate, filled with a kind of urgency that made Jesse's heart race.

Wyatt's fingers tangled in Jesse's hair, and the kiss became more intense, more desperate. Jesse could feel the heat between them rising, the connection deepening with every touch, every movement. It was like they were both trying to make up for all the time they'd spent apart, for all the fear and doubt that had kept them at a distance.

Jesse's hands roamed over Wyatt's back, feeling the muscles tense and relax under his touch. The kiss grew more passionate, their breathing becoming ragged as they lost themselves in each other. Jesse could feel the world around them disappearing, leaving only the two of them, here in this quiet, hidden place.

Wyatt broke the kiss first, but only to catch his breath. His forehead rested against Jesse's, his breath coming in short, shallow bursts. "I want this," Wyatt whispered, his voice thick with emotion. "I want us."

Jesse's heart pounded in his chest, his own emotions threatening to overwhelm him. "I want us too," he whispered back. "More than anything."

They stood there for a moment, breathing hard, their hands still clinging to each other like they were afraid to let go. The air around them was warm, but Jesse could feel the cool night breeze starting to settle in, wrapping them in a sense of quiet intimacy.

Wyatt pulled Jesse closer, their bodies pressed together as they stood in the clearing, the stars beginning to twinkle overhead. Jesse could feel every inch of Wyatt against him—the warmth of his skin, the rise and fall of his chest, the steady rhythm of his heartbeat. It was grounding, calming, and Jesse couldn't help but smile as he buried his face in the crook of Wyatt's neck, breathing him in.

"I don't know how we're going to do this," Wyatt murmured, his fingers tracing gentle circles on Jesse's back. "But I want you."

Jesse pulled back slightly, just enough to look into Wyatt's eyes. "We'll figure it out," he said softly. "We'll take it slow, and when you're ready, I'll be right there with you."

Wyatt smiled, his eyes filled with a mixture of hope and determination. "I want to do this together. When the time comes... I want you by my side."

Jesse nodded, his throat tight with emotion. "You won't have to face it alone. I promise."

They kissed again, slower this time, softer—more of a promise than anything else. It was a kiss that spoke of all the things they hadn't said yet, all the things they were planning to say when the time was right.

After a while, they sank down onto the grass, sitting side by side with their backs against the trunk of a large tree. Wyatt rested his head on Jesse's shoulder, and Jesse wrapped an arm around Wyatt's waist, holding him close. The sky above was darkening, the stars coming out in full force, twinkling like tiny lights against the backdrop of night.

They sat there in comfortable silence, the only sounds around them the rustling of leaves and the soft chirping of crickets. Jesse felt a sense of peace settle over him, a calmness he hadn't felt in days. It was like the weight of everything they'd been holding onto had finally lifted, leaving only the warmth of Wyatt's body against his and the quiet promise of what was to come.

"I love this spot," Wyatt said softly after a long stretch of silence. "It feels like our place."

Jesse smiled, pressing a soft kiss to Wyatt's temple. "It is our place. And it always will be."

They stayed like that for what felt like hours, just holding each other, talking quietly about the future—about what they wanted, what they were scared of, and how they planned to make it work. There was still so much uncertainty, so much they hadn't figured out yet, but in that moment, none of it mattered.

They had each other. And for now, that was more than enough.

As the night wore on and the air grew cooler, they finally stood to leave, walking back toward town hand in hand, their fingers intertwined. They'd part ways soon, heading home to their separate lives, but the connection between them was stronger than ever.

Chapter 36: The Conversation with Mom

Wyatt had been rehearsing this moment in his mind for days. Ever since he and Jesse had reconnected, since they'd shared that intimate moment at his favorite spot, the thought of telling his mom had been nagging at him, refusing to leave him alone. He knew it needed to happen. He needed to open up, to let her in on the truth of his relationship with Jesse. She was the only person in his family who might understand, who might stand by him. But it didn't make the idea any less terrifying.

The weight of his dad's disapproval hung over him like a storm cloud, casting a long shadow over everything. His father's beliefs were rigid, his expectations suffocating. And Wyatt had spent most of his life trying to fit the mold his dad wanted for him—obedient, strong, straight. But he couldn't do it anymore. He couldn't keep pretending.

As he stepped through the front door that evening, Wyatt felt his stomach twist with anxiety. The house was quiet, except for the familiar sounds of his mom moving around in the kitchen. The soft clatter of dishes and the bubbling of something cooking on the stove filled the space. The scent of spices lingered in the air, but instead of making him feel at home, it only heightened his nerves. This was the moment he'd been dreading.

He hesitated in the hallway, glancing toward the kitchen where his mom was busy preparing dinner. She hadn't heard him come in yet. Wyatt took a deep breath, trying to steady himself, but his palms were already sweating, and his heart was racing. He couldn't keep putting this off. He had to tell her, had to let her know the truth—not just about him, but about Jesse. About how much Jesse meant to him.

Wyatt took another deep breath and stepped into the kitchen, his footsteps softer than usual. His mom turned when she heard him approach, her face lighting up with a smile.

"There you are," she said warmly, wiping her hands on a dish towel. "I was wondering when you'd get back. How was your day? Hungry?"

The casualness of her greeting, the normalcy of it, almost made Wyatt want to retreat back into silence. But he couldn't. Not this time.

"Mom," Wyatt said, his voice a little shakier than he intended. "I need to talk to you. There's... something important I need to tell you."

His mom's smile faded a little, her brow furrowing as she turned off the burner and set the spoon down on the counter. She wiped her hands again, this time more slowly, like she was already bracing herself for whatever Wyatt was about to say. "Of course, honey. What's going on?"

Wyatt's mouth felt dry, and he swallowed hard, trying to gather the courage to get the words out. This wasn't going to be easy. "It's about Jesse," he began, glancing down at his hands before looking back up at her. "There's... there's more going on between us than you think."

His mom's face faltered, the smile fading completely now as a look of concern settled in. She crossed her arms, her expression careful, like she was trying to read Wyatt before he could continue. "What do you mean?" she asked, her voice quiet but tinged with worry.

Wyatt felt his heart thudding painfully in his chest. He shoved his hands into his pockets, not knowing what else to do with them, and forced himself to meet her eyes. "Jesse and I... we're not just friends," he said, his voice barely above a whisper. "We've been seeing each other. Like, as more than friends. I really like him"

For a moment, the room was completely still. His mom just stood there, staring at him like she couldn't quite process what he was saying. Wyatt felt the silence stretch between them, growing heavier with every second. He wanted to say something, anything, to fill the gap, but he didn't know what to say.

When his mom finally spoke, her voice was softer, almost hesitant. "You and Jesse are… together? Like… in a relationship?"

Wyatt nodded, his throat tight. "Yeah. We've been… we've been seeing each other for a while now. And I really like him, Mom."

The words hung in the air between them, heavy with truth and vulnerability. It was the first time Wyatt had said it out loud to anyone. His mom's face softened, but there was still a deep crease of worry between her brows.

She swallowed hard, her eyes flickering with a mix of emotions–fear, confusion, and something else Wyatt couldn't quite name. She glanced down at her hands, fidgeting nervously with the edge of the dish towel, before finally looking back up at Wyatt. "Wyatt… I don't know what to say," she whispered. "This is… a lot."

Wyatt could feel the tension building inside him, his emotions threatening to spill over. He had been so scared of this moment–scared of what his mom would say, of what she might think. But now that it was happening, all he could do was stand there, waiting for her to understand.

"Mom, I know this is a lot," Wyatt said softly, his voice trembling. "But I need you to know that this is real. Jesse and I... it's not just some phase. And I need your support. I don't know if Dad's ever going to accept this, and that terrifies me. But you... I need you on my side."

Tears pricked at the corners of Wyatt's eyes, and he blinked them away, his breath shaky as he continued. "I've spent so much time pretending to be someone I'm not, trying to fit into what Dad wants me to be. But I can't do it anymore. I can't keep pretending, and I can't lose Jesse."

His mom's face crumpled slightly at his words, and for a moment, she just stood there, staring at him with tears in her eyes. The silence between them was filled with a weight that felt impossible to lift, and Wyatt felt like he was standing on the edge of a cliff, waiting to fall.

After what felt like an eternity, his mom took a shaky breath and stepped closer, her voice barely above a whisper. "Wyatt... honey... I love you," she said, her voice trembling. "I love you so much. But this... this is so hard for me to understand."

Wyatt's heart clenched, and he could feel the tension rising again. "Mom, please," he said, his voice breaking. "I need you to try. I need you to understand. I can't do this without you."

His mom's eyes filled with tears as she reached out, placing a trembling hand on Wyatt's arm. "I'm trying, Wyatt," she whispered. "I'm really trying. But your father... he's not going to understand this. He's not going to accept it. And I'm so scared of what's going to happen if he finds out."

Wyatt swallowed hard, his throat tight. "I know," he whispered. "I know Dad's not going to accept it. But I can't keep hiding who I am. I can't keep hiding Jesse. I don't want to."

His mom nodded slowly, her face crumpling as she wiped her eyes with the back of her hand. "I know, honey. I know you're struggling. And I don't want you to feel like you have to hide. But I'm scared too. I don't know how to protect you from this. From what your father might say... or do."

Wyatt stepped closer, his voice soft but firm. "You don't have to protect me, Mom. I'm not asking you to choose between me and Dad. I just need to know that you're here for me. That you support me."

His mom looked up at him, her eyes filled with pain and uncertainty, but there was also a flicker of something else–something warmer, more determined. She reached up, cupping his face in her hands, her touch gentle and familiar.

"I'm here for you," she whispered, her voice breaking with emotion. "I don't understand all of this yet, but I'm here for you, Wyatt. I love you, and I'll always love you. No matter what."

Wyatt's breath hitched, and he closed his eyes, leaning into his mom's touch. The relief that washed over him was overwhelming, and he felt the tears spill over, falling silently down his cheeks.

"Thank you," he whispered, his voice thick with emotion. "Thank you, Mom."

They stood there for a long moment, the silence between them now filled with something warmer, something that felt like hope. His mom pulled him into a tight hug, holding him close like she used to when he was a kid. Wyatt clung to her, feeling the tension in his chest slowly ease.

When they finally pulled apart, his mom wiped her eyes again and gave him a shaky smile. "Just... promise me you'll be careful," she said softly. "Your dad... if he finds out..."

"I'll be careful," Wyatt promised, his heart still heavy with the knowledge of what his dad might do. "But I'm not going to hide forever. When the time is right... I'll tell him."

His mom nodded, though her eyes were still clouded with worry. "I'll be here for you when that time comes."

Wyatt smiled, a small but genuine smile, and for the first time in what felt like forever, he allowed himself to feel hopeful. It wasn't perfect, and there was still so much they hadn't figured out yet. But his mom was trying. She was standing by him. And that meant everything.

As they stood in the quiet kitchen, the weight of their conversation lingering in the air, Wyatt knew that this was only the beginning. There were still battles to be fought, still fears to be faced. But he wasn't alone anymore.

Wyatt lingered in the kitchen for a moment after his conversation with his mom, the weight of what had just happened still sinking in. He had been dreading this for days, unsure of how she would react, but now that it was over, he felt a mixture of relief and exhaustion. His mom hadn't pushed him away. She hadn't turned her back on him. It wasn't perfect–far from it–but it was better than he'd hoped for. She was trying.

And now, he needed to tell Jesse.

Wyatt made his way upstairs to his room, his thoughts swirling as he pulled out his phone. He sat on the edge of his bed, letting out a long breath as he opened his messages with Jesse. His hands were still trembling a little, the adrenaline of the conversation with his mom making it hard to focus, but he quickly typed out the first thing that came to mind.

Wyatt: *Just talked to my mom.*

He hit send, his heart pounding as he waited for Jesse's reply. He wasn't sure what he expected Jesse to say, but he needed to tell someone– needed to share this moment with the person who had been by his side through it all.

Jesse's response came almost instantly.

Jesse: *Really? How did it go?*

Wyatt smiled a little, his chest tightening with a mixture of nerves and excitement. He quickly typed back.

Wyatt: *Better than I expected. She didn't freak out. She said she's scared and doesn't understand everything, but she's trying. She said she's here for me.*

There was a brief pause before Jesse responded again, and Wyatt could almost feel the relief in his words.

Jesse: *That's great, Wyatt! I'm so glad. I know how nervous you were about telling her. It sounds like she's really making an effort.*

Wyatt felt his shoulders relax as he read Jesse's message. He hadn't realized just how much tension he'd been holding onto until now. It felt good–really good–to hear Jesse's reassurance, to know that he had someone to share this with.

Wyatt: *Yeah, I didn't expect her to be so understanding. She's worried about my dad, though. She doesn't know if he'll ever come around, and I'm scared he won't either.*

Jesse's response came quickly, as supportive as always.

Jesse: *That's understandable. But you don't have to deal with him right now. You told your mom, and she's on your side. That's a huge step. We'll figure out the rest when the time comes.*

Wyatt smiled at the message, feeling the warmth and support from Jesse radiating through the screen. Jesse had always known what to say, how to make everything seem less overwhelming.

Wyatt: *I don't think I could've done it without you. You've been my rock through all of this.*

The dots appeared almost immediately, and Jesse's response was quick and full of his usual kindness.

Jesse: *You give yourself too little credit. You were brave, Wyatt. I'm proud of you.*

Wyatt felt his chest tighten again, not from anxiety but from the overwhelming sense of gratitude he felt toward Jesse. He had been so scared to tell his mom, so worried that she wouldn't accept him, but knowing Jesse had his back gave him the strength he needed to push through.

Wyatt: *I'm just glad you've been here for me. I don't know how I would've gotten through this without you.*

Jesse's reply was soft, almost teasing, but still full of warmth.

Jesse: *You're stuck with me, so don't worry about that. We're in this together.*

Wyatt couldn't help but smile at the message. He'd been through so much with Jesse already, and knowing that Jesse wasn't going anywhere –that they were facing this together–made everything feel a little less terrifying.

Wyatt: *I'm scared about what's going to happen with my dad, but I feel better knowing I've got you and my mom on my side.*

Jesse's response was quick, filled with the kind of quiet determination Wyatt had come to rely on.

Jesse: *We'll take it one step at a time. You don't have to figure everything out right now. Just focus on this win–you told your mom, and she's on your side. That's huge.*

Wyatt nodded to himself as he read the message. Jesse was right. Telling his mom had been a massive step, and it had gone better than he could've hoped. His dad was still a looming threat, but for now, he didn't have to worry about that. He could just take it one day at a time.

Wyatt: *You're right. I'm just glad I'm not hiding anymore. It feels like I can finally breathe again.*

The dots appeared for a moment, and then Jesse's response came through, full of understanding.

Jesse: *I'm really happy for you, Wyatt. You deserve this. And you'll figure the rest out when you're ready.*

Wyatt leaned back against the headboard, staring up at the ceiling, a small smile tugging at his lips. Jesse had always been his steady, unwavering support through everything, and now, with his mom's tentative acceptance, he felt like he could handle whatever came next.

He typed one last message before putting his phone down, his heart full.

Wyatt: *Thanks for being there for me, Jesse. It means everything.*

Jesse's reply came almost instantly, simple but full of meaning.

Jesse: *Always.*

Wyatt stared at the screen for a few moments longer, feeling a sense of peace settle over him. Things weren't perfect, but they were better than they had been. His mom was trying, and Jesse was by his side. And for now, that was enough.

He closed his eyes, allowing himself to relax for the first time in what felt like days. He didn't have all the answers yet, but with Jesse and his mom supporting him, Wyatt knew he could handle whatever came next.

Chapter 37: A Weekend Away

Jesse couldn't stop glancing over at Wyatt in the passenger seat as they drove out of town, the excitement bubbling just beneath his calm exterior. They had been planning this weekend for days, days of mindless work at the pool, and now, as they headed further away from Brookwood and deeper into the hills, it finally felt real.

The late afternoon sun streamed through the windows, casting a golden glow across the landscape as the highway stretched out before them. Jesse's old, reliable car hummed along, packed with camping gear in the backseat. It wasn't fancy, but it was freedom—something they both desperately needed.

"You know," Wyatt said, breaking the comfortable silence between them, "I wasn't sure my mom would actually go for it."

Jesse glanced over, grinning. "Really? She seemed pretty on board when you asked her."

"Yeah, but she's never had to lie to my dad like this before," Wyatt replied, his voice softening. "I mean, she's been covering for me in little ways, but this is big. I half expected her to say no."

Jesse reached over and squeezed Wyatt's knee, feeling the warmth of his skin through his jeans. "She's trying, Wyatt. She wants you to be happy."

Wyatt smiled at that, a small but genuine smile. "Yeah. I think she's starting to get it, even if it's not easy for her. I think she knows I need this."

They fell into a comfortable silence again, the rhythmic hum of the car and the scenery passing by helping them relax. Jesse focused on the road, but his mind wandered to how different things felt now. It wasn't perfect–not by a long shot–but they were making progress. Wyatt had told his mom about them, Jesse's parents were okay with the trip, and now they were driving hours out of town, heading into the wilderness for a weekend where they didn't have to worry about anyone watching them, judging them, or forcing them to hide.

"I can't believe we're actually doing this," Wyatt said after a while, his voice laced with excitement. "Just you and me, no one else around. It feels... surreal."

Jesse smiled, feeling the same surge of anticipation. "Yeah, me too. It's gonna be nice to just... be. Without worrying about anyone seeing us."

Wyatt nodded, leaning his head back against the seat and closing his eyes for a moment. "No sneaking around. No pretending. Just us."

They had both needed this. The constant pressure of keeping their relationship hidden from Wyatt's dad, the rumors swirling around town, and the stress of going back to school had been weighing on them for weeks. But now, as the road stretched out before them, it felt like they were leaving all of that behind.

"You know what I'm looking forward to the most?" Wyatt asked, turning his head to look at Jesse.

"What?"

"Not having to look over my shoulder every time I want to hold your hand," Wyatt said with a grin. "Or kiss you."

Jesse laughed, his heart skipping a beat at the thought. "Yeah, that's going to be pretty great."

Wyatt chuckled, reaching over to take Jesse's hand. His fingers were warm, and Jesse gave them a squeeze, feeling a sense of calm wash over him. For so long, they had been forced to hide their affection, to sneak around like they were doing something wrong. But out here, in the middle of nowhere, none of that mattered. They could just be themselves.

"I'm not going to lie," Wyatt continued, his voice softer now, "I've been thinking about this trip all week. Just… being alone with you. No one around. No pressure. It feels like we can finally breathe."

Jesse nodded, feeling the same sense of relief. "Me too. It's gonna be nice to just… exist without worry."

They drove on in peaceful silence, the highway eventually giving way to winding country roads that led deeper into the forest. The trees grew thicker, casting long shadows across the road as the sun dipped lower in the sky. The further they got from Brookwood, the more relaxed they both became, the tension of their everyday lives slowly melting away.

It wasn't long before they reached the campsite–a quiet, secluded spot they had found online, far enough from the main camping areas to give them the privacy they craved. The site was nestled between a grove of tall trees, with a clear view of the mountains in the distance. It was perfect.

Jesse parked the car, and they both sat there for a moment, taking in the peacefulness of the place. The air was crisp, cooler than it had been back home, and the only sounds were the distant rustling of leaves and the soft chirping of birds.

"Wow," Wyatt said softly, his eyes scanning the campsite. "This is even better than I imagined."

"Right?" Jesse grinned, feeling a sense of accomplishment. "I thought we could set up over there," he pointed toward a flat patch of ground near the trees, "and have a fire pit here. There's even a trail that leads to a lake a little further down."

Wyatt looked over at him, his eyes full of warmth. "You planned this out pretty well, huh?"

Jesse shrugged, a little embarrassed. "I just wanted it to be perfect."

Wyatt leaned over and kissed him, soft and lingering, the warmth of his lips sending a jolt through Jesse. "It's already perfect," Wyatt whispered when he pulled back. "Because we're here together."

Jesse smiled, his heart swelling at the words. This was what he had been looking forward to–the freedom to kiss Wyatt without fear, to hold him without worrying who might see.

They got out of the car and started unloading the gear, setting up the tent and laying out their sleeping bags. It didn't take long to get everything organized, and once they were done, they stood back, admiring their work.

Wyatt stretched, his arms above his head, and Jesse couldn't help but notice how relaxed he looked, how different he seemed out here compared to when they were back in Brookwood. "This feels... good,"

Wyatt said, breathing in the fresh air. "Like we're miles away from everything."

Jesse nodded, feeling the same sense of calm. "That's because we are. No one to worry about. Just us."

They spent the next hour gathering wood for a fire, talking quietly as the sun dipped below the horizon, casting the sky in shades of orange and pink. As they worked, the conversation flowed easily–talking about school, their friends, and how things had been since Wyatt told his mom about them.

"I still can't believe she covered for me with my dad," Wyatt said as they sat down by the fire pit, their faces illuminated by the flickering flames. "I didn't think she had it in her."

"She loves you," Jesse said, leaning back against a log. "She's trying to understand. That's all you can ask for right now."

Wyatt nodded, poking the fire with a stick. "Yeah, I know. It's just... I wish things could be different with my dad. I hate that I have to hide this from him."

Jesse reached over, taking Wyatt's hand again. "We'll figure it out. Maybe he will come around. One step at a time."

Wyatt smiled at him, his eyes soft in the firelight. "Yeah. And for now... we have this, and it's perfect."

They sat in comfortable silence for a while, watching the fire crackle and pop, the stars slowly appearing in the night sky. For the first time in a long time, Jesse felt completely at ease. There were no walls between them, no secrets they had to keep. Just the two of them, together in the quiet of the wilderness.

"This weekend is going to be good for us," Wyatt said softly, his voice barely above a whisper. "It's what we need."

Jesse nodded, his heart full. "Yeah. It's exactly what we need."

As the fire burned down and the night grew darker, they settled into the tent, lying side by side in their sleeping bags. Wyatt reached for Jesse's hand, and they lay there in the quiet, listening to the sounds of the forest around them. It was peaceful, serene, and for the first time in a long time, they felt free.

"I wish we could stay like this forever," Wyatt murmured, his voice soft in the darkness.

"Me too," Jesse whispered back, squeezing Wyatt's hand. "I couldn't ask for anything more."

And in that moment, with the stars above them and the world far behind, they drifted off to sleep.

Chapter 38: A Day of Freedom

The soft light of the early morning sun filtered through the fabric of the tent, casting a warm glow over Wyatt and Jesse as they slowly stirred awake. Wyatt was the first to open his eyes, blinking sleepily as he realized he was wrapped in Jesse's arms, their bodies entwined in a way that felt both intimate and comforting. Jesse's breath was soft and steady against Wyatt's neck, and for a moment, Wyatt just lay there, soaking in the quiet peace of the morning.

They had fallen asleep like this, close and without worry, and Wyatt couldn't remember the last time he had slept so well. No tension, no anxiety, no need to hide. It was just the two of them, miles away from the weight of their everyday lives. Wyatt let out a contented sigh, pulling Jesse just a little closer, savoring the warmth of the embrace.

Eventually, Jesse stirred, his grip on Wyatt tightening for a moment before he woke up fully. He blinked, his eyes focusing on Wyatt, and a sleepy smile spread across his face.

"Morning," Jesse mumbled, his voice still thick with sleep.

"Morning," Wyatt replied, his own smile widening. "How'd you sleep?"

Jesse stretched, his body shifting against Wyatt's, and let out a satisfied hum. "Better than I have in… well, a long time. You?"

Wyatt nodded, brushing a lock of hair away from Jesse's forehead. "Same. I feel like I could stay here forever."

Jesse chuckled, his arms still wrapped around Wyatt. "I wouldn't mind that."

They lay there for a few more minutes, neither of them in any rush to leave the comfort of the tent, but eventually, the smell of the outdoors and the promise of breakfast lured them out of their cozy cocoon. They stretched and yawned as they stepped out into the crisp morning air, the forest around them waking up with the sound of birds chirping and leaves rustling in the breeze.

Jesse set to work getting the fire going again while Wyatt rummaged through their supplies, pulling out the bacon and eggs they had packed. The sky above was a brilliant blue, the morning sun casting a warm glow over the campsite as they worked together to prepare breakfast.

The scent of sizzling bacon soon filled the air, and Wyatt cracked the eggs into the pan, the fire crackling and popping as they cooked. Jesse handed him a cup of coffee, the steam rising into the cool morning air, and they sat side by side, listening to the sounds of nature around them.

"This is perfect," Jesse said quietly, his eyes scanning the trees. "Just us, out here. It feels like the world doesn't exist."

Wyatt smiled, taking a sip of his coffee. "It does feel like we're in our own little world, doesn't it? I don't think I've ever felt this... free."

Jesse nodded, leaning back against the log they were sitting on. "Yeah. It's like we can finally just be ourselves, without anyone watching or judging. I've missed that."

They ate their breakfast slowly, savoring each bite as they talked about nothing and everything. It was easy, the way they fell into conversation, the way they could just be together without any pretenses. Wyatt loved how natural it felt–like they'd been doing this forever.

Once breakfast was finished and the fire was doused, they packed a few things for their hike. Jesse had found a trail that wound through the forest and led to a ridge overlooking a valley, and they both couldn't wait to explore it.

As they started their hike, the air was cool and fresh, the scent of pine and earth filling their senses. The trail was peaceful, and the further they walked, the more relaxed they became. Jesse reached for Wyatt's hand, lacing their fingers together, and Wyatt's heart skipped a beat at the simple gesture.

It was so easy out here, away from everything. There was no need to check over their shoulders, no need to worry about who might be watching. They could just hold hands, talk, and enjoy each other's company without the constant fear of being seen.

"I could get used to this," Wyatt said with a grin, glancing over at Jesse as they walked along the trail, their hands swinging gently between them.

"Me too," Jesse replied, squeezing Wyatt's hand. "Just us and the trees."

They laughed, talked, and took in the beauty of the forest around them. The trail led them through dense groves of trees, across small streams, and finally up a steep incline to the ridge. When they reached the top, the view took their breath away–a sweeping panorama of the valley below, the mountains rising in the distance, and the sky stretched wide and endless above them.

Wyatt and Jesse stood there for a moment, hand in hand, soaking in the majesty of it all.

"Wow," Wyatt breathed, his eyes wide as he took in the sight. "This is... incredible."

Jesse nodded, a quiet smile on his face as he gazed out at the landscape. "Yeah. It's beautiful."

They stood there in silence for a while, just taking in the moment, before they sat down on a large rock near the edge of the ridge. Wyatt leaned into Jesse, their shoulders brushing as they sat side by side, and Jesse wrapped an arm around him, pulling him close.

"I wish we could stay here forever," Wyatt whispered, his voice barely audible over the sound of the wind.

Jesse rested his chin on Wyatt's shoulder, his voice equally soft. "Me too. But I'm so happy we have this."

They stayed up on the ridge for a long time, talking about the future, about school, and about their families. It was easy to open up out here, where the world felt far away and nothing seemed as complicated. Wyatt found himself sharing things with Jesse he hadn't told anyone else–his fears about his dad, his hopes for what life might look like once they were out of Brookwood, and the small moments that had made him realize just how much he cared about Jesse.

As the afternoon wore on, they made their way back down the trail, the sun beginning to dip lower in the sky. By the time they returned to camp, they were both tired but happy, the peacefulness of the day settling over them like a warm blanket.

That evening, they sat around the fire again, roasting marshmallows and making s'mores. The crackling flames cast a warm, flickering light over their faces as they laughed and talked, sharing stories about their lives, their childhoods, and the little things they hadn't yet had the chance to tell each other.

Jesse grinned as he bit into his s'more, the gooey marshmallow sticking to his fingers. "Okay, tell me something about you that no one else knows."

Wyatt chuckled, his own marshmallow a little too burnt but still delicious. "Hmm, okay. When I was a kid, I used to have this weird obsession with dinosaurs. Like, I knew everything about them. I even had a dinosaur bedspread."

Jesse laughed, imagining a young Wyatt surrounded by dinosaur toys and books. "That's adorable."

Wyatt shrugged, grinning. "Hey! It was pretty cool at the time."

Wyatt leaned back, his eyes fixed on Jesse. "Okay, your turn. What's something no one knows about you?"

Jesse looked thoughtful for a moment before a small smile tugged at his lips. "When I was around ten, I was terrified of swimming in lakes because I thought there were sharks in them. My older cousin told me there were freshwater sharks, and I believed him for way too long."

Wyatt burst out laughing, nearly dropping his marshmallow into the fire. "Freshwater sharks? Seriously?"

"Yep," Jesse said with a grin, shaking his head. "I was pretty gullible."

They kept trading stories like that, each one more ridiculous than the last, laughing until their sides hurt and the stars twinkled overhead. It was in these moments–sitting by the fire, sharing pieces of themselves with each other–that Wyatt realized just how much he had grown to care about Jesse. He felt completely comfortable, completely free, in a way he hadn't with anyone else.

The fire crackled softly as the night deepened around them. Jesse and Wyatt sat close to the glowing warmth, both lost in the quiet peace of the moment. The stars above twinkled brightly, and the cool air settled in around the campsite, but the heat from the fire and the sweetness of the s'mores made everything feel perfect.

Wyatt leaned back, his hands sticky with marshmallow, a grin spreading across his face as he looked at Jesse. "Okay, your turn," Wyatt said, still laughing from their last round of childhood confessions. "What's something embarrassing no one knows about you?"

Jesse thought for a moment, a mischievous smile playing at his lips. "Well, there was this one time I got my hand stuck in a vending machine at school. I was trying to reach for a candy bar, and I ended up having to get the janitor to come and pull me out. Took almost twenty minutes."

Wyatt laughed, shaking his head. "You really got stuck in a vending machine?"

"Yep," Jesse replied, laughing with him. "And the worst part? I never got the candy bar."

Jesse leaned back on his elbows, a playful smile tugging at his lips. "Alright, Wyatt. Your turn. You have to have at least one good embarrassing story. Spill it."

Wyatt chuckled, shaking his head. "Oh, man. I don't know if I'm ready for this level of humiliation."

Jesse nudged him gently with his knee. "It can't be that bad."

Wyatt groaned, rubbing the back of his neck, clearly debating whether or not to share. "Alright, fine. But don't judge me, okay?"

"No promises," Jesse teased.

Wyatt took a deep breath, glancing at the fire as if it might somehow distract him from the cringe-worthy memory. "So... this happened when I was in middle school. I was at a swim meet, and I was trying to impress this guy on the team who I thought was, like, the coolest person ever. You know the type–good at everything, always getting the most attention, that sort of thing."

Jesse raised an eyebrow. "Okay, I'm intrigued. Go on."

"Anyway," Wyatt continued, "I was trying to show off, which was already a terrible idea because I'm not exactly what you'd call a 'show-off' type. But, you know, I thought I'd make an impression. So, after my race, I decided to do this victory dive into the pool, thinking I'd look all cool and athletic."

Jesse grinned, already sensing where this was going.

Wyatt sighed dramatically. "Except, I completely misjudged the edge of the pool. I went to jump in, but my foot slipped on the wet tile, and instead of this graceful dive, I ended up belly-flopping right into the water. Like, full-on smack—loud enough that everyone in the entire pool area turned to look."

Jesse burst out laughing. "Oh no!"

"Yeah, and to make it worse," Wyatt added, his face flushing even in the firelight, "when I came up for air, my swim trunks had completely come off. I mean, they were floating halfway across the pool."

Jesse doubled over, laughing harder. "Wait, seriously?"

"Yup. I had to swim across the pool, completely naked, with everyone watching, and grab my trunks like nothing was wrong. I thought I was going to die of embarrassment."

Jesse wiped a tear from his eye, still laughing. "What did the guy you were trying to impress say?"

Wyatt shook his head, smiling ruefully. "He was the first one to start laughing. But then, afterward, he came over and was like, 'That was one hell of a dive.' So, I guess I made an impression after all, just not the one I was going for."

Jesse grinned, leaning closer to Wyatt. "I think it's a great story. At least you can laugh about it now."

Wyatt laughed, giving Jesse a sideways glance. "Yeah, well, I still get a little embarrassed when I think about it. I think it might be a little worse than getting your hand stuck in a vending machine."

Jesse nudged him again, this time more affectionately. "Don't worry. I think it's cute."

Wyatt chuckled, the sound carrying in the quiet night. The campfire flickered between them, casting soft shadows across their faces, and for a moment, everything felt easy and light. It was the kind of freedom they had both craved—just the two of them, miles away from the weight of the world. Sharing stories no one else knows.

But as the fire burned lower, and the night air grew cooler, the conversation shifted. The laughter faded, replaced by a comfortable silence. They sat there for a while, just enjoying the warmth of the fire and each other's presence, until Jesse glanced over at Wyatt.

"We should probably clean up before bed," Jesse said, breaking the quiet. "Can't go to sleep covered in marshmallow and dirt."

Wyatt nodded, though he hesitated for a moment, glancing at the small shower stalls next to the restrooms. The tension between them shifted, something unspoken hanging in the air.

"Yeah, you're right," Wyatt replied, rubbing his hands together. "But, uh... do you want to–" He trailed off, unsure of how to finish the sentence.

Jesse glanced at Wyatt, catching the same awkward energy that had suddenly filled the air. He could feel the weight of the question lingering between them: *Should they shower together?* The idea had been hanging over them all night, but now that the moment had arrived, neither of them seemed brave enough to bring it up directly.

"We could... I mean," Jesse started, then quickly backtracked, his heart beating faster. "I can go first, or... you can."

Wyatt let out a soft chuckle, clearly feeling the same tension. "Yeah, maybe we just... go in the separate ones?"

"Yeah, separate," Jesse agreed quickly, though the word felt heavier than he intended. "That's probably best."

They stood up, moving toward the showers, but the awkwardness followed them, making everything feel just a little off. As they each stepped into their respective stalls, Jesse couldn't help but think about how close they had come to something more–how the unspoken question of whether or not to shower together had left both of them hesitating.

The water hit his skin, warm and soothing, washing away the dirt and sweat of the day, but Jesse's mind was elsewhere. He could hear the soft sound of water running from Wyatt's stall, just a few feet away, and the thought of them standing there, so close yet so far, gnawed at him. He wanted to be with Wyatt, to feel that closeness again, but something had held them both back.

Wyatt, too, felt the tension. As he stood under the stream of water, he couldn't help but wonder why he hadn't just suggested they shower together. It wasn't like they hadn't been close before–after all, they had spent the entire day holding hands, laughing, sharing stories, not to mention the time they went skinny dipping in the clearing back home. But this felt different. There was an intimacy to it that neither of them had been quite ready to face.

The awkward tension lingered as they finished up, both wishing they had been braver, but neither wanting to admit it in the moment.

When they emerged from the showers, drying off in the cool night air, the silence between them was thick. They exchanged a few awkward glances, but neither said much as they made their way back to the tent, the fire now just glowing embers in the distance.

They crawled into the tent, settling into their sleeping bags side by side, but the unspoken tension still hung in the air. Wyatt lay there for a few minutes, staring up at the fabric of the tent, his mind racing. He wanted to say something, to break the silence, but he wasn't sure how. The hesitation from earlier was gnawing at him, and finally, he couldn't hold it in any longer.

"Can I tell you something?" Wyatt asked softly, his voice breaking the stillness of the tent.

Jesse turned to look at him, their faces just inches apart in the dim light. "Yeah, of course. What's up?"

Wyatt hesitated for a second, then took a deep breath, his voice barely above a whisper. "I... I wish we would have showered together."

Jesse blinked, his heart skipping a beat at the admission. A small, relieved smile tugged at the corners of his mouth as he processed Wyatt's words.

"Yeah," Jesse replied quietly, his own voice soft and full of emotion. "I do too."

The air in the tent was thick with the weight of Wyatt's words, the soft admission hanging between them like a thread that neither of them wanted to break. Jesse lay on his side, facing Wyatt, their bodies close but not quite touching. His heart raced in his chest, his pulse quickening as he replayed what Wyatt had just said: *I wish we would have showered together.*

Jesse swallowed hard, the tension from earlier still lingering, but now it felt different. It wasn't awkward–it was charged with something more, something deeper. He could feel the pull between them, the unspoken desire they had both been holding back. And for the first time, he felt brave enough to say something.

"Wyatt," Jesse whispered, his voice soft but steady in the quiet of the tent. "Can I kiss you?"

Wyatt's eyes flickered in the dim light, a small, breathless smile tugging at the corners of his mouth. He nodded, his voice barely above a whisper. "Yeah. I'd like that."

Jesse closed the small distance between them, his heart pounding as his lips met Wyatt's in a gentle, tentative kiss. The warmth of Wyatt's mouth against his sent a shiver down his spine, and for a moment, everything else melted away. It was just the two of them, lost in the quiet intimacy of the moment.

The kiss deepened, growing more passionate with each passing second. Jesse's hands found their way to Wyatt's waist, pulling him closer, and Wyatt responded by threading his fingers through Jesse's hair, their bodies inching toward each other as the intensity between them built.

There was a new kind of electricity in the air now–one that neither of them could ignore. The kisses grew hungrier, their touches more urgent, as they explored each other with a mixture of curiosity and longing. It was as if all the tension from the day, all the unsaid things, were finally being released, and they both knew where this was headed.

Jesse's breath hitched as Wyatt's hands moved over his back, pulling him closer still, their bodies pressing together. It felt like everything they had been holding back was finally pouring out, and the need to be closer, to feel more, became undeniable.

"Jesse," Wyatt murmured against his lips, his voice thick with emotion, "I... I think I want more."

Jesse pulled back slightly, searching Wyatt's eyes, his own heart pounding with the same desire. "Me too," he whispered, his voice trembling slightly. "But... are you sure? We can take it slow."

Wyatt nodded, his gaze steady and full of warmth. "I'm sure. I want this. With you."

Jesse's heart swelled at the words, and he leaned in to kiss Wyatt again, this time with more certainty. As their kisses deepened, their hands explored each other's bodies, the desire between them growing stronger with each passing moment. It was slow, deliberate, and full of tenderness–both of them taking their time, wanting to savor every second of this first time together.

Wyatt reached for his bag, pulling out what they needed with a small, nervous laugh. "I, uh, brought these just in case," he admitted, his cheeks flushing slightly.

Jesse smiled, his heart swelling with affection. "Good thinking."

What followed was a shared experience of discovery, full of soft whispers and tentative movements. The air between them was charged with something electric, something both of them had been feeling for weeks but hadn't fully acted on until now. They lay close, facing each other, their breaths synchronized as the anticipation between them built.

Jesse felt his heart pounding in his chest, his entire body tingling with a mix of excitement and nervousness. He could see the same uncertainty mirrored in Wyatt's eyes, but also the same hunger–the desire to explore this new territory together. Their hands found each other, fingers intertwining for a moment, grounding them both in the shared experience.

They started kissing again, slow, almost shy, as if neither of them wanted to break the fragile silence that hung in the air. Wyatt's hand slid up Jesse's arm, his touch featherlight, as though he was afraid of going too fast. But when their eyes met again, Jesse gave a small nod, letting Wyatt know that this felt right. That he wanted this.

Wyatt's lips met Jesse's in a kiss that was soft at first, a gentle press of lips that deepened with each passing second. It wasn't hurried; it wasn't rushed. Instead, it was deliberate–each movement measured, as if they were savoring every second. Jesse let out a quiet sigh as Wyatt's hand slid down to his waist, pulling him closer, their bodies now flush against each other.

Wyatt's movements were careful, tender, each shift slow, as though he was afraid of going too far, of losing the delicate balance they had created. They moved together, a slow, building rhythm, the sensation between them growing, deepening, but always guided by care. The vulnerability between them was tangible, unspoken, but it filled the space as they discovered this new closeness.

Jesse closed his eyes, letting himself fall into the moment, trusting Wyatt completely. There was no rush–only the steady, quiet understanding that what they shared now was more than physical. It was emotional, a connection that had been woven between them over time, and now, it was fully realized.

Jesse's breath hitched when Wyatt's hand traveled lower, lingering just at the edge of his waistline. His touch was light, teasing, as though Wyatt was testing boundaries, feeling for the silent signals Jesse gave. Jesse's eyes fluttered closed, his heart pounding in his chest, as he leaned into Wyatt's touch, giving him permission without a word.

Wyatt's fingers moved lower, slipping beneath the fabric of Jesse's waistband with a quiet, confidence. The touch was both gentle and commanding as if Wyatt wanted to explore but also ensure Jesse was comfortable. Jesse exhaled sharply, his body reacting instantly to the intimacy of Wyatt's hand. Every movement, every brush of Wyatt's skin against his own, sent a wave of pleasure coursing through him, heightening the connection between them.

Jesse's own hands wandered, sliding up Wyatt's sides and down the curve of his back, feeling the firm muscle beneath the soft skin, eventually landing beneath his waistband. The more he touched, the more he wanted to explore, to feel every inch of Wyatt's body against his own. His fingers pressed into Wyatt's hips, pulling him closer, until there was no space left between them, their bodies fully aligned. Jesse could feel Wyatt's breath, quick and unsteady, against his neck.

Wyatt's hand found Jesse's, their fingers intertwining, and in that moment, Jesse knew: this was what it meant to be seen, to be fully known. There was nothing more intimate than this, and as their bodies moved together, it wasn't just about what they were doing–it was about what they meant to each other.

They moved together slowly, carefully, always checking in with each other with every touch, every look. Wyatt's hands explored Jesse's body as though he was memorizing every inch of him, his fingertips tracing patterns across Jesse's chest and stomach, eliciting quiet gasps from him in return. Jesse could feel the tension building between them, the anticipation growing with each second.

Wyatt's lips moved down to Jesse's neck, placing soft, open-mouthed kisses along his throat, making Jesse's breath hitch in his throat. His hands roamed lower, brushing against Jesse's hips, his touch sending more shivers down Jesse's spine. Jesse closed his eyes, letting himself get lost in the sensation, the feeling of Wyatt's hands, his mouth, his body pressed against his.

There was a moment of hesitation, a pause in their movements as Wyatt pulled back slightly, his eyes searching Jesse's face for any sign of doubt or discomfort. "Are you okay?" Wyatt whispered, his voice barely audible, filled with concern.

Jesse opened his eyes, meeting Wyatt's gaze, his heart racing. He could feel the vulnerability in Wyatt's question, the fear that maybe this was too much too soon. But Jesse knew–knew in his heart–that this was exactly where he wanted to be, with exactly the person he wanted to be with.

"I'm okay," Jesse whispered back, his voice soft but sure. "I want this."

Wyatt's expression softened, and he nodded, leaning down to kiss Jesse again, this time with more urgency. The hesitation from before seemed to melt away as they both gave in to the moment, their bodies moving together in a rhythm that felt natural, instinctive. The world around them seemed to fade away, leaving only the two of them, connected in a way they had never been before.

As the intensity built, so did the emotional connection between them. This wasn't just about the physical—it was about the trust they had in each other, the safety they felt in each other's arms. Every touch, every kiss was a promise, a silent vow that they were in this together, that they were there for each other in every possible way.

Jesse's hands roamed over Wyatt's back, his fingers digging into his skin as the tension inside him grew. He could feel every inch of Wyatt against him, the heat of his skin, the weight of his body pressing him into the softness of his sleeping bag. It was overwhelming in the best way possible, every sensation heightened, every touch electric.

Wyatt kissed him again, deeper this time, their tongues brushing against each other as they lost themselves in the moment. Jesse moaned softly into Wyatt's mouth, his body arching into him as the intensity of their connection deepened. He could feel the emotions swirling inside him—desire, vulnerability, trust—all blending together in a way that felt almost intoxicating.

The moment they came together was slow, unhurried, as if they had all the time in the world. Jesse felt his body adjust, his heart pounding in his chest, but it wasn't fear—it was a rush of connection, of something deeper than anything he'd ever known. Wyatt's hands were on him, grounding him, guiding them both through the newness of the experience.

It was new for both of them, this level of intimacy, this intensity of connection, but there was an unspoken understanding between them. They didn't need to rush; they didn't need to force anything. Every touch, every kiss was intentional, full of meaning, full of the trust and vulnerability that had been building between them for months.

And when they finally reached that point of no return, when the tension between them snapped and they gave in to the moment, it wasn't just about the release. It was about everything they had shared– every look, every word, every quiet moment that had led them to this. It was about the way they trusted each other completely, the way they felt safe in each other's arms.

As they lay there afterward, their bodies still entwined, their breathing slowly returning to normal, there was a quiet sense of peace between them. Wyatt's hand rested on Jesse's chest, his thumb gently stroking the skin there as they both lay in comfortable silence, basking in the afterglow of the moment they had just shared.

Jesse turned his head to look at Wyatt, a small smile tugging at the corners of his lips. "That was..."

Wyatt smiled back, his eyes soft with affection. "Yeah," he murmured, leaning in to press a soft kiss to Jesse's lips. "It was."

There were no more words needed between them. They had said everything they needed to say through their actions, through the way they had treated each other with such care and tenderness. And in that moment, as they lay together in the quiet stillness of the night, Jesse knew that this was more than just a physical connection–it was something deeper, something real.

And for the first time in a long time, Jesse felt like he was exactly where he was meant to be.

It was everything they had wanted, and more.

They lay there for a while, the silence between them comfortable and full of meaning. Neither of them felt the need to rush or fill the space with words. It was enough just to be together, to feel the warmth of each other's presence, knowing that they had just shared something profound.

"I feel so close to you," Jesse murmured after a while, his head resting on Wyatt's chest. "Like... I didn't think it was possible to feel this connected to someone."

Wyatt smiled, his hand still tracing soft patterns on Jesse's back. "Me too," he whispered. "I didn't think it would feel like this."

The night stretched on around them, but in the quiet of the tent, everything felt still. Jesse could hear the soft rhythm of Wyatt's breathing, the steady beat of his heart beneath his cheek, and it filled him with a sense of peace he hadn't known before.

And then, just as Jesse was starting to drift off, Wyatt's voice broke the silence again, quiet and full of vulnerability.

"Jesse... can I tell you something?"

Jesse lifted his head, his eyes meeting Wyatt's in the dim light. "Of course."

Wyatt hesitated for a moment, his gaze soft and full of emotion. "I think... I think I love you."

The words hung in the air between them, and for a second, Jesse's heart stopped. He hadn't expected it–not so soon–but hearing Wyatt say it, seeing the honesty in his eyes, made everything feel right.

A slow smile spread across Jesse's face as he leaned in to kiss Wyatt softly, his heart full. "I think I love you too."

They lay there in the quiet of the tent, holding each other close, the weight of their words settling over them like a warm blanket. It wasn't rushed, or forced–it was simply the truth. They had found something special in each other, something that neither of them had been expecting, but now that it was here, it felt undeniable.

And as they drifted off to sleep, wrapped in each other's arms, they knew that this was just the beginning of something incredible. Something real.

Chapter 39: Coming Back to Reality

The car rumbled along the familiar roads of Brookwood as Wyatt and Jesse made their way back from their weekend away. The closer they got to town, the more the real world began to settle back over them, but neither of them was quite ready to let go of the peaceful bubble they had been living in. The weekend had been perfect—everything they needed and more—and now they were holding on to those memories like a shield, ready to face the challenges that lay ahead.

As they pulled into Jesse's driveway, both of them exchanged a look, silently acknowledging that it was time to return to reality. Jesse's parents were home, and as they got out of the car, Jesse spotted his mom waving at them from the porch.

"Back to the grind," Jesse muttered, though there was a smile on his face.

"Yeah," Wyatt agreed, returning Jesse's smile. "But at least we had that time together."

Jesse nodded, the warmth of their weekend still fresh in his mind. "Yeah. And no matter what happens, we've got each other."

Wyatt reached out and squeezed Jesse's hand, a small but meaningful gesture, before they both headed inside. The moment felt both heavy and light—like they were stepping back into their normal lives, but with a deeper connection than before.

The next day, they were back at work at the pool. It didn't take long for the familiar rhythm of their jobs to take over–the chatter of kids splashing in the water, the heat of the sun beating down on them, the hum of the lifeguard whistles blowing in the distance. Jesse worked at the concession stand while Wyatt sat perched in his lifeguard chair, but even with the busyness of the day, they shared quick glances and knowing smiles.

By the end of their shift, Jesse's phone buzzed with a message from one of their coworkers, Tori.

Tori: *Hey! Some of us are heading out for bowling after work. You guys down?*

Jesse showed Wyatt the message, and Wyatt's eyes lit up. "Bowling sounds fun. You in?"

Jesse grinned. "Yeah, let's do it."

They hadn't spent much time hanging out with their coworkers outside of work, but the idea of doing something fun–something that could help ease them back into their routine–sounded perfect.

That evening, they drove to the next town over, where there was a small but lively bowling alley. Tori, along with a couple of other coworkers–Matt, Rachel, and Evan–were already there when Wyatt and Jesse arrived. The lights inside the alley were dimmed, with neon lighting casting a colorful glow over the lanes, and the sound of pins crashing echoed in the background.

"Hey, you made it!" Tori called out as they approached, waving them over.

"Wouldn't miss it," Jesse said, smiling as he and Wyatt joined the group.

They spent the first hour laughing and bowling, the energy light and carefree. Jesse found himself relaxing in a way he hadn't expected–surrounded by his friends, and more importantly, by Wyatt. They were in a different town, away from the familiar faces of Brookwood, and for the first time, Jesse felt like they might be able to be themselves without fear.

As they finished up their second round of bowling, the conversation shifted, and Tori leaned back in her seat, eyeing Jesse and Wyatt with a knowing look.

"So," she began, a grin playing on her lips, "you two seem pretty close."

Jesse felt his stomach flip, and he glanced at Wyatt, who shot him a nervous but encouraging smile. They had been thinking about this moment–about telling their coworkers the truth–but now that it was here, Jesse's heart raced.

Wyatt shifted slightly, then spoke up, his voice steady but quiet. "Yeah, we are. Actually... we wanted to tell you guys something."

Tori, along with Matt, Rachel, and Evan, all looked at them expectantly. Jesse swallowed hard, feeling the weight of the moment settle over him, but Wyatt gave his hand a reassuring squeeze under the table. That small touch gave him the courage he needed.

"We're together," Jesse said, his voice a little shaky but filled with resolve. "Wyatt and I... we're dating."

There was a brief pause—just a heartbeat of silence—and then Tori broke out into a wide smile. "Oh my god, that's awesome!" she exclaimed, her voice filled with genuine excitement. "I knew something was going on between you two!"

Jesse blinked, a little stunned by how easily the words had been received. Matt, Rachel, and Evan quickly joined in, their faces lighting up with smiles and laughter.

"That's so cool!" Rachel said, clapping her hands. "I'm so happy for you guys!"

"Seriously," Matt chimed in, grinning. "You two are great together. I'm glad you told us."

Evan, who had been quiet, smiled warmly at them both. "Yeah, man. That's great. No need to hide it—we've got your backs."

Jesse felt a flood of relief wash over him, the tension that had been building inside him for so long finally breaking. Wyatt let out a soft laugh, his own shoulders relaxing as he looked around at their friends.

"Thanks, guys," Wyatt said, his voice full of gratitude. "We weren't sure how you'd take it, but... it feels good to be open about it."

Tori raised her drink, grinning. "Well, I say this calls for a celebration. To Wyatt and Jesse!"

Everyone raised their glasses, and Jesse couldn't stop the smile from spreading across his face. It felt surreal—being able to say it out loud, to share their relationship with people who genuinely supported them. For so long, they had been hiding, worrying about what others might think, but here, in this small moment, it didn't feel scary at all.

As the evening went on, the conversation flowed easily. They talked, joked, and bowled a few more rounds, but now, there was an added layer of freedom to everything. Jesse and Wyatt no longer had to pretend or hide; they could be themselves, and their friends accepted them wholeheartedly.

Later, as they were getting ready to leave, Jesse and Wyatt found themselves walking out of the bowling alley together, their hands brushing lightly as they stepped into the cool night air. The relief and joy of the night still lingered between them, and Jesse felt lighter than he had in days.

"Feels good, doesn't it?" Wyatt said quietly, glancing over at Jesse.

Jesse nodded, a smile playing at his lips. "Yeah. It feels... right."

Wyatt stopped for a moment, turning to face Jesse fully. "I wasn't sure how they'd react, but that was amazing. I'm glad we told them."

"Me too," Jesse replied, feeling the warmth of the moment settle over him. "It's nice to know we have people on our side."

Wyatt smiled, his eyes softening as he looked at Jesse. "We do. And we've got each other."

Jesse felt his heart swell at the words, and without thinking, he leaned in and kissed Wyatt softly, the gesture simple but full of meaning. It was a kiss of relief, of gratitude, of finally being able to be themselves.

As they pulled away, Wyatt grinned. "I think this is the start of something really good, Jesse."

Jesse nodded, his smile widening. "Yeah. I think so too."

And as they walked to the car, hand in hand, they both knew that no matter what challenges lay ahead, they had each other–and the support of those who mattered most. For the first time, it felt like everything was falling into place.

Chapter 40: The Consequences of Being Seen

The sun beat down on the pool as the familiar sounds of splashing water and children's laughter filled the air. Jesse and Wyatt had fallen back into the rhythm of their workday, trying to hold on to the freedom and peace they'd felt during their weekend away. After coming out to their coworkers during the bowling night, they both felt a sense of relief–a weight off their shoulders, at least with the people who mattered most to them.

But as the day wore on, something shifted. Jesse noticed a group of teens walk into the pool area. It was the group that had seen them in the pool after hours. His stomach tightened, and he shot a glance toward Wyatt, who was perched up in his lifeguard chair, scanning the pool as usual. Wyatt hadn't noticed them yet, but Jesse could already sense that something was coming.

The teens were louder this time, their presence more brazen as they walked closer to the lifeguard stand. Jesse tried to keep his eyes on his work at the concession stand, but he couldn't help but glance over as the group made their way toward Wyatt.

It started with a few snickers, low whispers exchanged between them, but then one of the teens–tall, with a smug look on his face–called out to Wyatt, loud enough for others around the pool to hear.

"Hey, Wyatt," the teen sneered. "How's your little boyfriend doing? You two planning another pool date after hours?"

Wyatt stiffened, his knuckles turning white as he gripped the armrest of his lifeguard chair. His eyes stayed on the pool, but it was clear the comment had hit its mark.

The others snickered, emboldened by their friend's words. "Yeah, are you guys gonna start making out again? 'Cause no one wants to see that."

Jesse's heart sank. His pulse quickened, and he felt the heat rising to his face as he watched the scene unfold. A few parents sitting nearby exchanged glances, some murmuring quietly among themselves, while others looked outright uncomfortable.

Wyatt clenched his jaw, his voice tight as he called down to them. "Knock it off. You're here to swim, not cause trouble."

But the teens weren't done. One of them, a younger boy with a baseball cap, laughed loudly. "Yeah, but it's hard to swim when we're stuck watching the lifeguard and his boyfriend play house. Maybe you should find somewhere else to do that fag stuff."

Jesse felt his hands tremble with anger, his blood boiling at the words. He could see the discomfort spreading around the pool. Parents were starting to glance over, whispering to each other. A mother nearby gathered her kids and stood up, walking toward the exit with a frown.

"I don't want you around that," she muttered to her children as they passed by. "Let's go."

The scene escalated quickly. More families began pulling their kids from the pool, some glaring at Wyatt and Jesse as they left, while others simply looked uncomfortable and hurried their children out without saying anything. Jesse could feel the judgment radiating from them, and it stung more than he'd anticipated.

Some were clearly leaving because of the teens causing a scene, but others... others were leaving because of him and Wyatt.

The lifeguards and other workers stood awkwardly by, unsure of how to intervene, but it was clear that the damage had already been done. Jesse looked toward Wyatt, who had finally climbed down from his chair, his expression tight with frustration and embarrassment.

Before they could exchange a word, Mr. Stevens, the pool manager, emerged from his office, his face set in a stern, unreadable expression. "Boys... time to leave! Get out of the pool and head home. We will not tolerate disruptions."

He motioned for Jesse and Wyatt to follow him, and the two of them exchanged a brief, pained glance before they complied.

They were led into the small, stuffy pool office, the door closing behind them with a soft click. Mr. Stevens leaned back against his desk, folding his arms over his chest as he sighed heavily. The tension in the room was palpable, and Jesse's heart raced as he braced himself for what was coming.

"Look," Mr. Stevens began, his tone weary, "I didn't want to have this conversation, but it's clear that we need to address what just happened out there."

Wyatt remained silent, his fists clenched at his sides. Jesse, standing next to him, could feel the frustration radiating from him, and he shared it. This wasn't fair, but they both knew what was coming.

"The behavior from those teens," Mr. Stevens continued, rubbing the bridge of his nose, "was completely out of line. I don't tolerate that kind of thing. But the problem is, it's not just about those kids."

Jesse shifted uncomfortably. "What do you mean?"

Mr. Stevens sighed again, looking down at the floor for a moment before meeting their eyes. "Parents are talking. They've been talking for a while, and what happened out there just now? It didn't help. Some families are uncomfortable with... the situation between you two."

Wyatt's voice was sharp, cutting through the thick air in the room. "You mean they're uncomfortable because we're together."

Mr. Stevens looked pained, but didn't deny it. "This is a small, conservative town. People talk, and not everyone is as open-minded as they should be. We've already had complaints from parents, and... well, families are starting to pull their kids out. It's affecting business."

"So what are you saying?" Jesse asked, his voice strained. "You want us to leave because we're making people uncomfortable?"

Mr. Stevens hesitated, then nodded slowly. "I know you both were planning to leave in a few weeks to go back to school. I think it's best if you finish up a little early."

Wyatt stared at Mr. Stevens in disbelief, his eyes flashing with anger. "You're firing us because we're gay?"

"I'm not firing you," Mr. Stevens replied quickly. "I'm suggesting that you leave early for your own sake. Look, I don't agree with the way those teens were acting, but I can't control how the parents feel. If they keep pulling their kids from the pool, it's going to hurt business. You are both welcome to work here next summer. Things have just gotten out of hand"

Wyatt clenched his fists tighter, his knuckles white. Jesse could feel the anger and hurt bubbling inside him too, but there was a sense of helplessness to it. They had known this might happen eventually–the town wasn't exactly known for its acceptance–but it didn't make the sting any less painful.

"Fine," Wyatt said through gritted teeth. "We'll leave."

Mr. Stevens shifted uncomfortably, but there was nothing more to say. The decision had already been made, and it was clear that they weren't going to win this battle. He opened the door to let them out, his expression still filled with awkward discomfort.

"Just know that I didn't want it to come to this," he said quietly. "You're both good workers. But this is just how it is around here."

Wyatt didn't respond. He walked out of the office, and Jesse followed, his heart heavy with frustration and hurt. They made their way toward the locker room in silence, the sting of their dismissal hanging in the air between them.

As they emptied their lockers, packing up the few belongings they had stored there over the summer, Jesse finally broke the silence.

"I can't believe this," Jesse said, his voice low but filled with emotion. "We didn't do anything wrong, and we're the ones who have to leave."

Wyatt slammed his locker shut, his eyes flashing with frustration. "Yeah, well, that's how this town works. People like us don't fit in here."

Jesse looked at him, his chest tight with emotion. "We'll get out of here soon enough. College is just a few weeks away. We'll be somewhere where people don't care about this."

Wyatt nodded, but the weight of their situation still pressed heavily on him. "Yeah. But it's not just the town I'm worried about."

Jesse knew exactly what Wyatt meant. He could see the fear and frustration in his eyes, and he knew that Wyatt wasn't just worried about what had happened at the pool. He was worried about what would happen when his dad found out.

They left the locker room together, walking toward the parking lot, but instead of heading home, they made a silent agreement to drive to their favorite spot—Wyatt's secret hideaway in the woods where they had spent so many quiet moments together. It was the only place where they could be themselves without fear of being judged.

The drive was quiet, but when they reached the familiar clearing and parked the car, Wyatt let out a long, shaky breath.

"I don't know what to do, Jesse," Wyatt admitted as they sat on the grass, the trees towering above them. "My dad's going to find out why I was let go. He'll know it's because of us."

Jesse reached out, placing a comforting hand on Wyatt's knee. "We can't keep hiding forever, Wyatt. Maybe... maybe it's time to tell him the truth."

Wyatt stared at the ground for a long moment, his jaw clenched. "I don't know how he's going to react. I'm scared, Jesse. I don't want to lose my family."

Jesse squeezed his knee, his voice soft but filled with quiet strength. "I know. But we can't keep living like this. We deserve to be who we are, without hiding."

Wyatt looked up at him, his eyes filled with uncertainty but also with determination. "You're right. I can't keep lying. I have to come clean with him. I have to see what happens."

Jesse nodded, his heart swelling with pride for Wyatt's decision. "No matter what, I'm here for you. We'll face it together."

Wyatt leaned into Jesse, resting his head on his shoulder as they sat in the quiet of the woods, the weight of the world pressing down on them but the strength of their connection holding them steady.

"I'll tell him," Wyatt whispered. "I don't know what's going to happen, but I can't keep hiding anymore."

And as the sun dipped lower in the sky, casting long shadows across the clearing, Jesse held Wyatt close, knowing that whatever came next, they would face it together.

Chapter 41: The Morning After

The soft morning light filtered through the curtains of Jesse's bedroom as he lay there, staring at the ceiling. The weight of the previous day still clung to him, the sting of being let go from the pool hanging heavy in his chest. The silence of the house only seemed to amplify his thoughts—everything that had happened with Wyatt, the confrontation with the teens, the conversation with Mr. Stevens.

Jesse knew that today he would have to tell his parents. They had been nothing but supportive since he came out to them, but explaining why he was let go from his job was going to be tough. He wasn't even sure how to put it into words. Still, he couldn't hide it from them. They deserved to know the truth.

With a deep breath, Jesse pushed the covers off and got dressed. He could already smell the coffee brewing in the kitchen, and the low murmur of his parents' voices told him they were already up. He lingered in the hallway for a moment, mentally preparing himself for the conversation that was about to unfold.

When he finally stepped into the kitchen, his parents were sitting at the table, his dad flipping through the morning paper while his mom sipped from her coffee cup. They both looked up when he entered, smiling warmly.

"Morning, Jess," his mom said, her voice light. "You're up early for someone who doesn't have work today."

Jesse hesitated, his heart pounding as he took a seat at the table. He wasn't sure how to begin, but he knew he needed to say it.

"Actually," he began, his voice a little shaky, "I don't have work today because… well, I don't have work anymore."

His dad lowered the newspaper, his brow furrowing in confusion. "What do you mean?"

Jesse glanced between his parents, feeling the weight of the words before they even left his mouth. "Mr. Stevens… he let me and Wyatt go yesterday."

The room fell silent, the tension thickening in the air. His mom set her coffee cup down, her eyes widening. "What? Why? What happened?"

Jesse swallowed hard, his throat tight. "It's because of those teens who've been giving us trouble. They showed up again yesterday and started making homophobic remarks about me and Wyatt, calling us some pretty messed up stuff. Some of the parents got uncomfortable and started leaving, and Mr. Stevens said it was affecting business. So he asked us to leave early… because we're gay."

His parents exchanged a glance, their expressions shifting from confusion to anger. His dad's jaw clenched, and his mom's face flushed with frustration.

"That's completely unacceptable," his dad said, his voice sharp with disbelief. "How could Mr. Stevens allow something like that to happen? You didn't do anything wrong!"

Jesse nodded, feeling the hurt and frustration well up again. "I know. But he said that parents were complaining, and he didn't want to risk losing more families. So… he let us go."

His mom shook her head, her eyes filled with a mix of anger and sadness. "That's not fair, Jesse. You deserve better than that. I can't believe he would do that, especially in a place that's supposed to be for the community."

Jesse's dad leaned back in his chair, rubbing his temples as he tried to process the news. "I want to talk to Mr. Stevens myself. He has no right to treat you like that just because some narrow-minded people don't approve of who you are. We could sue!"

Jesse reached out, placing a hand on his dad's arm. "Dad, it's okay. I mean, it's not okay, but... there's not much we can do about it now. I only have a couple of weeks left before school starts anyway."

His mom's eyes softened, though the worry was still evident. "I guess it might be for the best, Jesse. As much as it hurts to be let go like that, at least you won't have to deal with those awful people anymore."

Jesse nodded, his heart heavy. "Yeah, maybe you're right."

There was a brief silence, the tension slowly beginning to dissipate. His mom reached out, gently placing her hand on his.

"How's Wyatt handling all of this?" she asked, her voice quieter now, more concerned.

Jesse sighed, running a hand through his hair. "He's upset. Mostly because he knows his dad is going to find out why he was let go, and he's scared of how he'll react. We talked last night, and Wyatt said he's probably going to come clean to his dad about everything."

His parents exchanged another glance, this time filled with quiet understanding. They knew what that conversation would mean for Wyatt, and the fear he was carrying.

"How are you doing with all of this?" his dad asked, his voice softening. "It's a lot to go through in such a short time."

Jesse bit his lip, feeling the weight of his emotions swirling inside him. "Honestly… I'm trying to stay positive. The trip we took was amazing. It gave us a break from everything, and… I think I'm falling in love with him."

His mom's eyes softened, her expression shifting from worry to something more tender. "You think you're falling in love with him?"

Jesse nodded, feeling a warmth spread through his chest despite the heaviness of the conversation. "Yeah. I didn't expect it to happen, but I really care about him. And after this weekend… I think we're both realizing how much we mean to each other."

His dad leaned forward, resting his elbows on the table, his face filled with concern. "We're happy for you, Jesse. You know that. We want you to find love and be happy. But we're also worried. Life… life's not going to be easy for you and Wyatt. People are still cruel, as you've already seen."

His mom's eyes welled with tears, and she reached out to take his hand. "We're so proud of you, Jesse. For being true to yourself, for standing by Wyatt. But we're scared for you too. You'll face challenges that most people don't understand. And we just want to make sure you're prepared for that."

Jesse squeezed his mom's hand, his heart swelling with emotion. "I know, Mom. I know it's going to be hard. But... I have you and Dad. And I have Wyatt. I'm not alone in this."

His dad nodded, his face softening. "We'll always be here for you. No matter what. But you need to be careful, Jesse. There are going to be people who won't accept you. And as much as we want to protect you from that, we can't always be there."

His mom wiped her eyes, smiling through her tears. "Just promise us that you'll be careful. And if anything happens, if you ever need us... we're here. We love you, Jesse. We love you so much."

Jesse's chest tightened, a wave of gratitude and love washing over him. His parents had been nothing but supportive since he came out, and even now, as they expressed their fears, it came from a place of love and protection.

"I love you both too," Jesse said, his voice thick with emotion. "And I promise... I'll be careful."

They sat together in the quiet kitchen, the early morning light filling the room with a soft glow. Despite the anger and frustration over what had happened, Jesse felt a deep sense of comfort knowing that his parents were on his side. Their concern for his safety, their love for him—it was enough to remind him that he wasn't alone in this fight.

And no matter what challenges lay ahead, Jesse knew he had a family who loved him, a family who would support him through it all.

Chapter 42: The Confrontation

On a street one mile to the south, Wyatt sat at the kitchen table, staring out the window at the early morning light filtering through the trees. His stomach churned with a mix of fear and frustration, knowing the inevitable was about to happen. He had tried to prepare himself for this moment, but no matter how many times he went over it in his head, he couldn't shake the pit in his stomach.

His father had heard. There was no avoiding it now. He'd heard from some of the men in town about why Wyatt and Jesse had been let go from the pool. The small-town gossip had spread like wildfire, and Wyatt knew it was only a matter of time before his dad confronted him. He'd been dreading this conversation for as long as he could remember, but now that it was here, it felt more real and terrifying than he'd ever imagined.

The sound of the front door opening snapped Wyatt out of his thoughts. His father, gruff and tired-looking, stepped inside, his face set in a stony expression. Wyatt could tell by the tightness in his jaw and the way he moved that he was angry.

"Wyatt," his father said, his voice low and heavy. "We need to talk."

Wyatt swallowed hard, bracing himself as he stood up from the table. His mom was in the kitchen, her eyes flickering with concern as she glanced between the two of them. She knew this was coming too, but Wyatt wasn't sure if even she could stop what was about to unfold.

His father didn't waste any time. He walked into the kitchen, the tension radiating off him like a storm about to break. "I heard from some of the men in town," he began, his voice barely controlled.

"Heard you got fired from the pool. Heard it's because of... this relationship with Jesse."

Wyatt's heart pounded in his chest, his pulse quickening. He had known this moment was coming, but hearing it laid out so bluntly still sent a wave of fear through him.

"Yeah," Wyatt said, trying to keep his voice steady. "That's true."

His father's eyes narrowed, and for a moment, the room was silent except for the ticking of the clock on the wall. Then, with a deep breath, his father spoke again, his voice hard. "You've been lying to me. Hiding this from me. I didn't raise you to be like this, Wyatt."

Wyatt's fists clenched at his sides, anger and hurt bubbling up inside him. "I didn't ask to be like this," he shot back, his voice trembling with emotion. "This is who I am, Dad. And I didn't want to hide it anymore."

His father's face tightened with anger, and he took a step closer. "You're telling me that you threw away your job, your reputation, for some... some boy? You're going to ruin your life for this?"

Wyatt's heart pounded, and he could feel the anger rising in his chest. "I didn't throw anything away," he said, his voice growing stronger. "I'm finally being honest about who I am. And I care about Jesse. I love him."

His father's face darkened, his voice laced with disbelief. "Love? You think this is love? This is a phase, Wyatt. You'll regret this. You're ruining your life, and you're dragging us down with you."

At that moment, his mother, who had been standing quietly by the kitchen counter, stepped forward, her voice trembling with emotion but firm. "He's not ruining anything, Richard," she said, her voice shaky but strong. "Wyatt is our son. He deserves to be loved and accepted for who he is."

Wyatt's father turned to her, his face a mixture of anger and disbelief. "You knew about this?" he demanded, his voice rising. "And you didn't tell me?"

She nodded, her eyes brimming with tears. "I did. And I didn't tell you because I knew how you'd react. You're being unfair, Richard. Wyatt's trying to live his life. Why can't you see that?"

His father scoffed, his hands clenched into fists. "You're enabling this, Nancy. You're making it worse. You think supporting this is going to help him? He's throwing his future away, and you're just going to stand by and let it happen?"

Wyatt's mother's face flushed with emotion, her voice growing louder. "I'm not going to stand by and let you push our son away! He's not ruining anything. He's being who he is. And if you can't support that, then maybe you're the one who's going to ruin everything!"

Wyatt's heart pounded as he watched the argument unfold, his mother standing up to his father in a way he had never seen before. The room was filled with the sound of his father's heavy breathing, the tension thick in the air.

"You need to support him," his mom continued, her voice breaking. "Or you're going to lose him."

His father's face twisted with anger, and for a moment, it seemed like he might explode. But instead, he spat out his next words, cold and cutting. "Maybe I don't want him here if he's going to act like this. If he's going to choose to live this way."

The words hit Wyatt like a physical blow, and for a moment, he couldn't breathe. He looked at his father, his heart breaking, and then glanced at his mother, who had tears streaming down her face.

She shook her head, her voice trembling. "Richard, don't say that. Don't you dare say that."

But Wyatt had heard enough. He couldn't take it anymore—the anger, the disappointment, the way his father looked at him like he was something broken. Something to be fixed.

"Fine," Wyatt said, his voice cold and hard as he met his father's gaze. "If that's how you feel, then maybe I won't come back. Maybe when I leave for school, I'll just stay up there. I don't want to live like this anymore—afraid, hiding who I am. I'm not going to pretend for you or anyone else."

His father didn't respond. He just stared at Wyatt, his jaw tight, his eyes burning with anger and something else—something that Wyatt couldn't quite place. And then, without a word, his father turned and walked out of the room, the door slamming behind him.

Wyatt stood there, his chest heaving, the adrenaline still coursing through his veins. He couldn't believe what had just happened— couldn't believe that his father had said those things, that he had walked away.

For a moment, the room was silent, and then Wyatt's mom broke down, tears streaming down her face as she reached for Wyatt, pulling him into a tight hug.

"I'm so sorry, Wyatt," she whispered, her voice thick with emotion. "I'm so, so sorry."

Wyatt stood there, frozen for a moment, before the weight of it all crashed down on him. He wrapped his arms around his mom, burying his face in her shoulder as the tears finally came.

"I don't know what to do," Wyatt choked out, his voice breaking. "I don't know how to fix this."

His mom held him tighter, her own tears mixing with his. "We'll figure it out," she whispered. "I promise. We'll figure it out together. I'll do everything I can to help him see, Wyatt. You're my son, and I'm never going to stop fighting for you."

They stood there in the quiet kitchen, holding on to each other. Wyatt knew that nothing would be the same after this–that his relationship with his father might never be what it once was. But in that moment, with his mom by his side, he realized that he wasn't alone. He had people who loved him, who would fight for him. And even if his father didn't understand right now, Wyatt had hope that maybe, one day, things could change.

But for now, he needed to focus on living his life–his real, authentic life–and that was something no one, not even his father, could take away from him.

As the tears finally subsided, his mom pulled back, wiping her eyes. "I'm so proud of you," she whispered, her voice filled with love. "And no matter what happens, I'll always be here. I promise."

Wyatt nodded, his heart aching but full. "Thanks, Mom."

And as they stood there together, Wyatt knew that this was just the beginning of a new chapter in his life—one where he would no longer hide who he was, no matter the cost.

Chapter 43: Breaking Point

Wyatt's hands trembled as he stuffed clothes into his bag, his breath coming in shallow, shaky bursts. His father's words echoed relentlessly in his mind, cutting deeper each time they replayed.

"Maybe I don't want him here if he's going to act like this."

Each word felt like a punch, leaving him breathless and devastated. His father–the man he had looked up to his entire life–had essentially told him he wasn't welcome at home if he continued to live authentically. It was like a nightmare come true, and Wyatt wasn't sure what hurt more: the anger in his father's voice or the realization that he might never be truly accepted by him.

He grabbed his bag, slung it over his shoulder, and stormed out of the house. His mom's tearful voice called after him, but he couldn't stop. He couldn't stand to be in that house, not after what had just happened. His father's rejection was too raw, too overwhelming. Wyatt needed space–needed to breathe. He needed to be somewhere, anywhere, that wasn't filled with the suffocating weight of his father's disapproval.

His feet carried him to the small park down the street, a place he'd gone to when he was younger, whenever he needed to clear his head. The trees swayed gently in the breeze, and the distant sound of children laughing on the playground filled the air. But even the peaceful surroundings couldn't quiet the storm brewing inside him.

Wyatt found a bench near the edge of the park, away from prying eyes, and sat down heavily, his hands shaking as he buried his face in them.

The tears came almost immediately–hot, angry tears that he couldn't hold back. He cried for everything: for the way his father had looked at him like he was a disappointment, for the way his mother had tried to fix it but couldn't, for the overwhelming fear that he might never have his family's full acceptance.

The weight of it all felt unbearable. He knew what he had to do–he knew that standing up for himself was the right choice–but that didn't make it any easier. It felt like his entire world had been turned upside down, and Wyatt was terrified that things might never go back to the way they were.

For what felt like hours, Wyatt sat there, alone in the park, his sobs quiet but steady. Every time he thought the tears were done, another wave of emotion would hit him, leaving him feeling hollow and broken.

He pulled out his phone, his fingers trembling as he typed out a message to Jesse.

Wyatt: *I told my dad. It didn't go well. He said he doesn't want me there if I'm going to "live this way."*

The words felt heavy, final, as he hit send. He wasn't sure what Jesse would say, but he needed someone to know–someone to understand. The pain was too much to bear alone.

The minutes stretched out painfully as he sat there, staring at his phone, waiting for a response. He felt so lost, so unsure of what to do next. And then, his phone buzzed with a reply.

Jesse: *Where are you? I'm coming.*

Wyatt sent him a pin of his location at the park, his heart pounding with a mixture of relief and anxiety. He didn't know what he was going to say to Jesse when he arrived–didn't even know if he could explain how broken he felt–but knowing Jesse was on his way gave him a small glimmer of hope. Maybe he wasn't completely alone in this.

It wasn't long before Wyatt saw Jesse running down the street, his expression filled with concern. The sight of him, so determined, so ready to be there for him, made the tears well up in Wyatt's eyes again.

Jesse rushed over to the bench, barely saying a word before sitting down next to Wyatt and wrapping him in a tight embrace. Wyatt's whole body sagged against him, and the floodgates opened once more. He buried his face in Jesse's shoulder, the sobs coming harder now as Jesse held him, murmuring soft reassurances.

"I'm so sorry," Jesse whispered, his voice thick with emotion as he rubbed Wyatt's back. "I'm so, so sorry."

Wyatt clung to him like a lifeline, his breath ragged as he tried to speak. "He... he doesn't want me there, Jesse. He doesn't want me if I'm going to be... like this. Like who I am."

Jesse pulled back slightly, his eyes filled with pain for Wyatt. "That's not true. He's scared, and he's wrong. But you–" Jesse's voice cracked as he spoke, "you're perfect just the way you are. He'll see it eventually. He has to."

Wyatt shook his head, fresh tears spilling down his cheeks. "I don't know, Jesse. I don't think he ever will. He looked at me like I was... like I was nothing."

Jesse's heart broke at Wyatt's words, and he gently wiped away the tears from Wyatt's face. "You are not nothing. You hear me? You're everything. And no matter what he says or how he acts, I'm here. We'll get through this. Together."

Wyatt leaned into him, feeling the steady rhythm of Jesse's heartbeat against his chest. It was grounding, soothing, and for the first time that day, Wyatt felt like maybe he wasn't completely falling apart.

"I don't know what to do," Wyatt whispered, his voice raw with emotion. "I don't want to keep pretending, but I don't want to lose my family either. It feels like no matter what I choose, I'm going to lose something."

Jesse held him tighter, his voice quiet but resolute. "You shouldn't have to choose. You deserve to be who you are without losing anyone. But if he can't see that... if he can't accept you, then that's on him. Not you."

Wyatt nodded, his throat tight with unshed tears. "I just... I thought maybe my mom could help, but even she couldn't stop him. It was like he didn't even hear her."

Jesse's jaw clenched, anger bubbling up inside him at the thought of Wyatt's father treating him this way. "He's being stubborn. But your mom loves you, Wyatt. She's going to keep fighting for you. And so am I."

Wyatt took a deep, shaky breath, feeling a small flicker of hope amidst the pain. "Thank you," he whispered. "I don't know what I'd do without you."

Jesse smiled softly, leaning his forehead against Wyatt's. "You'll never have to find out."

They stayed like that for a while, just holding each other, the quiet of the park offering them a small moment of peace. But Jesse knew Wyatt needed more than just him. Wyatt needed to feel supported by the people who mattered in their lives.

"Hey," Jesse said after a long pause, pulling back slightly to look at Wyatt. "I think we need our friends right now."

Wyatt looked at him, confused. "What do you mean?"

"I mean, we need to be with people who get it. People who care about you," Jesse explained. "Let me text the group. Let's get together at the coffee shop. I think it'll help."

Wyatt hesitated, his heart still heavy, but the thought of being around their friends–around people who wouldn't judge or make him feel small–felt like something he could cling to. So he nodded.

Jesse quickly pulled out his phone, typing a message to their group of coworkers-turned-friends.

Jesse: *Hey, can we meet up? Wyatt's going through some stuff and could really use some support. We're thinking the coffee shop in about 30 minutes.*

The replies came almost instantly.

Tori: *Of course. We'll be there.*

Matt: *On my way.*

Rachel: *We've got you.*

Liz: Already out the door!

Jesse smiled at Wyatt, offering him a small sense of comfort. "They're coming. It's going to be okay."

Thirty minutes later, Wyatt and Jesse walked into the cozy coffee shop, the familiar scent of roasted coffee beans and baked goods enveloping them. The place was quiet, a few patrons scattered at tables reading or working, but it felt like the right kind of space for what Wyatt needed— calm and supportive.

Tori, Matt, and Rachel were already seated at a corner table, their faces filled with concern and warmth when they saw Wyatt and Jesse walk in. Tori immediately stood up, rushing over to Wyatt and pulling him into a tight hug.

"I'm so sorry, Wyatt," Tori said softly, her voice thick with emotion. "I can't imagine how hard this must be for you."

Wyatt hugged her back, the warmth of her support washing over him. "Thanks, Tori. It's... been rough."

Matt and Rachel both stood as well, each taking a moment to hug Wyatt, offering quiet words of support. The small gestures meant more to Wyatt than he could express, and as they all sat down together, he felt a little lighter knowing that his friends were here for him.

The bell over the door jingled as Liz stepped inside, her eyes scanning the shop until they landed on Jesse. She gave him a small smile and made her way over, balancing a large iced coffee in one hand and her ever-present phone in the other.

"Hey, sorry I'm late," Liz said as she slid into the seat next to Jesse, glancing around at the group. "I had to bribe my way past a line of coffee snobs for this," she added, lifting her cup with a grin.

Jesse smiled, glad to see her. "You made it. Guys, this is Liz. Liz, this is Tori, Rachel, Matt–and this is Wyatt."

Liz's eyes lingered on Wyatt for a second longer than the others, her expression softening as if she could sense the heaviness around him. "Hey, it's nice to meet you all," she said, her voice warm but not overly perky, sensing the mood without needing an explanation.

Liz sat down, shifting in her seat, leaning slightly closer to Jesse. "Everything okay?" she asked quietly, though she already had a good idea of the answer.

Jesse glanced at Wyatt, then back at Liz, keeping his voice low. "Wyatt left his dad's house. Things were... bad."

They ordered drinks, and as they sat at the table, Wyatt began to open up. He told them everything–how he had come out to his father, how his mother had tried to intervene, and how it had all fallen apart.

"He told me he doesn't want me there if I'm going to live this way," Wyatt said quietly, his hands wrapped tightly around his coffee cup. "I don't know if I can ever go back after that."

Rachel shook her head, her expression filled with sympathy and anger. "That's not fair. You shouldn't have to hide who you are just to have a relationship with your dad. He's the one who needs to change."

Matt nodded in agreement. "Exactly. It's not on you to make him feel comfortable with who you are. That's his problem, not yours."

Wyatt sighed, leaning back in his chair. "I just... I thought maybe, just maybe, he'd be able to understand. But hearing him say those things... I don't know if he ever will."

Tori reached across the table, placing her hand over Wyatt's. "You don't have to figure it all out right now, Wyatt. You've been through so much already. Just take it one step at a time. And remember, we're all here for you."

Wyatt's eyes welled with tears again, but this time, they were tears of gratitude. "Thank you," he whispered. "I don't know what I'd do without you guys."

Rachel smiled gently. "You don't have to do anything alone, Wyatt. We've got your back. Always."

The conversation flowed easily after that, a mixture of lighthearted banter and more serious talks about what Wyatt's next steps might be. As they sipped their drinks, Matt leaned forward, his expression thoughtful.

"You know what?" he said. "I've been thinking about it, and honestly... I don't feel right going back to the pool. Not after what they did to you guys."

Tori immediately nodded, her face set in determination. "Same. I'm done with that place. If they're going to treat people like that, I don't want to work there."

Rachel smiled in agreement. "Solidarity. We're in this together."

Wyatt blinked in surprise, his heart swelling at their support. "You guys don't have to quit for me."

Matt shrugged. "Maybe not. But it feels like the right thing to do. We're all in this together."

Jesse squeezed Wyatt's hand under the table, his heart full as he watched their friends rally around them. "See? We've got people who care."

Wyatt smiled, the pain in his chest easing just a little. The road ahead was still uncertain, and his father's rejection still stung, but knowing he had people in his corner—people who loved and supported him—made it feel bearable.

As the evening wore on, they laughed and talked, the heaviness of the day giving way to a sense of warmth and solidarity. By the time they left the coffee shop, Wyatt felt lighter, more hopeful than he had in hours.

Jesse wrapped his arm around Wyatt's shoulders as they stepped into the cool evening air. "How are you feeling now?"

Wyatt took a deep breath, the crisp air filling his lungs. "Better," he admitted. "I don't know what's going to happen with my dad, but... having you and our friends? It's enough for now."

Jesse smiled, leaning in to kiss Wyatt's temple softly. "That's more than enough."

As Jesse and Wyatt walked home from the coffee shop, the weight of everything that had happened still hung heavy between them. Wyatt had his hands shoved deep into his pockets, his face turned toward the ground as they made their way through the quiet streets. The warmth from their friends and the solidarity they'd felt at the coffee shop had helped ease the pain, but Wyatt's father's words lingered, gnawing at him.

Jesse glanced at Wyatt, his heart aching for him. He knew Wyatt needed a safe place, a place to figure things out without the crushing pressure of his father's rejection. Without a second thought, Jesse pulled out his phone and typed a quick message to his parents.

Jesse: *Hey, things got bad with Wyatt's dad. Can he come over? Will explain everything.*

He hit send, hoping his parents would be as understanding as they'd been in the past. They were good people, and he knew they wouldn't turn Wyatt away, but a part of him still felt nervous. This was different– this was real, and raw, and Wyatt was hurting in a way Jesse had never seen before.

By the time they reached Jesse's house, his phone buzzed with a reply from his mom.

Mom: *Of course, Jesse. He's welcome here. We'll get everything ready. Just come in.*

Relief flooded through Jesse as he slipped his phone back into his pocket and gave Wyatt a reassuring look. "We're almost there. My parents said you can stay as long as you need."

Wyatt gave a small, tight nod, though his face still looked clouded with sadness. "Thanks, Jess. I don't know what I would've done without you today."

Jesse squeezed Wyatt's arm gently. "You don't have to figure it all out tonight. We'll take it one step at a time."

They walked up the steps to Jesse's house, the warm glow of the living room light spilling out from the windows. As they opened the door, Jesse's mom and dad were waiting in the kitchen. His mom, always warm and welcoming, stepped forward with a gentle smile.

"Wyatt, it's so nice to finally meet you," she said, giving him a hug. "Come in, come in."

His dad, standing nearby, gave Wyatt a nod and a handshake. "You're welcome here. Whatever you need."

Wyatt managed a small smile, though Jesse could see the weariness in his eyes. "Thank you. I really appreciate it."

Jesse's mom ushered them into the living room, her motherly instincts kicking into high gear. "Are you hungry? Thirsty? I can make you something if you'd like. Anything you need, Wyatt."

Wyatt shook his head, his voice quiet. "I'm okay. Thank you, though."

Jesse's mom gave him a sympathetic look before motioning to the couch. "Why don't you both sit down? Let's talk about what's going on."

They all sat together in the cozy living room, the warmth of the house a stark contrast to the emotional storm that Wyatt had been enduring all day. Jesse sat close to Wyatt, their shoulders brushing, offering silent support as he began to explain everything to his parents.

Jesse spoke softly but clearly, telling them about Wyatt's conversation with his father, how it had spiraled into hurtful words and rejection, and how Wyatt had been forced to leave the house. As Jesse recounted the events, Wyatt sat quietly beside him, his face downcast, looking more vulnerable than Jesse had ever seen him.

When Jesse finished explaining, his mom and dad exchanged a glance— one filled with both understanding and concern. His mom turned to Wyatt, her eyes soft with sympathy.

"Wyatt," she began gently, "I'm so sorry you're going through this. No one should have to deal with that kind of hurt, especially not from their family."

Wyatt blinked, clearly overwhelmed but grateful. "Thank you," he said softly. "I didn't know where else to go."

Jesse's mom reached out and patted Wyatt's hand. "Well, you're here now. And we want you to know that you're welcome to stay with us for as long as you need. We have a spare bedroom that's all set up, and you can take some time to figure things out."

Wyatt looked up at her, his eyes filled with emotion. "I don't want to be a burden…"

"You're not," Jesse's dad said firmly, his voice filled with sincerity. "You're going through a lot, and we're happy to help however we can. We're all family here."

Wyatt nodded, a flicker of relief passing over his face, though the sadness still lingered in his eyes. "Thank you. Really. I don't know what to say."

"You don't have to say anything," Jesse's mom said with a kind smile. "We're just glad you're here."

There was a moment of quiet, the weight of the conversation settling over the room. Then, Jesse's dad cleared his throat.

"Now, we do have one rule," he said, glancing between Jesse and Wyatt. "You two can't share a bedroom while you're here. I know you're both adults, but this is still our house, and we have to set some boundaries."

Jesse nodded, understanding. "That's fine, Dad. We get it."

His mom smiled, standing up and smoothing out her clothes. "The spare bedroom is all set up for you, Wyatt. You can stay as long as you need to get your feet back under you."

Wyatt nodded, gratitude evident in his voice. "Thank you. I really appreciate it."

Jesse's mom gave them both a warm smile before heading toward the kitchen to clean up, leaving the boys to settle in. "If you need anything else, just let us know. I'll see you both in the morning."

As the evening wore on, the house grew quiet, and Jesse and Wyatt retreated to their separate rooms. Wyatt had been given the spare bedroom down the hall, and after a long, emotionally draining day, he collapsed onto the bed, his mind spinning with everything that had happened.

But no matter how hard he tried, Wyatt couldn't sleep. The events of the day played over and over in his mind–his father's harsh words, his mother's tearful defense, the overwhelming sense of loss that had settled over him. He stared at the ceiling, his thoughts racing, feeling more alone than ever, despite the kindness of Jesse's family.

Around 1 a.m., Wyatt's phone buzzed on the nightstand. He reached for it, his heart giving a small flutter when he saw it was a message from Jesse.

Jesse: *You awake?*

Wyatt hesitated for a second, then replied.

Wyatt: *Yeah. Can't sleep.*

A few seconds later, Jesse's reply came in.

Jesse: *Me either. Can I come over?*

Wyatt felt a small, warm smile tug at the corners of his mouth, the thought of Jesse being there with him easing some of the tension in his chest.

Wyatt: *Yeah. Come over.*

A few minutes later, Jesse quietly opened the door to the spare bedroom and slipped inside. He closed it softly behind him and padded over to the bed, where Wyatt was lying, staring up at the ceiling.

"Hey," Jesse whispered, slipping under the covers next to him.

"Hey," Wyatt whispered back, his voice heavy with emotion.

For a moment, they just lay there, side by side, in the dark room. The quiet felt heavy, filled with everything neither of them knew how to say. Wyatt turned his head slightly, his eyes meeting Jesse's, and in that moment, all of the pain, the confusion, the fear of what was coming melted away.

Jesse reached for Wyatt's hand, lacing their fingers together under the blanket. "I'm here," Jesse whispered. "I'm not going anywhere."

Wyatt's chest tightened with emotion, and he turned toward Jesse, pulling him close until their bodies were pressed together. They didn't speak, but the silence between them wasn't uncomfortable. It was filled with something deeper–an understanding, a shared grief, and a quiet kind of strength.

They lay there, holding each other, neither of them speaking, but neither of them needing to. The comfort of Jesse's presence was enough for Wyatt. It was enough to keep the darkness at bay for now.

As the hours passed, Wyatt felt the weight of the day slowly begin to ease. He was still scared–still uncertain of what the future held–but in this moment, with Jesse wrapped around him, he felt like maybe, just maybe, things would be okay.

"I don't know what's going to happen," Wyatt whispered into the dark.

Jesse tightened his hold on him. "Neither do I. But we'll figure it out. Together."

Wyatt smiled, a tear slipping down his cheek as he pressed his face into Jesse's chest. "I love you."

Jesse kissed the top of Wyatt's head softly. "I love you too."

They stayed like that for the rest of the night, neither of them sleeping, just holding each other, finding comfort in the quiet intimacy of the moment. No matter what happened next, no matter how uncertain the future felt, they knew they had each other.

Chapter 44: A Conversation of Hearts

The house was unnaturally still, the silence stretching across every room like a blanket that smothered everything in its path. Richard sat alone at the dining room table, staring blankly at the half-empty glass of whiskey in front of him. The ice had long since melted, but he hadn't taken a sip in over an hour. His mind was elsewhere, swirling with thoughts he couldn't quite get a grip on.

The argument with Wyatt kept replaying in his head, each moment sharper and more painful than the last. The words he had said—words he couldn't take back—clung to him, but instead of regret, they festered into something else. He didn't want to admit it, not even to himself, but fear and anger had twisted together in his chest, and he didn't know how to untangle them.

"Maybe I don't want him here if he's going to act like this."

He had meant it when he said it. He still wasn't sure if he didn't mean it now. The idea of Wyatt being gay, of choosing that kind of life, made Richard's skin crawl. It wasn't what he had envisioned for his son—it wasn't how things were supposed to be.

He rubbed a hand over his face, feeling the day's exhaustion creep up on him, but the tension in his chest wouldn't let him rest. There was a part of him, small and buried deep, that whispered doubts, that wondered if he had been too harsh, but he quickly shoved those thoughts aside. This wasn't about being harsh. This was about what was right.

Nancy's soft footsteps broke through his thoughts, and Richard glanced up as she stepped into the kitchen. Her face was lined with worry, and he could tell she'd been crying, though she'd tried to hide it.

She crossed her arms over her chest, lingering near the doorway as if she was preparing herself for a battle. Richard didn't say anything, waiting for her to make the first move. He knew what was coming–he could feel it in the air.

Nancy took a deep breath, her voice quiet but firm. "We need to talk, Richard. About Wyatt."

Richard's jaw tightened, and he glanced away, staring at the melting ice in his glass. "There's nothing to talk about. I said what I had to say."

Her lips pressed into a thin line, but she didn't back down. "You said a lot of things, Richard. Things I don't think you meant."

"I meant every word," Richard snapped, his voice harsher than he intended. He hated the way her eyes softened with sadness, hated the way she looked at him like he was someone she didn't recognize. But he couldn't stop himself. "He's making a mistake, Nancy. He's young, he's confused–he doesn't know what he's doing."

Nancy stared at him, her frustration bubbling just beneath the surface. She took a step forward, her hands trembling slightly, though she tried to steady them.

"He's not confused," she said, her voice breaking a little. "He's been trying to tell us this for months. This isn't a mistake. This is who he is."

Richard stood abruptly, the chair scraping against the floor as he began pacing the length of the kitchen. He couldn't sit still, couldn't just listen to this as if everything was normal. His chest felt tight, like he was being cornered, and he didn't like it.

"He doesn't know what he is!" Richard barked, his hands clenching into fists at his sides. "He's a kid, Nancy! He's just… he's going through a phase. It'll pass. This kind of thing doesn't last."

Nancy's eyes filled with a mixture of sadness and anger as she watched him. "You really believe that? That this is just some phase?"

Richard stopped pacing, his back to her, his shoulders tense. "Yeah," he said, his voice low but filled with certainty. "I do."

She shook her head, her voice trembling with emotion. "It's not a phase, Richard. This is who Wyatt is, and you can't just ignore it or hope it'll go away. He's gay. And he's been trying to tell you that for months, but you refuse to listen."

Richard let out a sharp breath, his frustration mounting. "Why does it have to be this? Why couldn't he just be normal?"

"Normal?" Nancy repeated, her voice incredulous. "He *is* normal, Richard. He's our son. He's the same Wyatt he's always been. He hasn't changed. The only thing that's different is that he's being honest with us."

Richard turned to face her, his eyes filled with anger and confusion. "It's not the same. He's not the same. You know what people will say. You know what he'll go through if he keeps this up. They'll tear him apart. They'll treat him like he's some freak. Is that what you want for him?"

Nancy's heart ached at the pain in his voice. She knew that beneath the anger, Richard was scared–scared for Wyatt, scared for their family, scared of what people would think. But that didn't make his words any less cruel.

"No," she said softly. "I don't want that for him. But you pushing him away isn't going to make any of this easier. You're only making him feel more alone."

Richard shook his head, his fists clenching tighter. "I'm trying to protect him."

"By telling him he's not welcome here?" Nancy shot back, her voice rising. "By making him feel like there's something wrong with him?"

Richard's chest heaved with the force of his frustration. He ran a hand through his hair, tugging at the roots as if trying to pull the thoughts straight out of his head. "I don't know what else to do, Nancy. He's throwing his life away for this."

"He's not throwing anything away!" Nancy said, her voice trembling with anger. "He's finally living his truth, and you're punishing him for it."

Richard's expression darkened, and he took a step closer, his voice low and cold. "You don't get it. This isn't the life we planned for him. This isn't what he's supposed to be."

Nancy's heart shattered at the words, but she didn't back down. She met his gaze, her voice filled with quiet, steely resolve. "No, it's not what *you* planned for him. But it's his life. And he gets to decide who he is and how he lives it."

Richard's breath caught in his throat, and for a moment, the room was thick with silence. He turned away from her, his mind racing. He didn't want this conversation. He didn't want to confront the possibility that he was wrong.

"I can't accept it," Richard said finally, his voice strained. "I can't pretend this is okay."

Nancy felt her heart break a little more with every word he said, but she took a deep breath, steadying herself. She wasn't going to let this go. Not this time.

"You don't have to accept everything right now," she said softly. "But you have to try. You can't keep pushing him away, Richard. If you do, you're going to lose him."

Richard froze, his body rigid as the weight of her words sank in. The idea of losing Wyatt–really losing him–sent a pang of fear through his chest, but he shoved it aside. He couldn't give in. Not yet.

"I'm not going to lose him," Richard said, his voice hard. "He's still my son."

"Then act like it," Nancy said, her voice sharp. "Love him like he's your son, not some stranger you're ashamed of."

Richard's eyes flashed with anger, but there was something else there too—something closer to guilt. He opened his mouth to argue, but the words caught in his throat.

Nancy stepped closer, her voice soft but filled with urgency. "I know you're scared. I'm scared too. But pushing him away isn't going to fix this. It's only going to make things worse."

Richard shook his head, turning his back to her. "You don't get it, Nancy. I can't just turn this off. I can't just accept this. He's ruining his life."

"No," Nancy whispered, tears welling up in her eyes. "You're ruining his life by refusing to love him as he is."

Richard's breath hitched, and for a moment, the room was filled with nothing but the sound of their breathing. The weight of her words hung between them, heavy and unrelenting.

"I don't know if I can do this," Richard whispered, his voice breaking.

Nancy's heart softened, and she reached out, gently placing a hand on his arm. "You can," she said quietly. "Because you love him. And that's all that matters."

Richard stood still, his chest tight with the weight of his confusion and fear. He didn't know how to move forward, didn't know if he could be the father Wyatt needed. But as he stood there, with Nancy's hand on his arm and her quiet strength anchoring him, he realized that maybe—just maybe—he wasn't as lost as he thought.

"I don't know how to fix this," he said, his voice hoarse. "But I'll try."

Nancy smiled softly through her tears. "That's all Wyatt needs."

They stood there in the quiet kitchen, the tension slowly easing between them. Richard still felt the weight of everything pressing down on him, but he knew that he couldn't keep running from it. Wyatt was his son, and no matter how hard it was, he couldn't lose him.

He wouldn't let himself.

Chapter 45: The Incident

The heat of the afternoon clung to the streets of town like a heavy blanket, making every breath feel thick and sluggish. Wyatt and Jesse walked side by side, their hands lightly intertwined, as they wandered past the familiar storefronts and shops of the small downtown area. For a moment, the world felt peaceful–quiet, even–with the faint hum of people going about their business. It was one of those rare days when Wyatt felt almost normal. Out in public, with Jesse, just being himself without the weight of everything at home pressing down on him.

Jesse leaned over, nudging him playfully. "You okay?"

Wyatt smiled softly, nodding. "Yeah. I'm good."

And he meant it. Despite everything that had happened with his father, despite the distance he'd had to create for his own sanity, being with Jesse always made things feel a little better. They weren't out of the woods yet, but right now, with the warm sun on their backs and the quiet chatter of the town around them, it felt like they could just be.

But as they approached a small diner on the corner of Main Street, the feeling of ease began to slip away. Wyatt noticed the shift before he even heard the voices–a tightening in his gut, a sense of eyes on him, like someone was watching too closely.

He glanced up and immediately saw the group of men standing near the diner's entrance. There were about five of them, leaning against a pickup truck parked at the curb, beers in hand, their voices loud and rough. Wyatt recognized a few faces–men he'd seen around town, men who worked at the local hardware store and garage.

One of them, Kyle, was the first to spot Wyatt and Jesse. His eyes narrowed, and then his mouth twisted into a smirk. Wyatt felt his heart skip a beat, dread crawling up his spine.

"Well, look at this," Kyle drawled, loud enough for everyone around to hear. "Ain't that a sweet sight. Wyatt Roberts, walking around with his little boyfriend."

The others turned to look, their smirks and laughter filling the air with a cruel undertone. Wyatt's stomach churned. He had expected this sort of thing, but it didn't make it any easier. There was always that lingering fear–fear of what people might say, what they might do.

He could feel Jesse's hand tighten around his, a subtle signal of support, but it didn't stop the knot of anxiety forming in his chest.

Kyle stepped forward, clearly enjoying the attention. "Does your daddy know about this, Wyatt? I always thought Richard Roberts was a tough guy. Guess I was wrong about that, huh? Must be real proud of you."

Wyatt's breath hitched in his throat, anger and shame battling for dominance. He wanted to say something, to fight back, but the words stuck. It was as if all the strength he'd mustered to hold Jesse's hand in public was now failing him in the face of this ugliness.

Jesse, on the other hand, didn't hesitate. He stepped in front of Wyatt, squaring his shoulders. "We're just minding our business, man. Why don't you do the same?"

Kyle's grin widened, but the look in his eyes was all malice. "Oh, I'm sorry. Did I hurt your feelings? You two queers think you can just walk around town holding hands like it's no big deal? What kind of world do you think we're living in?"

The group behind him chuckled darkly, clearly entertained by the show. Wyatt's hands balled into fists at his sides, his heart racing. He didn't want to make a scene, didn't want this to turn into something worse, but he could feel the anger bubbling up inside him, threatening to explode.

Before he could say anything, a new voice cut through the tension.

"What's going on here?"

Wyatt froze. He knew that voice, recognized it instantly, even though he hadn't heard it in days. His heart sank as he turned to see his father walking down the sidewalk toward them, his expression unreadable.

Richard stopped a few feet away, his eyes flicking between Wyatt, Jesse, and the group of men standing by the truck. For a moment, the air around them seemed to still, the tension thick enough to cut.

Kyle, who had been puffing up his chest with bravado, faltered slightly when he saw Richard, but he quickly regained his composure. "Hey, Richard. We were just having a little chat with your boy here." His tone was dripping with mockery. "Didn't know he was... you know, like *that*." He gestured vaguely toward Wyatt and Jesse, a look of disdain twisting his features.

Wyatt felt a wave of panic rise in his chest. His father had never been one to back down from confrontation, but he had no idea how Richard was going to react. Would he side with Kyle? Would he join in on the mocking? Wyatt had seen how deeply his father had struggled with accepting who he was, and part of him feared that this would only make things worse.

Kyle, sensing an opportunity to push further, chuckled. "I mean, I can't imagine you're too happy about it, right? Two boys like that, flaunting it in front of everyone. What's our world coming to?"

The silence that followed was suffocating. Wyatt's heart pounded in his chest, his mind racing with a million possibilities. He could feel Jesse standing beside him, solid and unwavering, but the weight of his father's presence was all-consuming.

Richard stood there, his face still unreadable, his eyes fixed on Wyatt for what felt like an eternity. Then, slowly, he turned to Kyle, his expression hardening.

"Kyle," Richard said, his voice low and firm, "this isn't your business. Let it go."

Kyle blinked, clearly caught off guard by Richard's response. He had been expecting Richard to side with him, to mock Wyatt, not to shut him down.

"What do you mean, let it go?" Kyle scoffed, crossing his arms over his chest. "I'm just saying what everyone's thinking. You can't be okay with this."

Richard took a step forward, his gaze sharp and unyielding. "I said, let it go. You don't need to involve yourself in my family's business."

Kyle's mouth opened and closed a few times, but no words came out. The other men exchanged awkward glances, clearly unsure of how to respond now that Richard had spoken.

Before Kyle could muster another response, Richard took another step forward, his voice growing colder. "Leave them alone. Now."

The authority in Richard's voice was undeniable, and Kyle's confidence wavered. His smirk disappeared, replaced by a flush of embarrassment. After a moment of hesitation, he muttered something under his breath and turned back to his friends. "Whatever, man. Not worth it."

The group quickly dispersed, climbing into the truck and driving off, their laughter fading into the distance. But the tension in the air lingered, heavy and suffocating. Wyatt stood frozen, still processing what had just happened.

Richard turned to him and Jesse, his face set in that familiar mask of sternness. His eyes flicked briefly to their intertwined hands, and Wyatt could see the flicker of disapproval there. But Richard didn't say anything about it.

"You two okay?" Richard asked, his voice gruff but not unkind.

Wyatt opened his mouth to respond, but the words caught in his throat. He didn't know what to say. He wasn't sure how to feel. His father had stepped in, had told Kyle to leave them alone–but he hadn't defended Wyatt. He hadn't stood up for him in the way that mattered. He had protected the peace, not his son.

"We're fine," Jesse answered for both of them, his voice steady but tight. Wyatt could feel the tension radiating off him.

Richard gave a short nod, his gaze lingering on Wyatt for a moment longer. "Good."

And just like that, Richard turned and walked away, blending into the crowd as if nothing had happened. As if this was just another day, another moment to be filed away and forgotten.

Wyatt stood there, his heart still racing, his mind swirling with conflicting emotions. He felt a strange mix of relief, disappointment, and anger. His father had intervened, yes. He had stopped the confrontation. But there was no pride, no acceptance in his actions—just a cold, calculated decision to maintain order.

"He didn't stand up for me," Wyatt whispered, more to himself than to Jesse. His chest tightened, the familiar ache of rejection settling in.

Jesse stepped closer, his hand still gripping Wyatt's tightly. "He stopped them. That's something."

Wyatt shook his head, the knot of emotion in his throat threatening to choke him. "It's not enough."

The words hung in the air between them, heavy with truth. Jesse didn't argue, didn't try to tell Wyatt how to feel. Instead, he simply stood by his side, offering silent support as the world moved on around them.

In that moment, Wyatt understood something he had been trying to ignore for too long: he couldn't keep waiting for his father to change. He couldn't keep hoping for something that might never come. His father's intervention today wasn't about love or acceptance—it was about maintaining control, about keeping up appearances.

But Wyatt didn't want to live his life waiting for someone else's approval, especially not his father's. He had Jesse, he had friends who loved and supported him, and maybe that had to be enough.

"I'm not going to let this break me," Wyatt said quietly, more to himself than anyone else. He felt Jesse's hand tighten around his, and that simple gesture gave him strength.

"You don't have to," Jesse whispered. "We'll figure this out. Together."

Wyatt nodded, the weight of the day still heavy on his shoulders, but a flicker of hope burned inside him. He couldn't control what his father thought, couldn't force him to see the truth. But he could control how he moved forward, how he lived his life.

And in that moment, Wyatt made a decision. He wasn't going to wait for his father's approval. He was going to live for himself.

PART THREE: BECOMING

Chapter 46: A Father's Promise

The sun was sinking lower in the sky, casting long shadows across the small town as Wyatt approached his parents' house. The late-summer air was thick, buzzing with the sound of cicadas, but all Wyatt could hear was the pounding of his own heart. He had thought about this confrontation all day, turning it over in his mind until the edges were worn down from overthinking. He wasn't sure what he expected to come out of this conversation, but he knew it was necessary.

As he stood at the front door, the familiar smell of his childhood home hit him, stirring a rush of memories—memories of safety, of simpler times when he hadn't had to worry about whether his father would ever truly accept him. But those memories felt distant now, tainted by the anger, confusion, and disappointment that had settled between him and Richard over the last few months.

Wyatt took a deep breath and pushed open the door, stepping inside. The creak of the old hinges sounded like an echo from his past, but there was no comfort in it now—only tension.

Richard sat in the living room, the television on but muted. He was hunched slightly in his armchair, staring blankly at the screen, but Wyatt knew he wasn't watching it. His father's thoughts were elsewhere, just like Wyatt's. They hadn't spoken since that ugly confrontation in town with Kyle, and the silence that had followed had been deafening.

Wyatt stood in the doorway for a moment, gathering his courage. He had come this far. He couldn't back down now.

"Dad," he said, his voice sounding smaller than he intended. Richard looked up, his eyes clouded with the weariness Wyatt had grown accustomed to seeing lately. For a moment, neither of them spoke, the air between them heavy with unsaid words.

"Wyatt," Richard said quietly, as if he had been expecting this but still wasn't ready. "You're here."

Wyatt nodded, stepping further into the room but keeping his distance. He shoved his hands into his pockets, trying to steady himself. "We need to talk."

Richard shifted in his chair, the familiar tension creeping back into his shoulders. "I figured we would."

Wyatt could feel the words pressing against the inside of his chest, desperate to escape, but he didn't know where to start. The incident with Kyle had been humiliating, but what had hurt more was his father's silence—the way he had shut down the confrontation without ever standing up for Wyatt as his son.

"I need to know," Wyatt began, his voice trembling despite his best efforts to keep it steady. "Why didn't you defend me today? Why didn't you stand up for me?"

Richard looked away, his jaw tightening. "I stopped Kyle from going any further. I thought that was enough."

"It wasn't," Wyatt said, his voice growing firmer. "You stopped him, but you didn't defend me. You didn't tell him he was wrong. You didn't tell him I'm your son and that you're proud of me."

Richard's head snapped up at that, his eyes narrowing. "Proud? Wyatt, I don't–" He stopped himself, clearly struggling to find the right words. "I didn't want things to get ugly. I thought it was better to stop it before it turned into something worse."

Wyatt felt a familiar anger rising in his chest. His father still didn't get it. "Keeping the peace isn't the same as standing up for me. You didn't defend me because you're still not okay with who I am."

Richard flinched, but he didn't argue. The silence stretched between them, thick and suffocating, until finally, Richard let out a long sigh and leaned forward in his chair, rubbing his temples as if the weight of the world had settled there.

"I'm trying," Richard said quietly, his voice sounding older, more tired than Wyatt had ever heard it. "I'm trying to understand, Wyatt. But it's not easy for me. I was raised to believe certain things, to see the world a certain way. And now… now I don't know what's right anymore."

Wyatt's chest tightened, the familiar ache of disappointment settling in. "So what? You're just going to keep seeing me as… as wrong? As broken?"

"No," Richard said quickly, his eyes flashing with something like guilt. "I don't think that. I don't think you're broken, Wyatt. I never have."

"Then why can't you accept me?" Wyatt demanded, his voice breaking. "Why can't you just be okay with me being who I am? I need you to be okay with it, Dad. I need you to see me."

Richard's face softened, the hard lines of anger and frustration melting away into something more vulnerable. "I see you, Wyatt. You're my son. I love you. That's never changed. But I'm struggling. This isn't what I imagined for you. It's not what I was prepared for."

Wyatt took a step closer, his heart pounding in his chest. He had heard variations of this speech before–his father's constant refrain of *I'm trying*, of *I don't understand*. But that wasn't enough anymore. He needed more than trying. He needed acceptance.

"I don't need you to understand everything right now," Wyatt said softly, his voice filled with a quiet urgency. "But I need you to stop holding onto the idea that I'm making a mistake just by being myself. You don't have to agree with everything, but you have to stop seeing me as something you need to fix."

Richard looked down at his hands, his knuckles white from gripping the arms of the chair too tightly. When he finally spoke, his voice was rough with emotion. "I'm sorry, Wyatt. For everything I said. I shouldn't have pushed you away. I don't want to be the reason you don't feel welcome in your own home."

Wyatt's breath caught in his throat. His father's words were soft, tentative, but they held a truth that Wyatt hadn't been expecting.

Richard looked up, his eyes filled with something that Wyatt hadn't seen before–something close to remorse. "I don't want to lose you.

I'm... I'm willing to try, Wyatt. I'll do whatever I can to make this work. I just need you to understand that it's going to be hard for me."

Wyatt blinked, his emotions swirling in a confusing storm. His father was offering him something–a chance at reconciliation, a sliver of hope–but Wyatt couldn't help but feel wary. It wasn't enough for Richard to *try*. Wyatt needed him to mean it, to truly accept him for who he was.

"It's hard for me too," Wyatt said quietly. "But I need to know that you're really going to try. That you're not just saying this to make things easier for yourself."

Richard nodded slowly, his face lined with exhaustion. "I'll try my best. I can't promise it'll be perfect. But I don't want you to feel like you have to stay away. I want you home, Wyatt. Spend the last week of summer here, with us. This is your home."

Wyatt's heart twisted at the offer. The idea of coming home, of reconnecting with his family, was tempting. But there was one thing he needed before he could say yes.

"I'll come home," Wyatt said slowly, his eyes locking onto his father's. "But I need you to say you're okay with me dating Jesse. I need to hear you say it."

Richard's face paled, and for a moment, Wyatt thought he would refuse. The silence that stretched between them felt endless, and Wyatt's heart pounded in his chest, waiting for his father's response.

Richard swallowed hard, his voice strained. "I don't know if I'll ever fully understand it. But if Jesse makes you happy... then I'll try to be okay with it."

Wyatt's chest tightened with a mix of emotions—relief, frustration, and sadness all swirling together. It wasn't the full acceptance he had hoped for, but it was a step in the right direction.

"I need more than 'try,'" Wyatt said, his voice cracking slightly. "I need to know that you'll accept me for who I am. That you'll accept us."

Richard looked at him, his eyes heavy with the weight of his internal struggle. Finally, he nodded, his voice barely above a whisper. "I'll accept it. I'll try to accept you and Jesse. I'll do my best."

Wyatt exhaled slowly, the tension in his chest easing, if only slightly. It wasn't perfect, but it was something. His father wasn't pushing him away anymore. He was trying, and for now, that had to be enough.

"I'll come home," Wyatt said softly, the words feeling both like a promise and a risk. "But I need to know that this is real, Dad. That you really mean it."

Richard's gaze softened, his face lined with exhaustion but also something like hope. "I'll do my best, Wyatt. I promise."

As Wyatt turned to leave, the weight of the conversation lingered in the air. He wasn't sure what the future held for him and his father, but for the first time in a long time, there was a glimmer of hope that things could change.

As he stepped outside, the evening air felt cooler against his skin, and for a moment, Wyatt allowed himself to hope that maybe, just maybe, his father would keep his word.

Chapter 47: Counting Down the Days

The sun had dipped below the horizon by the time Wyatt pulled up in front of Jesse's house. The orange and pink glow of the sky had faded into twilight, and the streetlights flickered on, casting long shadows across the quiet neighborhood. It was peaceful, almost eerily so, given everything that had happened that day. Wyatt parked his car and took a deep breath, steadying himself before heading inside to collect his things.

As he walked up the driveway, Wyatt felt the familiar knot of anxiety tightening in his chest. He hadn't been able to shake the conversation with his dad–Richard's reluctant but sincere promise to accept him, to try and support his relationship with Jesse. Wyatt wasn't sure what to make of it. His dad's words had been soft, careful, but Wyatt could still sense the hesitation, the discomfort. Richard had promised to try, but that wasn't the same as full acceptance, and Wyatt knew it.

When Wyatt stepped through the front door, Jesse was waiting for him in the living room, sprawled out on the couch with his phone in hand. As soon as he saw Wyatt, he sat up, concern etched across his face.

"How'd it go?" Jesse asked, his voice cautious.

Wyatt shrugged as he walked over to the couch, sitting down next to him. "It was... complicated."

Jesse's brow furrowed, and he shifted closer to Wyatt. "What do you mean? Did he apologize?"

Wyatt leaned back against the couch, running a hand through his hair. "Yeah, he apologized. Sort of. He said he was sorry for what he said, that he didn't want to lose me. He told me he's going to try to accept me and… us."

Jesse blinked in surprise, his eyes searching Wyatt's face for clues to how he felt about all of it. "Well, that's something, right?"

Wyatt let out a long sigh, feeling the weight of the day settle into his bones. "It's something, but it's not enough. He still doesn't fully get it, you know? He said he'll try, but I can tell he's still uncomfortable with the whole thing. Like he's forcing himself to say the right things, but I don't know if he really believes them."

Jesse frowned, reaching out to take Wyatt's hand. "That's rough. I'm sorry, Wyatt. I know you wanted more."

"Yeah," Wyatt said softly, squeezing Jesse's hand. "But I guess it's a step in the right direction."

They sat in silence for a moment, the quiet of the house wrapping around them like a blanket. Wyatt could feel the tension ebbing slightly, but there was still something hanging over them—something that neither of them had addressed yet.

"I told him I'd go home for the last week of summer," Wyatt said after a long pause. "He wants me to spend the week there, to try and make things right. I said I'd do it, but I also told him he had to be okay with me dating you."

Jesse raised an eyebrow, clearly impressed. "You actually told him that?"

"Yeah," Wyatt nodded. "I wasn't going to go back unless he could accept us. He was reluctant, but he agreed. I just don't know how real that is, you know? It still feels like he's saying it because he doesn't want to lose me, not because he actually supports it."

Jesse let out a slow breath, leaning back against the couch. "I get it. But at least he's trying. Maybe that's all you can ask for right now."

Wyatt nodded, though the doubt still gnawed at him. He didn't know what the last week at home would bring, but he hoped it wouldn't be more of the same strained, awkward conversations. He wanted to believe that his dad could change, but part of him was bracing for disappointment.

"What about us?" Jesse asked, his voice soft but serious. "I mean... we've only got a week left of summer, and then we go back to school. Are we okay?"

Wyatt turned to look at him, surprised by the question. "Of course we are. Why wouldn't we be?"

Jesse shrugged, glancing down at their joined hands. "I don't know. It's just... we've had so much going on this summer. All the drama with your dad, the stuff at the pool, worrying about what people think. It feels like we've spent most of our time dealing with everyone else's crap, and now the summer's almost over."

Wyatt sighed, feeling the weight of Jesse's words settle into his chest. He hadn't realized it until now, but Jesse was right. So much of their summer had been consumed by worrying about things they couldn't control—his father's disapproval, the homophobia in town, the endless stress of navigating their relationship in secret.

"We've wasted so much time," Jesse continued, his voice tinged with frustration. "We could've been enjoying our summer, just being together, but instead we've been tiptoeing around everyone else's problems."

Wyatt felt a pang of guilt. And now, with only a week left before they both headed back to college, it felt like they had lost something precious.

"I know," Wyatt said quietly, his chest tightening with regret. "I'm sorry. I let all of that get in the way."

Jesse shook his head quickly, his expression softening. "It's not your fault, Wyatt. We've both been dealing with a lot. I just wish we had more time."

Wyatt's heart ached at the thought. One week. That was all they had left before everything changed again—before college pulled them back into the whirlwind of classes, exams, and the distance that had always been hard to navigate.

"I wish we had more time too," Wyatt admitted, his voice barely above a whisper. "But we have a week. We can still make it count."

Jesse looked up at him, his eyes filled with that quiet determination Wyatt had always admired. "Yeah, we can. But no more worrying about what other people think. No more wasting time on things we can't control."

Wyatt nodded, a small smile tugging at the corners of his mouth. "Deal."

They sat in silence for a moment, the weight of the summer slowly lifting as they both allowed themselves to breathe, to think about the week ahead. Wyatt could feel the tension in his chest loosening, replaced by a new sense of resolve.

"We'll make this week about us," Wyatt said, his voice steadier now. "No more drama. Just us."

Jesse smiled, squeezing Wyatt's hand. "I like the sound of that."

Wyatt stood up, pulling Jesse with him. "I should probably go grab my stuff."

They headed up to the guest room where Wyatt had been staying for the past few days, the quiet of the house feeling almost surreal after the intensity of the day. Wyatt packed his things quickly, but as he folded his clothes into his duffel bag, he couldn't help but feel the weight of what this week represented–the last bit of freedom before they both returned to the real world.

Once everything was packed, Wyatt slung the bag over his shoulder and turned to Jesse, who was leaning against the doorway, watching him with a thoughtful expression.

"I guess this is it," Wyatt said with a small smile, though his heart felt heavy.

Jesse stepped forward, wrapping his arms around Wyatt's waist and pulling him close. "It's not 'it.' We've still got a week. And then we'll figure things out when we're back at school."

Wyatt leaned into the embrace, feeling the warmth of Jesse's body against his own. He didn't want to think about the end of summer, didn't want to think about how different things would be once they were back at college. For now, he just wanted to hold onto this moment, to the promise they had made to each other–to not let anything else get in the way.

"I'll see you tomorrow?" Jesse asked, his voice soft.

"Of course," Wyatt replied, pressing a gentle kiss to Jesse's forehead. "We've still got a week to make the most of."

Chapter 48: One Last Adventure

The air was warm with a slight breeze as Wyatt and Jesse walked side by side down the familiar streets of their town. The summer had flown by in a blur of emotions, and as the final days ticked away, the realization that this chapter of their lives was closing hit them hard. Their last week together had been spent soaking in every moment–trips to their favorite spots, quiet dinners with friends, and long talks about everything they hadn't been able to say during the whirlwind of the summer.

But tonight, their last night before they both went back to college, felt different. There was a weight to it, an unspoken understanding that things were about to change. In just a few short hours, they would be headed in opposite directions–Wyatt back to school on the West Coast, Jesse across the country on the East Coast. It wasn't the first time they'd been away for school, but this time, everything was more intense, more real. They weren't the same people who had started the summer. They were something more now.

"I still can't believe the summer's already over," Jesse said, his voice quiet as they turned down a familiar street. "Feels like we just got here."

Wyatt glanced over at him, a small smile tugging at his lips. "Yeah. It went by fast. Too fast."

Jesse nodded, his hand brushing against Wyatt's as they walked. "I keep thinking about how much time we wasted worrying about everything. Your dad, the town, people like Kyle… we let all of that get in the way."

Wyatt sighed, running a hand through his hair. "I know. But we made it through, right? We figured it out."

"Yeah," Jesse said with a soft smile. "We did. But still… I wish we hadn't let it take up so much space. We could've been doing this all along."

Wyatt gave Jesse's hand a gentle squeeze, his chest tightening at the thought. Jesse was right. So much of their summer had been spent caught up in fear.

"Well, we've still got tonight," Wyatt said, his voice filled with quiet determination. "Let's make it count."

Jesse's eyes lit up with a mischievous glint. "You have something in mind?"

Wyatt smirked, nudging Jesse playfully. "How about one last adventure?"

Jesse raised an eyebrow, clearly intrigued. "What kind of adventure?"

"The pool," Wyatt said, his grin widening. "For old times' sake."

Jesse laughed softly, his smile growing. "You want to sneak into the pool again?"

Wyatt shrugged, the memory of their previous pool escapades still fresh in his mind. "Why not? It's our last night. Let's do something we'll remember."

Jesse thought for a moment, then nodded, a grin spreading across his face. "Alright. But we have to be more careful this time. No getting caught."

Wyatt chuckled, his heart light with the promise of one final, reckless adventure. "We'll be quiet. Promise."

They made their way to the pool, the streets growing quieter as they ventured closer to the edge of town. The sky had turned a deep indigo, and the stars were just beginning to twinkle above them, casting a soft glow over the darkened streets. By the time they reached the pool, the place was completely deserted. The familiar chain-link fence stood between them and the water, but it didn't take long for Wyatt to find the spot where they could slip through.

As they approached the pool, Jesse couldn't help but feel a wave of nostalgia wash over him. So much had happened here–so many moments that had changed the course of his life, of *their* lives. It was where he met Wyatt. It was strange to think that just a few months ago, he had been so unsure of himself, so afraid of what people would think if they found out who he really was. And now, standing here with Wyatt, everything felt so much clearer.

They reached the locker room, and as they stepped inside, Jesse felt a rush of memories hit him–memories of the first time he had stood in this very spot, watching Wyatt from across the room, feeling that nervous excitement in his chest. Back then, Jesse had been so unsure, so lost in his feelings for Wyatt that he hadn't known what to do with them.

But now... now everything was different.

Jesse started to pull off his shirt, reaching into his bag for his swim trunks. As he changed, he noticed Wyatt watching him with a soft, thoughtful expression on his face.

"What?" Jesse asked, smiling as he tossed his shirt into his bag.

Wyatt shook his head, a small grin tugging at his lips. "Nothing. Just... I was thinking about the beginning of summer. How I used to see you in here, and I had no idea we'd end up like this."

Jesse laughed softly, shaking his head. "Yeah, I didn't either. I was a wreck back then. Could barely look at you without freaking out."

Wyatt smirked, pulling on his swim trunks. "Well, you're better at it now."

Jesse rolled his eyes playfully, stepping closer to Wyatt. "I guess practice helps."

They changed quickly, the locker room filling with the sound of rustling clothes and soft laughter. Once they were ready, they made their way out to the pool, the air cool against their skin as they stepped out into the night.

The pool stretched out before them, the water still and dark, reflecting the stars above like a mirror. It was quiet, the only sound the occasional chirp of crickets and the rustling of leaves in the breeze. Wyatt felt a sense of calm settle over him as he approached the edge of the pool, his heart light with the knowledge that this was their moment–just him and Jesse, no one else to worry about.

Jesse dipped his toes into the water, glancing up at Wyatt with a soft smile, the kind that always made Wyatt feel grounded, like everything was going to be okay. "Ready?"

Wyatt nodded, stepping into the water beside him. The coolness of the pool was immediate and refreshing, a stark contrast to the warmth of the night air that clung to their skin like the last remnants of summer. The pool was calm, the surface smooth and glassy, and it felt like they were the only two people left in the world. As they waded deeper, the water enveloped them, weightless and comforting, as if the pool itself was offering them a reprieve from everything they had been carrying for months.

They floated side by side in the water, their bodies suspended in the cool embrace as they stared up at the stars. The sky was a deep, velvety black, punctuated by twinkling points of light that seemed impossibly far away. It was a night that felt timeless, a quiet pocket of serenity in a world that had been anything but peaceful. The silence between them wasn't awkward or uncertain–it was the kind of silence that spoke of understanding, of knowing that words weren't necessary right now.

For a long time, neither of them spoke. They didn't need to. The gentle ripple of the water and the soft rustle of the trees in the distance were the only sounds that accompanied their thoughts. Wyatt let himself float on his back, arms outstretched as he gazed at the sky. He felt a sense of peace wash over him, something he hadn't felt in a long time. It was as if, for this brief moment, all the worries about the future, about school, about their families, had been pushed aside, and all that mattered was this–floating together, side by side, under the stars.

"This feels different," Jesse said quietly, breaking the stillness with a voice that was both wistful and reflective. His eyes remained fixed on the sky, but Wyatt could hear the deeper meaning in his words.

Wyatt turned his head slightly to look at him, sensing the unspoken emotion in Jesse's voice. "Yeah," Wyatt agreed softly, his own gaze returning to the stars. "It does."

There was something about this night that felt heavier, like it held more significance than either of them had anticipated. It wasn't just about sneaking into the pool for one last adventure. It was about the end of something–of this chapter, this summer, this part of their lives. It was about the uncertainty of what came next.

Jesse floated closer, his arm brushing against Wyatt's under the water, and then he turned to face him, his expression gentle and open, illuminated by the soft glow of the moonlight reflecting off the water. "But we're not saying goodbye to each other, right?"

Wyatt smiled, warmth blooming in his chest. "No," he said firmly, reaching out to take Jesse's hand under the water. "We're not."

Their hands intertwined, fingers locking together like pieces of a puzzle that fit perfectly. They stayed like that for a while, floating in the cool water, their hands held together beneath the surface as their hearts beat in sync. Wyatt couldn't help but feel grateful for this moment–for the quiet, for the stillness, for the chance to just be with Jesse without the weight of everything else pressing down on them. It was like they had carved out a small corner of the universe that was just for them.

Eventually, Wyatt swam toward the edge of the pool, pulling himself up to sit on the ledge. The cool night air hit his damp skin, and he shivered slightly as he settled on the concrete, letting his legs dangle in the water. Jesse followed a moment later, sitting beside him, their shoulders brushing as they gazed out over the still water.

For a long moment, they just sat there, the night wrapping around them like a blanket. The stars twinkled above them, the pool reflecting their light in ripples that shimmered on the surface. Wyatt felt a sense of calm settle over him, the kind of peace that comes after a storm. The drama of the summer–the tension with his dad, the fights, the constant worry–felt like a distant memory now. Here, with Jesse, it all seemed so far away, like it belonged to another life.

"This is nice," Jesse said softly, leaning his head against Wyatt's shoulder. His voice was low, almost like he didn't want to disturb the quiet beauty of the moment.

"Yeah," Wyatt agreed, his own voice barely above a whisper. "It is."

For a long time, they just sat there, the cool water lapping at their legs, the sounds of the night filling the spaces between their breaths. Jesse could hear the distant hum of crickets, the occasional rustle of leaves in the breeze, and the faint ripple of water as it moved against the edge of the pool. It was peaceful in a way that felt almost surreal, as if the world had finally given them a moment of quiet after so much chaos.

Jesse felt Wyatt shift beside him, lifting his head to look up at the sky. "You ever think about how small we are?" Wyatt asked, his voice thoughtful, almost philosophical. "Like, in the grand scheme of things. We're just... here. Tiny little specks in this huge universe."

Jesse smiled, glancing over at him. "Yeah. I guess we are."

Jesse let out a soft laugh, his fingers tracing absent patterns on Wyatt's arm. "It's kind of comforting, though, isn't it? Knowing that all the stuff we've been through... it's just a tiny blip in the universe. Makes it feel less overwhelming."

Wyatt nodded, understanding what Jesse meant. There was something oddly reassuring about knowing that, in the vastness of the cosmos, their problems weren't as big as they seemed. And yet, here they were, in this small town, in this pool, and it felt like everything.

Jesse turned his head to look at Wyatt, his expression soft and open. "We've come a long way, haven't we?"

Wyatt met his gaze, a smile tugging at the corners of his mouth. "Yeah, we have."

Jesse's hand found Wyatt's again, and they sat there, fingers intertwined, legs still dangling in the water. The night stretched on around them, vast and quiet, as if the stars were holding their breath, waiting for something. Wyatt didn't want to leave this moment, didn't want to think about the fact that in just a few short hours, they'd be heading off in opposite directions, back to their respective schools on different sides of the country.

"I'm going to miss this," Jesse said softly, his voice tinged with a sadness Wyatt recognized all too well.

"Me too," Wyatt replied, his throat tight with emotion. "But we'll figure it out. We always do."

Jesse smiled, leaning in to press a soft kiss to Wyatt's lips. The kiss was gentle, slow, filled with all the unspoken promises they had made to each other over the course of the summer. When they pulled away, Jesse rested his forehead against Wyatt's, his breath warm against Wyatt's skin.

"We'll figure it out," Jesse echoed, his voice full of quiet certainty.

After a while, they climbed out of the pool, drying off in the warm night air before slipping back into their clothes. The silence between them was comfortable now, filled with the quiet promise of everything that was yet to come.

Once they were dressed, they gathered their things and made their way to their special spot–the quiet clearing just outside of town, where they had spent so many nights together. It was their place, a place that felt like home in a way that nothing else did.

As they reached the clearing, Wyatt spread out a blanket on the grass, and they both lay down, staring up at the stars. The night sky seemed endless above them, the stars bright and clear, and for a moment, it felt like they were the only two people in the world.

"This is where it all started," Jesse said quietly, his voice filled with a mix of nostalgia and sadness.

Wyatt nodded, his hand reaching out to find Jesse's. "Yeah. Feels like it was forever ago."

Jesse smiled, his thumb brushing over Wyatt's knuckles. "We'll always have this place, a place to come back to, even if the world around us seems unbearable."

Wyatt smiled softly, his heart swelling with emotion. "Yeah, our place, just us."

They lay there for a while, the cool grass beneath them, the stars above them, their hands intertwined. Wyatt felt a sense of peace settle over him—a peace he hadn't felt in months. This was where he belonged. With Jesse. With the person who had seen him, truly seen him, and loved him for everything he was.

As the night wore on, the conversation between Jesse and Wyatt flowed effortlessly, like a soft current carrying them forward. They lay side by side on the blanket, staring up at the vast sky, feeling the weight of the moment but also the lightness of being together. The stars above seemed brighter here, far from the lights of the town, and each twinkle felt like a quiet reassurance that they were exactly where they needed to be.

Their talk meandered between the mundane and the profound—what classes they were excited for, what clubs they might join, and which late-night spots they were eager to visit once back at school. But woven into these lighter topics was the deeper, more pressing issue they were both thinking about: the distance. Two schools, miles apart, on opposite sides of the country.

"How do you think it'll be?" Jesse asked softly, his voice carrying a note of uncertainty.

Wyatt glanced at him, taking in the gentle curve of his smile, the way his eyes softened in the dim light of the stars. He didn't want to admit how nervous he was about the coming months, how the thought of not seeing Jesse every day made his chest ache in a way he hadn't expected. But there was a quiet strength in Jesse's presence, and Wyatt held onto that as he answered.

"We'll figure it out," Wyatt said, his voice steady despite the flicker of doubt in his mind. "It won't be easy, but we've gotten through so much already. We can handle this."

Jesse nodded, though there was still that hint of worry in his eyes. "I know we can. I just… I don't want to miss you so much it hurts."

Wyatt's heart clenched at that. He reached over, brushing his thumb gently across Jesse's cheek. "I'll miss you too, more than I probably know right now. But we'll make time for each other. We'll visit. We'll text, call, video chat. We'll make it work, because there's no way I'm letting what we have slip away."

Jesse smiled at that, a smile filled with a mixture of hope and love. "I feel the same. It's just… hard to imagine going back to normal life after all of this."

Wyatt knew what he meant. The summer had been a whirlwind of emotions, discovery, and change. What had started as a cautious, tentative connection had blossomed into something real, something strong. And now, as they faced the prospect of returning to their separate lives, the fear of losing that closeness loomed large.

But they weren't going to let fear dictate how their story played out. "I don't think we go back to normal life, not really," Wyatt said thoughtfully. "We've changed, Jesse. Everything's different now. But in the best way."

Jesse shifted closer, resting his hand on Wyatt's chest, feeling the steady beat of his heart beneath his fingers. "Yeah," he murmured, his voice soft, "you're right. I don't want to go back to how things were before. I like who we are now."

Wyatt smiled, wrapping his arm around Jesse and pulling him in closer. "Me too."

They lay like that for a while, their words growing softer and their breaths falling into a slow, synchronized rhythm. They talked about their dreams, their hopes for the future—about the new experiences waiting for them at college, and how, no matter how far apart they were, they would always have this bond between them. The distance would be hard, but they both knew it was worth fighting for. They had built something together that neither of them wanted to lose.

"I'm excited for what's next," Jesse said after a long pause. His voice was tinged with a kind of quiet wonder, as if he could already see the future unfolding before them. "It's scary, but... it feels like we're on the edge of something really good."

Jesse pressed a gentle kiss to Wyatt's forehead, the warmth of the moment wrapping around them like a protective blanket. "We are," Wyatt whispered. "We'll have hard days, but we'll have good days too. And I want to be there with you for all of it."

Jesse smiled against Wyatt's chest, his fingers tracing lazy patterns on Wyatt's skin. "You always know how to make me feel better."

They didn't need to say much after that. The weight of the conversation had settled between them, and the certainty that they could handle whatever came next was enough. Their voices slowed, their words trailing off into the cool night air, leaving only the sound of their steady breaths and the rustling of the trees around them.

Jesse shifted again, this time resting his head more fully against Wyatt's chest, listening to the soothing rhythm of his heartbeat. Wyatt tightened his arms around him, pulling him closer, and for a moment, everything else faded away. The worries of the future, the uncertainties about school, even the bittersweet feeling of the summer ending–they all melted into the background.

In this moment, there was only the two of them, lying under the stars, holding each other close.

As their voices quieted into comfortable silence, Wyatt could feel Jesse's breathing slow, becoming more even, more relaxed. He could sense the weight of sleep tugging at both of them, pulling them gently toward rest. But neither of them wanted to let go just yet. There was something sacred about this night, something they wanted to hold onto for as long as possible.

Jesse's head rose and fell with Wyatt's slow, steady breaths, and Wyatt's fingers brushed lightly through Jesse's hair, a soothing rhythm that lulled them both closer to sleep. The warmth of Jesse's body against his was a constant reminder of everything they had been through, everything they had shared. Wyatt couldn't imagine his life without Jesse in it, couldn't picture going back to a time when they hadn't been this close.

Eventually, the stars above them blurred as their eyes grew heavier. Wyatt felt Jesse's breath, slow and steady against his chest, and the soft rise and fall of his body as he drifted closer to sleep. Wyatt pressed a soft kiss to the top of Jesse's head, feeling the weight of the moment settle in.

"I've got you," Wyatt whispered, though he wasn't sure if Jesse was still awake to hear it. "I've always got you."

Jesse murmured something in response, his words slurred with sleep, but Wyatt didn't need to understand them to know what he meant. They had each other—that was all that mattered.

With one last deep breath, Wyatt allowed himself to relax completely, his body sinking into the soft blanket beneath them. He could feel the cool grass against his skin, the distant hum of the night around them, but most of all, he could feel Jesse in his arms, warm and safe.

And as they drifted off to sleep, their hearts beating in time with each other, the worries of the future melted away, forgotten at least for tonight.

Together, they slept under the stars, their bodies entwined, their breaths synchronized, as if the universe itself had aligned just for them.

Chapter 49: Is this the End?

The soft, golden light of dawn crept through the trees, warming the clearing where Jesse lay nestled against Wyatt's chest. The cool, damp grass beneath him, combined with the steady rise and fall of Wyatt's breathing, made him want to stay right there forever. For a moment, it was easy to pretend that time had stopped—that this was their world now, just the two of them, with no goodbyes on the horizon.

But reality was already pulling at the edges of Jesse's mind. Today was the day they'd been dreading—the last day of summer, the last day before they both had to leave. He could feel it like a weight in his chest, pressing down harder with every passing minute.

He didn't want to move, didn't want to acknowledge that this perfect, quiet moment was about to end. Jesse had spent the entire summer hoping for moments like these—moments of peace, of just being with Wyatt without the noise of the outside world intruding. And now, on the last morning of it all, he wasn't ready to let it go.

He stirred slightly, blinking his eyes open to find the world bathed in the soft glow of early morning. Wyatt's arm was still draped over him, his chest rising and falling with each steady breath. Jesse turned his head to look at him, his heart aching at the sight of Wyatt so peaceful, so content. There was something about seeing Wyatt like this—unguarded, free—that made Jesse's chest tighten with love and, at the same time, sadness. Because today, everything would change.

"Hey," Jesse whispered, his voice still thick with sleep.

Wyatt's eyes fluttered open, a soft, sleepy smile spreading across his face as he looked down at Jesse. "Hey," he whispered back, his voice gentle.

They didn't speak for a while after that, both of them content to lie there in the grass, tangled up in each other, holding onto these last few moments of calm. Jesse's head rested on Wyatt's chest, and he could hear the steady thump of Wyatt's heart beneath his ear. It was comforting, grounding. But it also made the day ahead feel all the more real.

"I don't want this to end," Jesse murmured, barely loud enough for Wyatt to hear.

Wyatt's arms tightened around him, pulling him closer. "Me neither."

The sun was creeping higher now, the warmth of it spreading over them, pulling them out of their dreamlike state. Jesse knew they couldn't stay here forever. They had to face the reality of what was coming, but that didn't make it any easier.

With a soft sigh, Jesse finally sat up, running a hand through his messy hair. He glanced around the clearing, at the soft blanket they had laid out the night before, now damp with dew, the grass flattened where they had slept. It was so peaceful here, so separate from the rest of the world, that it was hard to imagine they'd have to leave it behind in just a few short hours.

"We should probably head back," Jesse said, though the words felt heavy in his mouth. He didn't want to say them, didn't want to be the one to acknowledge that the day had started and their time together was slipping away.

Wyatt nodded, sitting up slowly beside him. "Yeah, we should."

They packed up in silence, rolling up the blanket and gathering their things. Jesse's heart felt heavier with each step they took toward the car, each step bringing them closer to the inevitable. The walk felt longer than usual, like they were trying to stretch out the time, but no matter how slowly they moved, the sun kept climbing higher in the sky.

When they finally reached the car, Jesse stopped and turned to Wyatt, searching his face. He didn't know what to say, didn't know how to make this any easier. The words that had been building up inside him all summer–about how much Wyatt meant to him, how scared he was to lose this–caught in his throat, too big to say out loud.

"So... what now?" Jesse asked, his voice small, almost fragile.

Wyatt stepped closer, taking Jesse's hands in his. "Now, we take it one day at a time," Wyatt said, his voice soft but steady. "We'll call, we'll visit, and we'll figure it out."

Jesse wanted to believe him. He wanted to believe that this wasn't the end, that they would be okay. But the weight of the distance between them–the miles and miles that would separate them in just a few hours–made him feel like he was standing on the edge of something huge, something he wasn't sure he knew how to face.

"I'm going to miss you so much," Jesse said, his voice trembling slightly, tears filling his eyes.

Wyatt pulled him into a tight hug, resting his chin on top of Jesse's head. "I'm going to miss you too. But this isn't the end. It's just the beginning."

Jesse held on tighter, closing his eyes as he buried his face in Wyatt's shoulder. He didn't want to let go, didn't want to face the day ahead. They stood there for a long moment, wrapped in each other's arms, holding on to this last bit of peace before everything changed.

When they finally pulled apart, Jesse wiped at his eyes, blinking against the sting of tears. He didn't want to cry, not now, not when he wanted to be strong. But the thought of leaving Wyatt, of not seeing him every day, was almost too much.

"You promise?" Jesse asked, his voice barely above a whisper. "You promise we'll be okay?"

Wyatt smiled, brushing a thumb across Jesse's cheek. "I promise. We'll make this work, Jesse. I know we will. Look at everything we've already overcome."

They climbed into the car, and the drive back to town was filled with a heavy silence. Jesse stared out the window, watching as the familiar streets of their small town passed by, feeling a strange sense of nostalgia for something that wasn't even over yet. The roads, the houses, the trees–everything looked the same, but it felt different. Maybe because he knew that after today, things wouldn't be the same anymore.

When they pulled up in front of Jesse's house, the weight in Jesse's chest grew even heavier. He stared at the front door, his hands resting in his lap, not sure how to make the next move. Leaving the clearing had been hard, but this… this felt impossible.

"This is it," Jesse said quietly, his voice barely above a whisper. "Our last day."

Wyatt didn't answer right away. He sat there beside Jesse, his own hands gripping the steering wheel tightly, his eyes fixed on the house. Finally, after what felt like an eternity, he turned to Jesse and with tears in his eyes said, "Yeah. This is it."

Jesse could feel the tears welling up again, but he blinked them away, forcing a small smile. "Come here," Wyatt said softly.

Jesse leaned over, and Wyatt pulled him into a slow, lingering kiss. It was tender and filled with everything they couldn't put into words–the fear, the hope, the love. When they pulled apart, Jesse's eyes were wet, but he smiled through it. "I'll see you soon," he said, though his voice wavered.

Wyatt nodded, his own eyes glistening. "Yeah. Very soon."

With one last kiss, Jesse climbed out of the car, his heart heavy as he grabbed his bag from the backseat. He stood there on the sidewalk for a moment, watching as Wyatt drove away, feeling the ache in his chest grow with each passing second. He wanted to run after him, wanted to tell him to stay, but he knew he couldn't.

Jesse stood there for a long time after Wyatt's car disappeared from view, staring down the empty street, feeling the weight of the summer settle over him like a blanket. The summer had been everything–messy, complicated, beautiful–and now, standing on the other side of it, Jesse wasn't sure how to let it go.

He finally turned and walked up the steps to his house, his heart heavy as he pushed open the door. The house was quiet, filled with the early morning light, but it didn't feel like home anymore. Not really. Not without Wyatt.

Jesse dropped his bag by the door and made his way to his bedroom, collapsing onto the bed with a deep sigh. He stared up at the ceiling, his mind racing with thoughts of Wyatt, of the summer, of everything they'd been through. It felt like the end of something huge, something life-changing, and now he didn't know what to do next.

But as he lay there, staring at the familiar ceiling, he reminded himself of what Wyatt had said. This wasn't the end. It was just the beginning.

And somehow, despite the sadness and the uncertainty, that thought gave him a little bit of hope.

Because no matter what happened next, Jesse knew one thing for sure— they'd figure it out.

Chapter 50: Into the Sunset

Jesse stood in the center of his bedroom, staring down at the last few things that still needed to be packed. The familiar smell of home filled the room, but today it felt different. The space that had once been his refuge now felt strange, almost foreign, as if it no longer fit him. The summer had changed him in ways he couldn't have imagined, and standing here, preparing to leave, he realized that he was no longer the same person who had come home just a few short months ago.

His duffel bag sat open on the bed, waiting for the final few pieces of his life that he needed to take with him back to school. As he folded his favorite shirt and tucked it into the bag, his mind raced with memories of everything that had happened over the past few months. This summer had started with so much uncertainty, so much doubt, but now, as he stood here on the brink of something new, he felt an unfamiliar sense of peace.

The Jesse who had returned home at the beginning of the summer had been hesitant, nervous about facing his own feelings and unsure of how the world would react if he let his guard down. He had been scared–scared of who he was, scared of what that meant, scared of how people would treat him if they knew. But now, after everything, after the challenges and triumphs of the summer, he felt... free.

With a deep breath, Jesse zipped up his bag and slung it over his shoulder. He took one last look around the room, his eyes lingering on the posters that had decorated his walls since high school, the sketches he'd taped up by his desk, the books stacked haphazardly on his shelf. It felt like he was saying goodbye to a version of himself–one that had been afraid to take up space, afraid to be seen. But as he stood there, a smile tugged at the corners of his mouth. He was ready to let that version of himself go.

He made his way downstairs, where his parents were waiting in the living room. His mom sat on the couch, her hands resting in her lap, while his dad leaned against the doorframe, his arms crossed but his expression softer than usual. They had been through a lot together this summer, and though there had been difficult moments, they had all come out stronger for it.

His mom was the first to speak, her voice gentle. "You all set?"

Jesse nodded, adjusting the strap of his bag on his shoulder. "Yeah. I think I've got everything."

His dad stepped forward, his usual stoic demeanor replaced with something warmer. "We're proud of you, Jess," he said quietly. His voice was rough with emotion, and Jesse could see the sincerity in his eyes.

It hit Jesse then, how much they had all grown—not just him, but his parents, too. They had struggled to understand, struggled to find the right words, but they had tried. And that effort, that willingness to meet him halfway, meant everything.

"Thanks, Dad," Jesse said, his voice steady but thick with feeling.

His mom stood up and crossed the room, pulling him into a tight hug. She held him close, and for a moment, Jesse could feel the weight of her love, of everything she hadn't been able to say over the summer but had shown in small, subtle ways. When she finally pulled back, there were tears in her eyes, but she smiled through them. "You'll call us when you get there, right?"

"Of course," Jesse replied, a soft smile tugging at his lips.

They walked him out to his car, the warm morning sun casting long shadows across the driveway. The air was still and quiet, and for a moment, Jesse just stood there, looking at his parents standing side by side, their expressions filled with a mixture of pride and sadness. This summer had been transformative for all of them, and as much as the thought of leaving weighed on him, Jesse knew he was leaving on good terms. They had all come out stronger, more open, more understanding.

His dad gave him a firm pat on the back as they stood by the car. "Drive safe, Jess. And remember–if you need anything, we're just a phone call away."

Jesse smiled, feeling a warmth spread through his chest. "I know. Thanks, Dad."

His mom reached out and squeezed his hand, her eyes soft and full of emotion. "We love you, Jesse. We're really proud of you."

Jesse felt a lump form in his throat, but he swallowed it down, not wanting to get choked up before he even got in the car. "I love you guys too."

With one last hug from his mom and a reassuring nod from his dad, Jesse climbed into the driver's seat and started the engine. The familiar rumble of the car filled the air, but it felt different today. Today, the sound was a reminder that something new was beginning. He waved one last time to his parents as he pulled out of the driveway, watching them get smaller in the rearview mirror as he drove away.

The quiet streets of his hometown passed by in a blur as he headed for the highway. The early morning sun was warm on his skin, and as he left the town behind, he felt a strange mix of emotions swirling inside him. There was sadness, of course—leaving this place that had shaped him, saying goodbye to the summer that had changed everything. But there was also excitement. Excitement for what came next, for the life that was waiting for him beyond the horizon.

As he merged onto the highway, the road stretching out endlessly before him, Jesse's thoughts drifted back to the summer. It felt like a lifetime ago that he had started working at the pool, trying to keep his head down, trying to ignore the feelings he had for Wyatt. He thought about the early days—the awkward, stolen glances, the hesitant conversations, the way his heart would race every time Wyatt came near. He had been so scared back then—scared of being found out, scared of what it would mean if people knew.

But over the course of the summer, everything had changed. He had changed. He had faced his fears head-on, had come out to his parents, had stood up to people who thought they had the right to shame him for who he was. And through it all, Wyatt had been there—steadfast, kind, always making him feel like he was worth loving, like he was enough.

Jesse smiled to himself as he remembered their first kiss—the way his whole body had buzzed with electricity, the way Wyatt had looked at him afterward, like he was the only person in the world. That moment had changed everything. It had been the beginning of something real, something powerful.

And now, as the miles passed by, Jesse realized just how much he had grown to love Wyatt. It wasn't just a crush, wasn't just the excitement of something new. It was deep, real, the kind of love that made him feel safe and seen. He loved Wyatt for his laugh, for the way he never took life too seriously, for the way he had always looked at Jesse like he was important.

Jesse's heart swelled as he thought about Wyatt, about all the moments they had shared, and about all the moments that were still to come. They were heading in different directions for school–opposite sides of the country, even–but Jesse wasn't scared anymore. Because he knew that no matter how far apart they were, Wyatt would always be there. Whether in person or on the other end of a phone call, Wyatt was a part of his life now, and that wasn't going to change.

The sun had begun to dip lower in the sky, casting a golden glow over the horizon as Jesse drove toward the next chapter of his life. The open road stretched out before him, wide and full of possibility, and for the first time in a long time, Jesse felt completely at peace with who he was.

He had spent so much of his life afraid. But now, after this summer, he had learned that there was nothing to be afraid of. He had learned to love himself, to embrace who he was, and that was something no one could take from him.

As the sun sank lower, painting the sky with hues of pink and orange, Jesse felt a tear slide down his cheek. But it wasn't a tear of sadness–it was a tear of happiness, of relief, of gratitude for everything that had happened. He wiped it away with the back of his hand, a smile spreading across his face as he thought about what was coming next.

Without a second thought, Jesse reached for his phone and dialed Wyatt's number. The phone rang a few times, and Jesse's heart skipped a beat when Wyatt finally picked up, his voice warm and familiar, like a lifeline that Jesse hadn't even realized he needed.

"Hey, miss me already?" Wyatt said, his tone immediately lifting Jesse's spirits.

Jesse smiled, his heart full. "Hey," he replied, his voice soft. "I was just thinking about you."

Wyatt laughed, and the sound of it made Jesse's chest feel light. "Yeah? What about?"

Jesse glanced out at the horizon, the last rays of sunlight casting everything in a golden glow. "Just everything," he said, his voice filled with quiet contentment. "Everything that happened this summer, everything we've been through. I don't know... I just wanted to hear your voice."

There was a pause on the other end of the line, and when Wyatt spoke again, his voice was soft, full of the same emotions Jesse was feeling. "I miss you," Wyatt admitted, his tone vulnerable.

Jesse's smile widened, his heart swelling with love. "I miss you too. But we're going to be okay, right?"

"Yeah," Wyatt said, his voice filled with certainty. "We're going to be okay."

As Jesse drove into the sunset, the open road ahead of him, he felt a deep sense of peace settle over him. This summer had changed everything–had changed *him*–and now, as he looked ahead, he wasn't afraid of what the future held.

Because this wasn't the end.

It was just the beginning.

Made in the USA
Monee, IL
12 December 2024